WHEN TWILIGHT BURNS

The Gardella Vampire Chronicles

Colleen Gleason

A SIGNET ECLIPSE BOOK

SIGNET ECLIPSE
Published by New American Library, a division of
Penguin Group (USA) Inc., 375 Hudson Street,
New York, New York 10014, USA
Penguin Group (Canada), 90 Eglinton Avenue East, Suite 700, Toronto,
Ontario M4P 2Y3, Canada (a division of Pearson Penguin Canada Inc.)
Penguin Books Ltd., 80 Strand, London WC2R 0RL, England
Penguin Ireland, 25 St. Stephen's Green, Dublin 2,
Ireland (a division of Penguin Books Ltd.)
Penguin Group (Australia), 250 Camberwell Road, Camberwell, Victoria 3124,
Australia (a division of Pearson Australia Group Pty. Ltd.)
Penguin Books India Pvt. Ltd., 11 Community Centre, Panchsheel Park,
New Delhi - 110 017, India
Penguin Group (NZ), 67 Apollo Drive, Rosedale, North Shore 0632,
New Zealand (a division of Pearson New Zealand Ltd.)
Penguin Books (South Africa) (Pty.) Ltd., 24 Sturdee Avenue,
Rosebank, Johannesburg 2196, South Africa

Penguin Books Ltd., Registered Offices:
80 Strand, London WC2R 0RL, England

First published by Signet Eclipse, an imprint of New American Library,
a division of Penguin Group (USA) Inc.

First Printing, August 2008
10 9 8 7 6 5 4 3 2 1

Copyright © Colleen Gleason, 2008
All rights reserved

SIGNET ECLIPSE and logo are trademarks of Penguin Group (USA) Inc.

Printed in the United States of America

continued . . .

For Linda,
for all those mornings and afternoons on the phone.
Every day.

And in memory of my grandmother,
Laura Genevieve.

Acknowledgments

As always, I owe big thanks to my agent, Marcy Posner, and my brilliant editor, Claire Zion, for the unwavering support and assistance for this book.

Everyone at New American Library, from the editorial staff to the art and publicity departments, as usual, has gone above and beyond in support of the Gardella Vampire Chronicles, and I thank you again for the great covers and promotional designs.

Special thanks to Devon Wolfe for putting Victoria and Sebastian in the sewers of London, and to Tammy, Holli, and Jana for keeping me honest during the writing process. Hugs to Trish M., Kelly, Kate, Jackie Kessler, and Kathryn Smith for their support. And a special thanks to Robyn Carr for just about everything.

My online friends and bloggers continue to support the series, and I'm wholly indebted to Carl Vincent, Nancy Horner, Cheya Weber, and the gals at Estella's. Also big, grateful shout-outs to Michelle Buonfiglio and her Bellas, Romance Novel.TV, Chris A., Bam, the rocking Smart

Bitches, Dear Author, Zeek, Book Fetish, and the wonderful ladies at AAR.

Thanks also to all of my fans, who keep in touch with their opinion on Victoria's love life, particularly MaryKate (I *so* don't want to have to throw down with you!), Danita, Beth, Jeannie, Shahenda, Andrea, Kristin, and everyone else. And also congratulations to Melissa and Deb, who won the chance to make cameo appearances herein.

Most of all, as always, I thank my family for their love and support and enthusiasm for everything from cover flat arrivals to typing *The End*. I couldn't do it without you.

WHEN TWILIGHT BURNS

Prologue

Wherein Our Heroine Has a Rude Awakening

Victoria opened her eyes.

A ring of faces looked down at her: Max, his face shadowed but sharp-eyed; Sebastian, golden-haired and tense; Wayren, near the foot of the bed, her pale oval face tight. Ylito and Hannever stood above Victoria's head, frozen and watchful. She knew from the pattern on the stone walls behind them that she was in the Consilium, the secret, subterranean space belonging to the Venators. The vampire hunters—of which she was the leader.

"What—" Her head felt soupy and her eyelids heavy, and suddenly she remembered. "Beauregard!"

As memory sliced through the fuzziness, she tried to pull up, but her ankles and one of her wrists were caught fast. Someone's—Max's—fingers tightened around her left arm, keeping it pinned onto the bed beneath her, and before she could react with the anger and confusion erupting inside her, a splash of water caught her over the face.

The cold seeped down into her hair and over the warm skin of her neck, and she jerked beneath her restraints.

"Why did you do that?" she said, glaring up at Ylito, who'd tipped the vial over her face. She raised her free arm, near Sebastian, to brush some of the water from her eye.

No one answered . . . yet, something in the room had changed. Eased. Sebastian glanced at Wayren, who was looking at Ylito over Victoria.

"Is it possible?" asked the ringlet-haired man.

"I don't know how it can be, Ylito," Wayren replied.

The tightness in her dear friend's face had softened, and her countenance had taken on more of that serene look Victoria was used to seeing.

What was happening?

And then the recognition of a searing pain in her neck, and the memory flash of shadows and blood and long, sleek fangs brought it all back to her. *Beauregard . . . she'd been with Beauregard, the master vampire . . . his cold and warm mouth on hers, his teeth sliding into her flesh . . . the brush of skin against skin . . . the rusty taste of blood . . . on her lips. Pooling, rich and heavy, on her tongue. Filling her throat. His hands, smooth and sure . . . everywhere. . . .*

He'd bitten her, fed on her. Had she drunk his blood? Oh . . . God . . .

Her heart was racing now, and she wanted to struggle, to whip off Max's firm hold on her arm, to sit up and demand to know what had happened. But the others were talking, above her, around her, as if she wasn't there.

For a moment, Victoria was afraid to know.

And then, Wayren was touching her, smoothing her hands down over Victoria's face, her wounded throat. Light and warm and sure, the pressure was soothing, spreading relief through her body. As she touched her, Wayren hummed a chantlike prayer deep in the back of her throat, and Victoria felt the vibrations coming through Wayren's fingertips, rippling through her body.

"The two *vis bullae.*" Max's quiet voice broke into the charged silence. He stepped back, releasing Victoria's wrist and, she noticed for the first time, the stake that rested on the table next to him.

Dear God, he'd been ready to stake her. She understood in an instant: they'd feared Beauregard had turned her.

Her mouth dried and she swiveled her face to look toward him, but Max was looking intently at Wayren. "She wears two of them, does she not?" he asked.

And then she realized what had happened, even as they discussed the situation above her head, above her prone body: it was only because of the two holy strength amulets that she wore, the badges of her Venator calling to hunt vampires, that she'd been saved from becoming one of the very undead that she vowed to destroy.

A chill wave rushed over her and Victoria closed her eyes, the conversation around her becoming a distorted buzz. When she looked again, she found herself caught by Sebastian's dark amber gaze. He was looking down at her, a frozen expression on his handsome face.

It took her a moment to remember what had happened, and for the anger at his betrayal to bubble up inside her aching body: he'd stolen from the Consilium, from the Venators.

Her sometime lover, sometime enemy had deceived her in even more ways than she had expected.

He *was* a Venator. Born of the Gardella family tree.

A Venator who had disdained his calling for years because of loyalty to his great-great-great-grandfather, Beauregard. One of the most powerful of vampires.

Her fury abated slightly as another scrap of memory slipped into place: *Sebastian, thrusting himself between her and Beauregard, shouting at her to leave, even as she shoved a stake meant for Beauregard into Sebastian's shoulder . . . and the blood, blood that wasn't supposed to be there. . . . She saw the crusty bloom even now on his sweat-stained shirt.*

And then another memory consumed her. *A dark, liquid one, of heavy, deep pleasure . . . lush shadows and dangerous pleasure and heat . . . hands, and lips, and tongue . . . And Sebastian, again, his face pale and desperate, pleading with Beauregard for her release.*

And her own laugh, welling up from deep inside her, husky and low. Derisive. Dismissive.

And then the handsome face of Sebastian's grandfather bending to hers, his fangs sleek and lethal, his lips warm and cold.

Oh God.

"What about Beauregard?" she said suddenly, her voice commanding their attention. She sat up and the room hardly dipped at all.

"He's dead," Max said flatly, his face still in shadow.

A modicum of relief seeped through her body, and she looked at Sebastian. From the expression on his face, she realized he'd done the impossible: he'd killed the six-hundred-year-old vampire who had been his grandfather.

She reached for his hand and his fingers closed around hers. She squeezed them: in thanks and apology. "Will you join us again, now?" she asked in the strong, demanding voice of *Illa* Gardella, the leader of the Venators.

"I will."

And then, with belated horror, she remembered: Max.

Victoria turned to look at him and their eyes met. The studiously flat expression there told her all she needed to know. Sebastian might be taking his rightful place within the ranks of the Venators, but Max no longer could. He'd given up his Venator powers in order to destroy the thrall Lilith the Dark, Queen of the Vampires, had held over him.

One

Two Dogs Circling

"Lilith won't know I've severed her hold on me until she tries to exert it," Max said. Exhaustion trembled in his muscles, and he swore he could feel his eyes sinking more deeply into their sockets.

The last time he'd felt so bruised and empty had been after the battle with Nedas, Lilith's son, last fall. Max had been forced to execute Eustacia, his mentor and Victoria's great-aunt. Eustacia was one of the most powerful Venators who had ever lived. She'd ordered Max to sacrifice her so that he could get close enough to Nedas to destroy him and the powerful, demonic obelisk in his possession.

It had been the hardest thing he'd ever done.

Now, here he was, ready to leave the Venators permanently.

Only an hour had passed since Victoria had awakened from her ordeal, and he and Wayren had slipped away to her library here in the Consilium, the subterranean headquarters of the Venators, in order to discuss his future.

They'd left Sebastian Vioget simpering over a pale-visaged, hollow-cheeked Victoria.

It was just as well, for that was quite obviously the way the wind blew. Although Max had had a moment of perverse satisfaction when he realized Vioget hadn't known that Victoria wore two *vis bullae*.

"But once Lilith realizes I'm free, she'll consider it a betrayal," he said, returning to the conversation.

"And she won't rest until she finds you," Wayren replied in her even voice. She looked at him with her cool blue-gray eyes, reality shining there. "Her fury will know no bounds."

"How fortunate I am to be the object of such passion." Max tasted bitterness.

At that moment, there was a knock at the door and then Vioget came in, uninvited.

Max glanced up, not bothering to hide the flash of animosity in his face. Still flecked with blood, dirt, and debris from his battle to rescue Victoria from Beauregard's lair, Vioget looked weary and uncharacteristically out of sorts. Max supposed that was only to be expected, after having been stabbed in the shoulder by the stake meant for a vampire. And by his lover, too.

Max's lips twitched. Victoria with one *vis bulla* was stronger than any man—but wearing two, her strength would be superhuman. Vioget had to be in pain, even being a Venator.

Despite the fact that Vioget had called Beauregard "Grandfather," the man was also a born Venator. Vioget's father had descended from Beauregard's mortal son, many generations after the vampire had been turned undead. And his mother had apparently carried some measure of Gardella blood in her, which had passed on to

Vioget in an ironic turn: the grandson of a vampire was called to be a slayer of the undead.

"So sorry to interrupt," Sebastian said in dulcet tones that didn't match his disheveled appearance. He barely glanced at Max, turning pointedly to Wayren.

She sat not behind her desk, but in a cushioned chair, dressed, as always, like a medieval chatelaine in a long, loose gown with pointed sleeves that brushed the floor. This night, the bulk of her pale blonde hair hung in two thick braids, with two finger-slim ones hanging from her temples. She wore no jewelry or adornment except for the braided leather girdle at her waist, upon which hung a ring of keys.

"I have a matter of some urgency which I must discuss with you," Vioget continued.

"I imagine you do. Beauregard's death at your hand probably won't be well received by his undead compatriots," Max replied pleasantly. "Especially since for the last decade you've fairly lived among them. You may actually need to bestir yourself to slay a few more in order to protect your hide."

He and Vioget had known each other for more than fifteen years, long before either even knew that vampires existed. The animosity between them had been put aside for the few hours it took to rescue Victoria, but Max saw no reason to hide his antipathy for Vioget and his years of denying his calling as a Venator. Cowardice or selfishness—Max wasn't sure which one had driven the man—but it didn't matter to him.

People had been mauled, killed, and Vioget had done nothing to help them.

Until Victoria came along.

And, as far as he was concerned, it was Vioget's fault that Max had had to carry a bloody, unconscious Victoria from Beauregard's bedchamber. If Vioget hadn't been balancing both sides of his loyalty—to the Venators and his grandfather—for years, Victoria would never have been caught between him and Beauregard.

The other man elected to ignore Max's comment, focusing his attention on Wayren. "The two *vis bullae* seem to have saved her from being turned," he said.

"A miraculous occurrence," she replied. "Completely unexpected. But, since I've never known of a Venator to wear two, there was no way to predict such a recovery. And who's to say another such event would have the same result. At least some of her recovery must be attributed to her own strength and determination. Who she is."

"Yes. But . . . how did she come to have two of them? I am fully aware of their rarity—that each *vis* is cast of precious silver from the Holy Land, and blessed only for its recipient," Vioget continued. "Victoria's was lost during the battle with Nedas last November, and I was able to retrieve Eustacia's and send it to Victoria to replace hers. . . . But where did the second one come from?"

Max settled back in his chair and bared his teeth in a condescending smile. "It's mine."

He was a bit annoyed it had taken him so long to figure it out, for, after all, it was imperially logical. He'd given his *vis bulla* to Victoria after the battle with Nedas, when he thought he was leaving the Venators for good. The irony was that, unbeknownst to Victoria, he had recovered the *vis bulla* that she'd lost when Nedas's creatures had torn it from her navel.

And it was her amulet that hung, now useless to him, from his areola. Max's moment of satisfaction evaporated.

"I see." Vioget's jaw shifted, and he turned once again to Wayren. "Then may I assume you've already discussed the situation? Is it possible it's merely a residual effect?"

Wayren looked at him with a slight frown. "Situation? I'm not certain what you mean, Sebastian."

"When Victoria awoke, she didn't react to the holy water splashed on her face, as any vampire would. She seems completely normal. Except . . ." Vioget looked at him. "Don't you feel it? The vampire chill at the back of your neck, or however you sense the presence of the undead?"

Vioget didn't know about him? Max shrugged off his surprise in order to focus on Sebastian's disturbing question. "What are you saying?"

"I still feel cold at the back of my neck in Victoria's presence." Venators could sense the presence of the undead by a chill that prickled the napes of their necks.

For the first time since he'd seen her sprawled on Beauregard's bed, blood trickling from her lips, Max was unable to breathe. Yet he kept his reply cool. "No. I don't feel anything."

Vioget looked relieved. "Well, that's promising. Perhaps it's only because Beauregard attempted to turn her, and I knew him so well, that I continue to sense his presence. After all, she did ingest his blood. It must be some residual effect." He looked as though he was ready to leave the room.

"You misunderstand me," Max was compelled to say. He would have rather let Sebastian go, let everything go, and accept the simple explanation. But. "I cannot feel anything. Any longer."

Vioget turned, his hand on the door. "Did you ever, Pesaro? Feel anything?"

Max's jaw tightened, but he plunged on. It had to be said. "I am no longer a Venator." But he was damned if he'd give Vioget the whole story, the reasons and the trials and the burdens. The fact that he'd had no choice but to give up his powers—not in order to be freed from Lilith; no, he would have continued to bear that burden as long as he had to. But because, in order to kill the demon Akvan, who'd threatened to take over the city of Roma, he'd had to become merely a man once again.

"When did this happen?"

"Yesterday."

Vioget's gaze sharpened with calculation. "That was why you were leaving the Consilium, when I came to ask you for help with Victoria." Max inclined his head, and Vioget looked startled, and grudgingly impressed. "You came with us unprotected by the *vis bulla*."

"I did what had to be done," Max replied. *Unlike you.* He left the words unspoken, but from the tightening of Vioget's expression, he knew they were understood.

In clear dismissal, the blond man turned his attention to Wayren, who'd remained silent throughout their exchange. Her smooth brow was furrowed and her eyes worried as he asked, "What do you think? Can it merely be a residual effect of the near turning?"

She lifted her shoulders gracefully. "I do not know. As you're aware, I cannot sense the presence of an undead as you can, nor could Ylito or Hannever, as they aren't Venators themselves. There was no one else in the room with us, and . . . methinks it would accomplish no good at this time if the other Venators were to be told what happened. Perhaps"—she glanced at Max—"the effect will subside as she grows stronger."

"Thus, the most prudent thing," Vioget said, his voice smooth, "would be to stay very close to Victoria and keep her under observation. And protected."

Max smothered a snort. Victoria, protected? She'd

sooner cut off her hands and give up the *vis bulla* than allow someone else to protect her.

"Apparently, that task is going to fall to me," Vioget continued in his rich tone. "Never fear, Wayren . . . I will make certain to stick very close to her. Day and night."

Two

Wherein the Stench of Sewage Is Preferred to Lily of the Valley

Victoria hadn't missed London in the least.

It held too many unpleasant memories. Beyond the sewage-lined streets and odiferous air, the swell of carriages and their nonstop clatter, there simmered the rest of it: Regents Park, where she'd ridden with Phillip, the Marquess of Rockley, and where he'd first kissed her. The grand residences, where she'd danced with him, fallen in love with him. The theater near Covent Garden, into which she'd sent him to fetch her supposedly lost shawl—so she could secretly stake a vampire.

The Silver Chalice, a pub patronized by the undead and owned by Sebastian, into which Phillip had followed her. And where, after they'd married, he had been captured by vampires.

St. Heath's Row, the grand London Town estate of the Marquess and Marchioness of Rockley, where she and Phillip had lived in marital harmony for little more than four weeks before he made that fateful visit to the Silver Chalice.

And where, in her bedchamber, she'd slain the vampire he'd become.

No. Victoria had not missed London at all.

Yet, she was back at St. Heath's Row after more than six months spent in Rome, for it was time for her to remove all of her belongings from the residence. The Rockley heir had been found at last, in a place called Kentucky, and he would soon take over the properties, leaving Victoria to return permanently to Rome—or wherever else the Venators needed her.

Thus, eighteen months after Phillip's death, here she sat: surrounded by his essence, stifled by the memories—and awash in thick, cream-colored, engraved invitations that she cared not a blasted fig for.

"But what do you expect, Victoria dear? You hadn't even come fully out of mourning for Rockley when you left for Venice," said her mother, Lady Melisande Grantworth. There was clear reproach in her voice even as the calculating gleam in her eyes boded no good for Victoria's solitude. She'd been rifling through the invitations as if they were her own, and her daughter still an unwed miss ready to debut into Society. "The ton is holding its collective breath, waiting to see who will be the first to host the Marchioness of Rockley in a year and a half. After the romantic tragedy of your short-lived marriage and Rockley dying at sea—"

"Stop it," Victoria said sharply. She caught herself, pulled back on the deep-seated anger that always seemed to be with her now, and closed her eyes. "Mother, I am not here to reenter Society in any manner. Except for Gwendolyn's wedding, I intend to make as few appearances as possible."

"But—"

"Please," she said between gritted teeth. Her head

pounded and her fingers ached from being curled so tightly. "I've only just arrived yesterday."

"And look how quickly all of the invitations have begun to pour in."

Victoria opened her eyes to see Lady Melly looking at her. The gleam had ebbed from her gaze, yet she didn't appear affronted by her daughter's edgy voice.

"I know that Winnie would dearly love to be the one to introduce you back into Society before Miss Starcasset's wedding. Please do think about how happy it would make her if you were to attend her fete on Friday."

"I'll consider it, Mama."

Barely a week later, Victoria found herself slogging through ankle-deep sewage deep beneath London. Stake in hand, she ducked to keep from scraping her head on a low dip of the tunnel ceiling. What had once been a small river tributary flowing south to the Thames had been enclosed by the City's construction during the last six centuries. The sluggish water now oozed with sewage, and only God and the toshers knew what else.

She considered herself quite hardened to repugnant images by now, but even she didn't particularly relish the thought of what her boots were crushing as she stepped through the muck.

Victoria knew that she could have been dancing at the Bridgertons' soiree, in a less damp—but just as odiferous—environment if she'd listened to her mother instead of Sebastian. (Lady Bridgerton was known for her exceedingly strong lily of the valley eau de toilette.) She hadn't yet concluded which was the better choice, although despite the obvious drawbacks, she was leaning toward vampire hunting in the sewers.

At least here she could eliminate any creature that ac-

costed her with the slam of a stake. It wouldn't be quite
that easy to dissuade the gossipmongers and fortune-
hunting bachelors of the ton.

"I don't sense any undead," she told Sebastian as she
stepped on something horribly squishy. A rank odor
squelched afresh into the air, and with her next step she
felt something hard and cylindrical roll beneath her boot.
A bone. Hopefully a canine one.

"Do you not?" he asked, his voice smooth and echoing
over the quiet splashing made by their stout leather boots.
"Perhaps there are no vampires about, then. Only the
harmless toshermen, which we may come upon if they
venture this far."

"Or perhaps you lured me down here for another
reason."

She could see the wickedness of his smile in the
torch's uneasy light. "Why should I ruin a perfectly good
pair of breeches—not to mention boots—by coaxing you
here, when I'd much prefer to have you . . . elsewhere."

His frank words caused a sudden swirl of pleasure in
her belly, and Victoria gave an unladylike snort to diffuse
the warm feeling—which had the added result of filling
her nostrils with putrid stench. She wondered how the
toshers could make a living, working down here day after
day, collecting copper, bones, rags, and anything else of
value to sell on the streets above. And how vampires
could stand to live among the odor when the mere smell
of garlic took them aback.

"Of course," Sebastian continued, "it's not as if you'll
be clutching at me and crying for protection, even in a
place as revolting as this. Much to my great regret." He
brandished a torch that cast sporadic shadows to break
the darkness, but Victoria found that she could see surprisingly well even outside the glow.

She was just about to make a wry rejoinder when she became aware of a new sound—that of rushing or falling water. Then she felt a faint prickle at the back of her neck. Her disgust with the dark, viscous environment slid away, replaced by the familiar rush of readiness and a cold smile.

"Ah," he said, cocking his head as if to hear better. "At last. Just when I thought we were well and truly lost."

"We're not alone," Victoria murmured, the prickle flushing into a full-blown chill.

"Undead?" His voice dropped to match hers.

She looked up at him. "Do you not sense them?"

"I do now that you say it," he said. "And it's no surprise, as we're near the place I was looking for."

A sudden splash behind them had Victoria spinning to meet the red-eyed vampire who'd come from nowhere. Presumably, he'd been expecting a slow-moving, malnourished tosherman, for the half demon had taken a moment to roll up the sleeves of his dull shirt, and that attention to grooming was his undoing.

"You should have worn cuff links," Victoria said conversationally the instant before she staked him into undead dust. She blew off the tip of her stake and turned back to Sebastian, who was watching her with an odd sort of smile.

But before she could wonder what it meant, his expression smoothed and he lifted the torch higher. "Take care," he said, gesturing ahead of them.

When she stepped further in the sloshing damp, she saw why. The filthy water fell away, only a few paces ahead of them, cascading into nothingness. A wall loomed beyond the falls, a clear dead end. "What now?"

"There." He gestured with the torch, and she saw a crude ledge slanting up from the sludge.

Carved into the wall, it was easily wide enough for a man to ascend into . . . "Is that an entrance?" Victoria peered up at the dark wall rising in front of them.

"You can see it from here?" Sebastian raised the torch, illuminating it more clearly.

"What's up there?" Victoria had already started to hike up the inclining ledge, keeping her stake at the ready. Water dripped from her boots at every step, splattering quietly on the rock beneath.

"Something that I'm certain you'll be fascinated to see," he said from behind her, suddenly very close. "Perhaps you'll even wish to reward me for showing you." His breath was warm on the side of her neck, which was exposed by the long, single braid she wore tucked into her coat.

"Unless it's Lilith's dust, I highly doubt that," she replied. Her heart beat a bit off as he moved behind her. "But you can certainly continue to hope."

Since they'd left Rome, Sebastian had made it abundantly clear that he'd be delighted to return to her bed—not that he'd really ever been there, for they'd only been intimate twice, and neither occasion had been in anyone's bedchamber.

And she wasn't quite ready to let him, for a variety of reasons—not least of which was that she still wasn't quite comfortable with the idea of trusting him.

At the top of the ledge, which was perhaps six feet above the tumbling waterfall, Victoria reached the opening. The entrance, camouflaged by the shiny darkness of the damp walls, and difficult to breach due to its position over the falls, was also at an angle. No one would notice it in this unpleasant, inky environment unless they were looking for it, or unless it was a vampire who could see in the dark.

Victoria wasn't certain what she was expecting when she stepped through the crevice, but it wasn't the narrow space she beheld. After her initial survey to ensure no one was waiting for them in the darkness—no chill at the back of her neck heralding the undead, nor the faint, putrid death-smell of a demon, nor even the presence·of another human—she stepped in and looked around.

With its stone walls and single flickering torch, the chamber reminded her immediately of the Consilium, the subterranean warren of chambers and corridors in Rome that served as the center of knowledge, history, and communication for the Venators. Created among the catacombs of the old city, where the first Venator had been called to serve in the fight against the undead, its location had been kept secret for centuries. This place, though much darker and colder, was similar in that it was obviously man-made, and not a natural cavern. And somehow, even the stench of the sewage below was filtered out. Or perhaps Victoria was simply becoming used to the smell.

Sebastian stepped in behind her, and then brushed past as he started further into the darkness where Victoria could see an archway of stone and the outline of a door. "As you can see, this was built long ago, around the time my gran—Beauregard was turned undead. It was originally beneath a Carmelite abbey, if you can believe the irony—although monks never actually lived down here. That's a story in itself."

"Which I'm certain your grandfather told you as he dandled you in your leading strings on his knee. What a terrible choice for bedtime storytelling."

"Bedtime story? Now that you mention it, I have a few I'd like to share with you."

Victoria heard his soft chuckle as she followed him

across the small antechamber, her lips twitching in spite of herself. At a solid stone door, he paused. Although his body blocked her view, she heard the faint clunks of something tumbling into place. "You know the way to unlock the door to a vampire lair. It is a vampire lair, I presume. Why should that not surprise me."

"Well, dash it all. My plan to fascinate and mystify you into a more accommodating mood is obviously not working. And yes, it is a vampire lair. One of the oldest in England." He turned to look at her, their faces close in the small yellow light. His eyes glowed like a hungry cat's. "No vampires around?"

"None that I can feel," she replied.

"Good." Before she could wonder why he had to ask, he grasped her by the shoulders, pushing her back against the rough wall. He followed the momentum of her movement, lining his warm body against hers as he lowered his face.

She met his mouth, her body pressed between Sebastian and the wall as their kiss eased into a long, loose tangle of lips and tongue. Heat seeped through her clothing, into breasts and belly and thighs as he pressed against her, just as the cold ooze from behind chilled her. She closed her eyes, let her knees give a little. It was good . . . good to be held, good to feel the spiral of desire curling through her, good to know that she was still alive. Still human and able to feel her own heartbeat lift and pound.

But the kiss dug up memories, frightening and dark images that threatened to overwhelm the pleasure of the moment . . . of needle-sharp fangs piercing her skin, the chill and warmth of the undead's lips as they mauled at her flesh, seducing and culling her consciousness . . . luring her into a funnel of malevolence and darkness. . . .

She nudged the unpleasant images away and delved

more fiercely into the taste of Sebastian, reveling in his smoky, lemony smell and the heat—heat, uninterrupted by chill or pain.

He pulled away, tugging her lower lip gently between his teeth in a little nick of surprise, then surging back to fully cover her mouth again, leaving her breathless. And then he eased back, releasing her from the kiss. She felt the curve of his lips as he smiled faintly against her, and the soft whisk of his clove-scented breath.

"Ah, then," he murmured, loosening his hold on her shoulders. "You haven't forgotten."

"No, of course not." Her voice was too husky, and, by God, her knees felt much too unsteady. She straightened them and stepped away from the supporting wall.

"I'd begun to wonder." He moved back, looked down at her. She hadn't even noticed when he slid the torch into a holder near the door, and now its light embraced them and their uneven breaths. His smile was crooked and his eyes burned amber, leaving no mistake about what he wanted.

"What's behind the door?" she asked briskly, to break the mood. "What are you looking for? Although it wouldn't surprise me to learn I was wrong, I'm fairly certain you didn't bring me here merely for seduction purposes."

"Of course not, but I couldn't resist the opportunity. You've kept me at such arm's length these last two months, since . . . since you woke up." His voice faltered in a rather un-Sebastian-like manner. She felt him draw in a breath and then he cautiously pushed the door inward. "And you're right, of course—I am looking for something," he said over his shoulder.

"And you needed me to help you." She followed him,

shifting out of his way when he reached to close the door behind them.

"Well, it might get a bit messy, and you know how I deplore drawing blood or exploding ash."

Her lips quirked in a smile as she looked around the room. There were no torches in here but she was able to discern more than shadows and shapes in the darkness before a tiny light flared to life in Sebastian's hands.

"Using the little light sticks Miro created, I see," she commented. "Do you carry them in your boot heel as Max did?"

"If I had," he replied, lighting a sconce near the door, "they'd be wet and sloppy after slogging through that mess. I did have the foresight to keep them in a dry place, my dear Victoria. Much as it might surprise you that I think ahead—"

"Oh, there's no doubt that you think ahead, Sebastian— usually about where to disappear to when things get dangerous." And that was why, even though she knew he was a Venator, Victoria couldn't quite trust him. He'd been too unreliable in the past.

As Victoria scanned the dark chamber, she saw the influence of the monks in the simplicity of what must have been some sort of main hall. The floor was uneven beneath her feet, and she could see some old furnishings— broken chairs, an upended table—near one end, as though they'd been tossed there during a bout of cleaning. Other than that, the room was empty but for a few tattered tapestries hanging from the wall, and a dozen scattered stones. The walls were the same charcoal and black shade as the sewer tunnel, slate discolored by years of dirt and smoke. There were, of course, no windows, and only a small fireplace that must have some sort of chimney.

There was only a single door, this one made of stout wood, beyond the one through which they'd come.

She followed him as he made his way across the abandoned room toward the door. And just then, the ruffle of a chill slipped over the back of her neck. Victoria readied her stake. Perhaps the place wasn't as abandoned as it appeared.

Sebastian didn't have to unlock this door and, when it cracked open, Victoria wasn't surprised to see a warm glow of light bleeding through. The chill on her neck had intensified slightly, yet she didn't think the undead— perhaps one or two of them—were in close proximity.

"Are you going to tell me what you're looking for before the vampires appear?" she asked.

"Perhaps. It may take a few moments. I'm not sure exactly . . ." Sebastian said this as he prodded the door open further, and Victoria saw a much more inviting setting than the chamber behind them. Though it might not be as comfortable as a parlor in St. James, with its upright chairs, tables covered with a variety of objects, and several torches, this smaller space was obviously occupied. Or had been recently, if the bundles of clothing and blankets littering the room were any indication.

Victoria followed Sebastian in, closing the door behind her to act as a warning for new arrivals—undead or mortal—as much as to keep the warmth and light contained within. Now that she had stepped inside, the first thing that struck her about the chamber was the smell permeating the air.

Blood.

Sharp, thick. Like iron.

Something hitched at the back of her throat, and her stomach lurched as she remembered being inundated with it—the taste, the odor, the heaviness on her tongue, the thick slide down her throat. Victoria gagged; yet even as she did so, her nostrils flared as though to drag in the smell, and saliva pooled in her mouth.

Her vision blurred, and a rosy haze filtered over the room as she forced herself to draw in a deep, blood-scented breath. Closing her eyes, she exhaled long and slow, pushing the smell away, then pulled in another breath, deep and easy. By this time, the sharp smell had softened and the nausea ebbed.

She opened her eyes. The red tinge was gone, and she stood steadier. The brush of chill at the back of her neck hadn't changed, indicating the vampires weren't yet in near vicinity. Looking over at Sebastian, she was gratified that he was too busy to have noticed her lapse. Or whatever it had been.

What *had* it been?

Tightening fingers that felt weak, she gripped her stake as if it were a talisman and walked toward Sebastian as he knelt at the base of a large stone chair in the center of one wall. With its dusty, torn cushions and white marble arms, it put her in mind of a masonry throne. Its white and red marble gleamed coolly in the light.

When she got close enough, she planted herself next to Sebastian, shiny muck still clinging to her boots. She looked down at the back of his thick, curling hair, watching the flex of shoulders beneath his coat as he worked. It wasn't until she stepped aside that she saw he was unbolting the chair's two front feet from the floor.

They weren't really bolts, she realized when he handed them up to her, but more like thick stone plugs that had been fitted through the clawlike curls of the marble feet and down into the stone-and-dirt floor. Cleverly designed caps on the bolts, when sunk into place, camouflaged them as part of the chair's design.

"The chair must hide something Beauregard told you about," Victoria said, rolling the finger-width cylinders in her palm. As they bumped together with a dull clunk, she realized the heavy bloodscent was threatening her again. She shook her head sharply, and concentrated on breathing steadily as the feeling passed.

"As usual," he muttered as he pulled gracefully to his feet, "you surprise me with your insight. If I thought we had the time, I'd kiss you senseless right here. Or perhaps"—he grinned lasciviously, glancing at the behemoth chair—"we could find other uses for this."

Victoria stepped back as though to put herself out of his reach, then felt ridiculous for doing so. He noticed, and although his smile remained fixed, the jest faded from his eyes. "Well then, since that's not your preference, let us see what lies behind this bloody thing."

Despite the great weight of the stone chair, it was easy for Sebastian, who of course wore the *vis bulla*, to move on his own. With a dull, gritty scrape, he shoved it aside so that he could approach the wall against which it had stood. Victoria heard his small sound of satisfaction just as the chill on the back of her neck exploded into a blast of cold.

"They're coming," she said, spinning around to face the door from which they'd entered. "Two or three, I think. I'll take care—"

But her words strangled in her throat as Sebastian leaped into place beside her, stake in hand.

An odd thing. So odd, after their debates time and again about the finality of sending a vampire to his death—to eternal damnation—and how Sebastian refused to be the one to pass such judgment on the creatures. So odd to see him holding a stake, ready to use it, instead of running the other way.

It was almost like being with Max.

The chill intensified and was now accompanied by deep, guttural voices just beyond the door. Sebastian whispered, "Get them before they see that the chair is moved."

Victoria was only too happy to oblige. She was waiting when the first undead stepped through the door, and the element of surprise along with the fact that he was turning to speak to someone behind him made it easy to turn him into a pile of ash.

His companions, a woman with long blonde hair and a man sporting a shiny head and a red beard, weren't quite as easily dispatched. However, the element of surprise and Victoria's quick decision to push between the two undead, back into the previous, darker chamber, at least brought the battle out of sight of the dismantled throne.

When she turned back to face the vampires, who had whirled after her, Victoria saw Sebastian emerge from the entrance behind them. The creatures rushed at her, fangs bared and eyes gleaming red, fairly glowing in this dark room.

She ducked and rammed her shoulder into the abdomen of the male in one smooth move, causing him to tumble over her spine and land with a thud on the floor. But his hand snaked out and grasped her ankle, tripping her as she slammed her stake at the female's chest. The stake drove into the vampire's shoulder instead of sliding easily into her heart, sending a shock along Victoria's arm.

Just as she began scrambling to her feet, a soft poof sent the bald vampire into an explosion of ash. She glanced over at Sebastian in surprise—until now, she hadn't been sure he'd really do it. She'd never actually seen him stake a vampire; when he killed Beauregard, she'd been too far gone to notice anything.

That left the female, and she began to back away, fear in her pale, gaunt face. But Victoria was too quick for her. Upright now, she started after her, following when the undead began to run. She had the extra moment when the creature had to pause to open the stone door leading to the small antechamber, and Victoria used it, leaping toward her.

They tumbled to the dirty floor, the vampire's long, blonde hair tangling about them like a greasy net. Victoria rolled on top and raised her stake, but the undead grasped her wrist in midstrike and flipped them both over so that she had the upper position. Her fangs were extended, digging into the full flesh of her lower lip as she struggled to force Victoria's hands to the ground behind her.

The odd rosy haze was beginning to feed into the corners of her vision when a shadow loomed above. The vampire jerked, and then the pressure on her wrists was released. A cloud of ash showered over Victoria, sprinkling her mouth and nose with the dusty, decayed smell.

Victoria jumped to her feet, shooting a glance at Sebastian. "Now that you've decided to slay vampires, you've really committed to it," she said, not quite successful in keeping all of the annoyance from her voice. "I didn't need your assistance." She spit out a mouthful of dust as she brushed the rest of it from her face and shoulders.

"Oho, so that's how it is. Shall I never please you? For months, you disparage my disinclination to slay vampires . . . and now that I'm doing so, you rebuff me. Tsk, tsk, Victoria. I thought that you, of all women, would not be fickle." He turned and walked back toward the comfortable room.

Victoria resisted the urge to tell him that it wasn't that he was staking the vampires; it was that he'd interfered when she hadn't needed him to. Max would have stood and watched, criticizing her technique all the while, but only stepping in if things got out of hand.

And she wasn't quite sure, as she stood there looking after Sebastian, which type she preferred.

The temperature at the back of her neck had returned to normal, indicating that there weren't any other undead in the vicinity, so Victoria decided she ought to examine the parlorlike chamber a bit more closely.

The oldest vampire lair in England, he'd said. Clearly, Beauregard had been busy educating his great-great-great-(some number of greats)-grandson about his demonic heritage.

Victoria pursed her lips as she looked over at Sebastian, who'd opened a small door that had been revealed with the movement of the throne. It would be best if she tried to find out what he was after, even though he was obviously not inclined to tell her.

She started toward him, but her attention was caught by what she had originally thought were bundles of clothing or blankets. But from this angle . . .

"Dear God."

She was at the side of the bodies in an instant, Sebastian and his cubbyhole forgotten for the moment.

He looked over. "What is—oh. Damnation."

There were three of them in heaps on the floor, tossed near the wall like trash. Blood—dried, congealed, pooled—was on their ravaged faces and hands, on the floor, spattered low on the wall. The stench filled her nose, and her fingers closed into each of her palms as she fought to stay steady, keep her breathing even.

"Victoria." Sebastian was there, his face suddenly close to hers.

She grabbed in a deep breath and shook her head. "I'm fine."

He knelt beside the bodies, heaped on top of each other haphazardly, and gently moved them so that their faces were revealed—or what was left of them. They were all men, and their clothing was in shreds. The vampires hadn't merely fed on them, they'd mauled and destroyed them. Even tortured them, if the rawness of the wrists was any sign.

"This is what you allowed to walk free when you turned your back on the Venators," Victoria said, her voice cold. "How many innocents have suffered like this when they could have been saved?" The fury burned through her, and her fingers were shaking. The haze colored her vision and she felt rage surging through her like a team of horses gone wild.

And then she turned over the last body, and saw the familiar face.

Three

Wherein Our Heroine Succumbs to a Maternal Threat

There was nothing to wrap the corpse in but her coat, and Sebastian's too, which Victoria immediately demanded. Although the body was cold, he couldn't have been dead for long, as the pools of blood around him had not yet completely dried. Oddly enough, neither bugs nor other vermin had yet discovered the destroyed flesh.

"Who is it?" Sebastian asked. His sensual voice was clipped, no doubt by anger at her sharp accusation. It wouldn't be guilt. Not Sebastian.

Victoria cared little for his sensitivities. She had said what needed to be said, even though it angered him.

"It's Briyani, Max's Comitator," she told him. "Kritanu's nephew."

Victoria carefully wrapped up the young man, who'd been perhaps only five years older than her own two decades. He'd been a smart, sharp fighter, brave and skilled. It had been he, along with his uncle, who had helped her and Max escape from Lilith during a terrible fire.

Not a Venator, no, but Briyani had been just as important in the fight against the undead. He had been Max's Comitator—his assistant, valet, and an expert who trained him in the Indian martial art of *kalaripayattu*.

Truth be told, both Max and Briyani had learned their skills at the hands of Kritanu, who had been Eustacia's companion and trainer for fifty years. But Briyani, who had been training since he was ten, had been working with Max to keep his skills honed for more than eight years.

And now he was gone.

She hoisted Briyani's body over her shoulder, frowning when Sebastian made a move to assist, and said, "I'll do it. Heaven forbid you should get blood on your shirt."

"I'm exceedingly appreciative of your consideration," he replied. But the usual self-deprecating tone was missing. "I'll just be a moment." He loped back over to the throne and began to put it all back the way it had been.

The burden heavy on her shoulder, Victoria walked slowly toward the exit as thoughts tumbled through her mind. She could find out later from Sebastian what he'd found behind the throne—if anything. But for now, she had other worries.

The last time she'd seen Briyani, he'd been in Rome. How had he come to be in London? Was he with Max? Did that mean Max was here? Why would he come to London when he hated England?

Did Max know Briyani was missing?

How was she to let him know about his trusted friend and companion if he was in hiding from Lilith? And she had to tell Kritanu, as well.

Tears welled at the corner of her eyes. She used her free hand to swipe angrily at them. This was part of her life, part of her choice. It would never get easier.

While the London ton danced and ate and copulated and gossiped, this evil happened. All the time, beneath their silken slippers and buffed boots.

Sebastian returned to her side, silent and grave.

"Did you get what you came for?" she asked, unable to keep a fringe of disgust from her voice.

He gave a brief nod and, to her surprise, held up a ring between his thumb and forefinger. She caught his gaze, one of those rich topaz eyes framed almost perfectly by the ring, which was thick and made of copper. She'd seen one exactly like it, braided with twisted copper strands, hidden away at the Consilium.

"One of Lilith's rings," Victoria breathed. There were only five in existence, and the Venators were in possession of one of them—now, two.

"I shall accept your gratitude later, once we're quit of this place." Head high, shoulders straight, he led the way from the underground chamber, back out into the foul sewers.

"I daresay, Victoria, I've asked thrice for your opinion on this lace." Gwendolyn Starcasset's voice at last penetrated Victoria's reverie. "You look exhausted, dearest. Are you certain you're feeling well?"

What could have been a petulant tone was as gentle and concerned as that of a young mother, drawing Victoria back to the gilded, laced, and overstuffed private sitting room of the Starcasset residence like a remonstrated child. An untouched tea service sat on the small walnut piecrust table next to the rose-upholstered divan on which she sat. Lemon biscuits and poppyseed scones, along with chestnut cakes, decorated a small, delicate platter. Despite her particular fondness for lemons and chestnuts, Victoria was unmoved.

Gwendolyn, one of the few young women Victoria had befriended during the Season during which she'd met and married Phillip, sat across from her in a wide-armed chair. Her spring green day dress and cornflower ribbons made her appear young and fresh in contrast to the maturity and weariness that seemed to weigh upon Victoria. Gwen's pale blonde hair was twisted high at the back of her head, with two generous locks rolled into sagging curls on either side of her face.

Victoria never had to worry about sagging curls, for her mane was composed of thick, springy ones, yet she knew that her coiffure wasn't nearly as elegant as her friend's. At one time, long ago, it would have been a task labored over with great care. But now, she barely allowed her maid to pin it into a chignon.

"I'm so sorry, Gwen," she said. "I must confess, I am a bit tired and still recovering from the headache that kept me away from the Bridgerton soiree last night." Not to mention the task of taking care of the corpse she'd brought home. She couldn't exactly walk across the front threshold of St. Heath's Row carrying Briyani's mauled body. With Sebastian's help, she'd managed to get it into the small chapel on the grounds, unseen. This morning she'd sent word to Kritanu, who was living at the town house Aunt Eustacia had bequeathed to Victoria. She didn't know when she'd have the chance to talk with Kritanu, but at least he could be with his nephew.

The only thing that had been simple about last evening's events was bidding Sebastian good night; she'd expected him to attempt to make his case for why—and how—she should thank him for finding the ring.

He must still have been angry with her for her cutting comments when she found Briyani's body, for he hadn't even tried to steal a kiss when he let her off. She couldn't remember the last time they were together that he hadn't attempted to tease or coax her into some sort of intimacy, even when she was angry or annoyed with him. Even earlier that evening, in the sewers, he'd made an attempt.

"We missed you, and of course everyone was asking everyone else if they'd called on you, or had seen you."

Victoria discarded all thought of Sebastian and smiled. "I hope you told them a great tale."

Gwen smiled back, showing deep, delicious dimples. She looked a bit weary too, or perhaps it was merely the stress of her upcoming nuptials. "Of course—I told them that you were remaining in seclusion until my wedding. Now, everyone will be even more eager to attend."

"As if marrying the Earl of Brodebaugh isn't enough of a reason to entice the entire ton and half the king's court to attend. His style and flair is superb, and his family is certain to spend hugely on the wedding."

Victoria may have been in Italy for nearly a year, but her mother had made certain she'd not fallen behind in Society gossip. And now that the Prince Regent would be crowned George IV in a matter of weeks, there was even more to gossip about—such as his wife, Queen Caroline, who'd recently returned from years of self-exile in Italy. Despite the scandal that had surrounded her over the affair she'd conducted with her Italian servant, Bartolomo Pergami, the queen had been welcomed back to England by the masses—purely because George was so unpopular, and he hated her.

Victoria dutifully pushed away her grief and weariness, and her potent dislike for nearly everything related to her old life of balls and fetes and musicales, and leaned closer to Gwen. "The lace is very fine, and I think it will be lovely on a wedding gown."

She wished she really did give more than a fig about

these things, but it was difficult to worry over tatting and trims when Briyani lay dead and she hadn't been able to see Kritanu yet. He was staying at the home he'd shared with Aunt Eustacia here in London; the place where Victoria would move upon leaving St. Heath's Row—which was yet another thing she needed to attend to.

"Oh, dear, Victoria," her friend sighed in mock annoyance. "But you haven't been listening to a word I've said, have you? This lace, this beautiful Brussels lace, isn't meant for my wedding gown . . . but for my wedding *night*. That is why I invited you *here*, to the *private* parlor. Why, see, I've even had the drapes drawn!" Her eyes sparkled with mischief.

"Ahh!" Victoria picked up the lace again. It was quite lovely—an eggshell white, shot through with shiny, glittering silver thread, tatted into the most intricate miniatures of loops and knots and scallops. "The earl will no doubt find himself speechless with delight."

"I do hope so." Gwen beamed, and for a moment, in the glare of her happiness, Victoria was shocked by pure, unadulterated *envy*.

It shot through her like a bolt of lightning: envy that she'd never have an ignorant life with a man she loved, and who loved her (for it was clearly a love match between Miss Starcasset and her wealthy earl, despite the fact that he was more than two decades older than she). The ugly feeling roiled inside her, threatening to burst free in the form of snide remarks and accusations that she didn't really mean.

Victoria dropped the lace when she realized her fingers had crumpled it, and a sting of tears surprised her. She forced herself to take a deep breath, to smile, to look at her friend's beaming face and ask herself: *Why shouldn't she be happy? Some of us have to be. I've more than enough angst for both of us.*

"And George may soon follow—as you can imagine, my mother has been nagging at him for years now," Gwendolyn was rattling on. Miraculously, she hadn't noticed or recognized Victoria's lapse, saving her from another explanation that would likely make no sense.

But Gwen's words served also to catch Victoria's attention, snatching her back to their conversation. "George? Your brother has returned to London?" She lifted her teacup.

The last time she'd seen George Starcasset had been in Rome, when he had imprisoned Victoria, Max, and Sebastian—capturing them for the demon Akvan. Victoria didn't know when or how George had become involved with the Tutela, the secret society of mortals that protected and served vampires, but he had become a nuisance. When he wasn't trying to seduce her, he was handing her over to the undead or a demon. And not doing it very capably.

When Max had taken on the task of destroying Akvan, George had disappeared during the melee that followed, and was presumed dead.

Apparently, that was not the case, if he was planning to attend Gwendolyn's wedding.

"Oh, yes. Mother and I hadn't had any letters from him for more than a month, then about three weeks ago he returned from his Grand Tour of the Continent. Then he spent a week at Claythorne Manor before arriving here in Town. I hope you don't mind my saying so," Gwen continued, "but I confess, I always harbored the hope that you and George might form an attachment, Victoria." She held up her hands as if to ward off any response her friend might make, adding, "Not now, of course, for it's not even been two years since Rockley died, but . . . well, he seemed quite smitten with you during the house party at Claythorne, and you didn't seem put off by him at all. And then he followed you to Italy, and I thought—"

"No, indeed," Victoria replied politely, thinking that the only off-putting thing about Mr. Starcasset was that he'd sneaked into her bedchamber during that very same house party—after inviting vampires to the estate. Oh, and that he'd planned to ravish her at gunpoint when they met up in Rome. No. She didn't find him terribly off-putting at all. More like an annoying gnat.

"But, alas, it appears my fondest wishes will never come to fruition . . . unless . . . you can distract him from that Italian woman he seems to have developed a *tendre* for."

"Italian woman?" There was only one person that could be. Victoria set her tea down—it was cold, and she'd put too much sugar in it.

"Signorina Sarafina Regalado," said Gwen. "Aside from the fact that she is disrupting my plans to have you as a sister-in-law, I rather like her myself. For all her English leaves much to be desired, her sense of fashion is quite good. She's been a blessing as I prepare my trousseau." If that was a veiled criticism of Victoria's inattention, it was belied by the sparkle in her friend's eyes.

Victoria raised her brows and reached for a lemon biscuit. "Blessing" was not quite the word she'd use to describe Sara Regalado. But Gwen was indeed right—Sara had a deep love for fashion, and debates about which lace to adorn which gown, new fabrics, and how long a hem should be dominated her every conversation. And the woman seemed to collect fiancés even more quickly than shoes. Less than a year ago, she and Max had been engaged.

Supposedly.

Victoria had never been able to get a straight answer from Max as to whether he had arranged the betrothal in order for him to be accepted by the Tutela, or a real engagement. It had been vital for him to pretend to be wholly loyal to the Tutela, as well as Nedas, in order to get into the inner circle of vampires and close enough to destroy the demonic obelisk. He'd even had to do the unthinkable in order to be accepted: execute Aunt Eustacia. Knowing that, it shouldn't surprise Victoria that he'd go so far as to get engaged to a woman who was part of the Tutela . . . but how much further would he have gone?

The one time she'd pressed him about whether he really would have married Sara, Max had replied, "If it was necessary, I would have."

Victoria had never actually asked Max if he'd loved his fiancée—for if he had, he must have been devastated by the fact that Sara's father, the leader of the Tutela, had been turned to a vampire.

Not to mention the fact that the lady in question seemed to enjoy being around and fed upon by vampires. Victoria had staked the newly undead Conte Regalado herself several months ago when he turned his attentions to wooing Lady Melly. But she wouldn't be surprised if Sarafina had taken her father's place—either as the leader of the Tutela, or as a vampire herself.

And now, Sara had arrived in London, ostensibly as George Starcasset's fiancée.

And Briyani had been found in a hidden vampire lair. In London.

It couldn't be a coincidence.

Because of her late nights patrolling streets where the undead might be found, Victoria wasn't often about during the day. Normally, she spent much of sunlight's hours catching up on her sleep, practicing her fighting skills with Kritanu, and avoiding her mother. But today she had to make an appearance.

Ironically, the cream of London Society lived much the same schedule as a Venator—sleeping late in the day, often till noon, then rising and dressing for afternoon calls. Late in the afternoon, they returned home to dress for the evening's events, which could include the theater, a dinner party, or a ball, wherein they ate and danced and gossiped until the early hours of morning.

Victoria's visit to Gwendolyn today had been made rather earlier than usual. They'd had luncheon together in the private parlor strewn with bolts of lace, silk, and ribbons.

After leaving the Starcasset residence, Victoria fulfilled her mother's demand to join her for her own afternoon calls. Lady Melly was no longer content to wait for her daughter to make her own entrée back into Society, and she'd threatened to bring droves of her friends down upon St. Heath's Row if her daughter didn't cooperate. Thus, she sat Victoria on the least comfortable chair—which also happened to be the focal point of a room overfilled with parlor chairs, twittering ladies, eaux de toilette of the most sweet scents, and poorly hidden nosiness.

"We are so pleased you've returned from your journey to Italy," crooned Lady Winnie, the Duchess of Farnham and one of Lady Melly's two cronies. She enveloped Victoria in a smothering hug against her shelflike bosom, her plump arms stronger than they looked. "We had a lovely time visiting you there, but the ton was calling, and of course, we had to return." When she released Victoria, she moved smoothly to scoop up three little ginger biscuits and a lemon scone.

Victoria smothered a smile. Fortunately, Lady Winnie wasn't able to recall just how much fun they'd had visiting her, thanks to Aunt Eustacia's special golden disk. With Wayren's help, Victoria had been able to eliminate any memories the ladies might have had about their attempt to hunt down and stake the Conte Regalado. Lady Winnie herself had carried a wooden pike as thick as her arm.

"It was quite exciting to be in Rome—or shall I say *Roma*?" added Lady Petronilla, rolling her R enthusiastically. Lady Nilly was one of Lady Melly's closest friends, and a surrogate aunt to Victoria. "The Carnivale was astonishing, but I daresay the King's coronation will be even more of an event. I've heard he's spending upward of forty-four thousand pounds . . . on his robe alone!"

"I never had the chance to give you my condolences personally, Lady Rockley," said Mrs. Winkledon, wedging herself between Ladies Melly and Nilly on the sofa. "About the loss of your dear Rockley. A love match it was, was it not?" Her sharp eyes matched her sharp nose, which nearly quivered with curiosity, as if she expected Victoria to admit that she hadn't actually loved Phillip. Not that it should matter, for few ton marriages were love matches. In fact, it was almost considered passé to love one's spouse.

"Thank you, Mrs. Winkledon," Victoria replied. "I do miss Phillip terribly." That was at least the truth.

"An accident on a ship?" asked Lady Breadlington, leaning in with a smile. Her teeth, flat instead of curved across the front of her mouth, looked as though they'd been kicked in by a horse. "How terrible that he perished in the cold sea, on his way to—where was it? Spain? His body was never found, was it?"

"No, indeed," Victoria replied. Unless you counted the

pile of ash that had poofed all over her bedchamber. She kept a bit of it in a small container on her dressing table. "But we had a burial service anyway . . . and, forgive me, but I cannot recall if you were in attendance?"

"Oh, no, I'm so sorry, my dear lady, but we had already repaired to the Country by then. Grouse season." Lady Breadlington had the grace to look abashed, which had exactly been Victoria's intention.

Most of the twenty or so women who crowded the Grantworth parlor were not close friends of Victoria's mother. They were here because they couldn't stand not to be the first to see the infamous Lady Rockley, who'd married, shockingly, for love, and whose husband had died tragically little more than a month after their wedding. And who hadn't been seen in Society since, even after her year of mourning.

"Odd," grumbled elderly Lady Thurling, her shiny, knobby fingers closed over the top of her walking stick, "last time I saw Lord Rockley, he claimed he would attend my granddaughter's wedding in four days, and yet two days later"—she paused to catch a wheezing breath—"sets off on a voyage without his new wife. And never comes back." She glared at Victoria with watery blue eyes gleaming with satisfaction.

She'd said exactly what had been on everyone's mind.

Victoria made what she hoped was a sad smile. "Yes, indeed, it was tragic. He was called away and hardly had the time to say good-bye, and I . . . well—"

"We thought at the time Victoria was in no *condition*," Lady Melly interrupted with a properly sad smile of her own, "to go with him."

There was a small chorus of sympathetic gasps, and then eyes became rounder and hands began to grasp at and pat Victoria's, and even a nose or two—the pointiest ones—tinged a bit red on the tips.

Nothing could have been further from the truth, except that it had been Lady Melly's baseless hope, but Victoria was delighted to have the conversation rerouted. She glanced surreptitiously at the watch pinned to Lady Thurlington's dress. It was the only one large enough to read from across the tea table, but it was fastened upside down so that the elderly lady could look down and easily read it.

Half past three. She'd been here only an hour.

Victoria endured another twenty minutes of sly queries and sympathy coated more thickly than the iced basil cakes before the opportunity for escape presented itself.

"A turn around the park?" she said. "Why, Mr. and Miss Needleton, I should greatly enjoy that." She was up and out of her seat before her mother could protest.

Mr. and Miss Needleton—a brother and sister—and their other companion, Miss Durfingdale, were the only visitors who had not been overly inquisitive, and were also in close proximity to Victoria's own age of twenty.

When Lady Melly opened her mouth—surely to argue—Victoria surged forward to hug her, effectively smothering anything she might have said. Her nostrils filled with the sweet yet comforting milk rose scent her mother always wore, she whispered, "I heard Mr. Needleton has more than forty thousand a year."

Lady Melly stiffened under her hands, but when she pulled away, Victoria saw that her mother had a most calculating look on her face as she examined the unfortunate Mr. Needleton, whose squashed nose resembled anything but his name. Even though Victoria had inherited a generous income from both her husband and aunt, Lady

Melly was of the mind that one could never have too much money. "Have a lovely time, my dear."

As Victoria left the room, the last thing she heard was, "—so glad to see her get out with young people her own age. It's been far too long, and—" The door closed, and she was with her new companions.

Victoria would have preferred driving her own curricle alongside the Needleton carriage, enabling her to divest herself of their company as soon as was polite. But Miss Needleton was to have none of it.

She was no more than a wisp of a girl, with flyaway hair of a nondescript brown, and soulful brown eyes. In addition, she had an excuse that made it impossible for Victoria to decline her request that she ride in the carriage.

"I knew Rockley when he was a young boy," Miss Needleton said. "Perhaps if you sit next to me, I could tell you some stories about him."

Curiosity won out, of course. Victoria climbed into the carriage with the help of Mr. Needleton, whose pale cheeks flushed with pleasure as their gloved hands skidded against each other. Smiling at him, and settling her day dress skirts so that they didn't infringe upon his sister's or Miss Durfingdale's, she realized how easy it could be for her to slip back into this world. Perhaps too easy.

If her mother had her way, Victoria would be intent on finding a new husband in order to provide Lady Melly with grandchildren (and an heir to the Grantworth estates). Instead all she could think about was what that copper ring meant to Sebastian, and whether he meant to give it to the Venators, or keep it for some other reason. And how to find Max to tell him about Briyani. And what George Starcasset was doing here in London with Sarafina. And how she felt about Sebastian.

How she really felt about Sebastian. A warm flush

spread through her. Whatever her feelings, it was clear that he made her skin tingle and her head light—even when he wasn't around.

Victoria realized with a start that her hands had clasped tightly together, and that Mr. Needleton—ignoring his sister's agenda for conversation—had been expounding quite profusely about the merits of a certain filly at the Derby, and why he expected she should take the cup.

The oaks and cottonwoods were thick and stately as the carriage turned past the stucco villas and into the Outer Circle of Regent's Park. When Victoria and Phillip had driven through here, John Nash had just begun the park's redesign. Though it wasn't near completion, the park already showed his influence, with its sweeping pathways and havens for waterfowl.

"Miss Needleton," Victoria said when the young woman's brother stopped for a breath of air, "did you say that you were acquainted with my husband as a young boy?"

"Yes, my lady," she replied. "His mother was a friend of my mother's, and we spent two summers together when I was seven and he was perhaps thirteen. He was frightfully fond of raspberries, though his mother forbade him to eat any, for they gave him a terrible rash. I recall how he convinced me to go berry picking with him one day—"

Her story was interrupted as the carriage approached that of another high-strung vehicle. As was expected, the Needletons stopped in order to greet the others. It was Gwendolyn and her earl, Brodebaugh. He seemed vaguely attentive to his adoring fiancée, but kind enough to agree with her when she pressed him for his thoughts on the weather. This was the first time Victoria recalled meeting him—although, according to Gwendolyn, he'd attended the Straithwaite musical the summer of their debut. They exchanged pleasantries for a short time. When the Needleton carriage was ready to move on, another conveyance had approached, and the conversation was extended. Victoria waved to Gwendolyn as Brodebaugh drove away, wishing she'd invited herself to ride back with them, for she didn't anticipate extricating herself any time soon.

For now that word had spread from carriage to rider to curricle that the Marchioness of Rockley was in the Needleton vehicle, everyone seemed to converge on their path.

Victoria's mouth was tired of smiling and her palms were sore from the score of her nails biting through her cotton gloves. She was just about to suggest that they return to the Grantworth home when someone screamed.

They all turned to look toward the terrified cry, which had been cut off in a sort of bubbling way. It had come from the direction of a far distant clump of thick bushes and grass that had not yet been subjected to Mr. Nash's attentions. Victoria bolted to her feet, causing the carriage to sway—but she caught herself before she hurtled out of the vehicle like a madwoman. Miss Needleton looked up at her in astonishment, for apparently it had never occurred to her that she might be of assistance.

Of course it wouldn't. Women of the ton let everything be done for and about them. Victoria remained standing, however, as Mr. Needleton and several other men leaped from their vehicles, dashing toward the cry of distress.

"Oh, my," Miss Durfingdale squeaked rather belatedly, and Victoria, who had nearly forgotten her existence, looked at her in surprise. Was she knocked for six by the scream, or the equally amazing speed at which the men had moved?

"Perhaps they may need assistance," Victoria said, lifting her skirts to climb carefully down from the carriage—

an unusual feat for a woman, but one that she was well accustomed to performing. "If she is in distress."

Miss Needleton's mild protestations ringing in her ears, Victoria hurried as quickly as she could through the tall grasses in the wake of the men. As soon as she was out of sight of the carriage, she thrashed through the brush, heedless of her new muslin day dress, and found herself running down a small incline. At the bottom, a creek trickled beneath scattered trees. Ahead of her, she heard the men running and calling to each other, but she remained silent as she ran pell-mell down the creek bank. There'd been no other cries from the victim, and at last Victoria came to a rushing halt when she reached the small stream.

Panting, she looked around for some sign of trouble, but saw nothing but dappled sunlight over the smooth stones scattered in the creek. Just then, a splash of pink caught her attention behind a massive, felled tree trunk.

It took her only a moment to reach the crumpled figure, and when she did, Victoria gasped in shock. Blood spattered the grass around her, staining the pink gown that had caught her attention. When she turned the young woman over, Victoria stared down at the horror.

The victim's bodice had been torn away, and the flesh of her chest and over her collarbones was marked with three large Xs, gouged into her skin. Fresh blood seeped through the fabric and oozed from her wounds. But what caught Victoria's attention were the four small marks on the girl's blue-white neck.

Vampire bites. Fresh ones.

In the middle of the day.

Four

Wherein a Bellpull Is Out of Commission

Despite the horrible fate of Miss Belvadine Forrest (as the victim's name was revealed to be), it turned out to be morbidly beneficial to Victoria. For, as a result of the traumatic discovery, she simply did not feel up to attending the Burlington-Frigate dinner party that night.

Lady Melly accepted the excuse with watery eyes and a tremulous smile. Armed with yet another fresh topic on which she would be the ultimate source, she took herself off to the dinner party in full regalia.

Victoria, meanwhile, took herself gratefully back to St. Heath's Row.

As the carriage pulled past the iron gates into the generous Rockley house, she glanced past the stables to the small family chapel cloaked by a cluster of maples. Almost two years ago, she'd hidden the Book of Antwartha there to keep it safe from Lilith, and now Briyani reposed in the same building until he was buried.

Vampires couldn't scale the stone walls surrounding the house, for the stone was stamped with crosses in honor of St. Heath, who, apparently, had died upon one (although the story was rather muddied, and no one other than her husband's family, the de Lacys, had ever heard of St. Heath, so there was no way to verify its accuracy). Another, larger, cross sat at the top of the iron gateway, splitting only when the gate was opened. And then of course, there was the fact that the chapel itself was too holy for any undead to enter.

Her groom helped her alight from the carriage, and Victoria hurried up the sweep of steps to the tall double doors. Her first order of business would be to send a message by pigeon to Wayren, in hopes of finding a way to notify Max about Briyani's death, and also to let her know about the events at the park today. The reality of a vampire attack in daylight gave Victoria a heavy, rolling feeling in her stomach. Vampires just weren't able to move about in the sunlight. Their flesh burned instantly, peeling away. Even a powerful vampire like Lilith the Dark couldn't stand pure sunlight.

And that reminded her of the copper ring Sebastian had retrieved. He hadn't offered it to her, nor had he indicated what he planned to use it for. But either way, she would feel much more comfortable if it were placed somewhere in the Consilium for safekeeping. After all, he'd teased her with the fact that she should show him gratitude for locating it—

"My lady," intoned her very proper butler, Lettender, as Victoria crossed the threshold into the vast foyer, "the master awaits you in the parlor."

His words brought her to a surprised halt. "Pardon me?"

"The master has arrived. He awaits you in the parlor," replied Lettender with agonizingly even tones, as though he regularly made such an announcement.

Her mouth suddenly dry and her palms springing moisture, Victoria pivoted slowly toward the twin doors of the sitting room. Absurdly, she'd never noticed before, but a wooden lotus blossom had been stamped in the center of each panel, its design a simple relief in an otherwise austere expanse of creamy white.

It shouldn't be that much of a shock; she'd known her husband's heir would arrive someday soon. She just . . . it had been a very long, trying day.

And she wasn't quite ready, yet, to meet the man who would take Phillip's place.

Victoria drew in a long, slow breath and reached for the glass doorknob. It was cool, even through her gloves, and she turned it.

Stepping in, she turned so as to ensure her skirts had made it completely through, and closed the door. She wanted no witnesses to this meeting.

She looked over.

He must have seen her carriage arrive moments ago, for he stood at one of the tall, narrow windows that faced the half-circle drive. His back was to her; perhaps he hadn't heard the door open and close . . . or perhaps he was merely preparing them both for the inevitable.

But Victoria shook that off. What would he have to prepare for? He, a poor American relation, had just inherited a title and estates that would propel him to wealth, status, and a seat in the House of Lords. He had nothing for which to prepare when meeting the woman who was now the Dowager Marchioness of Rockley.

He turned, the sunlight behind sending his face and features into shadow. At first, her impression was one of a tall puff of hair and angular shoulders, but then he stepped away from the window, closer to her.

"Mrs. Rockley," he said in long, easy accents. "I am

happy to meet you. I am James Lacy, and it is my pleasure to live with you under this roof."

The whole package—his drawling speech, the pure joy in his face, the sag of his ill-fitting clothing—was so different from Phillip that immediately Victoria felt a combination of relief and regret. And then his words sunk in.

Apparently they penetrated his consciousness at the same moment, for his tanned cheeks tightened and his eyes widened. "Oh, forgive me, Mrs. Rockley. I didn't mean what I said. I meant"—by now he was beginning to smile, and so was she—"that you are welcome to stay here with me as long as you wish. That you don't have to rush to move out," he amended hastily. "I've had my things put in a guest chamber."

And at that moment, Victoria felt her fears slip away. Not because he'd offered to let her stay, but because this man was so unlike Phillip, so far removed from the genteel, proper man she'd loved, that his taking over the title would never be as difficult and painful as she'd expected it to be.

He must be a very distant relation of the de Lacys, for, at least initially, she saw nothing reminiscent of her husband in the man's physical appearance. Where Phillip's hair had been the color of walnuts, this man's high sweep of hair was the color of deer hide. His brown eyes crinkled deeply at the corners, suggesting either frequent smiles, or much time squinting against the sun. Since his skin was tanned and weather-beaten, she presumed it was the latter. James Lacy, as he'd called himself, now Rockley to one and all in England, was perhaps five years younger than Phillip would have been had he lived. Victoria placed his age at about twenty-three.

If Lady Melly were there to see his attire, she would have been appalled. Although he wore pantaloons, a shirtwaist, and a coat like any other English gentleman, his clothing gave clear indication that he'd never sat for a tailor fitting. The pantaloons bagged at the knees and even above them, and his coat was too short for his long arms.

Her examination completed in an instant, Victoria now made a curtsy to him. "Lord Rockley, I am delighted to make your acquaintance, and I'd like to welcome you to St. Heath's Row."

"Thank you, Mrs. Rockley." Then he looked abashed, and smiled sheepishly. "Or is it Mrs. de Lacy? I trust you'll help me to sort out all of the things I must learn about society here—the titles, the manners, and whatever that heavy thing is that seems to be so important. I've only disembarked from my ship three hours ago."

"Heavy thing?" Victoria repeated as she tapped back a bit of panic. The last thing she needed was another task to add to her list. Despite the charm of his openly self-deprecating tone and his informal amiability, she had no desire to tutor him into his place in Society. Surely he didn't truly expect it of her. "Forgive me, but I'm not at all certain to what you're referring. And, the proper way to address me would be Lady Rockley, or my lady. And you will now simply be called Rockley, as you have thus taken on the title of the Marquess of Rockley."

"So in the eyes of London, I'm no longer James Lacy, Kentuckian?" He had a bemused expression on his face, as though he could barely conceive of losing his identity. "I become no one but a title?"

"Only your intimates would call you James," Victoria explained. "Your name will change so that all might attribute your title and estate to you, but you will still be yourself, James Lacy, the Kentuckian—whoever that might be." Just as she was still Victoria Gardella Grantworth de Lacy—yet also a born Venator.

He looked at her for a moment, long enough that she felt the urge to blush. "So perhaps my wife might call me by my given name."

"Indeed, I believe that is quite common . . . particularly in more private settings." Feeling as though the conversation had quite gotten out of her control, Victoria gave another little curtsy designed to be a farewell. "I will excuse myself now, my lord, and begin to make arrangements to give over the master's chambers now that you have arrived. I apologize for not having already done so, immediately upon my return here from Italy."

"No," he said, reaching for her—and then stopping, as if realizing he'd overstepped. "No, Mrs.—my lady. Please don't get your dander up over my account. I'm well used to a much smaller, less fancy abode than this. I'd feel very ungentlemanly if I felt as though I'd displaced you. There will be time enough for that later. There must be some other place that I could put my things." Whenever he said "I" it sounded as if he was suddenly comprehending something. It came out sounding like "ah."

"That is very kind of you," Victoria replied, unsure of how she felt about his protestations. Part of her had wanted an excuse to move from the chambers that belonged to the lady of the house, which attached to the master's rooms. And the other part of her wasn't quite ready to let them, along with their bittersweet memories, go. "And there are many very comfortable chambers available for your pleasure. I'll express your wishes to the staff if you like."

"That would be greatly appreciated. I must confess my ear is not used to hearin' the accents, and I have had a terrible time understandin' the butler—is that who he is? The one whose eyebrows stick out further than his nose?"

At Victoria's surprised smile and nod, he continued in his own oddly accented voice, "It took me three times to understand that I should let the groom take my horse, and that I couldn't have tea until three o'clock—although he did offer me some other food, something he called 'repast.' In Kentucky, we don't drink a lot of tea, but when we do, it's whenever the urge strikes us. Not at three."

Victoria couldn't contain the little amused smile that escaped, and immediately she bit her lip. The last thing she wanted to do was to offend him. His humor and charm were refreshing, absurd enough to make her forget that the rest of her life was too bloody dark. He would have the ladies in the ton eating out of his hand in no time. And then she realized what he'd meant earlier. "Oh, the heavy thing. Do you mean the ton?"

"Yes, ma'am, that's it. Where do we find the ton? And what do we do with it?"

Stifling another smile, Victoria explained that the haute ton was the nickname for the crème de la crème of London Society—and that he was now a member of "the heavy thing." By the time she was finished, they were both chuckling. Their conversation ended with James, as he'd insisted she call him—"for if you don't, I won't know who you're talking to!"—extracting a promise that she would join him for dinner that evening in the main dining room.

She would make a visit to Kritanu, who was with Briyani's body in the chapel, then have time to dress for dinner.

Despite the time it would take away from other matters, Victoria had a suspicion that the meal would likely be the most enjoyable part of her day.

*　　*　　*

That night, it was well past eleven by the time Victoria excused herself from James Lacy and his newfound enjoyment of a French brandy from Armagnac. Apparently he was used to something they drank in Kentucky called rotgut, which sounded as horrible as he claimed it tasted. She herself had had two glasses of sherry—one more than usual—and she was feeling more than a little loose-limbed.

Yet, as she climbed the stairs, it all came back to her: less than twenty-four hours earlier, she and Sebastian had been slogging through an underground river of sewage. And the rest of the day's events had left her even more worried, confused, and grieving.

Inside her chamber, she pulled the cord to summon her maid, Verbena, to assist her in preparing for bed. Or perhaps not. . . .

A lamp had been left burning low on her dressing table, and Victoria refrained from turning it brighter. Instead, she walked over to the tall window that gave her a view of the moonlit gardens below. Behind her, the room was lit with a bare glow, enabling her to see through the pane. There was only a quarter moon and clouds obscured many of the stars, so the grounds were painted mostly in heavy shades of black and dark blue. A pale sweep of gray designated a pea gravel path, and a cluster of lilac bushes rose in dark relief next to a glowing white bench that happened to catch the glare of the moonbeams.

She touched the cool glass, considering. Perhaps she should be on the streets tonight, trying to find out what she could about a vampire that attacked in the daylight.

Or perhaps it would be best to get a solid night's sleep and allow her mind to clear of sherry, as well as the reality of the problems she faced.

Alone.

Despite the fact that Sebastian was here in London with her, he came and went as he pleased, and Victoria felt utterly alone. She was without her Venator companions, far from the people who understood her and what her life was.

Max was gone, somewhere, God knew where. Wayren was in Rome, along with the other Venators Victoria had come to know and like—Brim, and Michalas, and others.

Aunt Eustacia was dead. Kritanu, though here, was grieving his nephew, and still reeling from the loss of Aunt Eustacia.

She also felt the loss of kind, gentle Zavier, a Venator who had made his desire to court Victoria quite clear. He had died at the hands of Beauregard.

She heard the faint snick of a door as Verbena came in behind her, entering through the sitting room that sat between the marquess's chamber and that of the marchioness. Still trying to decide whether to have her maid dress her in a night rail or in men's trousers, Victoria continued staring out the window.

She realized a fraction of a second later that Verbena was never so quiet, no matter what time it was or how tired she might be. Victoria's heart gave a little bump and the hair on her arms lifted.

Just as she started to whirl away from the window, a shadow moved behind her—a blurred reflection in the pane, and then it shifted out of sight. Strong hands closed over her shoulders, halting her in midpivot. Although he wasn't standing so as to reflect in the window, she recognized him now—by the way he touched her, the familiar scent that lingered on his fingers, the way his body brushed against hers. Her edgy nerves settled.

"Where's Verbena?" she demanded. She didn't attempt to turn toward him.

"Sleeping quite soundly, I believe," he said. "A comely girl, but repose is definitely not her most attractive state. Her snores are like to rattle the windows from their frames, and would be fairly off-putting to a gentleman who might wish to . . . er . . . *lie* . . . with her . . . though I'd venture to say that the poor beleaguered Oliver would seize the opportunity if offered."

"I rang for her. She'll be here any moment now."

"I'm afraid you're mistaken." In the window's reflection, his arm lifted from her shoulder and she saw that he was holding a slender rope.

"You cut the bellpull?"

"I didn't want to ruin your reputation, Lady Rockley," he said in a low purr. "At least here." He moved closer, brushing up against the back of her from shoulder blade to bum to heel. His proximity brought warmth to her bare shoulders. "Especially now that the new marquess has arrived."

"It would have served you right, Sebastian, if you'd sneaked into the wrong chamber. What if I'd had my belongings moved to a different one, as would be expected?"

He chuckled, his breath ruffling her hair. His hands had closed over the tops of her shoulders and began to rub them, gently moving the narrow bands of sleeves up and down over the curve. "Why do you think Verbena is sleeping so soundly? She had no qualms about chatting with me over a little turn of brandy—"

"—into which you no doubt slipped a bit of *salvi*, to help your cause. No wonder she's snoring." Victoria would have died before admitting it, but the gentle caresses over her arms lulled her from annoyance and edginess to . . . comfort. Perhaps something more.

"I'm nothing if not prepared—and resourceful."

Victoria pulled gently away and turned. "As much as I'm enjoying your attempts at seduction—"

"You are?" His sensual lips widened into a delicious smile. "And here I thought I'd lost—"

"—I must presume you have another reason for arranging this assignation." They were standing very close, slippers and boots staggered against each other. Her hem brushed the tops of his feet, and her full skirt edged between his ankles. He was looking down at her, his golden-brown hair a thick and wavy nimbus in the lamplight.

"You must? How . . . devastating." He tugged her into his arms at the same moment, pulling her close, so close that she could see his eyelashes, even in the low light.

"I thought you were quite angry with me this morning," she whispered, suddenly glad that he seemed to be no longer. Her heart was thudding in her chest, and the room felt very close and warm. Something seemed to have clicked inside her, opened, loosened. And she didn't think it was just due to the sherry.

"I was. And most likely still am," he replied, his breath warm on her face. "But right at this moment . . . I don't quite recall why."

She wasn't sure she did either.

Victoria stepped closer, her foot sliding between his large booted ones as she met his mouth. Warmth flooded through her as though it had been released from some strict reservoir, and she sagged against him. His body was lean and solid, and as their mouths melded together, she moved her hands to touch his chest. It was warm under the linen shirt he wore, and she felt the curve of the muscle flexing there.

Before she could protest, Sebastian was pulling at the buttons at the back of her gown. "Perhaps I could take Verbena's place this evening," he said after a particularly long, delving kiss.

Victoria snickered against his mouth. "I'm disappointed in you," she murmured, tugging away his neck cloth. "I thought you were more original. I imagine there must be dozens of eager lovers all over London offering to act as ladies' maids on any given day."

He huffed a small laugh against her neck, close enough to the sensitive part near her ear that she quivered. "If I've lost my rapier wit, it's only because of you, Victoria." She felt him draw in a breath, his chest expanding beneath her hands. He covered her lips again, drawing her sharply against him, plunging and twisting his tongue deeply into her mouth.

She allowed herself to taste him, the slick, sensual warmth flavored with brandy and clove, to let him coax and tease and seduce her with his mouth.

And then she pulled easily away, firmly stepping back. "I have something to tell you."

He smiled crookedly at her. "Ah, well, I knew it couldn't last. And, alas, I have things to tell you as well."

"So you didn't come here expressly to seduce me." She stepped away from the window and gestured to one of the two wingback chairs. "Perhaps you'd care to take a seat." Then she turned the lamp brighter.

"Ah, civility rears its ugly head," he sighed, taking her suggestion. "Would you consider me uncouth if I mentioned how much, at this moment, I despise civility?"

Victoria chose to ignore him. "Are you going to give me the copper ring? You took yourself off so quickly this morning that I didn't have a chance to ask—purposely, I'm sure."

"You certainly have the sound of your aunt in your tone, now that you've taken her place as *Illa* Gardella." He sat with one ankle positioned over his knee, lounging back into the depths of the chair.

"No prevarications, Sebastian. I take my role as the leader of the Venators—of which you are one—as seriously as she did. What do you plan to do with the ring?" She sat in the other wingback chair and faced him.

"The ring is one of the five Rings of Jubai that Lilith had made for her most trusted Guardian vampires," Sebastian explained. Guardians were undead who had eyes that glowed ruby pink when they were angry. They were part of the vampire queen's elite guard, and had the particular ability to easily enthrall mortals. They were very hard to kill. Beauregard had been a Guardian vampire. "Unfortunately, though you might expect otherwise, my grandfather was not one of the recipients of the five rings."

Victoria gave a little laugh. "To the contrary. Knowing Beauregard as I did, I'm not at all surprised Lilith didn't count him as one of her most trusted Guardians. Not only did there seem to be no love lost between them, but he also was clearly a creature concerned only with himself."

"I'll allow your disparaging comment about my grandfather to pass for now," Sebastian said in a cooler voice. "I'm not ignorant of his faults, but he was still my grandfather and he never caused me any harm. What he did to you—tried to do—was unacceptable, and I reacted accordingly."

"You do have my gratitude for that," Victoria replied, fervently meaning it.

"Your gratitude? Ah, what a wealthy man am I," he said dryly. Then his flippancy evaporated and a serious expression took over. "Before we talk further, there's something I must tell you. I'll get back to the Rings of Jubai in a moment, but first . . . Victoria, do you feel all of a piece? Since you . . . woke up, do you feel different?"

She looked at him and recognized something desperate in his face, and stopped her reflexive "I'm fine" response. "Most of the time, I feel . . . the same. But there are moments when I do not." Like when she was angry, her vision threatened to tinge red—literally. And earlier today, when Gwendolyn had been prattling on about her happiness and her wedding . . . how that surge of envy had caught Victoria by surprise, making her cold and angry. She'd been a lot more angry lately, come to think of it.

Or . . . when she'd smelled the blood in the underground abbey . . .

Now that she put it together, it made horrible, awful sense. She felt her face drain of color and feeling. "My God."

He seemed to understand, and reached for her arm. His slender fingers closed gently over the top of her hand. "Victoria, I'm certain you're not a vampire . . . but I do fear that you still carry some residue of Beauregard's attempt to turn you. I still . . . I feel the presence of an undead when I'm near you."

She stared for a moment without seeing as the pieces clunked into place. "That was why you didn't seem to notice the vampires down in the tunnels."

He nodded ruefully. "Your presence makes it difficult for me to sense other—er, the undead."

Victoria thought for a moment. "Does Wayren know? How about Max? And Ylito?"

"Wayren knows, and I'm certain she's told Ylito and Hannever, for if there's any hope of an antidote, they would help. As for Pesaro—well, he is aware of the situation. But . . . of course, he has his own concerns."

Yes, indeed he did. But she felt hollow anyway.

Sebastian remained silent for a moment as if to allow her thoughts to sink in, then he spoke. "The reason I wanted to find the underground abbey was not just to retrieve the ring, but also some old documents. The monks wrote not only holy pieces, apparently, but unholy ones as well—some vampiric history, as well as other information—and according to Beauregard, they might be of interest."

"Of interest to whom—the undead or the Venators?"

"Either one." He smiled ruefully. "I thought perhaps there might be information in them about another Venator who was nearly turned undead, and it might be relevant to . . . your situation."

Victoria had heard of the four Venators who had been turned to vampires over the ages. Only four . . . but still. Their *vis bullae* hadn't saved them . . . although each had been wearing only a single one. "Did you find the documents?"

"No. They weren't there with the ring."

"Do you plan to go back?"

He shrugged. "Perhaps. As you are aware, I generally prefer not to step into the lair of the lion, and it's quite obvious that the undead have been making use of the place. After you drove Lilith from London two years ago, the number of undead decreased greatly. But it seems they might be resettling here once again."

"What about a vampire who moves about and attacks in daylight?" Victoria asked.

"The only way that could happen is if the vampire drank of the special potion."

Victoria narrowed her eyes. "The recipe we found behind the Door of Alchemy in Rome? The one that you stole from the Consilium?" She tasted bitterness at the reminder of his betrayal.

Two months ago in Rome, she and Max had raced against the vampires and Tutela to find the keys that opened the door to an alchemical laboratory that had been locked for more than a century. They'd succeeded in being there first, and had retrieved the notes and papers hidden behind the door, but Sebastian had stolen one of the pages to give to his grandfather Beauregard.

"It's the only one I know of," he replied evenly, meeting her eyes without shame. "You can stop stabbing me with your eyes. You've already left a scar on my shoulder," he said, gesturing to where she'd stabbed him with the stake meant for Beauregard.

"You shouldn't have gotten in my way."

His mobile lips thinned; obviously, he read the double meaning there. "Speaking of prevarication—Victoria, are you saying you've seen a vampire in the daylight?"

"Not directly, but I saw the fresh remains of his—or her—attack on a mortal. During midday."

"Then it would appear that somehow, either you were mistaken—which of course is unlikely—or that the formula for the potion has fallen into the very hands from which you and Pesaro tried to keep it."

"Apparently. And if you hadn't taken it from the Consilium at the behest of your grandfather, it might still be there, safely ensconced. What did you do with it?"

"Do you not recall? Beauregard showed it to you when you were in his chambers," Sebastian returned, his voice softening slightly. "I meant to return to retrieve it, but when I did so, it was gone. Someone else found it first."

"So it's possible."

"Quite."

"But why did I not sense the presence of the undead in the park today?"

"Because that is the other important benefit of the potion. It gives the undead a mortal-like aura that keeps us from recognizing them, and allows them to move about as one of us."

Victoria felt a chill over her that had nothing to do with the presence of vampires. "That could be devastating to us," she murmured, standing abruptly. "If they can move about, and we can't sense them . . ." She paced over to her dressing table, where the lamp had begun to gutter in its low kerosene. "They could move about, anywhere, anytime . . ."

"It isn't a pleasant thought, indeed," Sebastian said. His voice was closer, and she heard the faint creak of a floorboard as he moved from his chair.

"Do you know where Max is?" she asked.

She felt him become still, and she turned back toward him. "Running from Lilith, I believe." His laugh had an odd note to it. "I don't blame the chap myself . . . if I'd been caught by that vile creature, and finally broke free, I'd do the same."

"He needs to know about Briyani. I've sent a message to Wayren."

"Then I'm certain she'll find a way to notify Pesaro. It seems to me you have other concerns now."

"Sebastian, why did you do it?" Victoria asked, suddenly feeling the pain of loneliness and betrayal. "Why did you steal from us? Why did you try to help Beauregard?"

He had the grace to look abashed—a decidedly unfamiliar expression on his face. "I acted irresponsibly and foolishly. I listened to him—he had the ability to enthrall me to some extent, even though I was usually aware of it and could control it. And he convinced me that it would be helpful in getting vampires and mortals to coexist."

Victoria gave an unladylike snort. "And you believed him?"

"Love can be blinding sometimes, Victoria."

She looked at him for a moment. It felt as though something in the air had shifted, broken . . . settled. "It can." She drew in a deep breath, let it out slowly. She'd made her own mistakes for love—marrying a mortal who had no idea about her secret life. And then lying to him, drugging him with *salvi* so that she could hunt vampires, thus endangering him and others that she loved.

Love was most certainly blinding.

Somehow, he must have understood what was in her face, for the next thing she knew, Sebastian was there again, drawing her into his arms. He lowered his mouth to hers, softly, as if in question.

She closed her eyes, kissed him back. She drew in his essence, his presence, pushed back the loneliness that had threatened her this day, these last weeks and months.

For this moment, this was comfort. This was Sebastian.

The kiss left her breathless, and suddenly Victoria felt the hip-high bed behind her, its edge pressing into the small of her back as Sebastian pressed into her front. Her gown gapped freely in the bodice due to his nimble fingers at the buttons along her spine. When he tipped her onto the bed, the coverlet was cool against her bare back.

His hands shifted smoothly to pull the fabric away as she looked up, dazed and desirous. It had been a long time. . . . The bed hangings were open, and beyond the heavy maple canopy frame, she saw the painting of Circe and Odysseus.

The fog of sherry and pleasure dissipated, and Victoria came back to herself. She sat up abruptly, nearly striking him on the chin.

"No," she said, looking around the room, remembering where she was. A chill raced over her, raising unpleasant goose pimples as she realized—oh, a myriad of reasons why she couldn't do this. "Sebastian . . . not here."

Not where she and Phillip had made love, only a few precious times during their short marriage.

Not here, where she'd kissed him for the last time, felt his hands on her body and the length of him next to her . . . just before she drove a lethal stake into his heart.

Not on this bed, or in this room . . . or in this house.

Five

In Which a Painting Is Criticized

Max moved with the shadows, alternating his quiet footsteps with the call of a night animal or the sift of wind
through the trees.

The last time he'd been here at St. Heath's Row, slipping silently across the trimmed lawn and between the
well-tended yew hedges, was nearly two years ago. That
time he'd had no trouble gaining access to the residence,
for Victoria had dismissed all of the servants for the
evening.

She had been expecting the return of her husband as
well.

Max had followed Rockley through the house, unseen
and unnoticed by the vampire who was driven purely by
the need for his wife's blood. He could have staked the
creature on more than one occasion—just beyond the
gates of the estate, as Rockley crossed the threshold of his
own home, as he mounted the stairs, drawn by Victoria's
scent and her heartbeat.

But Max had waited.

Instead, he'd followed, listened, paused outside of the door Rockley had left open. The door leading to the chamber where she slept.

The sounds, the unmistakable ones of shifting bed-clothes and sliding lips, of sighs, intimate murmurs, and ratcheting breathing at last forced him to peer into the room. The stake firm in his hand, Max tensed, tasting bitter disappointment . . . and a bit of self-righteousness. He had been right to come, for he was prepared to do what had to be done, what she was too bloody blind, too weak to do. . . .

Then he saw her arm raise high, an elegant, slender limb caught by moonlight above the rumpled coverlet. And she plunged the stake down into the dark.

He saw the small explosion of silvery ash, heard the faint sob of grief, and he lowered his stake.

When at last she pulled herself up to sit, her rich, black curls had poured over her shoulders and gauzy white gown. That moment, that colorless image of pale skin, shadowed eyes, a streak of tears, was indelibly printed in his memory. He'd never forget the glaze of moonlight over her features, haunted yet determined, when she turned to look at him.

At last, she truly understood.

And that was the moment everything changed.

Tonight, he had no need or desire to enter the house. His destination was the small chapel on the grounds, and it was this brick building that he approached after making his way beyond the looming house.

The wooden doors curved at the top, forming a gentle point, but they weren't locked. They made only a soft snuffing sound when Max eased through.

The space was small, barely larger than a parlor. Four

rows of benches lined each side of the aisle, padded with red velvet cushions. Candles of varying heights and widths burned around the altar and on the floor. The body, bound in white cloth, lay on a table in the center of the dais. Frankincense burning in a shallow bowl mingled its scent with that of the musky balm applied to the corpse's wrappings.

"Max." Kritanu pulled smoothly to his feet. Despite his seven decades, he was as agile and strong as a man half his age. His jet-black hair had held no hint of gray until the death of Eustacia, only six months ago, when a wide streak of white had appeared overnight. His face also showed the depths of his grief: hollow mahogany cheeks, his skin so taut it shone, the squareness of his jaw more pronounced. "You should not have risked coming."

"Of course I must." Max strode up the aisle, his long legs making short work of the distance. He paused at the altar, facing the body of the man who'd been his companion for eight years.

Death was nothing new to him; in fact, he would eagerly accept it for himself. He'd wished for it more than once. Eustacia had said that was part of the reason he was so skilled as a Venator.

But that didn't mean he didn't grieve for the loss of a friend.

After a moment of prayer and commendation, he turned to Kritanu. "I'm sorry." Those words, very simple, said many things.

The elder man's eyes shone with the understanding of all of them, the pinpoint of candlelight reflecting in his black orbs. "Briyani made his own choices, Max, just as you do. He fully understood the risk of staying with you. I'm glad he did. You should not be alone."

Max's lips pulled in a humorless smile. "Nor should you."

"You took a great chance in coming here tonight. I told you it wasn't necessary."

"I wanted to see him. To say good-bye." As he hadn't been able to do with Eustacia. Or Father. Or his sister Giulia. "I know how to move about unseen."

"But Victoria?"

"Is apparently otherwise occupied."

Kritanu looked at him, something suspiciously like pity in his handsome face. "And you shan't tell her you're here?"

"I have no desire to be ordered about, as she would be wont to do. To be at her beck and call. I'm no longer a Venator, and can be of little use to her or to any of you."

"Then why come to London? The world is vast, and there are many places to hide from Lilith that she would never suspect."

No one was more acutely aware of that fact than Max himself. But he'd been compelled to come to London, foolish as it had been.

He bloody well could have gone on, knowing that it would be safer for everyone if he went to Spain or Denmark or America, or even the wilds of Africa. Lilith would never find him there. But Vioget had raised the concern about Victoria, leaving Max with little choice but to assure himself all was well.

And, apparently, Vioget was still taking his job as protector quite seriously.

At least Max could give him credit for that.

He realized Kritanu was still watching him and selected a slightly easier topic. "Briyani and I were in Vauxhall, looking for vampires, when we got separated. I found some undead, but he never returned to our rooms.

I returned to Vauxhall hours later and found no trace of him."

"Briyani wanted to be a Venator," Kritanu said. "He was a better Comitator than he would have been as a Venator, but he was preparing to attempt the trial for the *vis bulla*. I suspect he would not have succeeded, for although he was very brave, and a skillful combatant, he lacked many necessary attributes, including a cool head under pressure."

Max looked at the swaddled corpse. Grief stirred again, more deeply. "I didn't know of his intentions." The flash of a memory of his own trial, where he knew the choice was either success or death, assaulted him. He'd been more prepared for death than for success, for only five men over the centuries had ever achieved the *vis bulla* without the blood of the Gardellas in their veins.

Kritanu turned from his nephew and looked up at Max. "How does your training go?"

"I've neglected it as of late." Yet, his body desired it—the quick, measured swipes with the *kadhara* knife, the kicks and leaps and thrusts of hand-to-hand *kalaripayattu* . . . and especially, the easy gliding of *qinggong*, where his body actually left the ground in long, sweeping arcs.

"Why should you do so? A lack of *vis bulla* does not eliminate what you have learned these years, Max."

A soft scuff drew their attention to the entrance to the chapel, and Max immediately began to slip into the shadowy alcove next to the altar. It was better for Victoria not to know he was here.

But it wasn't Victoria who moved toward them.

"Pesaro. Such an unexpected pleasure," Sebastian said as he drew near.

Max sensed an air of frustration about Vioget and saw no reason to let it pass. "It's rather early to be ending the evening, isn't it? I thought you'd be engaged much longer." He scanned the other man's well-tailored coat and the white shirt that, though still tied at the throat, was missing a neck cloth.

Vioget's eyes narrowed, but then he smiled coolly. "If it's Victoria for whom you're concerned, allow me to assure you that she's happily ensconced in her bedchamber. With a smile on her face."

"With. the painting of Circe and Odysseus in full view." He assumed the picture in its heavy gold frame hadn't been moved. "Not the finest rendition, but an acceptable one nevertheless."

Vioget's expression darkened, validating Max's assumption, but then his features rearranged into another smile, laced with contempt. "Does Victoria know that you've been skulking around London, unwilling to show your face?"

"There's no reason—"

"I disagree. She should know you're here, so that arrangements can be made to see to your protection. I'll be certain to advise her of your presence." Vioget fairly oozed condescension and confidence and Max felt a sharp pain shoot along his jaw as he ground his teeth. "I'm certain she'll want to see for herself that you're safe, particularly in light of poor Briyani's fate."

"It would delight you no end, wouldn't it?" Max was under no illusion. Vioget knew that he would show to his best advantage next to a weakened, *vis bulla*–less Max, who had been reduced to living on the run. Merely a man.

The other man's reply was nothing more than a bland smile.

Six

A Crowded Parlor

Victoria knew it would only be a matter of time before the news of James's arrival spread. But even she didn't account for the efficiency of the gossip trail spread by the house servants—as evidenced by the presentation of Lady Melly in St. Heath's Row's parlor scarcely past noon the next day.

She wasn't alone. She'd brought reinforcements in the form of Ladies Nilly and Winnie . . . and a bulging portmanteau.

"Hello Mother," Victoria greeted her, trying to sound more glad than she felt. "I thought you were going to the race today with Lord Jellington." Lady Melly's beau had nearly lost his position when she was in Rome, being wooed by a handsome vampire. A vampire who'd turned out to be Sara Regalado's father.

"I thought it would be best if I—we," she added, gesturing to Nilly and Winnie as if their presence might protect her from Victoria's annoyance, "paid a call to determine whether you'd recovered from your fright yesterday."

"Indeed," squeaked Lady Nilly, her pale, slender hands fluttering at her throat. "I cannot even imagine how you must have felt after seeing that poor girl! Why, I'm sure I'd not sleep for a week, for fear of the nightmares."

"Ah, nightmares," inserted Lady Winnie in a rather carrying voice. Her hand hovered over the plate of cinnamon-iced almond biscuits that had been summoned at the instant of their arrival—despite the fact that they were three hours early for afternoon calls. "I know all about them, I do. Why, I daresay, that visit to Rome put me in a state, for I've nary slept a wink since the trip. I spend all night tossing and turning, dreaming about vampires and other horrific things." She paused in her search for the perfect biscuit—namely, the largest and with the thickest swirl of icing—to pat her hand over the saucer-sized silver and gold cross she wore pinned to the side of her bodice. Its weight caused the blue floral muslin to sag slightly, pulling the scoop neckline off center just a bit.

"Vampires!" Nilly had no compunction about her selection. She slipped right in and swiped a most promising treat right from under the duchess's poised hand. "I declare, I'm certain we must have talked about this before and you're quite mistaken, Winnie. I'm the one who has been dreaming about vampires ever since Rome! You've only started since I told you about *my* dreams—the dark, cunning men, swooping down in dark halls, cornering me—"

Victoria found it necessary to interrupt and, from long experience, knew that the best tactic was to completely change the subject. "Mother, I'm feeling quite well today, after all. Thank you for your concern. I truly do appreciate it." She tried not to glance at the portmanteau. Perhaps if she didn't see it, it would leave with her mother without fuss.

Lady Melly leaned forward and patted her daughter's ungloved hand. "I'm delighted to hear it! Now, of course, since you've recovered, you'll be able to attend the Twisdale's garden party tonight with me. I'll call Melvindale in—she's waiting in the carriage with my trunks—and she'll—"

"Your trunks?" Victoria was aware that the pitch of her voice was sharp as a roof's peak, but she didn't care. Her control of the situation—along with the almond biscuits—was rapidly disappearing.

"Of course, my dear. You simply cannot go on as you have, even though you are a widow. One night is fine, especially if no one knows about it—which is possible, since I came as soon as I heard—"

"Mother. Thank you." Victoria struggled to keep her composure in the face of the runaway curricle that was her maternal parent. "I don't need a chaperone. I—"

"Oh, but Victoria, of course you do! You still must protect your reputation if you want to marry again," said Lady Nilly, spraying almond crumbs with abandon.

"Perhaps you might even catch the eye of one of the most eligible bachelors to grace our Society," added Lady Winnie with a familiar gleam in her eyes. "After all, you've already had the pleasure of meeting him, and it would be so much simpler—"

Whatever Victoria might have said to puncture the duchess's—and, clearly, Lady Melly's—outlandish hopes was forever lost as the tall white doors to the parlor opened.

"The Marquess of Rockley," intoned Lettender.

As one, the three older ladies surged to their feet and

turned toward the new arrival. Victoria steadied the tea
table, then turned to greet James.

He looked rough and windblown this morning, just as
unkempt as he'd done yesterday with the exception of his
clothing. Apparently the staff had seen to more than just
gossip, for he was dressed from head to toe as befit his
station.

Victoria refused to let herself look too closely, for fear
that she might recognize some of the clothing as
Phillip's . . . and it was just better not to. She still had his
cloak and one of his tall hats stuffed in the back of her
wardrobe, and she often used them when she went out at
night dressed as a man. She fancied they still carried the
scent of his lemon-rosemary pomade.

By the time Victoria rejoined the conversation, James
and his American drawl had been fussed over by the three
ladies, and he was on the sofa between Ladies Winnie
and Melly. In other words, exactly where they wanted
him.

"So you see, my lord," Lady Melly was saying, "we
certainly will take advantage of your hospitality while my
daughter sees to her personal affects being prepared for
removal—which I'm certain will take several weeks to be
done properly, of course—but it simply isn't done for her
to stay under your roof without a chaperone."

"I'd be delighted to have you here," James was saying
with what appeared to be complete sincerity. "I wouldn't
want to do anything to ruin Mrs.—er, Lady Rockley's
reputation."

"And aside of that, the duchess and Lady Petronilla
and I would be honored to help you sift through *those*"—
she gestured to a tray overflowing already with new invitations—"and determine which ones to accept, and which
ones might be best ignored, if you follow my thinking,"

Lady Melly said with a knowing look. "In fact, we were just about to discuss our plans for this evening, which include a garden party at the Twisdale residence."

Victoria could sit back no longer. "Thank you very much, Lord Rockley"—how horribly odd it felt to say that to a stranger—"for your hospitality, but I have already decided to move myself from St. Heath's Row, which I should have done immediately upon my return."

"Victoria, I can hardly bear to tell you this, but . . . the roof at Grantworth House—it's being repaired. A huge tree branch fell on it, just over the place where your chambers were, and it won't be habitable for weeks." Lady Melly looked over at James, who appeared to have the tiniest nag of a smile at the corner of his mouth. Thank God he seemed not to be as gullible as he appeared. "So there is no place for you to stay at Grantworth House—"

"I'm so sorry to hear about the repairs. That's the first I knew of them," Victoria returned with an exaggerated sweetness in her voice. "And what a sacrifice for you to offer to stay here when there is such a crisis at home. But, I meant to say that I have already begun to make arrangements to move to Aunt Eustacia's old town house. If you recall, she deeded it to me upon her death."

Lady Melly's face fell like a ruined soufflé, and Victoria could actually see the thoughts whirling about in her mind as she tried to extricate excuses and arguments. "Oh, dear, Victoria, but your aunt's town house is in such an unfashionable part of Town. Why, it would be much more convenient to stay here at St. Heath's Row. There's plenty of room—"

This time, it was Lady Melly's contentions that were cut off by the opening of the tall white doors.

"Miss Gwendolyn Starcasset, Mr. George Starcasset,

and Signorina Sarafina Regalado," said the butler in perfect pronunciation. He looked immensely pleased with himself.

Victoria realized her mouth had begun to sag open, and she snapped her jaws shut as she rose, along with the others, to greet these wholly unexpected guests.

George Starcasset looked much the same as he had the last time she'd seen him, when he'd been pointing a firearm at her as he ushered her through the hallways of the Palombara Villa in Rome, where the demon Akvan had made his hideout.

George was older than his sister, but his face bore a trace of youth that gave him dimpled cheeks and a cleft chin. He wasn't an unattractive man, by any stretch, but his hair was a flat flaxen helmet that curled up at the ends, and his sideburns were too short. Overall, he merely made Victoria want to pat him on the head and send him off to play with his wooden blocks.

He wasn't an especially adept villain either, for the one time he'd had Victoria alone and planned to ravage her at gunpoint, it had been much too simple to distract and disarm him. So much so that Victoria hardly credited herself with the escape.

But there was something different about him now . . . something harder and more confident as he swept his attention over her. There was a knowing look in his eyes, and a hint of challenge.

She had no worries that he might divulge the specifics of their last few meetings—not only would no one believe it (well, no one except Lady Winnie and Lady Nilly), but those events would definitely not show him in the most esteemed light. Perhaps his self-assured air was because he knew his presence had taken her by surprise, or perhaps it was because of the lovely young woman on his arm, who was clearly managing the event.

Sara Regalado flounced across the parlor in her perfectly tailored butter yellow day dress. Even Victoria, who was not one to care much for style—at least, not any longer—took notice of the fine Alençon lace dripping from the wrist-length sleeves, and the three rows of rosettes and lace decorating the hem of her skirt. The fabric alone was worth notice, for the design of bluebirds and spring green ivy wasn't stamped on it, but embroidered in painstaking detail.

"Victoria," Gwen was whispering once all the introductions were made, pulling a chair closer to hers. "I couldn't wait to meet him! I heard he arrived yesterday, and he seems divine. His accent is so . . . rustic."

Clearly, Lady Melly wasn't the only one who had designs on reinstating Victoria as the Marchioness of Rockley rather than merely the Dowager Marchioness. And since George appeared otherwise engaged, Gwendolyn wasn't wasting any time.

"Lady Rockley, is *splendido* to see you again," said Sara in her accented English. She smiled prettily, but Victoria didn't trust the glint in her brown eyes. "*Forse*, we might do the shopping together, on Via Fleet, is it? Perhaps you and I and our mutual friend?"

"Our mutual friend?" Victoria replied. She was damned if she was going to talk to her about Max—let alone admit that she had no idea where he was hiding. For all she knew, Sara had aligned herself with Lilith and was looking for Max herself.

The thought—absurd as it was, for how would Sara find Lilith? And why?—made her blood run cold.

"Why, *si*, was it not . . . Mrs. Withers, *ci credo*. Mrs. Emmaline Withers?" The glint turned to laughter in those brown doe eyes, hard and knowing. "Did I not meet her in Roma? Is she not a friend of yours? The *povero* widow?"

Before Victoria could reply, her mother leaped into the fray. "Emmaline Withers? Why, I don't know any Mrs. Withers, Victoria. What have you been keeping from us." It was quite pointedly not a question, but a statement. The crease between her eyebrows clearly told Victoria what her words did not.

But Lady Melly had nothing to fear, and Sara was well aware of it, for Mrs. Withers was merely the name Victoria had used during her visit to Rome. She had done so in order to keep her identity as Aunt Eustacia's great-niece, a Venator, secret.

"I'm so sorry, *signorina*," Victoria replied. "Mrs. Withers is no longer with us."

"Pardon me, I am so sorry for your loss," Sara replied in a voice as thick as the honey Lady Winnie liked to slop in her tea. "I have suffered a recent loss myself." She lowered her face as if to hide a sudden tear, a flimsy lace handkerchief suddenly appearing in her hand.

Victoria had a sudden suspicion that she spoke of her father, the Conte Regalado, who had been wooing Lady Melly. But before she could divert the subject, Lady Nilly interrupted. "Oh, my dear, I'm so sorry. Who was it?"

"My father," Sara replied, her face still obscured except for the hard, deadly look she lifted to Victoria. "He recently met his end because of a horrid woman who destroyed his heart. She is a murderess!"

Namely, Victoria. The one who had driven the stake into Regalado's undead chest.

Well, at least she no longer had to wonder how Sara perceived her.

"Oh!" Lady Melly squeaked as if she'd just seen a

mouse. "Regalado. Conte Regalado? Alberto Regalado?" Her face had drained pale except for the spots of red in her cheeks. "I feel rather . . . faint . . . could I . . . could it . . . he was . . ." Another handkerchief fluttered, appearing, surprisingly, from the tanned hand of James Lacy.

Victoria's lips firmed. "Nonsense, Mother. I'm quite certain you had nothing to do with his . . . er . . . broken heart. Any man's heart as fragile as dust is not worthy of your esteem. Now, shall I pour you some tea, Gwen?"

"Lady Rockley," said George in his easy voice. "Understand you had an unsettling experience in the park yesterday."

"It was horrid," Lady Nilly announced, her spoon clanking against the sides of her teacup. "Why, there was blood everywhere."

"And markings on her chest!" Lady Winnie added. "Three Xs, and her clothes were torn everywhere . . . as if some animal had mauled her."

George's eyebrows rose in unadulterated surprise. "You were there as well? You saw this horrible sight? Daresay, a sight like that would send m'mother to bed for a week."

"No, we weren't there, but I—"

"It was a terrible sight," Victoria interrupted firmly. She didn't know what George and Sara were up to, but she suspected they were quite aware of the details of what she'd seen. It was too much of a coincidence for them to arrive unannounced at her residence the day after she'd seen the results of a vampire attack—in the sunlight, no less. They were both members of the Tutela, and the only conclusion she could draw was that either they were well aware of the attack and wanted to see what Victoria had figured out, or they suspected there was vampire activity, and they were trying to confirm it. Either way, she was understandably disinclined to assist them.

But before she could respond by changing the subject, the parlor door opened again. "Monsieur Sebastian Vioget," announced the butler, his nose lifted as though he smelled something a bit unpleasant. Lettender had not been fond of the French since his brother was killed at Waterloo.

Sebastian, a rakish grin on his face, and not one whit of surprise that the parlor was becoming overcrowded with members of two elite groups—the ton and the Tutela—strode easily into the room and went directly to Victoria's side.

"Hello, my dear," he said, bending over to place a kiss that screamed intimacy on her cheek. "You look lovely today."

She was tempted to pull away, just to showcase the effrontery of it, but the look on her mother's face was too much a work of art to destroy it. Lady Melly looked as though she'd swallowed a biscuit whole, and Lady Winnie, who was swallowing gamely and trying not to cough, probably had.

"Sebastian," she said, giving him a sincerely melting smile. His was a friendly face, and at least she had no illusions about what he wanted from her.

She patted his properly gloved hand and gestured to a chair next to her. "Would you care to join us for tea before we take our ride?" Her voice was full of charm and invitation, but the look she sent him was pointed. They'd made no plans for a ride, or any other activity, but he was sharp enough to follow her lead. "I do realize it is a bit early for tea . . ."

If he sat down instead of taking her subtle cue to leave, she'd never kiss him again.

"Of course I should. We can ride later," he said, sending her a disarming smile that, nevertheless, sent a little pang through her. Perhaps she should have let him coax her into bed last night. "I can always enjoy tea. And with such esteemed company." He gave a little bow, then he turned to look at her, his eyebrows raised innocently. "You haven't announced our wonderful news yet, have you, dearest?"

She was going to stake him again—and this time in the heart, mortal or not. Lady Melly's breath was coming in short, wheezing pants, and her fingers had somehow curled around Victoria's wrist in a death grip.

Before Victoria could extricate herself from that conundrum, there was a knock at the parlor door. All heads turned. The door opened, and Lettender's long face appeared. "My lady, we have another visitor. He . . . er . . . wishes to speak with you."

Victoria tensed, then felt suddenly jittery. Max, of course. He was the only person missing from this odd arrangement. "Please, show him in," she said.

The butler stepped in and opened the door. The visitor followed him. "Mr. Bemis Goodwin. Of the Magistrate's Bow Street Runners."

Mr. Goodwin was tall and dark-haired. He had a face as sharp and angular as Max, but the arrangement of his features, though just as haughty, wasn't nearly as attractive. His chin and nose were matching jutting points, his cheekbones like slanted plateaus, and his lips thin and red. But his eyes: they were sharp and dark and darted about as if determined to miss nothing. They flitted around, skittering over the little gathering, and finally settled onto Victoria.

"Lady Rockley, I require a word with you."

*   *   *

"Thus, Lady Rockley, you were the one to find the remains of Miss Forrest," said Mr. Goodwin. For the third time.

"As I have explained now twice, sir, yes, I came upon her unfortunate remains."

"But there were others who had begun the search before you. They were, so to speak, ahead of you." His eyes were narrow and black. She fancied they gleamed like those of a snake, ready to strike. Yet, they were intelligent. "So how could you know just where to look if they had not found her?"

Leaving the others in the parlor, Victoria had taken Mr. Goodwin to the marquess's study, thinking she was making an escape. But the demeanor which pervaded the whippetlike man and his questions annoyed and unsettled her. "Are you suggesting that I somehow knew where Miss Forrest was before I discovered her?"

"You seemed to locate her quite easily."

"She was beneath a tree, half hidden by a rock, near the creek. Anyone could have found her." Victoria settled back in her chair and forced her fingers to uncurl. Ridiculous that he should rouse her as he had. The man was just doing his job.

The Bow Street Runners were the only sort of police-detectives in London, for Victoria's countrymen had long been leery of giving up their freedoms by formalizing a police force. In fact, London was the only city in Europe without a formal police force. Certainly, there were the few members of the Night Watch, and a constable for every parish, but their responsibilities were only to report criminal activity if they witnessed it. The Runners were responsible for investigating any grievous crimes—such as murder or rape—and bringing the felons to the magistrate. They were also able to help victims of other crimes, such as fraud or robbery, to recover their losses—at their discretion. Regardless, it was unfortunate the Runner would be unable to help in this particular instance.

Vampire crimes weren't recognized by the magistrate.

"Is there anything else I can help you with, Mr. Goodwin?" Victoria asked, ready to end the conversation.

As if recognizing her change of demeanor, he stretched his lips in a smile. "You came upon the mauled and destroyed body, and you had the presence of mind to call for assistance, Lady Rockley. Immediately. Apparently the sight of her torn flesh and spilled blood had little effect on you."

"It wasn't a pleasant sight, but I am not one to be overcome by feminine vapors."

"What do you think happened to Miss Forrest?"

"I'm certain someone of your expertise would have come to the same conclusion as I: it appears that she was attacked by something bent on killing her."

Mr. Goodwin's eyes narrowed. "A vampire, perhaps?"

Victoria caught herself in midbreath, then exhaled slowly and evenly. "A vampire?"

"Do you believe in vampires, Lady Rockley?"

"I fail to see how my belief—or nonbelief—in the supernatural is relevant to the investigation into Miss Forrest's death, Mr. Goodwin. I'm certain you must investigate every aspect of the situation, which is why it doesn't follow that you're wasting my time and yours asking me such questions." The edge of her vision began to waver and she drew in an even breath through her nose.

Mr. Goodwin stood. He took up his black hat with long fingers and placed it precisely on his scalp. "Thank you, Lady Rockley. I wish you a good day." He started to turn, and then slowly swiveled back to face Victoria, who had stood. "What happened to your husband, Lady Rockley?"

She felt her heart give an unpleasant little lurch. "He died at sea," she replied automatically.

"That is the story that's been given out." He nodded. "What ship was he sailing on?"

"Your questions are not only becoming tiresome, but an outright waste of my time. These matters are of the public record. And, as they can have no relevance to your investigation regarding Miss Forrest, I believe we are done." Victoria looked pointedly at the study door, gesturing the man toward it. "Good day, Mr. Goodwin."

"The ship *The Plentifulle*, it was, or so has been reported. And your husband left his new wife less than a month after the return of your wedding holiday? Suddenly? Without notifying even the servants?"

Victoria drew herself up in all haughtiness. "Mr. Goodwin, I'm not certain how your household is run, but here at St. Heath's Row, the servants do not grant permission for the master's comings and goings."

"I see." He pulled his hat brim even straighter, and gave a little bow. "Thank you very much for your assistance, Lady Rockley."

With loathing, Victoria watched the man go. Such a prig, and he had pulled on her strings enough to make her feel unsettled. She, a Venator of two years, who had faced demons and vampires and multiple undead, had been set off balance by a mere Bow Street Runner.

But why on earth had he been asking her about vampires?

Seven

Of Stone-filled Wicker Baskets, Meeting at the Altar, and Confessions

After Mr. Bemis Goodwin, Bow Street Runner, made his exit, Victoria did not return to the parlor. She decided that it was more than fitting to leave Sebastian to face the ferocious Lady Melly and mop up the pieces of his little charade.

Of course, there was always the risk that he might complicate matters further . . . or that Lady Melly might be won over—Sebastian, after all, was as charming as they came—and leap heartily into planning the second wedding to which he had alluded.

But for now . . . Victoria had so many things to think about, to worry on, that she absolutely couldn't sit in that crowded parlor and pretend to be civil any longer.

She'd already given Verbena, her maid, the direction to pack some of her belongings and to have the footmen take them over to Aunt Eustacia's town house. She wouldn't sleep another night under James Lacy's roof, where Sebastian felt as though he could invade her chambers at will, with disregard for whoever might see him.

Taking care to stay away from any window that might reveal her location to those visiting in the parlor, Victoria took a pea-gravel path along the side of the mansion. She suspected that Kritanu was still in the chapel where she'd left him yesterday afternoon, before joining James for dinner. She'd meant to visit again last night, but the sherry, along with Sebastian's visit to her chamber, had sent her to bed earlier than she planned.

"Victoria." Kritanu greeted her as her shadow spilled into the chapel. She closed the door behind her and moved down the aisle toward her trainer.

He was on the altar arranged in one of his more complicated yoga positions: balanced on shoulders and chest with his arms extended along the floor and legs bent up around. His feet rested gently on the top of his head and his arms splayed strongly beneath his raised torso, extended on the ground in a stabilizing vee. As she watched, he moved slowly and smoothly out of what she recognized as the *shalabha-asana*.

Although Kritanu had taught her some of the positions, or asanas, of yoga in order to help her learn to concentrate and breathe more efficiently, Victoria had never been able to arrange her body thus. Neither had Aunt Eustacia.

"I meant to come again last night," she began, but he was already shaking his head.

"You've much to attend to, child. I know well how difficult it can be."

Indeed he would, for he had been Aunt Eustacia's trainer, companion, and—as Victoria had recently learned—her lover for more than fifty years.

Victoria closed her fingers over his smooth, tea-colored hand and squeezed. "When will you bury him?"

Kritanu shook his head. "We do not bury our dead. His

body, worn out like that of an old chariot, will be burned. I will take his ashes back to the Consilium, where he would want them to be." He straightened, and she saw that although grief still lived within his gaze, it had softened. "But I have wanted to talk with you about continuing your training. We've done little in the last months, and I fear that you'll become weak and slow . . . and fall back into using predictable moves."

Victoria smiled, though for some reason she wanted to cry. "I have made arrangements to move to Aunt Eustacia's house—which I should have done immediately upon returning to London. It was foolish of me to stay here."

Kritanu nodded. "I will take my nephew today, then, so you needn't worry on that. And I'm glad that you'll be back with me. We'll hone your *ankathari* skills, for you must become more adept with a blade. It's a worthwhile skill for fighting Imperials."

Imperial vampires were the oldest of the half-demon race, often having been created more than a millennium ago. Their eyes burned red-violet, and they were faster and stronger than even the Guardians. They carried swords, and had the ability to glide through the air. Some of them could also shape-shift or pull the life force from a person with their mere gaze.

Victoria had fought Imperials only twice, and only with help. They were horrible, fearsome creatures.

"When will I be ready to start *qinggong*?" she asked.

She'd seen Max's graceful, gliding movements through the air, swooping and leaping as though he was bewinged. As a novice Venator, she'd observed him use these skills in a battle he'd fought against an Imperial vampire two years ago. Max's strength and skill were well matched to the vampire's, and the battle had been almost beautiful to behold as they matched blade to wooden pike, feet brushing the ground then rising again, swirling and sliding in great arcs through the night air.

Kritanu gave her a fatherly smile. "If you wish, we can begin tomorrow. But, I must warn you, it will take years, perhaps decades, for you to master it. Unlike other combat skills, *qinggong* is not enhanced by the *vis bulla*. It is mostly the strength and power of your mind that will make you successful with *qinggong*."

But Max had mastered it, and he couldn't have been doing so for more than a decade himself. Victoria knew she could learn it as well.

"I see you are skeptical." Kritanu tipped his head in a gentle nod. "*Qinggong* is an art from China, not of the Venators. And you will begin, tomorrow if you wish, in the same manner of all who study *qinggong*."

Victoria had visions of leaping off chairs or tables, stake in hand, and her lips twitched at the thought of her mother witnessing such a sight. Of course, Lady Melly would faint dead away if she saw the manner in which her daughter already kicked and spun and rolled during her other combat.

"We will fill a large woven basket with rocks," Kritanu explained. There was a glint of humor in his eyes as if he knew what she'd been thinking. "You'll walk around the rim of the basket, balancing on its narrow edge. Every day you'll do this until you can do it perfectly. Then we'll remove one stone. And you'll do it again until you can do it perfectly.

"And then," he said, raising a finger as if to forestall any question about leaping off the sofa, "we'll remove another stone. And again you'll walk around it. We'll continue to do this until the basket is empty, and you can still walk around its rim."

Victoria stared at him as the force of his description sunk in. "That is how you trained Max?" How could one walk around the rim of an empty woven basket without collapsing it, or tipping it?

His blue-black hair gleamed. "Indeed. As I said, Victoria, it's the power of your mind . . . not your muscle or speed."

She gave a spare nod. "I'll do it."

Light broke into the small room as the door opened. They both turned to see Sebastian standing at the other end of the aisle. Sunbeams shone over his golden hair from behind, and then he stepped into the darker room and closed the door.

"I wondered where you'd gone off to," he said. "It was only a bit of luck that I looked out one of the windows and saw the flutter of your skirt as you slipped in here."

"Never say my mother allowed you to slip from her clutches." As Victoria watched him walk up the chapel aisle, she was struck by the memory of doing the same thing herself: to meet Phillip at the altar.

Her throat burned. She swallowed hard, and found herself needing to blink rapidly. Meeting her at the altar. Taking Phillip's place? He'd made it clear he'd like to. At least, in the bedchamber.

She realized with a start that Sebastian had reached her side. But unlike a meeting of his bride, he didn't reach for her hand and close warm fingers around it. Instead, he replied, "It was quite a feat, getting away from her—but not because she was suddenly overcome with fondness for me. Rather, it was because she was determined to undermine me, and keep me from your side. She sent Rockley off in search of you."

"Hm. I was rather hoping for a bit more torture," she

replied, shaking off the discomfiting thoughts. "It's only fair, after that little performance you gave."

He settled his smile on her. "Torture? But, *ma chère*, you needn't leave that to your mother. You have the skill well in hand." There was a gleam in his gaze that unsettled her . . . and made her stomach squeeze pleasantly. She still could not repress her physical attraction to Sebastian.

Victoria felt her cheeks warm and she shifted her attention toward Kritanu. As if her acknowledgement gave him the impetus to speak, he looked at Sebastian. "You and Victoria have more in common than simply being Venators born."

"But of course. The Gardella blood runs deeply through us both—but as I've told you before, my dear"—Sebastian bowed briefly to Victoria—"it's from my mother's side of the family. The Gardella name is so far back in my family tree that you and I needn't worry about our branches crossing. We aren't closely related at all." His face lit with joviality, but his eyes . . . they were sharp with apprehension.

"But that is not what I meant," Kritanu said in his precise tones. "I am speaking of Giulia."

Silence.

Victoria looked at Sebastian, whose face had settled into an odd expression of chagrin and annoyance. When he didn't speak, she turned to Kritanu. He, too, remained silent, watching Sebastian with an expectant look.

She folded her arms over her middle. "Another secret, Sebastian? Aren't you through with them?"

He was silent for a moment, then he spoke at last, in a low, tight voice. "Max was a member of the Tutela, years ago."

"That's no secret to me." Although Max had shown

Victoria the marking on his skin from his days with the Tutela, he'd told her little else. She had had to get more information from Wayren, when Max had left the Venators after executing Aunt Eustacia.

"He exposed his father and sister to the Tutela," said Sebastian.

"I know about that . . . it was a terrible mistake, but he was trying to protect them—they were sick, and his father was old, and dying," Victoria replied evenly. "Max was young, and the Tutela was smart—"

"Then you must know that the Tutela killed his father . . . and allowed the vampires to turn Giulia to an undead."

"Giulia?" Victoria felt as though the bottom of her stomach had opened and her insides were tumbling out.

"Giulia," he continued in that tight voice, "was the first vampire I slew after receiving my *vis bulla*. She was my . . . I loved her. Max's sister." Then he looked steadily at her with empty golden eyes, his mouth angled into a humorless smile. "So you see, Victoria, Kritanu is right. You and I have much in common. We've both had to send the one we loved most to Hell."

Eight

Wherein the Delights of a British Chef Are Discussed

Victoria forced her lips into a polite smile and nodded to Lord Bentworth as he and his triple chins extolled the virtues of his new chef in comparison to the one here at the Hungreath residence.

"Don't skimp on the salt, either," he said, emphasizing his pleasure with the slice of pheasant skewered on the tines of his fork. "Told him not to, and listened from the first day. And the sauces. None of that Frenchy stuff—like this here—told him that. Don't need the beef swimming in it, said." He slipped the fowl in his mouth, and his jaw ground furiously as he chewed, cheeks bulging.

Her mind distracted by other matters more pressing than an appropriate level of seasoning or the cultural influence thereof, Victoria glanced down the table. Sara Regalado was indeed watching her, sharp brown eyes and mysterious smirk all aimed in her direction. Victoria firmed her lips to let the other woman know she wasn't intimidated, then turned back to her own roast pheasant.

Although she could have manufactured an excuse for

staying home tonight, Victoria had decided to attend the dinner party at the Hungreaths' for a variety of reasons. First, because Lady Hungreath was Gwendolyn's godmother and was giving the party in honor of the happily affianced couple, and Gwen had extracted Victoria's promise to attend. Secondly, because George Starcasset and Sara were to be in attendance, and Victoria felt that it might be prudent to keep an eye on them. And finally, because it gave her a bit of space from Sebastian and his shocking revelations.

It was no wonder he and Max could barely stand to be in the same room.

"Don't like green food, either," Bentworth said. He pushed away a bowl of soggy spinach in favor of stabbing a boiled potato bursting from its skin. He plopped it on his plate and beckoned the footman to bring the butter. Apparently Bentworth was a frequent guest at the Hungreaths', as the servant seemed well aware of the man's delight with the dairy confection, and apportioned a generous pale yellow slab onto the potato. "Don't care for the sweets, and told him too. M'wife has a sweet tooth, loves sugar biscuits, but don't care for 'em myself. Just meat and potatoes and bread. Stewed carrots, beets, onions. Can't abide hard or crunchy."

"He must be a versatile chef in order to prepare those items in an agreeable way," Victoria commented in a voice as bland as the food she was eating. Perhaps the Hungreaths ought to speak with Lord Bentworth about hiring a better chef. But she wasn't all that hungry, and, unlike in Italy, the food here was pale in color and mostly the same texture. And thankfully, as long as she kept nodding every so often and adding a comment once in a while, she could try to comb through her tangled thoughts.

It was no news to her that Max had been involved with the Tutela when he was younger. She'd seen the secret society's mark on the back of his shoulder: a whiplike, sinuous dog curved in a writhing circle. As abhorrent as the society it represented, the tattoo was symbolic of the mortals who acted, as Kritanu had once said, like subservient bitches and whores for the undead.

The Tutela coaxed and lured people of all ages into their alliance, preying on the mortal fear of death by promising a chance for immortality and protection from the undead. Max had been one of them for a time, but now she knew without a doubt that the experience, and his early, naive choices, had given him an unflinching and deeply rooted hatred of the undead and the Tutela.

Victoria realized with a start that the people around her seemed to be looking at her, waiting for something. "Pardon me," she said with a little smile, "I seem to have been woolgathering. What was it you asked, Mrs. Cranwrathe?"

The woman across the table cleared her throat in a grating, rough manner that sent Victoria reaching for her own wine. "I was saying, Lady Rockley, how delightful it was for you to encourage the new marquess to join us this evening." There was a sparkle in her light eyes that made Victoria straighten up in her chair. "I understand you are still in residence at St. Heath's Row? And he arrived yesterday?"

She glanced down the table and saw that James, who'd been seated clear at the other end near his hostess, was buffeted on both sides by eager mamas. The poor man. "I'm afraid you're mistaken, Mrs. Cranwrathe. I'm no longer in residence at St. Heath's Row, but have taken over the home of my mother's deceased aunt."

The footman slipped in between her and Lord Bentworth and removed their rose-patterned dishes: the man's fairly gleaming in its emptiness, and Victoria's roses still obliterated by blobs of potatoes, carrots, and a bit of stringy pheasant. Frivolous confections towering on small plates replaced them, and everyone's dessert was dispatched with great enthusiasm, except for Bentworth's.

"Shall we ladies repair to the parlor for sherry?" said Lady Hungreath from her position further down the table. "There are sugar biscuits as well."

Victoria made her way between the other guests, slipping her arm around Gwendolyn, who'd just returned from refreshing herself. As they walked to the parlor, she glanced out at the gardens behind the house. It was barely eight o'clock, so the sun had slipped near the horizon, but was still at just the top of the trees in the distance. She would stay for another hour, perhaps ninety minutes, and then would make her excuses.

Once the flurry of skirts and crocheted wraps and reticules were settled, along with their owners, in the parlor, Victoria realized that Sara Regalado was missing. Drat and blast! She should have hung back and waited to enter the room until she was sure the other woman had joined them.

That faintly supercilious smile during the soup course had implied the Italian chit was up to no good. But now Victoria was in a fix. The men were in the study, enjoying their cigars and brandy, and until they came in to join the women in the parlor, she was going to be stuck here, playing whist or listening to wedding plans or gossip about who was fornicating with whom.

Or at least, if she weren't Victoria Gardella Grantworth de Lacy, she would be stuck in this green and gold parlor, playing the polite Society matron. But being *Illa* Gardella, and having other matters to deal with besides gossip and fashion, she would take matters into her own hands.

Victoria stood, excusing herself to freshen up.

And, as luck would have it, as she started out of the room, she glanced toward one of the hip-level square windows that faced the Hungreaths' enthusiastic gardens of pergolas flanked by clusters of lilies and hyacinth bushes, decorated with climbing roses. She saw the flutter of a rose-colored fabric as it passed behind the statue of a water-spouting cupid.

Sara had been wearing a rose-colored frock.

Moments later, Victoria was hurrying along the slate pathway, staying out of sight of the house windows as much as possible. Although she had to enter from the other side of the garden, she found the cupid fountain and started off in the direction in which the fluttering skirt had disappeared.

Victoria avoided dry sticks and rustling leaves, peering around trees and hedges before turning a corner. One arm of the path took her through the herb garden, where she passed clumps of silver-leafed sage, yellow hyssop, and miniature myrtle. She paused often to look through a filter of climbing rose vines and decorative wrought iron, or clusters of tall grasses and equally tall blooms.

Everything was still but the spray of water from the cupid's mouth, rumbling in the distance. A bird chirped a warning, then fluttered to its nest, sending a few dried leaves drifting down. The sun lowered, its orange ball blazing through the treetops in the distance, still clearly lighting the garden.

Victoria increased her pace, and found herself retracing her steps through the four large circular pathways of the garden, all of which intersected at the cupid fountain. There was no one about.

Frowning, she pivoted at last to return to the house, admitting defeat. Either she hadn't seen what she thought she had, or Sara had made her way back inside. Or she was hiding somewhere that Victoria couldn't find—but there was really no place for her to do so.

Other than the small gardener's shed.

Victoria's heart rate kicked up as her attention landed on the small, well-kept building—hardly larger than an old-fashioned outhouse. It was situated in the far left corner of the garden, next to the stone enclosure that bordered the grounds. Her skin prickling, she crept up to the small building, listening for any human sounds. What could Sara Regalado be doing out here?

But when Victoria came close enough to sidle alongside the small building, her mouth began to water and her heart started to thump hard. The scent of blood filtered through the air. Her vision clouded at the edges.

No. Not again.

Easing her way around the corner of the shed to the front, she found the door. It was locked . . . but the aroma of thick, rich blood was stronger. It was as if it weighted the summer evening air, clogging the delicate essence of roses and lilies with rust. Her head pounding, Victoria blinked hard and moved along the front of the shed, following the smell and her instincts around the corner toward the back . . . and then she needed to go no further.

It was just as bloody a mess as the last one she'd found, in the park. Her mouth salivating so that she had to swallow back, twice, Victoria bent shakily next to what remained of the body.

It wasn't Sara Regalado. Victoria didn't recognize her, but based on the simple worsted wool of her dress—now bloodied and torn—the victim appeared to be a chambermaid or some other servant. The puncture wounds on her throat and claw marks on the top of her shoulders clearly indicated an attack by an undead.

Victoria's hand shook as she reached to close the woman's sightless eyes. Her lids were still warm, and Victoria let her fingers move gingerly over cheeks so pudgy they could belong to her own maid, Verbena. The vampire probably hadn't gone far.

A sound behind her had the hair on the back of her arms prickling, and Victoria half turned as she looked automatically for something that could be used as a stake.

"Lady Rockley?"

Victoria looked up into the face of Brodebaugh, Gwen's earl, who was flanked by Baron Hungreath and George Starcasset. She pulled to her feet and swallowed again. "She's dead."

"So it appears." Hungreath was looking at her with something like apprehension tinged with suspicion. "How did you come to find her?"

Victoria glanced at George, instinctively looking to see if he was somehow responsible for the trio discovering her and the mauled maid. His soft face was bland, but she saw a glint in his blue eyes that made her tighten her lips. And while the other two men were looking at the bloodied body with a combination of disgust and horror, George appeared unmoved.

As if recognizing her suspicions, he said, "The other women are in the parlor enjoying their sherry. When they said you'd been gone for some time, and no one knew where you were, we thought it would be best to check the gardens." His deceptively sweet dimples appeared.

Smoothing her skirt, which she realized now had streaks of blood on it, Victoria said, "Someone had best send for the magistrate. And perhaps the housekeeper, to see if she recognizes the poor thing."

"What ho," said George, bending toward a bush. When he stood, he was holding a long shawl, stained with blood. "What is this?"

Victoria stared at it, feeling light of head. Her vision blushed with red as she recognized her own shawl. The one that she'd left on a small table in the foyer, upon arrival this evening.

"Poor gel," Brodebaugh said, with real sincerity in his voice as he looked down at the victim. Then he turned and offered Victoria his arm, cementing her affection for the man that her best friend was to wed. "And for you, Lady Rockley, to have found her in such a state. Lean on my arm, and I'll assist you back to the house."

Victoria did as he suggested, not because she needed his support, of course . . . but because the expression on George Starcasset's face made her uneasy. When he'd produced the shawl, there was an unmistakable smugness in his expression that suggested he knew that it was hers. Not that she would deny it of course, but she wondered how it had gotten there—and who had moved it.

It was most certainly not beyond the realm of possibility—and in fact, was likely—that Sara had lured her into the gardens so that she would discover the remnants of another daylight vampire attack, and had planted the shawl nearby.

Which then begged the question: was it Sara or George who had turned undead?

Or someone else?

Victoria came awake sharply.

She didn't move, kept her breathing easy and regular, and slitted her eyes a crack. Someone or some*thing* was in the bedchamber with her.

The room was all shapes and shades of dark gray, any

detail that might be discernable in the predawn light distorted by her narrow view. She'd have to turn her head. . . .

"Good God. You might as well open your eyes, Victoria. A gnat could do a better job feigning sleep than you."

Victoria's eyes flew open. She sat up abruptly, her fingers tightening around a stake as she pulled it from beneath the coverlet. She hadn't slept without one since the night she'd killed Phillip.

"Well, Max. It's been quite some time since you've visited my bedchamber."

Her voice was rough with slumber, and she wasn't quite certain why she said such a provocative thing . . . unless it was because there was nothing else one could say to a man who sneaked into one's bedchamber in the hours just before dawn.

Particularly a man who'd kissed one against the stone wall of a Roman villa, then had given up his role as a Venator and disappeared without saying good-bye.

Something fluttered deep in her stomach.

He was standing in a dark corner of the room, well in the shadows. It was only his voice that had given him away. None of the windows were open, nor was the door, to indicate how he'd managed to enter.

"I don't think you'll need that," he said, obviously noticing the stake. "Unless it's become an addition to your nighttime bedchamber activities."

"What are you doing here?"

He stepped more fully into view. Max was taller than most men, looming over the bed, and he preferred black clothing. Neither factor did much to reveal the details of his form or countenance tonight; he remained an elegant shadow with only the bridge of his long, straight nose outlined by the pale light glazing the window. "I wanted to talk to you."

Victoria gave an impatient jerk of the stake against the coverlet's whitework embroidery. "I mean, what are you doing in London? Of course you came to talk to me. What other reason would you have to be in my bed-chamber?"

Silence descended and stretched for a moment, then Max replied, his voice smooth, "Perhaps your imagination is a bit stunted." He shifted, removing his hands from his pockets to cross them over his middle. Victoria realized her heart was thumping hard at the base of her throat. And she was remembering the way he'd kissed her, against that cold, wet stone.

He continued, "Vioget informed me of your find in the park. The vampire attack during the daylight."

"You've spoken to Sebastian?"

"Last night, as a matter of fact. After he left you." Max shifted, spreading his long-fingered hands to emphasize his words. "A bit of advice, Victoria. Keep away from the windows when entertaining in your bedchamber."

"I didn't take you for a voyeur, Max. But perhaps watching is more to your liking than doing."

Now she saw the gleam of white teeth in a humorless smile. "Mmm . . . no." Then the smile faded. "Do you mind covering up a bit? That's a ghastly-looking gown."

Victoria looked down and saw that not only had the bedclothes drifted into her lap, but the growing light from the window seemed to shine directly on her and the lavender night rail she wore. The fine lawn material and deep lace trim of the plunging neckline—one of her favorites—hid none of the curves of her torso. "I'm terribly sorry to have offended your fashion sensibilities, Max. I didn't realize you had any." She shrugged, pulling the covers up. "But after all, I didn't invite you into my bedchamber."

"Quite true. Please accept my deepest gratitude." He made an insolent bow, leaving her to wonder whether he was thanking her for pulling the bedclothes up to her collarbones, or for not inviting him into her room. "I must also commend your efficiency."

"My efficiency?"

"From dinner with the newly arrived marquess to . . . er . . . nocturnal entertainment in the marchioness's bedchamber the very same night, and then a move to another bedchamber in a different house the next day. Quite efficient, and much coming and going. Thus I felt it necessary to take precautions that Vioget would be otherwise occupied this evening." Now she saw a flash of white teeth in the dark. "Far be it for me to cause an interruption."

"How very accommodating of you, Max. What did you do to Sebastian?"

"Oh, you needn't fear for the man's safety. He's merely on the tail of a woman who, from a distance, bears an astonishing resemblance to you."

"And what is this woman doing?"

"I'm not quite certain, but I do believe she's having an assignation in Vauxhall Gardens." His smile gleamed again. "I don't think Vioget was pleased."

Victoria hid her own smile. It would serve Sebastian right to be following a false trail—especially after his blithe announcement in the parlor today, chosen, of course, for timing and audience. "Perhaps now might be a good time to reveal exactly why you've made it a point to invade my chamber. But, truly, Max," she said, her voice softening from the haughty edge she'd adopted. "I am glad to see that you are safe and well. And . . . of course you must know about Briyani."

He nodded, and she saw his shoulders relax. "I spoke with Kritanu last night as well."

"Kritanu too?" Victoria felt a swell of annoyance again.

"Don't be angry with him," Max said. "I told him I'd speak with you . . . and as you're aware, he's been otherwise distracted."

"I notice you don't defend Sebastian's lack of communication about your presence in London."

"In fact, I'm shocked that he didn't rush to inform you of it, knowing that it would annoy me. He threatened to do so."

"Your fiancée is here as well. Did he tell you that?" Even though Max's engagement to Sara had been a false one—at least, Victoria thought it had been a false one—she'd never been able to resist the urge to needle him about it.

"Vioget didn't see fit to tell me that—unless he wasn't aware."

Victoria shook her head. "He is fully aware, for she and George Starcasset were there when he fairly announced our engagement to my mother this afternoon. And I'm terribly sorry, Max, but it appears you've been replaced in her affections by Gwendolyn's brother George."

"I'm devastated."

"I used to feel sorry for the woman, for you made her believe you loved her," Victoria chided.

"Did I?" Max sounded amused.

"You certainly appeared to be promoting such a conviction when I met you at the home of the Conte Regalado." She'd come upon a rumpled Max leaving an obvious tête-à-tête with Sara.

"That must certainly have made an impression on you, Victoria, for you bring that incident up nearly every time we talk."

"You looked ridiculous, with your hair mussed and your neck cloth crooked. It was more than obvious what you'd been doing. And will you please *do* sit down," Victoria said in exasperation. "Your hovering is quite annoying, and if you don't, I shall be forced to stand myself—and I daresay you don't want to be treated to the full sight of my ghastly nightgown."

He made a sound that could have been a strangled laugh or a cough; but in either case, he took her advice and sat—in the chair farthest from the bed, placing himself back in the shadows. "I daresay I don't."

"Now, tell me, why are you in London when you should be running as far from Lilith as possible."

She actually felt the tension settle back in the room, chilling whatever lightness their banter had brought to bear. "Ah yes . . . my unfortunate circumstances. We needn't discuss the banalities of why I came back to this drafty, wet country—but more to the purpose, how I might be of assistance in your current dilemma. The daylight vampire attack."

Victoria nodded, focusing her attention on that instead of flinging one-sentence barbs back and forth. It did become wearying after awhile, and, truth to tell, she was relieved to see Max. If only he didn't have to be so prickly. And arrogant. And rude. "There was another one today."

She told him, and ended with her suspicions about Sara and George. "But it seems rather heavy-handed for them to taunt me so blatantly, if indeed one of them is the daylight vampire."

"I tend to agree. Although Sara is not known for her subtlety."

"It is not pure chance that I was the one to discover both victims, within the space of two days."

"Indeed. And we must presume that they've obtained the elixir that was described in the writings we found behind the Magic Door in Roma." He moved; she heard rather than saw it. "The formula Vioget stole from the Consilium."

Victoria pushed a long curl back over the crown of her head. "I've not forgotten that, Max. But he did take me to a secret abbey under London, where he retrieved one of the Rings of Jubai."

"But he didn't give you the ring, did he?"

"No. But he made no attempt to hide it."

Max snorted. "Well, one can always find a straw at which to grasp if one looks hard enough."

"He killed Beauregard. That's done much to build my trust in him," Victoria said, ignoring the fact that she trusted Sebastian hardly at all.

"He had no choice," Max said flatly. "After what he allowed to happen to you."

"Allowed?" She shook her head. "No, Max. It wasn't Sebastian—the fault lay with me. I followed him to Beauregard's lair, I went after him. Sebastian tried to stop me—that was how he was injured, by me with my stake, and then by the other vampires. He knew what Beauregard wanted. He wanted me. And the only reason he succeeded in subduing me was because of the copper armband."

Copper was the only material that did not disintegrate when a vampire was killed. Everything else the creature was wearing exploded into ashes and dust, except for items made of copper. That was why Lilith had forged her

Five Rings of Jubai from the soft metal, and why Beauregard's special armband had been imbued with the ability to sap the strength of a mortal. Even if the vampire was killed, the metal—and any powers that had been bestowed upon it—would survive.

"And why did Beauregard want to turn you, Victoria? Because of Vioget. He gave his grandfather too much— too much freedom, too much loyalty, too much support." He moved again, and she saw that he'd stood once more. "I would have killed him myself if necessary."

"Beauregard?"

"Vioget. And he was well aware of it. That was why he finally did the right thing by staking Beauregard. He made no move to do so until I came on the scene."

Victoria felt a cool chill ripple over her. The animosity between the men was frightening; yet she'd known them both for two years, and never, until now, had it been so overt. So dark, as though it were preparing to erupt. "When you went with Sebastian to save me, you were . . . you no longer had the power of the *vis bulla.*"

"And?"

"You didn't tell him, Max. You might have been killed."

"I wasn't."

"What will you do now?"

He shifted, and now the glowing sunrise illuminated half of his face, outlining a high, sculpted cheekbone and part of his sharp jaw. His dark hair brushed the underside of his chin, gleaming in thick waves where the light touched it. "I'm here to assist you, and then I'll move on to somewhere else where Lilith won't find me."

"How?"

"I can still stake a vampire, Victoria."

"Of course you can," she replied tartly. "Before you

took the *vis bulla* you killed many vampires—a fact which you've made certain to impress upon me more than once. But you'll be no match for Lilith if she finds you, and you can be certain she's looking for both of us. It's possible she's even here in London. One bite is all it would take to put you back under her thrall—"

"No it wouldn't. There's more to the process than a mere bite from her—or else everyone she feeds from would be so. And I certainly see no need to revisit those memories."

"Even if it's more than one bite—"

"I'm gratified by your concern," he said, "but I have no intention of being entrapped by that creature again. I have my own protection." He lifted his hand, and in the dim light she saw that he wore a heavy silver ring.

He didn't need to explain; she knew him well enough to understand. There was something in the ring that would send him to his death if need be. He seemed almost eager to put it to the test. "Practical, practical Max." She felt her lips move in a false smile. "So, how do you anticipate being able to assist in our endeavors?"

"It's simple. You and Vioget rely on the power of the *vis bulla* to sense the presence of a vampire, and to fight them. Perhaps too much, in this case. I no longer have that burden, and can instead rely only on intuition and senses—skills that I used before I became a Venator. Simple observation, and other instincts, have worked well for me in the past."

Victoria had crossed her arms over her middle. Her hackles had begun to rise at the beginning of his speech, but by the end she was nodding in agreement. "I'm nothing if not practical myself," she said. "I think it's an excellent idea."

He didn't respond and she could only conclude that

even Max couldn't think of a snide remark in this case. After all, she'd agreed with him.

"So, do tell, Victoria. What prompted your move from the very comfortable home of the Marquess of Rockley to this smaller residence, in a most unfashionable part of town?" he said, moving away from the window.

She drew in a deep breath, then released it slowly. Sadness settled over her. "I no longer belong there. My life has changed completely."

"A sentiment I fully understand." His voice had lost its crispness.

Silence descended.

Victoria had often thought about what her life would be like—how empty, different, bland it would be—if she no longer wore the *vis bulla*. As horrible as that event would be for her, how much more difficult it must be for Max.

He had not only been stalking the undead for longer, but also had a penance to pay for giving his family to those immortal creatures. He'd given up his Venatorial powers not only to break the hold Lilith had over him, but also in order to slay the demon Akvan. It had been prophesied that no Venator or demon should ever harm him—so Max had cast off his supernatural powers and become merely a man in order to destroy the creature.

But Max would never be merely a man.

"How is your hand?" he asked suddenly, standing at the foot of the bed.

"My hand?"

A sudden, quiet *snick*, and then a tiny light flared in the room, cupped by one of his hands, held aloft by the other. "Miro's light sticks are quite convenient," Max said with a little bow. "Your right hand, Victoria. Let me see it."

Now she understood. Victoria hesitated, curling her fingers into her palm.

He was closer to the bed now, and she swung her feet out from beneath the coverings and sat on the edge as if that position would give her more stability—yet her feet dangled nervously above the floor. Holding the flickering flame on a stick, he reached for her wrist.

"Open."

She did, and the yellow glow illuminated the faint bluish cast over the plump parts of her palm, up along the inside of her thumb.

Their eyes met and she felt warmth billow through her, from her chest out into each of her limbs. The room pressed in around them.

"It won't wash off." Her voice was soft.

"I told you it would not."

The blue tinge was from a shard of Akvan's Obelisk, the demonic stone that had been shattered by Max the previous November when they battled Nedas. Victoria had retrieved one of the pieces and brought it back to the Consilium, where, unbeknownst to her, the power of the obelisk had called Akvan back to earth—and the power of the splinter directed his minions to the secret location of the Consilium.

When she'd removed the shard from the hideaway, returning it to a safe place behind the Door of Alchemy, Max had been there as well.

That was when Victoria, influenced by the malevolent power of the piece of obelisk that she'd held, had goaded him into kissing her.

The blue on her hand was indelibly connected to the memory of her fingers curling into the rough stone wall as Max fit his mouth to hers.

She closed her hand into a fist. It was a good thing she had to wear gloves in polite society.

"I've often wondered if that also contributed to the failure of Beauregard's blood to take root in you." He nodded brusquely at her hand as he released it, then moved slightly away.

She breathed a bit easier now, and stopped her leg against the edge of the bed. "I hadn't thought of that, but it's possible. Vampires and demons are immortal enemies. I obviously had been somewhat influenced by Akvan's power when I was holding the shard. Perhaps some essence of it remained."

He nodded. "That and your two *vis bullae*." His eyes focused on her, and even in the shadowy light, she could sense the sharpness of his gaze.

Her two strength amulets were not a topic on which she cared to speak. She didn't want to discuss or acknowledge the fact that one of them was his. It was simply too uncomfortable. Strange, to think about the intimacy of wearing an amulet pierced through her own skin that had once hung from his.

The silence snapped when he shifted away with spare, smooth movements. His hand closed over the doorknob, answering at least one of her questions: how he'd entered the room. "Perhaps you'd best get some sleep now, Victoria," he said. "I'm certain Vioget will return soon enough."

"He hasn't open access to my bedchamber," she said sharply. "Much as he might wish to."

"Do I detect upheaval in paradise? A bit of a tension between two lovers?"

"Sebastian isn't my lover."

His brows rose. "Indeed." He turned the knob, but refrained from opening the door. "Another word of advice,

Victoria. For all of the enmity between Vioget and my-self, I know that he means well by you. His greatest weakness is blind loyalty. He is a worthy match for you." His words were short and clipped. "It's . . . important that you think of the future."

"You begin to sound like my mother," Victoria replied, feeling bewildered. Why was Max encouraging her to-ward a man he loathed?

"Whereas your mother is concerned only with titles and wealth and grandchildren, my interest relates to the well-being of the Venators. You are the last of the direct line, and should consider what will happen if you die without issue. Or prematurely."

Victoria slid down from the edge of the bed, her feet landing on the soft woolen rug. The brush of silk from her nightgown shifted sleekly against her calves, swishing down from her thighs. "This from a man who, two years ago, was furious that I chose to wed? Make up your mind, Max." As she stood in front of him, she saw him draw back . . . subtly, almost imperceptibly putting distance between them.

"My mind has been made up. Don't be a fool, Victo-ria. Remember your duty." He pulled the door open, then paused halfway out of the room. "I do hope you'll be con-siderate and keep any—er—activities in here from being too strident."

She looked at him, enlightenment dawning as the urge to tamper with him disappeared. "You're staying here?"

"Kritanu suggested it." His sardonic smile flashed again. "But you needn't worry that I'll disrupt things . . . I'm staying in the servants' quarters." The door closed behind him with a firm click as he made his escape.

Nine

In Which Our Heroine Is Interrogated Yet Again

Victoria did not go back to sleep after Max left.

Instead, she found herself staring at the ceiling of the bedchamber that used to belong to Aunt Eustacia. As ceilings went, it was patently uninteresting—there was nary a mural nor a small plafond to relieve its eggshell color. It was flat, unmarked, and without flaw.

Thus Victoria had nothing to distract her from her churning thoughts.

Max was somewhere in the house, a fact which alone made her feel odd. He was suggesting that she marry—or at least have a long-term, child-bearing affair with—a man he loathed. The man who'd killed his sister, in fact, sending her, as an undead, to an eternal damnation that Max had caused. A man that Max had disparaged for his cowardice on more than one occasion, who had declined to accept the role of Venator, yet who had kept the knowledge and power of one for more than a decade.

A man that Victoria had been intimate with on more than one occasion, although, as she'd informed Max, she didn't consider Sebastian her lover. Not really. Not in an ongoing or permanent way. Not as if she was ready to wed the man.

Since she'd first met Sebastian, he'd projected an aura of mystery and untrustworthiness. Yet, from their initial conversation at the Silver Chalice, there'd been a connection between them, a flare of attraction on which he never wasted an opportunity to act. Or attempt to act.

And she'd been willing. A few times.

She shivered, smiled, remembering.

In truth, he had made her *feel* when she'd otherwise been numb. When she grieved, he soothed and awakened her. When she raged, he enraged her further, drawing forth that energy and massaging it into passion. His sense of the absurd, his ability to turn every situation into a prospect for seduction, his fit, golden body . . . the one, she remembered now, with a tinge of bitterness, that he'd kept fairly hidden from her until two months ago, when she'd discovered that he wore the *vis bulla*.

Nothing could change the fact that he'd turned his back on the Venators. He'd lived with a powerful vampire for years, protecting and serving him while watching the vampire hunters from a distance.

He'd ignored his duty.

Yes, he'd had to slay the woman he loved. Giulia had no longer been the girl he'd known, just as Phillip had no longer been the man Victoria had wed. It had been the hardest thing she'd ever done . . . but it had not drawn her from her responsibilities.

If anything, it had made her stronger and more determined to eradicate the undead.

Her thoughts were interrupted by a knock at the door. Victoria sat up, surprised that Verbena would bother her so early. It wasn't yet nine o'clock. "Yes?"

Verbena's puff of wiry orange hair poked around the door. "Oh, thank'od my lady, ye'r awake. I'm so sorry to bother ye, but there's a man on the front stoop who's de-mandin' to speak t'ye."

"Who is it?" Victoria swung her legs out of the bed and slid to the floor.

"I dunno, but says ye'd want t'talk to him. He says as he'll stay there all th'day if'n ye don' come down." Verbena came in the room, carrying a fine white chemise and Victoria's corset. "The nerve o' him an' his sharp-edged beak. I d'clare, th' man looks like a ferret."

Frowning, Victoria pulled her nightgown over her head as her maid ruffled quickly through the wardrobe for a frock that could easily be slipped over her corset and fastened quickly, without having to be pressed. Whoever it was, it must be important for him to call on her so early.

Many possibilities shot through her mind as Verbena helped her to dress quickly, then looped her thick, heavy hair into a loose knot at the back of her neck. Within min-utes, Victoria hurried down the stairs.

To be sure, there wasn't another lady of the ton who could have been dressed so quickly, so early in the morning—let alone already be awake when the sum-mons came. And yet, when Victoria opened the front door to the stoop, she found her guest pacing the small space with an air of deep impatience.

She recognized the familiar, sharp-faced man right away, even as, without a bow or even the pretense of one, he said, "Lady Rockley. I understand you had another harrowing experience last evening. How dreadful for you." His tone, his countenance, and even his posture ex-posed his words as sarcastic. Instead, Mr. Bemis Good-win's pale gray eyes appeared cold. "And I'm certain you'd want this conversation to take place inside, rather than here on your front stoop."

Annoyance buffeted her, but she tasted a bit of apprehension as well. The look in his eyes held suspicion along with unfriendliness. She stepped away to allow him entrance, and gestured to the tiny parlor. "What do you want, Mr. Goodwin?" she asked, following him in and closing the door.

"I have some questions to ask in regards to your discovery last evening, at the home of Baron Hungreath." He looked pointedly toward one of the chairs. Victoria ignored him. "Of course, the magistrate is quite concerned."

Victoria, having been the one to suggest contacting the magistrate, felt like kicking herself. But she refrained, and instead replied, "As well he should be. Someone is attacking innocent women and leaving their mauled bodies for dead."

"Someone? Or some*thing*?" Mr. Goodwin's slender nose gleamed like the mother-of-pearl handle on a spoon.

"If you continue to make such vague statements, my butler will show you the door."

"The magistrate has sent me to ask you some questions, Lady Rockley. It will be best for you if you cooperate. I should hate for you to end up in Newgate, waiting for the noose, due to some . . . misunderstanding . . . in regards to your involvement. I understand it's quite a loathsome place, even for a prison."

"Who are you working for?" she asked.

"Why, the magistrate, of course. Although Miss Forrest's family is, and quite rightly, devastated and determined to find out who or what is behind the horrible attack on their daughter." Victoria saw him glance toward the chair again, but perversely, she remained standing. "You came upon this young woman's body hidden behind a gardener's shed. Her name, incidentally, was Bertha Flowers." He looked at her as if to challenge whether she cared that the woman had a name.

"Yes, I found her behind the shed."

"What were you doing in the garden during a dinner party, Lady Rockley?"

"I had excused myself to get some air. The gardens were lovely."

"But the other guests were playing cards. Why would you be so rude as to leave the party?"

"I thought I saw one of the other ladies in the garden, and I went to join her."

"And who was that? According to Lady Hungreath, all of the other ladies were in the parlor with the exception of you."

"Miss Sara Regalado, from Rome, was not in the parlor when I quit the room."

"Miss Regalado returned almost immediately after you disappeared. Lady Hungreath noted it especially as she thought it would be you, and was quite confused when you didn't return."

So that had not been Sara's pink gown, flashing behind the cupid statue? It was impossible for Sara to have returned to the parlor so quickly without Victoria seeing her.

"How did you know where to find the body?"

"As I wasn't looking for a body," Victoria replied shortly, "I didn't know where to find it."

"You had blood on your skirt and hands when the gentlemen found you. And your shawl, covered in blood, was found at the scene as well, as if it had been . . . discarded. Nor, again, did you scream or make any other sound of distress—according to the others. Who, certainly, should have heard you. It's almost as if you expected to find it, and knew where to look." He rocked back on his heels, as if delivering some great pronouncement.

"There was blood everywhere, Mr. Goodwin. When I knelt next to the girl to ascertain whether she was dead—"

"Lady Rockley, I saw the condition of her body. You must be foolish in the extreme to believe that she might have been alive. Regardless, no woman would have the constitution to come upon a person in that condition and not make any sound of distress." He didn't speak further, but exaggerated dubiousness was written on his face.

"Perhaps you could desist from dancing about the Maypole and say whatever it is you mean," Victoria replied.

"Very well, then, Lady Rockley. I believe that you are somehow involved in these attacks. Either you are the perpetrator, or are somehow involved with the person— or creature—who is."

"Mr. Goodwin, do you have any idea how ridiculous you sound?" Victoria found it easy to laugh, although an uncomfortable feeling had begun to settle in the back of her mind. "How would a woman such as I make those kinds of wounds on another person?"

"A woman such as you?" Mr. Goodwin's eyebrows turned into dark, inverted vees, drawing together above the bridge of his nose. "I have a feeling that a *woman such as you* just might be able to."

Victoria's mouth dried. Who was this man? The discomfort in her middle turned cold and heavy. Yet she responded coolly. "Accusations toward me are merely a waste of your time and energy. The real monster who is doing this is escaping your notice while you point the finger at me."

"Of course you would say that, Lady Rockley. You are

very clever, I do give you credit for that. After what happened with your husband, I would expect you to react in such a fashion."

She must have frowned in question, but, in truth, her anxiety was turning to anger at the skinny man before her. Victoria's vision blurred and began to pinken. She felt her fingers close in on themselves, her nails scoring deeply into her palms.

"Yes, indeed," he continued in an unhurried voice. "The circumstances under which your husband disappeared are exceedingly odd, indeed. I shall not be overlooking them in my investigations. And do not think that your status will protect you, Lady Rockley."

"Get out of my house."

"Of course, Lady Rockley." He started toward the door, moving as if he had all of the time in the world and as if Victoria wasn't ready to do something violent to his person. It must have showed in her face, despite the fact that she tried to control it. The anger bubbled and simmered and she felt it in the way her knees shook beneath the fall of her skirt, and her teeth ground down on themselves.

"Perhaps you recall the fate of Baron Clifton's heir? It wasn't even murder, Lady Rockley. He merely stole some jewelry." Mr. Goodwin smiled with great pleasure. "Stealing is still a hanging offense. As is assault, and accomplice to murder."

Now his hand was on the knob, and he turned it. Then he stopped, just like Max had earlier this morning. "Did I mention that one of the servants at St. Heath's Row told me that Rockley had left the home days before you claim he left on *The Plentifulle*, after a great row between the two of you? And that the day you say he sailed on that ship, that same servant saw his master enter the house in the dead of night? The same night that you dismissed all of the servants?"

He stepped through the door as Victoria's vision began to burn. She felt her heart beat and her breath increasing in speed, and herself wanting to move toward him . . . to stop him. Stop him from these snide remarks, these thinly covered accusations.

He had one more thing to say. "I believe you had something to do with his disappearance, Lady Rockley. Just as you had something to do with the attacks on Miss Forrest and Miss Flowers. And a man left for dead in the Dials more than a year ago. He had been repeatedly stabbed.

"I've been awaiting your return from Italy for nearly a year now." He smiled and slammed his hat onto sleek, smooth hair, looking at her with the same insolence that Nedas, the vampire son of Lilith, had. "I've seen many of your class behind the bars of Newgate, Lady Rockley, and watched them on the scaffold. It's my opinion that you will soon join them, and then how long will your lush, dark beauty last?"

And he closed the door so quietly it was ominous.

Despite the uneasiness from her meeting with Mr. Goodwin, Victoria was clearheaded enough to order Charley, Aunt Eustacia's trusted butler, to follow the odious man.

Once she was alone, standing in the foyer, Victoria shook off the foreboding and fury that had billowed through her during their meeting. Her vision cleared, and she looked down at her hands—one scarred and creamy, the other faintly blue, as though she'd been out in the cold for too long. They showed the marks of her nails, but none had drawn blood.

And her fingers no longer shook.

Despite his threats, she had no real fear of the Bow Street Runner. What could he do to her? Not only was she a member of the ton, but she was *Illa* Gardella. And most importantly, she'd done nothing wrong. She'd certainly not had anything to do with the deaths of Miss Forrest and Miss Flowers, and the situation with Phillip was utterly different.

But . . . there had been that incident in the Seven Dials neighborhood.

As she stood in the entrance of Aunt Eustacia's home, Victoria couldn't help but remember the night she'd come into this very same space. Well past midnight, nearing the dawn, only a month after Phillip's death, she'd eased through the front door, blood-spattered and insensitive.

There wasn't supposed to be blood.

That phrase rang through her memory again, just as it had done that night, over and over. Aunt Eustacia, roused by her niece's arrival, had listened with calm, dark eyes as Victoria described how she'd come upon a large man attempting to ravish a young girl in the filthy, poverty-stricken, and mean streets of the Dials. It was her first night out hunting for undead after Phillip's death, and grief for him and hatred toward herself had burst forth as she attacked the man bare-handed.

When he turned on her, a dagger in his hand, she'd wrested the unfamiliar weapon from him and used it against him—plunging it into mortal flesh and bone in an awful parody of slaying an undead. A berserker had overtaken her.

The man had been breathing when she left him, but, nevertheless, Victoria had inflicted grave harm on a human. A mortal, of the very race she was bound to protect.

After that incident, she'd removed her *vis bulla* and let

it languish. She mourned Phillip for a year, struggling to contain and control her need to destroy and avenge. It was then that she realized how terrible and dangerous her Venatorial gifts were—how they could be used to destroy those she was meant to save.

When she replaced the *vis bulla*, she did so with the full understanding of who she was, and what her limits were. And with the vow that her powers were not to be used against her own race. That was not her role to play.

She took a deep breath and unclasped her hands, stretching her fingers, tried to ease the tension. The oddest thing of all was that Mr. Goodwin even knew of the incident in the Dials. After all, in that area of town, violence and murder happened so regularly that it was difficult for the authorities to bring the criminals to justice, if they were even notified of every death or injury—which was impossible.

I've been awaiting your return from Italy for nearly a year now.

Those words hung in her mind, leaving her with a greasy lump in the back of her throat.

She had to find out who—or what—Bemis Goodwin was.

Ten

Wherein a Highwayman Engages in Social Frivolities

In Victoria's mind masquerade balls weren't so terrible, as far as Society events went. After all, she wore her own kind of mask every day, and she'd only ever attended one other such Society event—shortly after she and Phillip had announced their engagement. The mystery and intrigue reminded her of a safer, more lighthearted version of her nightly hunts on the streets. Certainly, masked dances with many rich-blooded potential victims were liable to attract some of the undead, due to their ability to hide behind a domino or other facial obstruction, but it wasn't as though a vampire could enter a home uninvited.

That aspect did cut down on the number of vampires that crashed these soirees.

As she alighted from the sleek, midnight blue carriage, Victoria adjusted her mask and slung her small reticule over the other wrist. She'd purposely elected to use a plain carriage and arrive alone so that her identity would remain unknown for as long as possible. Despite her mother's transparent attempts to engage James Lacy as her escort, Victoria had slipped firmly out of any such mazes, warning her mother not to reveal the nature of her costume to the new marquess—or even that she planned to attend. She didn't want anyone to know she would be there, particularly George Starcasset and Sara Regalado.

"If you do, I promise you, Mother, that I'll never accept another dance or invitation from Rockley again. And then how on earth will you ever get anyone to believe we've developed an attachment?"

Apparently, Lady Melly believed her—and the fallacy that there was a chance for the two to form an attachment—for she clamped her lips and nodded. "But you must promise to dance with him at least twice, and most definitely once after the masks have been removed." Victoria had made some vague reply, helped in her attempt to prevaricate by the industrious Verbena, who'd been working on her hair in a most enthusiastic manner.

Now, as she took measured paces up the steps to Landross House, the residence of Lord and Lady Philander, Victoria felt a little knit of excitement trip down her spine. Unlike a few months ago, during the Carnivale in Rome where the streets were packed with costumed revelers, this would be a bit more sedate. The masks and costumes wouldn't include long beaks or ungainly papier-mâché animal masks; likely, most of the garb would be gowns or dress clothing fashioned to represent the personage portrayed.

Because it was a masquerade ball, and the attendees' identities were to remain secret until midnight, when the masks were removed, the butler did not announce Victoria by name as she entered the ballroom. It was busy, but not thoroughly crowded. Since the fascinating new Marquess of Rockley was due to attend, Victoria knew the room would soon be a complete crush.

Fortunately, Landross House not only boasted a high-ceilinged anteroom next to the ballroom, where the food and drink had been laid out (along with some chairs for the chaperones and other matrons), but a generous terrace that ran along the entire length of the residence. The doors from the ballroom were opened to the night air, and small lanterns festooned potted fig, lemon, and olive trees throughout the patio.

Feeling secure behind her large cream-and-silver mask, which covered her from hairline to over the top of her nose, and curved down over the sides of her face like a medieval helm, Victoria strolled through the room. Most of her hair had been twisted into a long coil, then wound in a large, intricate knot at the back of her crown, but a thick wave had been left to hang freely over her shoulder and down over one side of her torso.

The dancing had not yet started, and Victoria held her dance card and its little dangling pencil as she examined the other guests. She fully expected George Starcasset and Sara Regalado to be in attendance, and her main goal was to remain unrecognized by them so that she could observe.

In keeping with the theme of an underwater grotto, lighting was scarce and often obscured by false rocks inside the ballroom. Illumination threaded through the silver and blue strips of silk that hung from the ceiling, glittering and shifting the light as if it were under the ocean. The footmen, butler, and serving girls all wore livery decorated with glittering green, blue, and silver sequins, as though they were fish swimming silently among the guests. Victoria took a small glass of something pink and sparkling from one of them. It turned out to be effervescent water flavored with sugar and grapefruit peel—rather unusual and delicious, if a bit warm for her taste.

As she sipped, she turned in a slow arc from her vantage point across from the patio. From here, she could see the dance floor to her left, the orchestra positioned behind a thrush of papier-mâché rocks studded with fake seaweed and glittering fish, and beyond, in the anteroom, the long tables of food and drink.

Her eyes snagged on a man with blond hair that was long enough to just brush the back of his neck.

Romeo, if his doublet and slashed pantaloons were any indication. His cleft chin and the familiar movement of his shoulders betrayed his identity. As she watched George without appearing to do so, Victoria wondered if, somewhere, Sara was dressed as a matching Juliet.

As she considered whether to approach him directly or merely to observe, George turned and looked in her direction. Victoria held her breath and forced her attention to move casually away as though she didn't recognize him. She felt the weight of his attention skim over her and, out of the corner of her eye, watched it settle on one of the Fates, who happened to be holding a pair of shears.

The glint of her blonde hair and the puffy pink lips beneath Atropos's mask, along with her diminutive stature, identified her as Gwen Starcasset. Victoria hadn't realized that Gwen was going to be in attendance tonight, and she eased back behind a nearby cluster of potted plants disguised as seaweed in an effort to keep out of her friend's view. Watching as George approached his sister, she strained to see if she could hear anything. Even from a distance, and in the untrustworthy illumination, she recognized the pure delight in Gwen's smile when her brother greeted her. And the surprise evident in his physical reaction, which gave Victoria something to think about.

"Ah . . . Diana the Huntress," murmured a silky voice from behind Victoria. "How apropos."

She stepped slightly to the side, angling half toward Sebastian while keeping her attention focused on George. Her left shoulder brushed against the right side of his chest. She smiled. He'd guessed correctly that her flowing, silver-shot gown and Roman-styled hair depicted Diana. But perhaps the small bow and arrow hanging from her heavy belt had given him a clue.

The whisper-thin fabric of her togalike gown gathered over one shoulder with a wide silver clasp, leaving the other bare. Her skirt, made of the same material, fell in many deep folds to the floor, but wrapped around in such a manner that it split to well above her knee, just below a vee-shaped girdle of silver studded with cabochons. The slit gave her ease of movement when she walked, yet the yards of fabric camouflaged the opening when she was standing, as now. And Verbena, in a moment of brilliance, had created two separate skirts with the frothy fabric. The overskirt could be removed easily—for it was tucked into the belt—to reveal a shorter, less voluminous skirt in the event that Victoria needed more freedom of movement, which happened more often than not, it seemed.

"You have the advantage of me. I can't place your costume. Cupid perhaps? Odysseus?"

"Adonis, of course." His chuckle tickled her ear; he was standing much closer than was proper, and she did not move away. Under the cover of shadow, his arm slid around her from behind, tugging her gently back against him. Her heel stepped between his feet, and her light, silky gown gusted around his legs. The metal fastening on his toga was cold against her bare shoulder.

Victoria couldn't hold back a smile at Sebastian's

boastfulness. Of course the man would dress as a perfect specimen of the male species—he certainly considered himself such. And from what she'd seen, he had the right to do so. She couldn't help a little flutter in the pit of her belly, and focused her attention strictly on George. He had bowed to Gwen and was leading her to the center of the ballroom for what looked to be the first dance of the evening—a short, traditional line dance. The orchestra slid into the opening notes, led by two violins.

"Why does that not surprise me. But what are you doing here?" she asked.

"Same as you, my dear. Enjoying wearing a mask, and anonymously keeping a watch over our acquaintances Romeo and Juliet. I missed you last evening," he murmured into her ear.

"Did you?" she asked, remembering that, according to Max, he'd been in Vauxhall Gardens on a false trail. "I returned early after the dinner party at the Hungreaths'."

"No hunting of vampires?" he asked casually.

"No, indeed." She hadn't yet had a chance to tell him about the events at the dinner party, and at this moment she felt rather like keeping them to herself. As if she would have an assignation with another man in the gardens when she and Sebastian were . . . well, what? She hadn't allowed Sebastian into her bed for months, and his frustration was becoming evident.

And truth to tell, she'd begun to wonder exactly why she'd been holding him off. Even now, his strong body eased up behind her and his firm arm around her waist reminded her of their intimacies . . . and of how she missed the touch and affection of a man who understood her. And now that he had joined the Venators, she thought she knew where his loyalties lay.

There in the shadowy corner behind the clump of fake

seaweed, he brushed his lips and then the tip of his tongue along the delicate skin behind her ear. She shuddered lightly, and felt warmth flush through her. Perhaps tonight . . .

Sebastian smoothed his hand over the silk of her gown, murmuring, "Might I say, your gown is quite—"

"Drafty."

Victoria started and turned to find dark eyes looking down at her from behind her right shoulder. Max was dressed as a highwayman; there was no mistaking his garb, from the black cape and high black boots to the white shirt and red leather jerkin. A wide-brimmed black hat covered his thick hair, and a mask completely obscured the top half of his face, stopping just above his upper lip. He hadn't shaved, and his chin and jaw were dark with stubble. Despite his height, she might not have recognized him immediately if he hadn't spoken.

"That wasn't quite the word I had in mind," Sebastian replied, his arm tightening ever so slightly against Victoria's belly as he shifted to the right, behind her. "Convenient. That's more what I was thinking."

"Regardless, I'm disappointed."

Victoria adjusted her mask and looked at Max. "What do you mean?"

"Diana? I expected something less . . . obvious. Scheherazade, perhaps? Or even Zenobia."

Victoria drew herself up, moving slightly away from Sebastian and aware that her neck was moist from his ministrations. "It was Verbena's doing, not mine."

"Blame it on the maid, shall we."

"And who chose your flowing black cape? Surely you wouldn't have made such an unfortunate choice. Besides, I rather like my costume," she added.

"As do I," said Sebastian. His voice was as easy and

smooth as the thin fabric, and to her shock and surprise, she felt his hands smooth along the sides of her hips and . . . down. . . .

"Sebastian," she breathed, and stepped away, her silk-stockinged leg lunging out from the slit. She turned to face the two men, who were standing at angles to each other.

"Perhaps you could save it for later," Max said agreeably. "There's not a carriage in sight."

Victoria glared at him from behind her mask. He'd never missed an opportunity to comment on the fact that Sebastian had seduced her in a carriage—although how he had ever found out that bit of information, she'd never been able to learn. "It's more than a bit risky for you to be here. Do you think that even though you wear a mask and hat, Sara wouldn't recognize you?"

"Ah, that. No disguise can obscure true love." He was laughing now, sardonically but also with real humor. It was a rare sight, and one that made her distinctly uncomfortable. "Your theory is wrong, Victoria, for I passed directly next to Sara, and she flickered not an eyelash." He turned to Sebastian. "And how did you find Vauxhall? Such a convenient place for an assignation."

Sebastian looked at him, and then his mouth tightened. "I was not the one engaged in an assignation."

"Ah." Max inclined his head in full mockery. "A case of mistaken identity, perhaps. I was fairly certain—but never mind. Victoria and I had a pleasant chat in your absence."

"I do hope I'm not intruding."

Victoria was both grateful for the interruption and startled as she realized that James Lacy, the Marquess of Rockley, had somehow approached, unnoticed. Unerringly, he'd found her—despite the fancy mask and her solitary arrival. Unfortunately, she knew just who to blame for that happenstance. She considered—and immediately rejected—the option of prevaricating, but knew it was useless. Her mother would find another way to manipulate them together. Thank God Lady Melly hadn't planned to attend tonight, although she'd obviously found a way to communicate with James about Victoria's costume.

The fact that the three men with whom she was acquainted had found her, recognizing her so quickly and easily when she'd taken such pains to remain anonymous, gave Max's criticism new credibility. She hoped that George hadn't seen through her disguise as easily.

"Good evening, my lord," Victoria said when she realized her two other companions had not responded, and made a brief curtsy. James was dressed as a medieval knight, complete with woolen hose—which had to be stifling in the warm summer evening—and a loose tunic, belted and boasting a wooden sword.

"Perhaps you would grant me this waltz," James said, giving a disjointed bow. She noticed that he'd positioned himself so that he was between Sebastian and herself.

"I certainly would—"

"But she's already promised it to me."

Victoria could not have been more surprised if Lilith had walked into the room and asked to be staked. She might have expected Sebastian to make such a statement—and if the strangled look on his face was any indication, he had intended to—but not Max.

Max? Dance?

Max? Engage in social frivolities? It was just as well that Victoria couldn't speak right away, for that gave James the opportunity to respond. "But is there another spot on your dance card, Mrs.—er, Lady Rockley?" And before she could respond, he plucked it out of her hand, complete with the tiny pencil and its silvery blue ribbon. "But there is nothing written on here," he began.

Max smoothly relieved him of his possession and glanced at it. "Indeed there isn't." Victoria couldn't see his brows raise in that way he had, but she knew they did, beneath his mask. "My mistake." He returned the dance card to James, adding, "Be my guest, my lord. We shall return."

Max directed Victoria none too gently to the dance floor. "Do close your gaping mouth," he said. "People will begin to think I've dragged you out here."

"But you have. I never thought you would be one to engage in—"

"Social frivolities?"

Had she said those words aloud?

Max positioned her firmly, his hand at her waist, his legs nearly brushing hers. Their hands clasped, glove to glove, and were angled properly, bent and apart from their bodies. Very correctly, in fact. And the first steps into the waltz, which brought them fairly into the center of the room, he executed so smoothly and perfectly between the other dancers that she could not help but look up at him in surprise. Again.

"You needn't look so bloody shocked," he said as they whirled past another couple. "I may dislike dancing, but I'm quite good at it."

Indeed. And as he eased them in and around the other couples as if they were cogs within a well-oiled watchworks, without hesitation, without lurching or shifting, or even coming within inches of anyone else, she realized she'd been foolish to expect anything other than grace and timing from a man who fought like Max. After all, a man who could glide through the air could surely navigate the dance floor.

In fact, gliding through the air was something she had been unable to fathom ever doing, after having spent only one day practicing her *qinggong* under Kritanu's direction. She wondered if Max knew about that. She realized she was gripping his shoulder more tightly than she needed to, and eased her touch.

"If you dislike dancing, why are we out here?" she asked impertinently.

"How else can we talk without being overheard?"

She looked up, realizing again how tall he was. She wasn't a short woman, and she barely reached to Max's broad shoulder. But he was looking down at her, and she could discern the expression in his eyes. He didn't look as though this social frivolity was much of a hardship at all. Victoria felt suddenly breathless and flushed, so she spoke. "Did you have something you wished to tell me?"

"I had rather hoped the opposite. What have you done about that Bow Street Runner?"

She didn't bother to ask how or what he knew of Mr. Goodwin's second visit and ensuing interrogation. "I've set Barth and Oliver on the task to spy on the man and find out what they can. Charley followed him today when he left, and returned with his direction. Now Oliver and Barth are taking turns watching him."

Barth was Verbena's cousin, and the hackney driver who habitually took Victoria to the unsavory parts of town when she was hunting vampires. After all, she could hardly take the Rockley carriage—or any other carriage that might be identified as hers. And Oliver, who was Barth's friend and the bane of Verbena's existence, had traveled to Italy with Victoria and her maid. He was a large man who more often than not was cowed by Verbena's sharply wagging finger and tart tongue—though she barely reached to his elbow.

"But he is a legitimate Bow Street Runner? Not that it matters; they're so bloody corrupt anyway."

She nodded as he directed them through an unexpected, complicated maneuver between two other couples—one of which was completely out of step with the music—and felt the surprise of cooler air over her leg when her skirt swirled wide and open. "When Charley followed him, he returned to the magistrate's office. Someone will need to make inquiries about him, however, to see what else we can learn."

Max nodded, used gentle pressure at the center of her back to ease them into a spin, and Victoria nearly gasped aloud as she came face-to-face with Sara Regalado. Max's hands tightened on her, and they twirled again, away from Romeo and Juliet, who were waltzing in a much more structured manner.

"I wonder," he said after a moment, breaking into her enjoyment of the elegant flow of their steps and the confident touch of his hands guiding her movements, "if it has occurred to you that the new marquess might be our daytime vampire."

"James?"

"James, is it? Such familiarity with a man to whom you have no attachment." He managed, somehow, to lift his chin while looking down at her, annoying and arrogant even behind the mask.

"Of course it's occurred to me," she replied. It was at least partly true. "And it's also occurred to me that it could be you as well."

Ah! She'd succeeded in surprising him—she saw it in the sudden glint in his eyes and felt it when one of his steps wasn't quite as perfectly smooth as the previous.

"After all, for all I know, you've been captured by Lilith, turned undead, and have come to London for some nefarious purpose—drinking the special elixir, of course, so that you can move about in daylight and so that I cannot sense your vampirism."

"Very good, Victoria." He nodded gravely, but there was reluctant humor in his eyes. And she swore she saw his lips twitch. "But I suggest you might keep a closer eye on the man. He recognized you rather quickly and easily tonight, without knowing that you are, indeed, a huntress. Unless, of course, he does know who you are."

"I rather think it was the hand of my mother that assisted him in his recognition of me." She lifted her chin, but looked over his shoulder. James Lacy was standing near the edge of the dance floor, where they'd left him. "He knows no one else here, and acts otherwise indifferent to me."

"Are you trolling for compliments? There's not a man in this room who's indifferent to you, Victoria. Particularly in that gown."

She looked up at him, startled by his tone. "Then you must include yourself in that group."

He gave a little laugh, rare humor lighting his eyes again. "If you consider the fact that I've wanted to wrap my hands around your elegant little neck since that moment two years ago when you mistook me for a vampire then, yes, I am most definitely not indifferent to you."

"But you've kissed me."

"That I have." His eyes were very dark.

"And you rather enjoyed it."

"Did I?" he sounded amused. "I seem to have forgotten the details."

Victoria felt a rise of annoyance, and she tightened her

grip on his shoulder. But she made her smile sweet and knowing. "Are you trolling for a reminder?"

She imagined that, behind the mask, his eyebrows rose in that sardonic manner. "What would be the point? Sebastian, Zavier, Beauregard, James Lacy . . . I have no desire to be one of many, Victoria." And now all humor vanished from his expression. "No man does. So, if you would like my advice—"

"No, I don't—"

"—then I suggest," he continued smoothly, "if you wish to keep Vioget, that you keep your kisses, and suggestions of them, confined to him. And most definitely away from the Marquess of Rockley."

Eleven

Dinner Is Announced

After their waltz, Max deposited Victoria at the edge of the dance floor where Vioget and Rockley waited. It was a bloody relief to let her go and step away. He bowed curtly and took himself off to investigate whatever the hell he could find to investigate.

She'd be too damned busy to do so herself for awhile, if the expectant expressions on the faces of her two panting suitors were any indication. It looked as though Vioget might have a bit of a fight on his hands, although Max had no concerns that Victoria would make the same mistake with this Rockley as she had with the previous one.

Max's scalp was hot under his hat, and his mask felt stifling. His fingers still remembered the warm, delicate feel of her spine through that scandalously thin gown—if one could call it a gown. Hadn't she been wearing a damned corset?

Some years ago, he'd been witness to Parisian women dampening their thin muslin gowns so that they clung to the very outline of their entire body—a Madame

Gorhomme and her luxurious form sprang immediately to mind, prompting his tight mouth into a smile. But a glance at the dance floor stopped it. Christ, the fabric of Victoria's long toga was just as thin and revealing as Madame Gorhomme's—without benefit of water.

Hard to believe, he thought as he sidled his way through the warm crush of guests, that the lithe, light body he'd just handled was the possessor of such power and skill. A man could hardly fathom it . . . yet he'd experienced it firsthand: the strength and grace of her slender arms, the whirl of a powerful leg slamming into a vampire twice her size, the fire in her eyes and the flush of battle reddening her cheeks . . . all of which simply made her more fascinating to men like Vioget and Zavier. And even ones who had no idea who she was, and what she was capable of—like her husband and the new American marquess.

Even creatures like Beauregard, whom she was bound to slay.

All thanks to the two *vis bullae*, hidden somewhere under that gown. And one of them was his.

While he wore only one, even though it was useless to him.

Max had an urge for whiskey to cleanse the bitterness in his mouth. He gestured for a sequined footman to pour him one, and turned back to watch the dancers.

God damn Lilith for taking away his only passion, the single purpose in the life he'd salvaged after Papa and Giulia were gone. When he was done here in London, he was going after the vampire queen. He'd send her to Hell and, God willing, would die himself in the process. And at last he'd find out if he'd paid enough penance for destroying his family.

He took a healthy swallow of whiskey.

"Good evening, Maximilian."

Damn.

"Sara." Bloody hell. He'd been so damned distracted he nearly walked into the chit.

"I knew that had to be you," she said, her full lips curving under her rose-colored mask. She spoke smoothly, in their native Italian. "I haven't forgotten how beautifully you waltz. Shall we, for old time's sake?"

"No."

Sara's lips formed a generous pout. "Whoever she was, not only did she get you to dance, but you were completely captivated. I shall have to be jealous, Maximilian. Or . . . perhaps it is Lilith who will be jealous." The pout had disappeared, along with the manufactured teasing in her voice.

Max's body drained of heat. Sara and Lilith? Good God. "So you have allied yourself with Lilith the Dark. A dangerous proposition. She's not known for constancy to her minions."

"Are you concerned for my well-being, then, Maximilian?" She leaned into him, confident and bold. Her fingers wrapped around his arm and her leg brushed against his.

"Not in the least." He grasped her wrist and set her away. "Have you turned undead?"

She smiled, looking up at him from under her lashes. "Would you like me to drink from you, Max?"

The whiskey in his belly churned. Lilith's bites on his neck had finally disappeared, but the memories assailed him: red, hot, pain, pleasure.

His mouth dried; his head suddenly felt light. He was weaker now; he had little power and only mortal strength. To be trapped by her fangs and her thrall would be so much worse. He felt for the silver ring that bulked out his gloved finger, and the feel of it steadied him. He'd die before he would submit to her.

"I see that the idea excites you," Sara murmured, and he felt her close to him again. "Perhaps I can arrange—"

"You are a foolish young girl," he said sharply. "If you continue on this path, you'll end up like your father—a pile of ashes at the other end of a stake."

And then he noticed Victoria. Something had caused her to stop in the middle of a waltz. She was looking over the crowd of people—

Max realized he smelled smoke. Something was burning.

Victoria was hurrying toward the patio doors, and he saw movement out there, beyond the openings: tiny red lights glowing. Many of them.

Good Lord. Vampire eyes.

He started to move, and someone screamed from behind him. "Fire!"

"It's in the hall!" someone else shouted, and suddenly there was a wave of panicked people, pushing and shoving onto the dance floor, toward the patio doors.

In an instant he realized what was happening, and he looked down at Sara, who'd grabbed his arm and leaned back into him. She had a pleased smile on her face as she looked up.

"I do believe it's dinnertime." And then she moved against him. Something hard and metal poked into his ribs. "But never fear. I've other plans for you."

Tearing off her mask, Victoria burst out into the summer night, stake in hand. Immediately, she saw at least a dozen pairs of vampire eyes swimming in the dark.

As she launched herself at the nearest one, she heard screaming behind her. The first vampire poofed into dust with little fanfare, obviously not having expected an attack. But when she turned, Victoria found herself facing three more undead.

Her loose gown whipped about her legs as she leaped onto a stone bench near the edge of the patio. The smell of smoke filtered through the air. She was aware of the flood of people coming out of the ballroom, running and shouting, but her attention was on the trio of vampires who clustered around her perch.

Kicking out with one foot, she caught a vampire in the chin as he lunged for her, and followed the momentum by jumping onto one of his companions. As they tumbled to the stone paving, she slammed the stake down, missed the creature's head, and found herself rolling onto her back, tangling in her filmy skirt and the loose length of her hair.

The vampire came with her, his red eyes angry and glowing. He grabbed her by the shoulders, pinning her arms down. His fangs gleamed as he lunged toward her. Victoria gave a great buck and twist and used his own upended weight to set him off balance, then flipped him over on the uneven stones. Her elbow planted against the ground, she made a quick slash. The stake slammed into his chest, blasting a poof of dust and ashes into her face. She took a moment to tear away the long overlayer of her skirt, leaving a shorter, less hampering amount of fabric. Her vision had tinged filmy pink and she was vaguely aware of the harder pounding of her heart, and a sharp, driving anger.

Before she could rise, something landed heavily on her back. The air exploded from her lungs and her face ground into grittiness. Cheek scraping against the rough patio, she levered her feet up behind her, kicking her second assailant in the small of the back as he lunged on top of her. The force of her heels sent the vampire sprawling toward her head, and she used the moment of imbalance to shove him to the side.

Quickly she slipped out from under him as he closed his hand over the loose length of her hair, yanking her back to the ground. Pain shot through her scalp as she twisted toward him, her hair wrapping around his arm as he reeled her closer. His eyes were rose pink, and when her gaze flashed over them, it snagged for a moment. She felt a warm tug, and everything began to slow. The agony in her scalp eased, and the stake felt loose in her fingers.

Victoria drew in a deep breath and jerked her chin in order to strain the thrall. She was able to force her eyes closed even as the vampire's free hand closed around her throat. She felt his fingers and their sharp nails tighten, clogging her breath. Hers steadied the stake in her hand as she fairly hung there, with him holding her by the throat. She went limp.

His fingers tightened and that was her cue: she slugged him with a foot, just enough to catch him off guard and force him to turn, and then automatically drove the stake into the target of his chest as it pivoted in front of her.

Victoria gulped in a breath as he froze, then billowed into a cloud of musty undead dust. Catching herself before her knees hit the ground, she had that split second to take stock. The burning smell was stronger, and black smoke billowed from the upper windows of the house. Seemingly unaware of the battle between mortal and vampire going on behind them, people stared in shock at the building, where, even from the outside, orange flames could be seen licking at the closed doors from the ballroom to the hall behind it. Still costumed and masked, they were shouting and calling out, and many of them were unaware of the red-eyed danger that lurked behind them. There had to be more than a dozen undead, watching, fighting, and attacking in the small clearing as the gardens became thick and dark.

As Victoria watched, a duo of vampires lunged forward and snatched two spectators away from the rear of the crowd, dragging them toward those dark garden shadows. One of them was still masked, and looked like a medieval Crusader dressed in a dark red tunic. The other was a woman in a cream-and-gold gown in the Grecian style.

She started toward them, only to be yanked backward by a fist at the rear of her gown. Stumbling, she twisted around to meet a red-eyed undead.

She rammed her elbow up under the chin of the vampire that held her gown, and heard the slam and crack as his jaws came together. He tripped back and she helped him with the point of her stake, then turned back as he exploded into dust.

Someone whirled sharply next to her, followed by a soft poof of vampire. Sebastian, with bare legs as beautiful and golden as Adonis himself, leaped onto the bench. He glanced at her with a sharp nod, and, as two undead rushed at them, Victoria spun one way and Sebastian leaped . . . and they both found their targets.

Victoria glanced around, realizing that the pinkness of her vision had eased a bit. People crowded the area, standing on the damp grass and ringing the patio, unaware that vampires lurked in the shadows, waiting to snatch them to feed. What was holding them back from rushing in en masse and grabbing their victims? Or corralling them and marching them off?

Perhaps it was the realization that she, Max, and Sebastian were there, slinging stakes about. Then Victoria stopped. She was wrong. There was no sign of Max's tall, dark figure.

The last time she'd seen him was just as James brought

her out to the dance floor. He'd been moving toward the tables of food and drink, far from the entrance to the patio.

Then she remembered with a pitch of her stomach that he no longer wore the *vis*.

Something shoved her from behind and she stumbled deeply. She used her forward motion to roll over in a somersault—a very unladylike technique that Kritanu had just taught her—then sprang to her feet, stake still in hand. The vampire had lunged after her, and when she steadied herself and turned, she went after him. Fool, she thought as he exploded.

As she turned back to the crowd of people, she remembered the two partygoers who'd been taken off by the vampires. With a glance at Sebastian, who seemed to have taken to vampire staking with surprising vigor, Victoria dashed off down the brick pathway where the two vampires had dragged their prey.

Down the dark path she barreled, unfamiliar with the garden. Smoke tinged the air, and large black ashes wafted and swirled like small bats. She tripped over a stone, falling half into a boxwood or some other prickly hedge. Catching her balance, she paused, listening. She'd left Sebastian to handle the group of vampires back there, choosing to go after the ones who were already feeding from their prey, and she wasn't sure that was the right thing to do.

But she couldn't leave them to be killed in the shadows of a rosebush.

And Max could take care of himself. Wherever he was.

A soft gurgling cry met her ears, and Victoria spun to plow through a thick bush too dark to identify. She rammed her knee into something sharp and metal, felt it gouge and drag over her thigh. She kept going, heedless of the noise as she shoved the thin, sharp branches out of the way. Then she saw the shift of movement ahead.

With a cry meant more to distract than anything else, she sprang the last few feet forward. The vampire released his victim, who crumpled to the ground in a puddle of white-and-gold fabric. Victoria launched herself at the vampire, and saw the dark drool of blood from the corner of her mouth.

The undead was a tall, corpulent female, her arms as bulky as those of a burly man. She smiled at Victoria, her fangs gleaming, and faced her, ready. "The female Venator," she grunted.

The smell of blood tickling at her consciousness, Victoria swallowed hard. And focused. She smiled back at the female, feeling the feral curl of her own lips—but she didn't have time to waste looking ferocious and confident. With a quick snap, she broke off a wrist-sized branch as long as her leg, and swung out powerfully.

The female grabbed at it as Victoria expected she would, and Victoria gave a hard yank, pulling the vampire off balance. As the heavy creature lurched forward, Victoria leaped out of the way and tripped the lumbering undead, then spun to slam the stake deep into the back of her evil heart.

Before the dust had settled, she stumbled over to the victim collapsed on the ground, and turned her over. Her mask was gone and she recognized the shy Miss Melissa Keitherton, who spoke of little but her beloved cat Damian. She was still warm and breathing, and despite the blood oozing from her neck, she wasn't terribly hurt. It was a small wound, a single bite, with a relatively meager amount of blood. She would live to spoil Damian with catnip another day.

Victoria ripped a piece of silk from her gown and tied it firmly, but not too tightly, around the neck wound, and she then flung Miss Keitherton over her shoulder.

When she reached the patio again, she came upon a scene that could only be described as Hell. The house was in orange and red flames, throwing eerie shadows threaded with a dancing golden glow over the figures standing at the horizon of light and darkness. Smoke poured through the eaves and chimney, through upper windows open to the summer air. The ballroom, which appeared to be the last room on the lower level broached by the fire, was filled with black smoke. Flames ringed the far wall, making their way relatively slowly through a room that was fairly empty of fuel.

Releasing her burden gently to the ground, Victoria turned back and saw that the last pair of vampires, unengaged in battle and seeing that their companions had been vanquished, had turned tail. They bounded into the darkness, slick and dark and fast, and Victoria couldn't resist. She preferred that there be none to tell the tale to Lilith, or any other creature who might be there.

But as she dashed into the shadows again, heedless of the now-tattered gown and the slipping silver brooch on her shoulder, she heard a loud noise behind her. Faltering in her chase, she turned just in time to see the house's roof fold in on itself. The sound of screams, dulled by the roar of fire and distance, reached her . . . and urged Victoria to return.

She let the vampires escape, realizing, suddenly, that she hadn't seen Gwendolyn. Had she made it out of the house? Were there others trapped inside? Max?

And what about George and Sara? There and at that moment, in the middle of the melee, Victoria realized how this whole tragedy had been executed—and why.

Panting, Victoria sped back to the clearing in time to hear the tolling of the fire bell as the wagon arrived. It was impossible to pump a large volume of water fast enough to keep the fire from destroying the house—it was too hot and too strong of a blaze. But at least the nearby buildings and fences could be dampened to keep it from spreading.

But now that the threat of the undead was gone and the house was evacuated, Victoria knew she needed to find George and Sara. It was obviously no accident that vampires had been waiting in the walled garden when a blaze forced a group of rich-blooded partygoers outside. As invited guests with access to the house, and members of the Tutela, George and Sara had obviously had a hand in this.

She scanned the crowd of people who'd quieted down and were now merely staring with soot-streaked faces—some even unaware they were still wearing their masks. Shadows of light and dark danced over their smoke-tinted costumes and faces. Many of them spoke quietly to each other, shock turning stoic facial expressions into long, drab ones. The household staff clustered off to one side, some of them still in their glittering livery; others, in plain dress, watching their home and livelihood eaten alive by flames.

Victoria didn't see a Romeo or Juliet anywhere, nor an unmasked George or Sara. Nor, come to think of it, did she see Gwen.

Or Max.

Her heart thumping hard, she hurried forward, realizing she was limping from the gash on her leg. She shoved through the crowd of people to get between them and the house—the only way she could see their faces and recognize anyone. Sebastian came up next to her. A slight sheen of sweat glistened on his face in the flames, and he put his arm around her, pulling her close.

"Are you hurt?" he asked, his face in her hair.

"I can't find Gwendolyn," she replied, pulling away. "Or Sara or George. Have you seen Max?"

He shook his head. "No, none of them."

Victoria looked around and left Sebastian. She walked along the inside of the ring of people, looking sharply at the clusters of faces turned to each other. Some were being embraced and others were crying. But there was no sign of Max. Or Gwen.

"Have you seen Gwendolyn Starcasset?" she asked, at last coming upon a matron she vaguely recognized as being an acquaintance. She recalled that she had an odd fascination with science and chemistry, and often spoke endlessly about things that Victoria didn't understand.

Mrs. Debora Guyette-Foster had tears running down her face, making glistening white lines in gray ash streaks. Her costume appeared to have been that of a gypsy, but her flowing scarves sagged, and her rainbow-colored frock was dark and torn. Glitter sparkled weakly in her straight, dark hair. "She's not here. She left before—before—" The woman's sobs obliterated her words, but Victoria had heard enough to feel easier about Gwen.

But Max.

He would tower above most everyone here. She stood on the empty patio, close enough that the heat of the fire from the house blazed against the back of her legs and her one bare shoulder. Looking for the tall dark head.

A deep unease flowered inside her as she searched in vain. He had to have gotten out of the house.

But it would be just like him to be a hero, trying to rescue someone.

Damned man.

Why couldn't he be a hero by staking vampires?

Then she remembered the vampire that had dragged off the Crusader. Maybe Max had seen him, and gone after him.

Ignoring the people around her, who seemed to be coming out of their daze and once more were talking in full sentences, she ran into the dark garden again. This time she drove to the left, away from where she'd rescued Miss Keitherton, and found herself abruptly against a tall hedge.

She smelled blood. Tasted it in the air.

Victoria could have followed the hedge around, but impatience and need won out and she plowed right through it, heedless of the nasty branches. When she stumbled through to the other side, she landed on her knees next to a sprawled dark figure. The blood-iron essence filled her mouth and nose and she found herself struggling to breathe normally.

Groping frantically at him, for it was a man, she shoved him onto his back and saw vaguely that the dark red tunic of the Crusader merely looked black in the low light, with the dirt and soot and blood.

Her hands were wet with it, the cooling lifeblood of the man who would never wear another costume, ride another horse, eat another meal. Victoria pushed the hair from her face and pulled to her feet. There was nothing she could do for him. And she knew faintly that she had to leave him and get away from here. Her vision clouded darker in the night as saliva pooled in her mouth. The blood's essence tugged at her.

Her heart pounded, ramrodding through her body so that her fingers trembled and it felt as though her whole chest was moving. Time churned sluggishly.

All at once, she realized she was not alone.

Victoria looked over. Three figures had come around the bushes and stood clustered together as though afraid to move any closer. She felt their shock and fear, and her heart pounded more strongly. She swallowed.

"He's dead," she managed to say. Gestured to the Crusading knight. "There's nothing to be done now." She thought her words came out normally. But no one replied. They watched her, and she noticed that one had a gun. It wasn't pointed at her . . . but he had a gun.

A shout drew her attention. Her name. It was as though her ears were stuffed with cotton. She turned to see Sebastian. Slowly. The blood was so thick, it clogged everything. Even her movements.

"Victoria." He came toward her, and she recognized the expression on his handsome face: worry, relief. He was soot-streaked and his hair was sticking out in thick waves. Before she could protest, or even think, he pulled her away from the small clearing, back toward the blazing house.

"Victoria," he said as soon as they were far enough away, almost to the patio. She could breathe now. The blood-smell was gone and her head was a little clearer. The fire had quieted a bit, though the golden light flickered through the trees. The muted sounds from the crowd reached her ears.

Clarity.

She sank into his arms, felt them wrap strong around her, buried her head in his sweaty neck. "So much blood," she whispered. "I couldn't think."

"I know," he said. He lifted her face. The kiss tasted like smoky Sebastian and sweat and it chased away the lingering essence of iron. He pulled away and looked down at her. "I thought you'd gone back in the house."

His eyes were tigerish, the blaze turning them gold even in the dark. His fingers curled tight on her arms.

"No."

But she thought of Max. If he wasn't outside, he had to be in the house.

"Victoria," said Sebastian. "I . . . let me take you home."

She knew what he meant. But she didn't answer.

Though she didn't need to be steadied, didn't need to be held up, she let him put an arm around her. Moments later they were back with the others, but, by now, the crowd had begun to thin out. Some had been able to find their carriages and had left in disheveled, smoky clothing.

Others still stood, talking, describing in loud, important voices, what had happened. How they'd escaped the fire, what they'd been doing prior to the alarm, how they'd helped pull out Mr. or Miss or Lady So-and-So.

She felt clearer now. Stronger.

Victoria turned toward the house, which had crumbled in on itself in some areas and still blazed angry orange and red. An elegant poplar that grew too close to the building had all its leaves burned off. The heat still blasted, but there was little to be done. The fire would burn itself out; keeping it from spreading was the only reasonable objective.

No one could get close enough to the structure to even pour water on it. There could be no survivors inside. How many people had perished?

Who?

Victoria turned, not yet ready to leave with Sebastian, still searching, and she noticed a tall, dark, blade-nosed figure. Her heart leaped, and she lurched toward him— but then he moved from the shadows.

Mr. Bemis Goodwin.

He saw her and she felt the ugly weight of his eyes on her, sweeping over her. She could only imagine what he saw—a torn gown, blood streaks everywhere, her hair in dishabille. His gaze narrowed and although he said nothing, did nothing to acknowledge her beyond an arrogant nod—she felt it.

The animosity.

Sebastian folded her into his arms; she'd told him nothing about Goodwin, so he couldn't know. But she felt a wave of foreboding sweep over her.

"Let me take you home, Victoria," Sebastian said. His chin brushed the side of her head and she raised her face to look over his shoulder.

"Not yet," she said, still scanning the darkness.

At that moment, a dark figure came into view, making a wide skirt from around the front of the house. Appearing not to see her off to the side, he moved quickly, yet unsteadily, disappearing into the crowd of people. There was no mistaking it.

"Max," Victoria breathed, her whole body going soft with relief. Then she felt jittery and warm. "Thank God." She stared after him, trying to determine if he was hurt or wounded. Where had he been?

"And so it goes," Sebastian muttered, so quietly she wasn't certain he'd really spoken. Then she realized she'd stepped away from him, toward the crowd of people. And Max.

"What?" Victoria looked back up at him.

His face was drawn and hard. His lips formed a humorless smile. "Ah, Victoria . . . don't be a fool. He doesn't want you. He doesn't want anyone."

Twelve

In Which Sebastian and Victoria Have an Uneventful Carriage Ride

The carriage rumbled down the night-dark street. The smell of smoke lingered inside, clinging to all three of its silent occupants.

Victoria sat next to Sebastian, across from a grim-faced, bedraggled Max.

But they were all weary, their throats and lungs skimmed with smoke, eyes dry and stinging, clothing torn and soot-streaked. Victoria's thigh continued to ooze blood, and the scratches on her face still stung.

She'd had to fairly shove Max into the carriage for the ride back to Aunt Eustacia's home, reminding him that they were going to the same place. Since he'd settled grumpily into his seat, arranging himself so that no one could sit next to him even if they'd wanted to, he'd remained silent.

Yet his eyes were not quiet. Still sharp, they scanned over her—yet never met her gaze—and Sebastian, then moved to stare out the window of the vehicle. His mask was long gone, as was the hat he'd worn, and the cape she'd teased him about. Stubble made his face darker and more shadowed. His eyes were sunken in their sockets, and his skin seemed to have tightened in the last hours. Those elegant hands hid in the shadows.

Sebastian shifted next to her, bringing a gentle waft of smoke and clove, and she felt his ungloved hand settle on her knee. Lightly, half pinned between their thighs . . . but it had eased there stealthily and smoothly. As if to keep from drawing attention.

Yet it was there. Warm.

He doesn't want you. He doesn't want anyone.

Victoria glanced at Max, who continued to watch out the window. Sebastian's words had opened whole recesses in her mind. Had he guessed that the great weight, the awful, heavy mood that had settled over her as he encouraged her to come home had been from worry and grief over Max?

As she was turning to leave with Sebastian, knowing that there'd been no hope for anyone left in the flaming building, knowing that if Max hadn't been in the house he would have been fighting with them, realizing that this time he had to be gone . . . had Sebastian realized how empty and weary she felt? How lost?

Would she have felt the same way if things had been reversed—if Max was leading her away from a missing Sebastian?

And so it goes.

"Sorry to intrude on your carriage ride, old chap." Max's curt voice cut the silence. He had shifted and was looking at them. Down at the hand on Victoria's knee. "But my lady insisted."

"Where were you?" Victoria asked.

He lifted his gaze to her languidly, as though contemplating whether to respond. "As it turned out, Miss Sara

Regalado required my escort. It took some time to extricate myself from the situation."

"You left with her?"

One side of his mouth twisted. "The lady was most insistent, and I do hate to disappoint. She had visions of reacquainting me with an old friend, believing that she'd be rewarded for doing so. However, I found the idea quite distasteful."

"So Lilith is here? In London?"

Max's eyes gleamed with appreciation. "Apparently that is the case, although I cannot confirm it."

"And in what condition did you leave Miss Regalado?" asked Sebastian.

Max transferred his gaze. "As I usually do—quite distraught." His smile was pale and humorless in the shadows. "But nevertheless mobile."

"What about George?"

"I didn't have the pleasure of his company; I assumed he was herding the evening fodder out to the vampires. Did you not see him?"

Victoria shook her head. "No, although I was otherwise . . . engaged. He could have been there for some time, and later took himself off once it was clear the battle wasn't to be won."

"And did you bestir yourself to stake some vampires, then, Vioget?"

Victoria felt Sebastian move. Ever so slightly, tension rippled along the arm and leg that pressed against her side. Then, as the hand on her knee lifted, the tension eased. "A few," he replied negligently. "We . . . Victoria and I . . . took care of most of them."

She felt a gentle tug on the loose part of her hair and thought it had caught between them . . . but then she realized he'd taken a lock of it and was rubbing it between a forefinger and thumb, twisting it softly around a digit. A most intimate gesture, and one that made her distinctly uncomfortable.

Before she could pull away or otherwise respond, the carriage gave the fortuitous lurch that announced their arrival.

Victoria stood quickly, causing Sebastian to release her hair. Max had the same idea and they fairly collided in the center of the small carriage, shoulder to chest.

"In a hurry, my dear?" he asked with a grim smile. "Don't let me get in your way."

He settled back into his seat as the carriage door opened. Barth was there to help Victoria climb down, which she did with little fanfare—and without waiting for Sebastian.

The dawn had come, and her mind was spinning.

As she walked up the house's walkway, she heard the low murmur of a male voice behind her, and the carriage door close again. A quick glance behind told her she was alone, and that Max and Sebastian had remained in the carriage.

Only hours later, with the sun blasting its heat through a rare, cloudless London sky, Victoria was awakened by a knock on her bedchamber door.

With bleary eyes, she looked next to her. The bed was empty, but rumpled. No, she hadn't dreamed it—the warm slide of Sebastian's body next to hers, the hands on her hair, the gentle kiss before he gathered her close to sleep. He'd murmured something unintelligible into the top of her head.

She'd drifted off thinking how unlike him that was . . . and wondering what had transpired between him and Max after she left the carriage.

Verbena entered at her bidding.

"My lady," she said, her lips pursed in a tight circle that barely moved when she spoke. "I'm sorry to wake ye, but that Ol'ver claims he needs to speak t'you right away." She shook her head, tsking in disgust. "I told him you'd only been abed for a few hours, but he 'nsists."

"Send him up to me," Victoria said. An uncomfortable feeling opened in her stomach. Any news from Oliver would likely pertain to Mr. Bemis Goodwin.

"Up here?" Verbena fairly screeched, her eyes springing wide open. "Why, m'lady, it's not proper. That man can wait while I dress ye, for sure, my lady. 'E has no call t'be—"

Victoria shook her head. "No, it cannot wait, I'm afraid. Call for him to be sent up, and if you're quick, perhaps you can help me into a day frock before he gets here.

Verbena muttered something about Langford, who happened to be the personal maid to Duchess Farnham and who most likely would require smelling salts should her mistress have ordered her to bring a man to her bedchamber. Even, Victoria suspected, the late duke. But Verbena disappeared from the room for a brief moment, and her mistress heard the reverberation of her voice and its direction to Oliver. Then she returned and threw herself into Victoria's wardrobe.

"I never heard o'such a thing," she muttered as she bustled about, pulling forth a clean chemise and a new corset for her mistress. Victoria had bathed the night before, to cleanse herself from the smoke, blood, and soot, so the small ewer of water on her night table would suffice for her to freshen up.

"'Avin' a man no better'n a footman into the lady's chamber! Why, the on'y time I ever knew o' such a happenin' was when Lady Meryton was tuppin' her groom on the sly o' her husband, y'know. An' it wasn't long afore such was all the talk o' the belowstairs!"

She pulled the cotton shift down over Victoria's head, jerking it into place as she emphasized her words. "An' the groom, well, 'e was no prize, if ye ask me. I seen'im once an' he had big eyebrows that looked like spiders. I'd not be wantin' that face too close t'me, ye know, wit' them squiggly things. An' on 'is ears, too! But"—she pulled on Victoria's corset to hook it in place beneath her breasts as there came a knock on the door. "Ye can jus' wait a minnit," she hollered.

"Come in, Oliver," Victoria said.

Verbena straightened in shock, barely missing clipping Victoria's chin. She fairly flew to the chair over which she'd hung the chosen frock. "Do not come in here, Oliver," she ordered as the door cracked. "Only one more—" Her words became muffled as Victoria's ears were filled with the swoosh of fabric and rustle of lace and other gewgaws. She wouldn't have chosen such a decorated dress, but it was too late now.

At last Oliver came in, the large red-haired man half skulking as if in fear of Verbena's wrath. And rightly so. Victoria wondered what would become of them if they ever admitted their attraction for each other and actually had a normal conversation. He hunched a bit, twisting his cap in his large hands, and gave three bows in a row. "My lady, I've come wi' some news."

"O' course ye have," Verbena railed, tugging roughly at the buttons lining the nape of her mistress's neck. "Else why would we let ye in 'ere? Now, spit it out, my lady's not got all the day to wait for ye to figger out what t'say."

"Come in, Oliver," Victoria said. "What have you to tell me about Mr. Goodwin?"

The process was excruciating, working around Verbena's

bossy interjections and Oliver's hesitant narrative, but Victoria at last reeled the information from his depths.

It wasn't the least bit comforting.

Last night's events had fixated Goodwin's suspicions more sharply on Victoria—as if they hadn't already been sharp enough. The fact that she'd been at the affair had been only part of it. Vague stories of her acting in an unladylike manner had blossomed. As Oliver told it, when Goodwin learned that she had been found crouched next to a ravaged man alone in a sequestered part of the garden with blood everywhere, including dripping from her mouth and an odd expression on a scratched face . . .

Blood dripping from her mouth?

It took her a moment to remember pushing the hair away from her face. Maybe blood had been on her hands and smeared near her lips.

And apparently the scratches on her face had been, not the result of blasting through a hedge of boxwood, but in self-defense from her victim as she'd bent to drink his blood.

Victoria had a healthy enough imagination to know that was exactly what Goodwin would be thinking.

"'E's goin' to come here an' take ye right to the magistrate. Today," Oliver concluded, still worrying his hat. "An' he'll listen t'Goodwin, and put ye in Newgate. M'lady, ye can't go in there. It's no place—"

"I have no intention of being put into Newgate," Victoria said. "And I've no fear of the place anyway." Yet a shiver skittered over her shoulders. Even for *Illa Gardella*, it would be unpleasant.

But the worst of it was that she wouldn't spend much time in Newgate at all, for murderers were tried quickly. She'd be on the scaffold with a noose around her neck within a week, if Goodwin had his way.

She turned to Verbena. "I'm indisposed for the day. I will see no one. *No one*, Verbena. Not Max, not Kritanu, nor Sebastian Vioget." She looked at Verbena sharply. "And don't drink *anything* with Sebastian—or Max, for that matter. And you're to tell no one of this conversation—either of you." She glared at both of them, fixing the strength of *Illa* Gardella in her gaze. "I cannot risk having any of you carted off to Newgate for trying to protect me."

"But what will you do, my lady?"

Victoria stood. "First, I will borrow your cloak. And . . . could you perhaps cut off a bit of your hair for me?"

The short puff of orange hair peeking from the low-hanging hood of Verbena's cloak easily disguised Victoria out of the back of the house, through the mews, and onto the street nearby. She met Barth in his hackney a few blocks away, feeling as though she was making the secret assignation that Sebastian had suspected of her.

The ride to Gwendolyn Starcasset's home gave Victoria a few moments to remove the disguising cloak, and to think about Bemis Goodwin. It wasn't possible that coincidence kept bringing him to the places where vampire attacks happened.

Near the Starcasset residence, Victoria alighted from the hack and walked a half block to the walkway. She preferred not to have to answer queries as to why she used a public hackney instead of one of her own carriages. Victoria actually wondered why she even kept her own carriages. She never used them.

"Victoria!" Gwendolyn shrieked and threw herself into her friend's arms. In any other case, a young woman such as Victoria would have staggered back under the force of her onslaught . . . but of course one as strong as *Illa* Gardella did not.

Gwen's eyes were red-rimmed and her nose tinged pink. Her face looked as though she hadn't slept all night. Her embrace included a damp handkerchief.

"Gwendolyn," Victoria replied with as much heartfelt emotion as the other woman. "I just had to see for myself that you were uninjured."

"I sent a message to your house this morning to ensure myself that you'd escaped the tragedy, but had no response! I've been simply distraught, Victoria. And George too," she said, with a covert look at her friend.

Ah, a convenient opening. Victoria smiled inside but kept a sober expression. "Then Mr. Starcasset is well? I was able to learn that you'd left early—which surprised me, Gwen, for I know how you adore such parties—but I did not see your brother anywhere during the horrible fire."

"Was it truly frightening?" Gwen asked. She looked sincerely upset—rather than greedy for the sordid details. "I've heard that at least eight people are unaccounted for, Victoria, and I so feared that you were one of them. And poor Mr. Ferguson-Brightley was burned so badly, it's certain he won't live." Her eyes welled with tears. "I cannot fathom how I was so lucky as to have been called home early, even if it was a misunderstanding."

"You were called home?" The pieces clicked into place. Had George made certain his sister was spared?

"It was quite Providential that George recognized me, for he had no idea that I was meant to attend last night. I thought . . ." Gwen actually blushed, looking away from Victoria for a moment. "I told no one that I was to attend, for I thought that it would be amusing . . . well, I am to be married in a few weeks, and though I do love Brodebaugh . . . but, Victoria, he is just not quite so handsome and dashing as your Phillip was . . . and, oh, I'm making a cake of this, am I not! You must think so poorly of me, but truly, it was a harmless thought I had . . . to spend one last night as a debutante. I was masked, so no one would recognize me, and I only wished to dance." Her voice trailed off as Victoria nodded encouragingly.

"It doesn't matter now," she told Gwen soothingly. "How did it come about that you left the party early, though?"

"Well, George espied me and he told me that Brodebaugh had come to the house looking for me . . . and of course, I left immediately." She twisted her hands together, looking altogether miserable. "I do love him, Victoria. And I never meant to do anything to harm him. It really was for innocent fun."

Innocent fun that nearly got her killed . . . or fed on by a vampire. At least George had had the conscience to send her home before executing his Tutela plan.

But that answered one question. A vampire would just as soon walk away from their dying lover or mother as feed on them, should the urge arise. It would be hard to believe that George was the daytime vampire . . . for the one thing the undead didn't have was a conscience.

Thirteen

Wherein Our Heroine Makes a Telling Decision

Victoria left Gwendolyn's house relieved that her friend was unhurt, but deep in thought.

She'd realized that there could be more than one daytime vampire, as she'd begun to think of the creature. After all, if an undead merely had to drink the special elixir, what was to stop more than one of them from doing it?

Or many of them?

She sat in the hackney, her shoulder slamming against the side every time Barth made a right turn, and her head bobbing every time he urged the horse forward. His vulgar language peppered the air as he navigated them down Fleet Street—a mistake in itself, for the road was clogged with other carriages and conveyances, as well as shoppers, shopkeepers, and street urchins.

But it gave Victoria a bit of time to consider the situation.

From what she knew about the elixir, it could only be made from the stamen of a special plant that bloomed rarely—perhaps once per century, or no more than twice. Since little could be made, more vampires must want it than could have it. That didn't preclude more than one undead from using it, but the supply couldn't last forever. And there couldn't be an entire army of undead drinking it, which gave her some measure of comfort.

Still, both Sara and George could be daytime vampires.

Of course, as Max had suggested, James could be the daytime undead. She hadn't missed the fact that the incidents had begun to occur the day he arrived at St. Heath's Row.

Sara and George, as well as James, had been at the Hungreath dinner party, and also at the masquerade ball. And while she'd seen none of them in Regent's Park when Victoria found the first victim, that didn't mean they hadn't been around. She had, after all, spoken with Gwen and Brodebaugh, who could have told them Victoria was in the vicinity.

Or, it could simply be that the daytime vampire was someone she didn't know or hadn't noticed. After all, it didn't have to be someone she'd seen. It could be any minion of Lilith.

And, yes indeed, it could also be Mr. Bemis Goodwin.

Oh, how she wanted it to be him.

Even now, thinking about how his sharp, angry eyes examined her, searching for something that wasn't there, she felt tension rise. Her fingers itched for a stake, ready to plunge it into his chest. He had made it clear he wanted nothing more than to see her hang.

But why?

Victoria turned the ugly thought over in her mind. It wasn't easy; the fury tinged her vision, and her mind rebelled at the very thought . . . but she had to consider it.

Why would a man she didn't know want to harm her?

Several deep breaths later—ones she'd had to focus on, draw in deeply, hold, and then release—Victoria had pared her scattered, berserker thoughts down.

He either truly thought she was a murderess and wanted to see justice done—in which case, she was innocent and should have nothing to worry about. But that wouldn't explain his pointed comments about the undead.

A woman like you.

No, he knew something about her. He could be a vampire himself and be drinking the elixir. Obviously a vampire would want her, *Illa* Gardella, to die. But that didn't follow—for he'd said he'd been watching her for over a year. Since she nearly killed the man in the Dials. The elixir hadn't been in existence for that long, and he appeared to have been living a normal life as a Bow Street Runner for longer than that.

She concluded he couldn't be undead himself.

He could believe she was a vampire herself, and want to destroy her. If Barth and Verbena had known about vampires before Victoria did, before she became a Venator . . . it was possible that he did too. But . . . if he knew anything about vampires, he would know that hanging her would do no good. So why focus on getting her to the magistrate?

If that were the case, if he believed she was a vampire, that should be easy to address—after all, then they were fighting on the same side.

Or . . . this was the most interesting, and worrisome thought: perhaps he wanted revenge. Perhaps he knew someone she'd killed—a vampire she'd staked, who'd once been someone he loved. A wife or a brother, or anyone.

So that would mean he knew that she was a Venator,

and knew that the undead had tried many times to destroy her without luck. And he would try another way.

After all, bullets, blades, nooses—they would all work equally well to slay a Venator.

Victoria felt an unpleasant shiver ripple over her shoulders. Whatever the reason, Bemis Goodwin loathed her, and he was essentially an unknown opponent.

These thoughts settled in her mind, leaving Victoria uncomfortable, but not panicked. After all, she knew she was a formidable adversary herself.

But when the hackney dropped her off a block from Aunt Eustacia's house, and Victoria slipped into the mews that led into the small yard behind the house, she found herself confronted by Bemis Goodwin and four burly men. On seeing them, her first thought was that he clearly knew her strength.

She'd already stepped out of sight of Barth, who'd rattled off in the carriage as soon as her slippers touched the ground. And the thick hedge of the mews, which ran along behind the row of houses, obscured the view from any of the residences—should anyone happen to be watching, which was in itself unlikely.

Any further considerations evaporated as she braced herself, ready for battle. "What do you want?" she asked, aware that her heart was racing.

"Come now, Lady Rockley," Goodwin said with a supercilious gesture. "It should be no surprise to you that the magistrate awaits your presence. I'm merely here to see that he gets it."

"For what reason?" She inched to the side, eyeing the thug closest to her as a feeling of urgency began to build, and her heart to pound. He couldn't be as strong as a vampire. Or a Venator. None of them could be. Confidence surged through her. She was also smaller and could slip through the hedge more easily. . . .

"It will do you no good to run, Lady Rockley. You may be quick and strong, but you cannot outrun this." He pulled a gun from his pocket.

No, she couldn't. But the bullet would have to find her first.

Red glazing her vision, she ducked and rushed at the first of the burly men, knocking him into Goodwin. The sharp retort of a pistol shot sounded, and something whistled through the air much too close to her.

Victoria spun and began a mad dash through the hedge—if she made it through, she'd be in sight of the rear windows of the house and there was a chance someone would see her.

Something yanked hard at her cloak, and she flew backward, landing with the jolt of her skull on the ground. Head spinning, heart pounding, veins pumping, she rolled and leaped to her feet. Rage blasted through her, and she kicked out, tearing into the man closest to her. She felt her nails pare the skin from his face and her foot connect with something soft.

Her red-hued world became a cyclone of movement and ferocity in that narrow, dark walkway until suddenly something wafted down over her. It was clingy and heavy and she realized a net had been thrown over her. It wrapped around her legs, restricted her arms, and before she could fight her way out of it, the net tightened and Victoria felt herself falling.

She crashed to the ground, her head slamming onto a rock. Someone shoved her into a spin. She rolled, tangling further in the net, shouting now—hoping that someone—Max, Verbena, Kritanu, *someone* would hear.

Something dark went over her head, muffling her

voice and smothering her gasps for air, and, like a bundle, she was lifted. The heavy cloth tightened over her face, cloistering her nose and mouth, making her struggle for every bit of air. She struggled, bucking and kicking . . . the red of her vision faded, consciousness ebbed, and she knew no more.

When Victoria became aware again, she found herself sitting in a hard wooden chair. Her hands were bound behind her and she slumped forward. The only things preventing her from tumbling off the chair were her arms bent over the top of it. They ached, and her fingers were cold and numb. Her feet were in a similar condition, tied to the rung of the chair.

She wasn't alone. She kept her eyes closed and listened. It took her only a moment to realize that she'd awakened in the middle of Goodwin's meeting with the magistrate. Her hearing, such as it were.

Her mind was fuzzy, and she knew little about the workings of the Bow Street Runners and their responsibility to the magistrate. But she did know that there were few honest magistrates. And fewer honest Runners. Which did not ease her anxiety in the least.

"I find your evidence against Lady Rockley compelling, Mr. Goodwin," intoned a voice, presumably that of the magistrate.

"The woman is exceedingly strong," now spoke Goodwin himself. "She will have to be transported in chains, and in secrecy. She has some fairly able friends."

Victoria's mouth went dry. Chains? Good God. But surely they would have to bring her to public trial. And by that time, Max, and Sebastian, and Lady Melly—

But did any of them know where she was?

Barth and Oliver would know. They'd still be watching Goodwin. Or they would be able to figure it out.

She lifted her head. Its throbbing was so harsh it had to be audible. "Who brings the charges against me?" she said. Her voice . . . it was not one she recognized. It was . . . dark, heavy, rough. A shiver rattled down her arms and she pulled on her bonds as rage shuddered through her. "Someone must charge me."

She knew at least that much about crime and punishment in London. A victim or family member must press charges for a trial to occur. There were no representatives, or prosecutors, for the general public.

"Ah, she is with us again." Goodwin's face came into her view, blurred and clouded with the red haze. His breath smelled of stale ale.

"Who charges me?"

"It is I who bring the charges," Goodwin replied.

"You?" Victoria blinked rapidly, trying to alleviate the distortion. Her thoughts were scrambled. "Why?"

His face came in front of hers, his long sharp nose shining, eyes dark with loathing. "My brother. You killed my brother."

"Your brother? Who is your brother?" Victoria demanded. "I've killed *no one*."

A loud crack sounded, a hammer slamming onto a wooden surface. "Take the prisoner to Newgate. I'll arrange for the trial to be held tomorrow." The magistrate's voice was filled with malice. "The assizes judge is in my debt and will be happy to hurry things along in this case."

Tomorrow?

Victoria raised her head to protest, but something hard slapped against her cheek. Her head whipped up and back so hard the chair tottered.

"I have no sympathy for murderesses, especially those who mutilate their victims first." Goodwin's ale breath was hot on her face as he bent in front of her. His eyes glowed with triumph. "Cutting them up and tearing them to pieces. What did you do with your husband, Lady Rockley?"

Her cheek throbbed, and the room wavered, but she fixed her gaze on him. "I've done nothing wrong."

Goodwin rose upright, crowing. "The proclamation of innocence—but of course. You've used your powers and strength to do whatever you choose . . . and you'll pay recompense and hang by your lovely neck, dear lady."

She would have responded again, but the black hood came down over her face, obstructing her vision. As she breathed, the cloth became more smothering, as if her need for air drew it closer and closer about her face, plastering it to her nose and eyes. Victoria struggled to dislodge the hood, but something tightened about her neck, holding it in place.

She heard the clink of chains. Her arms were loosened from the back of the chair, and she fell forward, dizzy and still bound by her ankles. Crashing onto the ground, she realized the ties at her wrists were no longer as tight. Someone moved next to her; she felt the bump of a leg or knee against the side of her hip, and heard more clinking.

Dragging in a hot, muffled breath, Victoria lurched onto her face and shoulders and, using her legs, raised the sturdy chair, snapped her heels toward the back of her head. The powerful swing whipped the seat onto the man kneeling next to her, and she heard—and felt—it smash into pieces. Chunks of wood splintered, raining down on them. Goodwin groaned as he slumped to the ground, heavy against her.

Still fighting for air, Victoria pulled at the ropes

around her wrists and frantically began to jimmy her hands free. Someone shouted, and she heard quick, hard movements in the room. One wrist popped free and she tore at the hood and its tie.

Something smashed into her shoulder blades, and she fell face-first down against something warm and soft—Goodwin, she realized. The other movement must be coming from the magistrate. A heavy weight lunged onto her, and he was shouting for assistance in her ear. One of her arms was captured, yanked up behind her back—but the other one was safely under her, tearing at the tie at her throat until at last it came loose.

With a guttural cry, she yanked the hood off and gulped in fresh, clean air.

And then she was ready to fight.

Able to breathe, and see, she was galvanized by fury. She moved like furious lightning, rolling to the side, striking fast and hard. The magistrate tumbled back under her assault, and Victoria bent to tear the ropes from her ankles. Thus released, the last vestiges of the chair clattered to the floor as she heard the sounds of thundering footsteps.

Scrambling to her feet, she saw Goodwin dragging himself up under the wreckage of the chair, and the man who had to be the magistrate trying to pull to his feet. Next time she would hit them harder.

Victoria dashed toward the dark window, smashing the glass with the chains with which they'd meant to bind her. The ground wasn't far below, and as she leaped through, a jagged edge of glass sliced the underside of her thigh and she heard the door slam open in her wake.

Landing on the ground in a neat crouch, she sprang to her feet. The fresh night air was like ambrosia, despite the stench of garbage and other waste. The building from which she'd escaped was on a narrow street, and if she'd jumped at the wrong angle she could have slammed into one the nearby walls.

Looking at the night sky, Victoria realized how late it was. She must have been unconscious for hours, and it had taken that long for Goodwin to arrange for the meeting with his crooked magistrate.

She hesitated, warring between the driving desire to go back and destroy Goodwin and his magistrate, and the need to get away. If she left, they would come after her again. She knew it.

A door opened, spilling light into the darkness, and she saw the tall figure of Goodwin outlined. He held a pistol. Two of his henchmen loomed behind him, and they burst out into the night.

Hesitation gone, she turned and dashed away. She couldn't fight against a bullet. Shouts told her they were following, and she ran pell-mell down the dark street, turning onto another, and then another. She realized belatedly that this was not a pleasant area of town, or one that would boast a magistrate's office. Her suspicion that the magistrate was just as corrupt as Goodwin, and that they had had to meet in secret, solidified.

Pushing past prostitutes and drunkards, dodging carts and dogs, Victoria slowed her pace when she turned onto a dark street that was curiously empty.

The thick crescent moon shone high and seemed to beam down the center of the narrow street. Her vision still blurred faint red, and rage bubbled through her.

And then Victoria realized that the back of her neck was abnormally cold.

Which could explain why the street was empty.

Pounding footsteps slapped to a halt behind her, and she turned to see Goodwin, and one of his men, half a block away. He raised his arm, and she saw the gleam of metal in the moonlight, pointing at her.

"Stop there, madame."

The chill on the nape of her neck was colder, and she sensed the arrival of an undead. Or two.

"Who was your brother?" she called back to Goodwin, taking a step away from him. The farther she was from that bullet . . . The prickles at the back of her neck were growing worse. Where was it? Or they?

"Frederick Goodwin, Baron Truscott."

Her gazed darted around as she looked for something to use as a stake, but she saw nothing of use. Then she felt, rather than saw, something shift—just out of her vision.

"You don't remember him? But of course . . . why should you? He was only one of many that you've destroyed." He took another step toward her, and she backed up slightly. They were separated by perhaps five carriage lengths, but she stood in the center of the street, well lit and unprotected. A bullet in the heart or head would kill her, just as it would any other mortal.

"I remember him." She did indeed remember Lord Truscott—a Society man she'd danced with more than a year ago, and then only days later had been forced to stake. In that time he'd turned to a vampire and coaxed Miss Emily Colton from a party and into the dark gardens.

Victoria had been receiving Phillip's proposal when she realized what was happening, and had needed to duck away.

She was not likely to forget Lord Truscott.

"You killed him. After all I'd done to protect him."

The chill sharpened, and Victoria spun just as a shadow turned into the figure of a man in front of her. As she ducked the undead's attack, ramming into his gut, a gun fired. For the second time that day, a bullet whizzed much too close to her head.

She flipped the vampire over her shoulder and whirled around, still looking for something to use as a stake. The undead crashed to the ground, and she looked up to see Goodwin facing a cluster of vampires. Three of them. That made four total.

Red eyes glowing, the undead in front of her scrambled to his feet and launched himself at Victoria. As she kicked out, catching the vampire in the chin, she saw Goodwin pitch his firearm wildly at the one closest to him.

When the creature near her attacked again, she pummeled him back, allowing all of her red rage to burst free with kicks, punches, elbows, and head butts. The last time she smashed him to the ground, he had enough and scrambled to his feet, running away.

Victoria turned and saw Goodwin pinned to a brick wall by the hand of a vampire. His legs thrashed wildly and anything he might have screamed was reduced to faint gurgles. Two others were closing in on his large companion, who brandished a heavy club.

It wouldn't be long before he was relieved of the club.

The rest of the street was quiet and empty.

Victoria looked at them through red vision, heart pounding, hatred surging through her. Then turned her back on the scene and walked into the darkness.

Fourteen

Victoria Faces the Music

"I never thought to see you in such a state, Vioget. If there's one woman who can take care of herself, it's Victoria," Pesaro drawled.

Sebastian turned away from the supercilious prick, who lounged long and dark in an armchair, a book open in his lap. Not only was his neck cloth a disgrace, but he looked supremely unconcerned about the fact that Victoria seemed to have disappeared. The hackney driver, Barth, claimed he'd let her off a block away from the house in the early afternoon . . . but no one had seen or heard from her since.

But what did he expect from Max Pesaro? The man was utterly useless except for slinging insults and veiled comments now that he'd lost his Venator powers.

He was an unfeeling bastard, but he'd made his opinions clear to Sebastian last night, when Victoria left them alone in the carriage.

I'll be gone soon. You'll need to stay with Victoria. I

know you loved Giulia, and though you may not believe it, so did I.

The sentiment had been implicit: take care of Victoria without overtly taking care of her. It smacked of Pilate, but Sebastian's annoyance grew from the fact that Pesaro felt it necessary to make it an order. Yet, the fact that Pesaro had felt the conversation a necessity at all made it clear that Sebastian's warning to Victoria had been accurate: *He doesn't want anyone.*

"You'd be better off learning that now," Pesaro continued, holding a glass of brandy that was as full as it had been when poured. "She doesn't need to be taken care of. Nor does she desire it." *But take care of her regardless.*

Sebastian took a drink of his own liquor instead of replying the way he wanted to. He was better equipped to know Victoria's desires than Pesaro was, by God. Once he swallowed the burning liquid and leashed his instinctive response, he replied, "That may be the case—which remains to be seen—but since I've been in such close proximity to her, I've noticed that all is not well. She's acting differently."

Pesaro glanced sharply toward the door, and Sebastian stilled for a moment. Had that been a sound in the front entrance? By silent communion, they waited for another beat, but they heard nothing else.

Sebastian sipped again, rolling the brandy over his tongue. Unease tickled when he looked at the clock and saw that it was midnight.

"Differently?" Pesaro sounded bored, but Sebastian noticed that he was resting the glass on the table next to him.

He could barely stand the sight of Pesaro sometimes, for the shape and color of the man's dark eyes reminded him of Giuilia's, along with the sharp peaks that formed the dip in his upper lip. On her, the Pesaro eyes had been huge and overwhelming in her pale, delicate face, and her lower lip a lush complement to the well-formed upper one. . . .

Giulia had been a sickly girl, thin and delicate, with a cough that never seemed to ease. Sebastian had fallen completely, foolishly in love with her the first time he laid eyes on her at fifteen. Plagued by illness, she might not have lived to her twenties, but her life had been shortened even further by her brother's naive decision to bring her to the Tutela. Pesaro had thought vampirism's immortality would be the cure for her illness, but he'd been horribly tricked.

Sebastian steeled his thoughts, returning from the past to the present concern. God help him—he couldn't bear to lose Victoria as he had Giulia. But he wouldn't.

She was so much stronger.

"She reacts to the smell of blood," he told Pesaro, returning to the conversation. He hated having to share his concerns with him, but there was no one else. And, like it or not, Pesaro had been a fierce, capable, knowledgeable Venator who had given even Beauregard concern.

Sebastian's statement snared the other man's attention. The glass clunked softly as Pesaro released it completely onto the table. Though he didn't move otherwise, Sebastian noticed that his eyes sharpened in a way Giulia's never had. "What do you mean?"

Sebastian explained what had happened in the sewers, and also at the masquerade ball when he'd come upon her next to the dead Crusading knight. "She told me she has moments where she doesn't feel the same."

"And you've just now decided to share that important detail?"

Before Sebastian could reply, both men cocked their

attention toward the door. That had been a definite sound in the front hall. Glancing at the clock, which now read well past midnight, Sebastian listened.

A low murmur of voices told him someone had arrived, and then the parlor door opened.

Victoria tottered in.

Taking in Victoria's appearance, Sebastian stepped quickly toward her. He wanted to drag her into his arms, but the closed expression on her face held him back. "My God, Victoria, where have you been?" He settled for taking her hands—they were gloveless. Her hair was a disaster, her clothing—

"You do look frightful," Pesaro agreed.

Sebastian would have twitched a smile if the moment hadn't been so tense. Pesaro not only had no taste for fashion, he had no idea how to speak to a woman, no concept of charm. He had the glass in his hand again and remained in his nonchalant position, yet . . . something in his demeanor had changed. It was on edge.

Sebastian felt it, but he turned his attention back to Victoria. Her face was scraped up—there were long red scrapes along one cheek as if she'd ground it against something—and there was blood everywhere. Her hair was matted and tangled, a bushy black mess hanging in her eyes and face.

But it was the look on her face that arrested him. Cold, marblelike. Her rich green-brown eyes hard and empty. Long lashes dark against pale skin. Even her lips were pale, almost the color of lavender.

"I was taken to the magistrate. They were going to have me hung."

"Drink this." Pesaro thrust a hand between them, shoving his glass at Victoria. "You let them take you?"

"I didn't bloody *let* them take me," she replied, ignoring the glass. Her eyes flashed now, hot and furious, at Pesaro.

The men listened as Victoria explained, quite clearly and concisely despite her obvious anger.

"Then you left them?" Pesaro said at the end. He rose from his chair, smooth and tall, and stood over Victoria.

"What the hell else was she to do?" Sebastian snapped. He had taken Victoria's hand during her story, and felt the chill in her fingers. "He was going to have her hung. I'd have killed him myself."

"Where did this happen?" Pesaro said in a calmer voice than Sebastian had expected, shrugging into his coat. "Where did you walk away?"

Victoria's lips seemed to have a hard time moving, but she replied, giving him the direction of an address in Whitechapel. "I couldn't," she said, pulling away from Sebastian. "I had to leave."

"Leave them to die?" Pesaro turned back to her, and for a moment they stood, facing each other as if ready to come to blows. Something snapped in the room, tightened, and stretched. He looked as though he was about to wrap his fingers around her throat, and Sebastian closed his fingers into his palm. "I thought better of you, Victoria. It was as good as murder."

"They were alive when I left."

"With no chance of survival. Their fate was sealed." Pesaro turned away, then stopped suddenly, pivoting back to Victoria, his eyes narrow and sharp. He looked at her again, delving long and hard, then he raised his eyes to meet Sebastian's. The bald condemnation Sebastian expected to see had gone; instead, it was a knowing look, filled with meaning. And then Sebastian understood.

This wasn't Victoria—not the Victoria he knew.

Pesaro pushed between Sebastian and Victoria, marching toward the door.

"Where are you going?"

Pesaro didn't break stride. "To see if there is anything to salvage."

"I'll go with you," she said. "You can't go alone."

That insult stopped Pesaro, who turned back, his hand on the doorjamb. Even Sebastian was taken aback by the ferocity in his expression. "No. I don't want you with me." He flung the door closed behind him.

The room settled into quiet again. Sebastian saw Victoria's stricken face, and familiar discomfort curdled in his belly. The way she looked after him, the way she'd looked when Pesaro had miraculously appeared after the fire . . . Sebastian didn't like it.

He didn't like it at all.

Which was why he was very glad he'd told Pesaro that Victoria knew everything about Giulia, and what her reaction had been.

A bit of an exaggeration, of course, but all was fair in love . . . and war.

Victoria dreamed of blood.

Rivers and ribbons of it, the smell, the thick coagulation . . . it filled her nostrils, settled on her tongue. She bathed in it. Choked on it.

She opened her eyes to find the sun streaming into her bedchamber. The bedclothes were twisted and wrinkled, cocooning her legs and wrapped togalike around her middle. Her head pounded, and her face felt tight and sore.

But she had to rise.

Even knowing that her wounds would heal within a day, seeing herself in the mirror did little to improve

Victoria's spirits. Her face was mottled with bruises, and there was a long scrape on the side of her jaw.

Downstairs, dressed in a simple gown that was barely more than a chemise, her hair pulled into a single braid, Victoria found Kritanu in the *kalari*, the room they used for training. It was a large space for the small town house, for Aunt Eustacia had had a wall removed between the music room and a parlor. The chamber was well lit, spacious, and covered by a shining wooden floor, which Kritanu claimed was the best surface for training. There were piles of huge cushions in the corner, used not only for seating or reclining, but also for padding during training sessions.

She didn't expect to see Max, but he was there in a mock battle with Kritanu. Both men held long slender swords, blades curved in a gentle arc, and they clashed and slid and gleamed.

When she stepped into the room, Max stepped away from the exercise, letting the tip of his weapon bump to the floor. He was dressed in loose, ankle-length brown trousers and a cream-colored tunic streaked with sweat. His hair was pulled back like a pirate's. His large feet were bare, but a slender cord encircled one of his ankles. A small silver cross hung from it.

"I found nothing last night," he said abruptly. "I wonder if you gave me the correct direction."

"Of course I did."

"There was no sign of any destruction, nor had anyone heard any unusual disruption."

"Does it mean nothing that they would just as easily have hung me?" Victoria asked, suddenly wanting a sword in her own hand. She'd like to make Max dance at the other end, and she knew she had the strength and speed, if not the skill.

He must have understood her desire, for he glanced at Kritanu. "Would you care to surrender the blade to Victoria? I do believe she wishes to stab me." His smile was nothing more than a flash of teeth.

Kritanu relinquished his weapon and stepped back as Victoria hefted it in her hand. She was used to the shorter *kadhara* knives, or a long slender épée. But this was a much more serious blade. Heavier, and it would move differently.

"Perhaps you'd best don some protection," she returned, slicing the blade experimentally in front of her, from shoulder to floor. She adjusted the angle of her wrist and felt the weapon balance more comfortably.

Max snorted. He riposted back at her with a deep swipe that stirred the air. "I look forward to fighting unfettered—for I have no reason to hold myself in check matched against you." He moved neatly to the side when she brought her blade up again, and the metal weapons smashed together. "And . . . to answer your question . . . it does mean something that they wished to hang you."

The hem of her chemise would limit her from taking great steps, but it was full enough for her to lunge forward. He skimmed easily aside, his feet leaving the ground in a low glide, and she watched in chagrin. Max landed on the floor, and she saw that he was grinning.

Max grinning was a sight that riled her to the core.

Victoria met his blade and forced him back several steps. "Does it?"

"Yes," he replied, surprising her by pressing forward into her space. Their blades slid and then he neatly stepped to the side. "But you cannot forget—you are bound to protect mortals from the undead, Victoria. You cannot walk away just because one of them angered you."

"Angered me?" She sliced more viciously than she'd

intended, and he leaped back under her onslaught. "He would have shot me on the street. Or hung me at New-gate."

"An unpleasant occurrence, to be sure. I don't fault you for wanting to save your skin. But . . . it was the man-ner in which you did." He slashed and she felt the gust of air next to her face. "Venators have superhuman powers. If we—you—begin to use those abilities to pass judg-ment on mortals . . . that is wrong. It is nothing more than abuse of the gifts given."

"I've never abused my gift," she replied, knowing that it was untrue. "I wouldn't."

Max lunged. "But you did. Last night."

"And what about your own foolish actions?" she replied, whipping her blade viciously through the air so that he was forced to leap back. His smile flashed, as if pleased that she'd caught him off guard, and he moved forward.

"What foolish actions do you speak of?" he asked, dip-ping to the side and bringing his blade up sharply. She re-acted and the metal clanged and rang in the room.

"Max, Lilith is here in London. Clearly, she would love nothing more than to get her hands on you again."

She saw his mouth tighten, the glimmer of humor gone. "And of course, I cannot protect myself." He lunged sharply and Victoria dodged, hearing the blade whistle next to her ear.

"You must admit," she said, starting back toward him, "that it might be a bit more difficult now." He met her blade without backing up, and their arms strained against each other before the force of her blade caused his to slide away.

"I have the means to take care of myself." He came at

her again, this time gliding on the air, and she was forced to raise her blade higher to stop his onslaught.

"But if she caught you again . . . and bit you, put you back under her thrall—"

"I won't give her the opportunity. She cannot do it with a single bite . . . and it required some participation on my part."

"What?" Victoria stopped, and he caught her unawares, slicing down the side of her arm. The blade brushed along her sleeve, but did nothing more than scrape the fabric. "Participation?"

"Christ, Victoria, it wasn't willing participation," he snarled. "If I'd known the salve she was putting on the bites would cause them to never heal, and to bind me to her, don't you think I would have stopped her?" He slashed violently.

They fought in silence for a moment, Max's feet back on the ground, and Victoria aware of the trickle of perspiration down her spine.

"Incidentally, I don't believe he's dead," Max commented, easing back after a particularly feisty tip-to-tip dance of their swords.

"Who?"

"The Runner."

"What?"

"I told you . . . I found nothing and could locate no one who'd seen or heard any disturbances. And," he said, shifting to the side, and then suddenly around her, dragging the tip of her blade with him, "I have a recollection that might interest you and may clear up the matter even more."

Victoria pivoted after him, striking out with her weapon as he brought his down. Their blades smashed, caught, and with a great jerk, she gave a powerful twist.

Both blades tangled, their guards twisted, and flew through the air, landing a few feet away with a dull clatter.

"A draw," he said, looking down at her, barely breathing hard. He'd pulled his hair back in a short, thick stub at the back of his head, but one strand fell over his face. He pushed it back and planted his hands on his hips. His brown feet spread wide, making him look more like a pirate than ever. All he needed was a gold hoop in his ear—although Max would probably opt for silver, if he was thus inclined.

"Your recollection?" she asked, noticing how the vee of his tunic revealed dark hair brushing the curve at the base of his throat. He'd drawn her hand there once, beneath the warm cotton of another shirt, over flesh and muscle, to touch the *vis bulla* for strength. She stepped back.

"Goodwin, yes? Frederick Goodwin was the Runner's brother?"

"Yes, Lord Truscott."

"There was a Goodwin in the Tutela. It may have been him. If so, then I doubt he met his end—he or his cohort—at the hands of the undead."

Victoria understood, and a flare of anger sparked. "But if not, I'm nevertheless absolved from my sin of passivity if Goodwin was a member of the Tutela? Mortal or no?"

"If he was a member of the Tutela, Goodwin would have been safe with the vampires," Max reminded her. "You wouldn't have been leaving him to his death. If he wasn't Tutela, it wasn't your place to determine whether he lived or died."

"So I should have let him—"

"And," Max continued smoothly, "if he was Tutela, it

would explain his animosity toward you. The Venator who took his brother's life."

She didn't like the train of this conversation, for the condemnation from Max still weighed heavily on her. Perhaps she shouldn't have left Goodwin at the hands of the vampires . . . but at that time, it was the only thing she could do . . . wanted to do.

It was as if all concepts but self-preservation had evaporated from her mind. Leaving only a single-minded need for survival. Red-tinged anger, blind wrath. Conscienceless fury.

Then she remembered. "He did say something . . . something about protecting his brother. 'After all I did to protect him.'"

"He could have helped him turn undead to protect him. It's been done before." Bitterness.

Victoria looked at him sharply and recognized that he was speaking of himself. "As you did with your father and sister."

"But Vioget has told you all of the sordid details, has he not." Max's voice was staccato and hard, and he turned to pick up the tangle of blades.

"I know enough from Wayren to be aware that you were young and had been tricked into believing in the promise of the Tutela. You did it to save your father's life, and your sister's too. They were both weak and ill."

"Immortality. Protection from illness. Power." He stood, holding the weapons. "Only a naive boy would believe there was no cost for such a prize." Max turned, walking toward the cabinet where the weapons were stored.

Victoria realized that Kritanu had gone, and they were alone. "The way I understand it, the Tutela is more than a match for a naive boy. Mature and learned people like John Polidori have succumbed to their machinations."

"Never fear, Victoria. I've come to terms with what I did. Why do you think I've dedicated my life to hunting the undead? I see no reason to wallow in self-pity or flag-ellate myself. There's too much work to be done." Max lifted one of the swords, fitting it onto its pegs inside the cabinet. He didn't look at her as he latched it into place. "And I certainly don't need your sympathy or pity."

Victoria opened her mouth to reply, but Max was already out of the room.

Fifteen

Wherein Victoria Breaks a Trust

"We called yesterday," Lady Melly sniffed, "after we'd heard about that terrible fire. But that Verbena insisted that you were indisposed." She glowered at Victoria. "She made us wait here in this room for an hour. Without tea."

Victoria thought it was more likely that Lady Melly and her two cronies had refused to budge for that hour, rather than being forced to sit there . . . but then again, Verbena was just as strong-willed. Perhaps it had been a game of who would blink first.

Apparently, the ladies had blinked—or perhaps hunger had won out.

"I wasn't feeling at all up to visitors yesterday, Mama," she told her with a placating pat on her hand. In reality, Victoria felt a bit guilty for her mother's worry— for the lines on her face seemed deeper, and the way she'd gasped upon seeing the scrapes and bruises on her cheeks and chin bespoke her concern. "But Verbena told me that you'd come, and it made me feel much better."

"You do look rather worse for the wear," Lady Melly said, her tone and her face softening. "Fires are terrible things."

Victoria nodded and squeezed her fingers around her mother's wrist. Lady Melly's father had died in a stable fire when she was a young girl, and she'd often described the terror of the furious blaze and the screams of the horses trapped inside. "But I survived with only a few scars, and all is well."

Lady Melly sniffed again, the tip of her nose tinged suspiciously pink. "When your maid wouldn't allow us to see you—and I must say that I am quite offended that she should disallow your own flesh and blood to visit— we called on Rockley." She looked at Victoria, the calculation back in her blue eyes. "It seemed the right thing to do."

Victoria smothered a sigh. "Mama, you must understand—"

As if to forestall any declaration of her disinterest in the marquess, Melly interrupted. "He is quite besotted with you, Victoria. There's no need to feel uncomfortable about it. It's not as though he and Rockley—your Rockley— were brothers or any such thing. As I hear it, they're very distantly related and it wouldn't be odd at all. And then you would be a marchioness."

"I'm still a marchioness," Victoria reminded her dryly. "But, Mama, you really must cease this matchmaking. I'm a widow now, and I haven't any real desire to marry again. Nor do I need to."

Even as she said those words, and registered the bald disapproval in her parent's face, Victoria felt an odd nudge deep inside. Marriage in the way Society expected of her was most definitely out of the question. But there was the fact that she was the last direct descendant of the

Gardella line—as far as she knew. If she died, as Max had said, without issue . . .

And, if she examined things even more deeply, she couldn't deny that being a Venator, especially *Illa* Gardella, was a lonely, terribly lonely, life. Even Aunt Eustacia had had a partner, someone to share it with, to sleep next to, to be held by when times became dark and frightening. Someone who understood her, and loved her. After all, Aunt Eustacia had had a brother, who had been Melly's father, and thus she knew the line wouldn't die with her. Perhaps it really was time for Victoria to think in that manner, and to stop taking the special potion that kept her from getting with child.

Sebastian flashed into her mind, and she smiled. He had made it more than clear how willing he was to be with her. Intimately. Whether he loved her or not wasn't clear, but he certainly cared for her.

Unlike Max.

Victoria focused back in on her mother, who had launched into a breathless diatribe about how terrible it was to remain unmarried and alone. She let her go on for a moment longer, then said, "But Mama, you've been widowed for more than four years now and I haven't heard you speak once of wedding Lord Jellington."

Lady Melly's barrage of platitudes abruptly stopped and she blinked at her daughter.

And then, thankfully, before she was able to gather up a full breath to respond, a knock came at the parlor door. Charley opened it and Victoria saw that behind him were not only the ladies Winnie and Nilly, but the tall, rumpled figure of James Lacy.

"Ah," Lady Melly said, standing. The tea table rattled in her wake. "At last."

Victoria realized that the trio of women had implemented

a divide-and-conquer campaign. Lady Melly was to ascertain her daughter's condition, and the two other ladies were to retrieve the prize and deliver him in a timely manner.

"And it was such a frightfully frightening event!" Victoria didn't know for certain what Lady Nilly was babbling about, but whatever it was, it had been . . . frightening.

"Good afternoon, Mrs.—Lady Rockley," said James. He smiled warmly at Victoria. "I'm right glad you're feeling better today."

She returned the smile, but without the depth of warmth. How was she going to make her mother understand that James was not going to be her next son by law? "How kind of you to call," she said a bit stiffly.

"What a pleasure to see you again, Lord Rockley," crooned Lady Melly. As if she were the hostess, she gestured for him and the others to sit. "Victoria and I were just agreeing that September is a lovely time for a wed—mmph!" She gasped and jerked her leg out of range of Victoria's pointy slippers.

"Are you quite all right, ma'am?" asked James.

"Oh, yes, indeed, pardon me, my lord," she said. "Er . . . a bit of arthritis, and I'm never quite certain when it will kick"—she glared at Victoria—"in."

"Perhaps you ought to return home and rest a bit if it's too painful, Mama." Her daughter smiled blandly. Then she turned to James. "I see that you recovered from the fire with nary a scratch."

"I was lucky. And it 'pears that although you didn't completely escape injury, you're feeling better today. I'm glad to hear it." His blue eyes twinkled. "I was afraid you'd be feeling too ill to join me tonight."

Victoria opened her mouth to explain that she was, indeed, feeling the renewed throb of a headache. But Lady Melly's strident voice overruled anything she might say, claiming that her daughter was of strong constitution and had fully recovered from her fright of the previous night.

Victoria considered whether speaking even louder than her mother would negate her claim of a headache.

"That's quite a shame, ma'am, Lady Rockley," James said, all charm and dimples, speaking easily over the volume of Lady Melly. "Mr. Starcasset and his friend Miss Regalado invited me to join them this evening. They claim there is some special comet that can be seen tonight in a certain location, near one of the parks. I confess, I'm not altogether sure I care about stargazing, but I thought it was a splendid excuse to see if you'd join me for a drive later tonight."

Victoria closed her lips around the automatic declination. George and Sara had invited James to join them for an evening ride? "Of course I'd be honored to attend with you," she replied, aware that she had just sent Lady Melly over the moon.

What more could a matchmaking mother hope for? Victoria was certain her maternal parent was imagining a romantic carriage ride by moonlight, whereas the reality was likely something much more disagreeable. Namely, a ruse to entrap someone.

But who was the intended prey: James . . . or Victoria?

"And where might your paramour be this evening?" asked Max. His tone implied that Sebastian's appearance would relieve him of the taxing obligation of conversing with Victoria. "Tell me there hasn't been a lovers' spat. You do seem a bit . . . distracted."

Distracted was one word to describe Victoria's state of mind, but not the one she would have chosen.

It was after dinner. They had settled in the only sitting room on that floor—the small parlor that had entertained not only Lady Melly and her friends, but which also held the cupboard wherein the Gardella family Bible was kept. When Aunt Eustacia had been alive, and first acclimating Victoria to the world of the Venators, the three of them— four, when Kritanu was there, and sometimes Wayren— had sat here many times.

"I'm pleased to inform you that your plans for my future are still intact. Sebastian and I have done nothing but share wistful glances, swoon at the sight of the other, and spout poetry—all since you've given your blessing to the match." Her smile was sweeter than the double-iced pink sugar biscuits favored by Lady Winnie.

Max's lips twitched. "Ah, if only I had been witness to such a spectacle. I expect it would have provided me amusement for weeks to come." He stretched his long legs, crossing them at the ankles. "Did Vioget position himself on one knee so as to look up into your crystalline eyes whilst waxing rhapsodic?"

"I believe I shall have a bit of sherry," Victoria said. "Would you like me to pour you some whiskey? Apparently my aunt had a fondness for it, but I can't say I share her taste." She closed her mouth with a snap, realizing how close she was coming to babbling nervously.

"By all means."

Victoria stood at the sideboard and prepared their drinks, then turned back to deliver the amber liquor to Max. Then she took herself to the chair near a small piecrust table where she'd sat, sharpening stakes, nearly two years ago, defending her decision to marry Philip.

A glance at the clock told her it was after nine. James was due to arrive at ten o'clock. Victoria took a significant gulp of sherry, despising the watery liquid for its weakness. And herself.

"Am I to understand that you haven't any intention of going out tonight?" Max asked. He was looking at her over the rim of his glass. Then he drank, and put the glass back down.

"Perhaps later," Victoria replied.

He raised his brows. "No social engagements? No vampire hunting?"

"James is to call for me later."

"James, is it? And what does Monsieur Vioget think of this? Or are you hunting the daytime vampire?" His eyes narrowed in speculation. "You believe it's he, don't you. I'm not so certain."

"Truly? How odd, since you were the one who suggested that it might indeed be he."

"Ah, so you hadn't considered him before my mention." He looked utterly pleased with himself.

She stood abruptly and walked over to the cabinet which housed the Bible. "I have not seen this since the first time Aunt Eustacia told me about the legacy of the Gardellas."

Feeling Max's attention on her, she fumbled the small gold key into its slot. Click, click, *clunk.* She swung open the bifold doors, heavy and slick.

Inside the cabinet, on its gently inclining display, rested the elderly Bible.

It was heavy, with gilt-edged pages that shone stubbornly despite its age. The leather corners were rounded and bumped, but the spine was as rigid as Aunt Eustacia's own had been. Three faded silk bookmarks fell lifelessly from their places.

She pulled out the book and placed it on the larger table in the middle of the room. She needed something to focus on, rather than the thoughts and questions running rampant through her mind.

Opening the front cover, Victoria smoothed her hand over words written in ink of varying shades of black, brown, and sepia. Listed there in the front pages were the names of the Gardellas who had accepted their calling as Venators. She touched one of the last names scribed there: *Eustacia Alexandria Gardella.* Below it was her own name: *Victoria Anastasia Gardella.* Seeing it there, its ink relatively fresh and bold, Victoria shivered.

Would there be any other names beneath hers?

Feeling the weight of Max's gaze, she was compelled to lecture. "Aunt Eustacia told me that the original pages of this Bible were given to the family during the Middle Ages. Six hundred years ago." She looked up, saw that he was silently sipping his drink. "A Gardella monk scribed this book in the twelfth century. I wonder if there was any connection to the monks who built the subterranean crypt Sebastian and I visited by the sewers."

"One could contemplate the beautiful irony of monks scribing a Bible in chambers next to those penning vampire secrets," Max said gravely. "It would not surprise me, as the monks and undead have intertwined—usually at odds—for centuries."

The Bible's pages had been bound, and rebound, and more pages added to include the growing family tree as the decades passed. Victoria carefully turned the crisp brown sheets. They crackled like a gentle fire. She saw images on some of them, and fading script on others, line after line. Ornate lettering, patterns, and illustrations in faded colors decorated the first letters of each book of the Bible.

Turning back to the front, she resumed scanning the list of Venator names. *Catherine Victoria Gardella.* An image of a vivid redhead with a flashy emerald ring and a saucy expression came to mind, and Victoria nodded to herself. Yes, she'd seen her portrait in the hall at the Consilium in Rome.

Another name, faded and further up the list, drew her attention. *Rosamunde Joanna Gardella.* The mystic who wrote pages of prophecy during her youth in an abbey . . . before she learned of her calling as a Venator.

A thought struck her, and she turned back to the end of the list. "Sebastian's name isn't written here," she said, looking up at Max.

"Nor is mine." He sipped, swallowed. "That list in the front is confined to those who have descended directly from Gardeleus, with strong Gardella blood—such as yourself."

An odd expression crossed his face and he stopped, blinking hard. Victoria tensed. But then he continued, "I believe the back of the book shows a full family tree, and also every Venator from the extended branches of the family tree—and those of us who can't claim one drop of Gardella blood. You'll find Zavier there, I suspect, and Brim, and Michalas as well. Or so I've been told."

"I see." A little shiver worked its way over the back of her shoulders. It wouldn't be long now. "If I had looked more closely at the book early on, I would have known the truth about Sebastian much sooner, since you and Aunt Eustacia chose not to tell me."

"There was no point in telling you." Max shifted in his seat. "And Vioget should have been struck from the list years ago. He had no cause to be there."

Knowing that this could be the last conversation she and Max ever had, Victoria closed the book and looked at him. "Why do you hate him so?"

"You ask because you know why he loathes me . . . but

you can't help but wonder what possible reason I could have for enmity toward him. I know he's made his case to you."

"There is no case to be made, Max. I understand why he . . . dislikes . . . you, and holds you responsible for Giulia's death—even though it was by his own hand. But I also know that you've forgiven yourself for the horrible mistake, and that you didn't bring her to the Tutela to hurt her. Only because you thought to help her, and that you've done everything you can to atone for it. But I do want to know what it is about him that makes you so disgusted."

He looked at her, and she saw the signs lingering in his gaze. "Vioget has the calling—the blood, the innate skills, to be a Venator—and yet he rejected it. For years. I can't forgive him for that. Nor can I understand it."

"At first, I couldn't either. But I've come to realize why he lost the urge to hunt vampires. Knowing that I'm responsible for sending a creature who—no matter how abhorrent he became—was once a mortal, loving and loved, to his eternal damnation, does give me pause sometimes."

"Yet you still do it," Max said quietly. His words were firm, steady. "As do I. Because you must; because we're charged to protect our own race. Do you think it hasn't occurred to me that not only did I cause Giulia to turn into an immortal half demon, but I also gave her a sentence of eternal damnation? I live with that knowledge every day."

Victoria looked at him, at last realizing why he wore such a cold, harsh persona; why he seemed so brittle and emotionless most of the time. That made what she was about to do all the more difficult. "It was hard enough for me to slay Phillip," she said, her heart breaking for him, "but it was that much easier, knowing that he'd not be sent to eternal Hell because he'd not yet fed on a mortal."

"Indeed."

"And yet," she said, echoing words he'd said himself, "you've never wavered from your decision to hunt vampires. Despite knowing the sentence you—we—thrust upon them."

"No. For what choice do we have? If we don't slay them, strive to put an end to them, what would happen to our race? They're stronger and faster than we are, immortal, and their instinct—their driving need to survive—is to take from humans. If we did nothing, if all—or even many—Venators rejected their calling as Vioget did, it wouldn't be long before the undead would take over. We have no choice. As Venators—you especially, as a Gardella—it's our calling. Our duty and responsibility. But it's not our role to make judgments about whether the undead should live or die. Or whether there truly is no chance that an undead's soul might be spared damnation."

"Is there?"

He shrugged, lines deep in his face. "It's a hope I live with every day, that perhaps . . ." He shook his head as if to clear it. "It's not for us to question our calling." He looked at Victoria. His eyes were bleary. "If Phillip had drunk from a mortal before you had the chance to slay him, would you still have done it, knowing you'd be sending him to Hell?"

How many times had she wondered the same thing? Countless times, over the last two years, sometimes waking from a deep, twisting slumber, damp and heart pounding, with her fingers curled around an invisible stake. She knew the answer.

"Yes."

Max nodded. "And that is the difference between you and me—and Vioget. We fulfill our God-given purpose no matter how difficult or painful it is." He raised his glass to drink again and stopped, his hand in midair.

Their eyes met and, in that moment, a burst of clarity flashed into his. "By God, you didn't." He surged to his feet and swayed. Fury darkened his face, fury the likes of which she'd never seen before. He looked carved from stone.

Her stomach tipped and roiled as she pulled slowly to her feet. Guilt was plastered all over her face. She remained silent. She had no words.

He lunged toward her, unsteady from the effects of the quick-working *salvi*, and bumped into the table. Glasses clinked ominously. *"Why?"* His chest moved in quick, hard jerks, as if he'd been running for hours.

She couldn't answer; her mouth was devoid of all moisture. She could barely swallow and her tongue seemed to be glued to the roof of her mouth.

Max slashed out at her, clumsy and slow, and she moved easily out of reach of those strong fingers. "What are you doing tonight? Where are you going?" His words were slurred; the *salvi*, once it took hold, worked quickly.

Victoria shook her head. "Max, I wanted to pro—"

"My God, Victoria . . ." His voice trailed off, weakening, and he turned away, staggering slightly. "I will . . . *never* . . . forgive. . . ."

His proud shoulders slumped and she saw his fingers closing into lethal fists. He half fell into the chair he'd recently vacated, the force of his uncontrolled weight shoving it against the wall.

Max looked up, fixing his dark eyes on her in one last look of loathing before he slumped into unconsciousness.

Sixteen

In Which the Marquess of Rockley Acquires a Chaperone

The night still hoarded some of the sun's warmth, eliminating the need for a shawl or wrap. The moon was a bit more slender than the night before, when Victoria had stood on the empty street and faced Bemis Goodwin, but the stars were twinkling in a great wide swath overhead and helped to light the inky blue sky.

James sat next to her in the curricle, holding the lines and bumping his solid arm against hers every time he moved. The open-faced, two-seater vehicle rumbled along the deserted pathways of Regent's Park, the awkward, random shapes of bush and shrubbery adding to a slightly eerie feel. The faint essence of wood smoke sifted through the air.

Victoria couldn't get Max out of her mind. Taking a deep breath, she looked up obediently when her companion commented on the array of celestial bodies, but her thoughts churned like the swill at the bottom of a fishing boat.

He would never understand, never forgive her. She

knew that. But, more than that, she feared what could happen if he followed her tonight. It had been worth taking the chance, knowing she wouldn't have to worry about his safety.

"Oho, and here they are," crowed James in delight. "Over here!"

Forced from her unpleasant thoughts, Victoria looked up and redirected her mind to the matter at hand. She had not come on this little excursion without preparation and planning. In fact, as she peered in the dark toward the sprightly vehicle that presumably carried Sara and George, she was actually looking beyond it. If all had gone as expected, Sebastian and Kritanu would be there, somewhere in the darkness, having been delivered by Barth and his hackney. They would be watching and waiting, ready to help quell any problems that might arise.

As Sara and George moved closer in their vehicular conveyance, Victoria became aware of the telltale chill on the back of her neck. Complacence and anticipation settled over her. She'd been right to suspect something.

"Good evening, Lord Rockley . . . and Lady Rockley." George's voice held faint amusement, presumably at the linking of their names.

Behind the other carriage, Victoria saw shadows moving. The corresponding barometer at her nape indicated a fair number of undead in the vicinity. She tensed beneath her skin, careful not to indicate her reaction to James. If he were a daytime vampire, he didn't need to drink the elixir at night—unless he wanted to keep her unaware of his condition until now. Which would make sense.

Or, just as likely, he and she were both planned victims.

But now that other vampires had arrived, obviously without masking their undeadness to her sensitivities, why was nothing happening? Sara and George—and whoever else—certainly would know she was aware of the presence of vampires. Unease prickled over her.

Just then, a third carriage moved into view from behind the one carrying George and Sara. Victoria heard a familiar laugh . . . one that sent horrible shivers down her spine. What was Gwendolyn doing here?

Indeed, the tableau played out with all of the societal niceties one might have expected, if one were unaware that at least some of those present had a propensity for drinking blood.

"I must apologize for our tardiness, but my darling sister and her betrothed insisted upon joining us for tonight's excursion," explained George, maneuvering his carriage so that the third one could pull forward.

"Victoria!" Gwendolyn cried, lurching forward in her vehicle to wave. The moonlight slivered over her blond hair and outlined round cheeks curved in a delighted smile. "Is this not the most delightful thing? A ride in the park at night?"

"It is most delightful," Victoria replied, managing to keep the trepidation from her voice. George had sent his sister safely away from the fire two nights ago; why had he allowed her to come tonight?

"It was a last-minute decision," Gwendolyn said, as if knowing explanations were in order. "I do hope you don't feel that Brodebaugh and I are intruding. George didn't think I should be out in the cool night air, but I convinced Brodebaugh that it was no worse than sitting in the dinner room with the windows open. And George and Sara simply couldn't be out without a chaperone." Gwen couldn't seem to stop smiling. In fact, she fairly glowed with happiness as she leaned companionably against her fiancé, who looked down at her with his own indulgent smile.

"Indeed," Victoria replied faintly. She was still waiting for something to happen . . . although what, she wasn't certain.

"So where is this comet you wanted to show us?" James said, his voice booming.

Instead of looking up, as the others automatically did, Victoria scanned the darkness. The small glowing eyes, floating like red lightning bugs in the depths of brush and shrubbery, watched them expectantly. One of her stakes was wedged beneath her thigh, inside the hidden pocket Verbena had sewn into her gown. She shifted to adjust it, and to make it more easily retrievable. Her fingers itched to close around the small wooden pike and slam it into the variety of hearts surrounding them.

Prudence held her back; prudence and discretion. Not until she had to. Gwendolyn and her earl didn't need to be frightened, or exposed to the violence that would occur.

But though she waited, nothing untoward happened. The drive through the park went on as though it were nothing other than what it had been put out to be: an opportunity for several young couples to have a romantic interlude.

It wasn't until nearly a half hour later, after George had pointed out simply every constellation and planet known to man—along with the Comet Encke, as it had been named—that the air changed.

She sensed an expectation building, a feeling of anticipation. Victoria remained alert, but other than the insistent chill on her neck and the sense of waiting, she felt and saw nothing.

She needed to do something to get Gwendolyn and

her earl away before whatever was going to happen happened.

They were trotting along the easy, curving path lit by the moon's skirt. The odd lumps of dirt and out-of-place boulders, groupings of trees and brush, and piles of paving stones that bespoke John Nash's ongoing redesign of the park reared up in the dark, sending awkward shadows over the road.

The three carriages were moving along at a good clip, not quite in a single file, but staggered across the path. George and Sara were in the lead, Victoria and James slightly to the left behind them, and Gwendolyn and Brodebaugh in the rear directly behind her brother, almost next to Victoria.

She turned in her seat to call back to Gwendolyn, planning to make an excuse—a headache, weariness, something—so that her friend would accompany her home.

But before she could even hail her friend, there was a great lurch and all at once, everything was falling. The horses shrieked and James shouted, and Victoria felt everything tipping as if in slow motion. Then, as she hit her head, a moment of darkness and pain.

When she opened her eyes, only seconds later, she heard Gwendolyn screaming. James was heavy atop her and everything was dark and awkward. It took her only an instant to realize that somehow the carriage had tipped or fallen, and that she was trapped beneath James. The vehicle was half on its side so that everything concentrated on her corner of the conveyance.

She had the wherewithal to grip her stake, and even though she felt discomfort from the fall, Victoria wasn't injured. But she was fully aware that this could not have been an accident.

And when she heard the screams growing louder, and saw the flash of red eyes glowering into the curricle above her, she knew she was right.

Victoria shoved at James, pushing his weight from hers. He seemed to be unconscious, and his legs were caught under the ledge of the carriage, making it difficult to move him. The awkward pose had fairly trapped her in the corner of the seat. The horses were still squealing, and the carriage lurched and lunged in its place as they struggled to pull loose and run free.

The vampire grabbed James and yanked him off Victoria—which was a bad choice on his part. No sooner had the weight been extricated and lifted from her than she clambered out awkwardly, her feet fumbling around her skirts. She landed on the ground just in time for the vampire to turn back to her. Meeting him with the point of her stake, she sent him to his destiny in a poof of ash, then spun to take note of the situation.

Sebastian and Kritanu had already made their presence known. As Victoria looked, she saw that Sebastian was engaged with numerous vampires. Kritanu was making use of his *qinggong* skills to glide and leap from tree to boulder to tree. He harassed the creatures, swiping at them with a long, gleaming sword as he moved above them and lopped off an undead head when the opportunity arose. Gwendolyn sat in her carriage, screaming, her hands plastered to her cheeks as her fiancé attempted to beat off the undead with a whip.

Sara and George, along with their carriage, were nowhere in sight.

Gone. Victoria would have thought they'd stay to watch the results of their trap. Her brows furrowed as she pivoted to meet a feral female vampire, blocking the creature's lunge with her arm, then slamming the stake into her chest beneath it.

Sara and George had left as soon as the battle started. As soon as everyone was flushed out and engaged.

But Victoria wasted no further time in contemplation. There were at least a dozen vampires about, and she launched herself into the fray, stepping in to relieve Sebastian from a trio that had attempted to corner him near a large boulder.

With a passing-by poof, she cut his attackers down to a duo, and then continued over to Gwendolyn and Brodebaugh. With a shout meant to draw the attention of the undead, she rushed toward the cluster of red-eyed vampires as Kritanu's wiry body landed gracefully on the top of the curricle's roof. His sword whistled, lopping the head from an undead at a distance safe from its inhuman strength, and then he turned to the other side.

He kicked a particularly insistent undead back so that the creature tumbled to the ground in front of her, and Victoria paused to stake him as she moved into the melee about her friend's carriage.

Why would George and Sara have left? To escape?

Or to attend to some other task?

And then a horrible feeling rumbled inside her. Max. He was alone, and . . . incapacitated.

"Kritanu," she cried, her voice rising above the pandemonium. The trainer's jet eyes found hers amid the battle. "Max! He's unprotected."

With relief, she saw Kritanu immediately leap up, then disappear into the higher branches of a tall maple. She was aware of branches and leaves shaking gently as he moved away, presumably toward the hack that would take him back to the town house.

For now she could concentrate on the matter at hand. And worry about Max later.

Despite the tangle of skirts, and Gwendolyn's screams ringing in her ears, Victoria was quite successful in her endeavors, staking three more vampires before she realized the battle had waned.

Breathing heavily but by no means winded, she turned and found Sebastian standing behind her. He looked down at her, stake outlined in his hand, blond hair tufted and mussed in the moonlight. He was breathing harder than usual, but he didn't have more than a sheen of sweat on his forehead.

"I know I shouldn't ask—and in light of the fact that while I made no move to help you in your battles, you insisted upon interfering in my fight," he said, his lips quirking in a smile, "but, consider it merely a sign of my affection for you when I *do* ask . . . were you injured when the carriage fell?" His voice, deeper than usual, belied the humor in his words.

"Not enough to matter," she replied, suddenly aware that she didn't mind so much that he cared enough to ask. Max certainly never would.

"James?" she called, glad to be distracted by the dark form rising from where he'd been flung by the vampire. "Are you hurt?" She hurried to his side, aware that Sebastian watched after her.

She was finding it easier, more comfortable . . . to be with Sebastian, to trust him, to fight side by side with him. She looked back and saw that he was still watching her, even though he was speaking with Gwendolyn and Brodebaugh.

"What happened?" James asked. "That was one helluva—excuse me, ma'am—hole there!" He glanced cursorily at the carriage, which Victoria now saw had the whole front half sunk into a hole in the ground. His attention focused on the horses, which, although they were still snorting and rolling their eyes, had ceased trying to pull the conveyance free.

She agreed, and walked over with him to look at the situation.

The cause of the accident was clear. Someone had taken advantage of Nash's construction to obscure a deep impression left in the ground with some sticks and leaves. The carriage being wider than the two horses, they had managed to walk on by unscathed, but the left front wheel had slipped off into the hole.

The resulting crash had been enough to jar and shock, but not enough to injure. She wondered if that had been the intent.

Or, she wondered again, had this all been a way to distract her while Sara and George went after Max—after ascertaining that he hadn't been lying in wait to help Victoria?

If either one of them were vampires, they wouldn't be able to get to Max inside Aunt Eustacia's house, because they wouldn't be able to enter. But if one of them wasn't, they could go in after him . . . if indeed that was the intent.

She knew that Kritanu and Barth, along with a feisty Verbena, could easily handle one or two nonvampires that might try to break into the house.

Of course, Max would have been able to handle any such threat on his own . . . if she hadn't drugged him.

Victoria ignored the niggle of guilt in favor of the larger matter at hand. Was it that simple? Was all this merely to grab Max for Lilith? Or was there something else going on?

Maybe Max didn't figure at all into any of the reasons

for these attacks, or the daytime vampire. Maybe she was
focusing her attention in the wrong place. After all, she'd
been the target of Bemis Goodwin—although there was
no definite connection between him and the Tutela, only
Max's recollection of a vampire sympathizer named
Goodwin.

Maybe Max was the daytime vampire himself.

That was patently ridiculous.

"We'll have to get help to pull 'er back out," James
said, scratching his head in a way that a London gentleman never would. "Guess that won' be until tomorrow."

"Sebastian and Brodebaugh could do·it, I venture,"
Victoria said. She waved the two men over, and with their
combined efforts—especially Sebastian's *vis bulla*
power—it took only moments before the carriage was
righted again.

Then she and Sebastian looked at each other. "Do you
feel any other undead?" he asked privately.

She grimaced. "You still sense my presence?" He nodded. But that was neither here nor there at this time. "I
don't feel any undead about any longer. And I don't know
what happened to George and Sara. But, somehow, we
must get James, Brodebaugh, and Gwen home safely. I
don't trust this situation."

"Starcasset whipped his horses into speed as soon as
your vehicle fell," Sebastian told her. "I saw them dash
off, and from the looks of it, they aren't coming back."

"We can't all fit in one carriage. I sent Kritanu and
Barth back to my house." She wasn't ready to give him a
full explanation, and, to his credit, Sebastian didn't ask.

"Perhaps it would be best if I took the marquess home,
and you could go with Gwendolyn and her earl." Sebastian's casual suggestion threatened a smile from Victoria.
She couldn't hold it back and looked up at him teas-

ingly. "Is that because you don't trust the marquess in the moonlight . . . or me?"

That surprised a smile out of Sebastian. "He can try anything he likes. . . . I have no concerns that the big, uncivilized oaf might charm you blind, Victoria. He's not man enough for you." He looked at her slyly, his smile suddenly hot and promising there in the moonlight. "I miss being with you."

"Victoria!"

Gwen's voice broke into the moment, and Victoria wasn't sure if she was disappointed or relieved. Sebastian would not be held off much longer . . . and tonight . . . well, tonight, she just wasn't sure if she was up to it. Although . . . Sebastian was quite adept at distraction of the most pleasant type. An unwilling smile tugged at her lips . . . then faded as she worried again about Max. "Yes, Gwen?"

"Are you going to tell me what happened?" her friend was all aflutter—apparently the shock of the attack had worn off, and what she'd seen had at last penetrated. "Who those people were? Why their eyes were so odd?"

Oh, how Victoria wished for her Aunt Eustacia's golden disk! The one that was able to pull select memories from the minds of people who shouldn't know about the presence of the undead. Which was most of the world.

"What am I going to tell her?" She looked at Sebastian, and he must have read her mind.

"I'll see them home. You can ride with the marquess and ensure his safe return. Poor devil. I almost pity him in any endeavor he might make." His grin flashed, cocksure and sexy.

That was good—St. Heath's Row was closer to home. She could drop James off and then hurry back to Aunt Eustacia's to see if Max was all right.

"Thank you for taking Gwen home. You spin a better yarn than I do, and I'm sure she'll fall for whatever tale you choose to paint," she said, smiling prettily at Sebastian.

"Flattery, my dear, will get you everywhere with me." He pulled her into his arms, strong and warm, fitting his mouth possessively over hers.

The kiss was long enough that it caught at her breath, so that when he released her, she had to drag in a deep gulp of air. It had been a lovely, perfect melding of lips and tease of tongue, rife with the promise of much more to come.

And, of course, it had been Sebastian's clear message to James Lacy that Victoria was spoken for.

Seventeen

Wherein the Smell of Roses Portends an Unpleasant Evening

Victoria realized, of course, that she still hadn't identified the daytime vampire . . . and that the man sitting next to her in the scraped-up, creaking curricle could very well be the undead in question.

It could also be George, Sara, or any one or all of them.

She didn't really believe it was Max, but he'd taught her to consider all possibilities.

Oh God. Max.

Victoria realized she was curling her fingernails into her palms. She didn't like to imagine the way he'd look at her the next time she saw him—if indeed she ever did. When she'd made the decision to give him the *salvi*, it had been a single-minded, tunneled response to a very simple, real fear.

She could not bear for Lilith to have him again. Victoria had never been able to erase the memory, seeing him—always so powerful, so arrogant and in control— under that creature's domination. Bare-chested, kneeling at Lilith's side, a submissive Max with empty eyes and no will of his own . . . then the way he had jerked helplessly, convulsing, his torso shuddering as the vampire queen bent to sink her teeth into his neck. And drink.

The image haunted her.

And now, he was free—free of a hold Victoria knew she couldn't begin to comprehend. Even though he was still brusque and arrogant and commanding, she'd noticed an easing in his face, a lessening of the darkness in his eyes. A few more smiles, even. Being released from the vampire queen's thrall had—not softened him; that wasn't the word. Max wasn't soft in any sense of the word.

He'd become . . . easier. Just a bit easier.

"Would you like a rose?"

James's voice broke into Victoria's thoughts, and she realized the carriage had traveled from the park and was now rolling along the street. Other vehicles filled the thoroughfare, and ladies and gentlemen walked along arm in arm, likely returning from Vauxhall or Covent Gardens.

There was a young woman hawking roses on the corner. Victoria had never noticed street vendors about at night—although orange sellers and the like were thick in this area during the day. But how enterprising of the woman to take advantage of couples out for an evening in the Gardens, or other less innocent assignations.

James hadn't waited for her response; he guided the curricle over to the side of the street. The young woman stood under a lantern, where its light gleamed over her blonde hair. Victoria might have been worried for her safety, there on the street by herself, despite the number of other people about. But when she noticed the hulking silhouette of a man propped against a building behind her, her fears eased.

"Which one would you like, my lady?" asked the girl, thrusting the bunch of roses in her face.

As Victoria leaned forward to select one of the blooms, two things happened: she realized that the back of her neck had chilled, and something sprayed in her face from the midst of the flowers.

She groped for her stake, but it was too late. The sickly sweet smell that had been atomized into her face filled her nostrils and seared the inside of her mouth and throat. She coughed, shaking her head, feeling the increased chill at the back of her neck, struggled to keep her fingers around the stake . . . saw the dark figure from the building move into the lantern light . . . and then everything went black.

Max forced himself to sit, unmoving. If he dared rise again, he feared what he'd do—to the room, to the furnishings, to the locked and barred door, to himself.

He kept his mind focused on inane things—counting the lines in the wood-planked floor, the number of neat pleats on the ruffles around the pillow on the bed that had been made so bloody comfortable for him.

A prisoner.

Every time he allowed his thoughts even to start in that direction, his stomach tightened and dangerous bile burned the back of his throat. He couldn't let himself think about why she'd done it . . . or even the fact that she had.

Locked him here. A prisoner.

He knew why.

Oh, he knew why, and the fact that he did made it all the more disgusting and loathsome.

Bad enough that she'd broken his trust . . . but even worse—so damned much worse—was that she'd felt the need to do it.

He forced his attention to the pattern of rosebud wallpaper on the wall and began to count the blooms.

The *salvi* had not completely relinquished its hold on him, or so it seemed . . . for he began to feel heavy-lidded in the eyes and weary in the muscles.

The next thing he knew, he was lying on the bed.

And Wayren was there.

She stood in the small room, tall and serene. Her beautiful elfin face bore traces of concern and also a hint of challenge. Thick silver-blonde hair hung, for once, unfettered by small braids or leather thongs. Simple, straight, melding into the pale gold of her gown, which seemed almost to glow. Her whole person seemed almost to glow. "Why do you fight it, Max?"

He sat up, still exhausted. "Get me out of here."

"I can't do that."

"The hell you can't. I've seen what you can do, Wayren." His head was splitting and pounding at the same time; it was a wonder he could form words.

She smiled, but there was a trace of sadness there. "You deserve happiness after so many years of darkness and self-recrimination."

"I can't."

"You refuse to, Max. Let it all go and stop thinking about it. Stop denying yourself."

"I won't."

"She loves you."

"She loves Vioget."

Wayren nodded briefly. "Yes, she does."

Max closed his eyes. When he opened them, she was gone.

"Get me out of here!" he said to the empty room.

"You must do that on your own." Wayren's voice penetrated . . . from somewhere.

And then Max woke up.

*   *   *

Victoria opened her eyes.

Her first impression was of a warm room, filled with dancing red and orange lights. Smelling of roses. The back of her neck was unbearably frigid and the stone wall close to her nose was immediately recognizable to her. She was in the subterranean abbey Sebastian had shown her, lying in the exact place she'd found Briyani's body.

"Ah, at last. Our guest awakens."

Victoria realized she was lying crumpled on the ground, and, from the feel of the intense ache throughout her body, flung there like a sack of grain. Unfortunately, beyond the radiating aches, there was no uncomfortable, hard roundness under her hip or leg that would indicate the presence of her stake. She squeezed her eyes shut, then opened them again, focused . . . and pulled herself up on her hands, then her knees, and then proudly to her feet. The ache and lingering weakness ebbed into nothing, and she felt a surge of power when she concentrated on the *vis bullae*, groping for them through the special slit in her gown.

She hadn't needed to concentrate on the power of the *vis bulla* for a long time, but now she was flooded with it.

As her mind started to work more sharply, her first thought was of James. Had he been part of the trap, or an unwitting accomplice?

She turned to face Lilith, who had been silent since her greeting.

The room looked much more comfortable than it had when she and Sebastian were there. Fires roared in massive saucers throughout the room, giving off the reddish glow and warmth Victoria had first noticed. There must be some kind of ventilation that allowed the smoke up and out, as in the Consilium. A rug lined the stones in the center of the room.

The vampire queen sat on the thronelike chair Sebastian had moved to find the Ring of Jubai. She looked no different from the last time Victoria had seen her—nearly two years ago, when Victoria had offered the Book of Antwartha as a bargaining chip to free Max.

Lilith was still horribly elegant, still skeletally slender with the whitest skin marked by an occasional blue vein. Her eyelids were onionskin thin, colored bluish-purple, and her lips the gray-blue of someone who cannot get warm. Five dark marks dotted the side of her face, creating the path of a half-moon's curve.

But her hair and her eyes . . . they burned, in horrible contrast to the frigidity of her flesh. Brilliant copper, her curls fell about her like a glorious nimbus, and her eyes: Victoria glanced at them just long enough to see the sapphire blue ringed by red.

"I see that you've recovered from the accident of our last meeting," she told Lilith coolly, wondering if the stake buried in her coiffure had been located and removed. She reached up to feel through the mass of curls there . . . and pulled out the slender stake. Aha. They'd missed that one.

The vampiress's eyes narrowed, either at Victoria's taunt or the sight of the stake. "My skin healed from the burn of sunlight . . . but even so, you'll not walk away from me again."

"You've gone to much trouble to bring me here. What do you want?" The stake, no more than the thickness of her thumb, was comforting in her hand.

Lilith forbore to answer. Instead, she merely watched Victoria from her negligent pose on the throne. Her body angled in the massive stone seat so that one elbow rested close on an armrest, and she positioned her wrist on the other arm. "So it is you." She sounded contemplative, but

Victoria knew better than to look closely at the vampire to confirm.

Instead, she scanned the room. Clearly, Lilith meant her no immediate harm—otherwise she would not have been left to awaken on her own—or, even, to awaken at all.

They weren't alone in the room. Two Guardian vampires stood like stoic statues at the door through which Victoria and Sebastian had entered less than a week ago.

Lilith rose from her throne, the pale blue of her long gown whispering over her gaunt figure. "You are the one. I should have known it from the beginning. Who else could capture him?" She was talking as if to herself, but moving closer to Victoria. The smell of roses accompanied her movements, the cloying sweetness nothing like the delicate tea rose Lady Melly wore.

"It's your *vis bulla* that he wears."

Victoria forgot herself, and her gaze snapped to the undead queen's. Malice burned in those blue-red eyes; she fairly saw flames leap and dart in there. She dragged her eyelids closed even as the vampire's words rang in the room.

Max wore *her vis bulla*.

She heard the rustle of silk and forced her eyes open. This was not the time to think about it. . . . Lilith stood much too close. Victoria could see each hair of her slender brows and the tiny pores of her skin. She smelled roses as if her face was buried in them. And something . . . malevolent . . . tugged at her—pulled from the center of her torso, as if a rope had wrapped around her rib cage, drawing her closer.

Victoria let out the breath she'd been holding, and sidled the stake between them.

"How brave you are, Venator." Lilith smiled. The expression was one of such depravity that it sent an ugly, chilling shiver down Victoria's spine and shooting through her limbs. Her fingertips suddenly felt as though they'd been submerged in icy water for hours. "But in vain."

Victoria's heartbeat struggled, fighting to keep its own rhythm in the face of the vampire queen's power. Her lungs felt heavy, clogged, paralytic . . . yet she stayed steady, forcing the breaths, focusing on the power radiating from the two holy silver crosses in her navel.

Lilith moved, and suddenly Victoria felt vises close around her arms, yanking them to the side. The Guardian vampires flanked her, one of them jerking her off balance as the other kicked her legs far apart so that she stood as if straddling a wide river, unable to raise a leg to lash out.

She still held the stake, though the grip of the Guardian on her left wrist threatened to squeeze it from her fingers.

Victoria looked defiantly at Lilith, careful not to be ensnared by that enthralling gaze, fighting deep within to remain the mistress of her breath and heartbeat. "Surely you jest. You, the queen of the vampires, cannot face me without assistance?"

Lilith stepped closer, her breath warm on Victoria's face. She turned away, but the vampiress's fingernails closed around her chin and forced her head back to face her. Victoria didn't waste the energy trying to fight it. Her heart was pounding now, as though ready to leap from her skin . . . toward the sudden gleam of long white fangs.

"I prefer to feed in peace." In a sudden, horrific movement, she reached up and yanked the top of Victoria's head to the side, releasing her chin, and baring her throat. "We shall see what he thinks of you now."

Victoria couldn't move; she was held firmly from wrist to shoulder, and her ankles were spread apart and kept immobile by heavy boots planted next to them. Only her hips were unhampered; but she could do little but twist and turn—and even that was ineffectual against the strength of her undead captors.

Lilith moved closer, her breath hot on Victoria's bare neck, where the vein lurched and throbbed, pulsing as though ready to surge free. Dimly, she felt her fingers loosen and the stake fall as she struggled minutely, desperately.

The slide of fangs into flesh is rarely painful. They cut so cleanly and smoothly that the incision is little more than a terrifyingly joyful release . . . the warm blood at last free from its confines, flowing into the waiting vessel.

Victoria was stupidly conscious of the warmth of Lilith's upper lip and the chill of her lower one . . . of the way her tongue lapped against her flesh and the fangs bored deeply . . . the suction of cold and heat tugging deeply through her as Lilith drank, swallowing against her in an absurdly gentle manner.

And, suddenly, the vampire queen pulled away. She stepped back, staring at Victoria with wide eyes. All at once her guards dropped their hands, and she was free.

"So it's true."

Victoria lunged for her stake, forcing herself to ignore the warm trickle of blood leaking down her neck. From the corner of her eye, she saw the darkness staining her yellow gown as she surged upright.

She faced the vampiress, her fingers tight around the stake. "Is my blood too pure for your taste?"

The shocked look faded from Lilith's face, to be replaced by one of unadulterated pleasure. "Oh no, not at all. It was my error . . . for I discounted the tales told me. I could not believe you could drink from Beauregard, and he from you, and the turning not take place." Her eyes narrowed with malice. "But I have tasted the truth. You have vampire blood rushing through your veins, Victoria Gardella."

She turned and walked back to her throne as casually as if she were entertaining a guest. "I meant to destroy you . . . but there's no need. If I let nature take its course . . . not only will you become despicable to him, but you'll become bound to me."

"I'm no vampire."

Lilith looked at her again, her full blue-gray lips curling into a smile. "I see it in your eyes. You know that I speak the truth. Already you feel it, don't you? You've been fighting it, likely for months now. And it's getting stronger." She shook her head, the smile tickling her mouth like that of a coquette. "But how could it be?" she murmured, almost to herself.

"I'm too strong for it."

The laugh surprised her—eerie, high, and yet, like smoke. It curled and disseminated itself through the room, chasing away any other sound for the moment. Filling Victoria's ears, and her consciousness. It echoed there, and settled itself in place as if to confirm her own deep-seated fears.

Eighteen

Wherein Our Heroine Conducts an Unsuccessful Interrogation

Settled in her massive stone chair, Lilith seemed to feel far more companionable toward Victoria now. Her odd eyes lit with unholy humor and anticipation, and she seemed almost relaxed.

As though they were having tea.

Seeing the vampire queen in such a state unsettled Victoria. Her veins were still humming, though not as violently. But her breathing and heartbeat had eased into a more normal rhythm.

Could Lilith be right?

She drew in a deep breath, the scent of roses and wood smoke filtering into her nostrils and lungs, and calm crept slowly over her. She was obviously in no danger at this moment, nor did Lilith seem inclined to release her . . . so, at the very least, Victoria felt that the situation should be used to its advantage regardless of what was to come.

Boldly, she walked over to one of the heavy wooden chairs that lined the wall and sat. Lilith's chin lifted, but with a nod of acceptance rather than condemnation. "Of course . . . do make yourself comfortable."

"I will indeed. Perhaps while we wait—for whatever it is you await—you'll assuage some of my curiosity about the vampires that move about in the daylight. Clearly, the formula for the elixir found its way from Beauregard into your hands . . . but I'm mystified as to how that happened."

The queen slanted her an arrogant look. "It was brought to me by that blonde Regalado girl. She obtained it from one of Beauregard's followers, who meant it as a token to her as the new leader of the Tutela. Apparently you killed her father?"

"Is she drinking the elixir then? And what about you, Lilith? Don't you wish to see the sunlight again?"

Now the creature laughed again, this time more contemptuously. "I? Drink of that poison? Of course not."

"Poison?"

"My, how naive you are, Victoria Gardella. I shall quite enjoy watching your innocent veneer crack and dull." Lilith sat upright in her chair, her bony wrist resting on the curved arm. "The plant which makes up a large portion of the formula is very rare, and grows only once or twice per century. It also happens to be poisonous to the undead."

"It doesn't kill them."

"Not immediately . . . but the benefits of the potion last for only a short time—no more than a few hours. The daytime vampires, as you so quaintly call them, drink it as needed—whenever they wish to move about in the sun, or to remain undetected by you and your comrades. But for every use of the elixir, those who consume it age one year, perhaps more . . . it is not an exact—science, so to speak. If one uses it enough, one ages, and eventually cannot stop the aging process, even if the elixir is stopped . . . and the undead dies quite rapidly and unexpectedly. Without the unpleasantness of your stake or sword." She smiled, her fangs dipping gently into her lower lip. "Of course, I did not tell them of the hazards . . . for, as you can see, I had use for undead that could move about in the day. And the elixir is more addictive than opium."

"Them? Sara and George?"

"The elixir would do Sara no good," Lilith admitted. "She has not turned undead. And as for the others . . . well, I do not feel like being charitable. If you do not know, then I don't care to enlighten you."

"But why not? If I am soon to join your ranks."

Lilith made a sound almost like a giggle . . . but more ominous. "Ah, you are a clever one. But, no. I'll divulge no more. I will be amused watching you attempt to figure it out."

Victoria was not about to give up her chance to extricate more information from the vampire queen, even as the back of her mind formulated possible ways of escape. If she could get away, she would send for Wayren and tell her of Lilith's awful prediction. She'd find some way to stop it.

"And so you have come to London for what purpose? Do you not recall how you fled the last time you were here and believed you had me in your power?" Victoria asked with great condescension in her voice.

The creature's face mottled blue and gray, but she responded evenly. "Oh, do not think that it was only you, or Maximilian, who drew me to this cold city. I was not even certain he was here until Sara discovered him at that masquerade party. The two of you are only added little trinkets to this business." Her expression challenged Victoria to ask more.

"Was it you who set Bemis Goodwin onto me?"

"It was not that I made the request, but that I gave him

leave to do it. He is a valuable member of the Tutela, and though I haven't all that much use for them—mortals, I've found, are not as predictable as undead, to my great dismay—I saw no reason to disallow it. He has kept you busy, and distracted . . . and nearly incarcerated," she added with a pale smile. "That has left me free to put my other plans in place."

"You dare not tell me, for fear that your prediction doesn't come to pass," Victoria said dismissively.

Lilith narrowed her eyes, then they lit with malicious humor. "You already feel the tug of consciencelessness, Venator. The seed of everything evil begins with self. When one places oneself before every and all, evil sprouts, and spreads, taking over. And already, you've done so, even when you knew it was wrong . . . have you not?"

Suddenly, the door behind Victoria opened. She turned to see a pair of vampires dragging in two struggling, crying young women.

Her heart began to race, and she tightened the grip on her stake as Lilith stood.

"Ah, how lovely," said the vampire queen. She inclined her head regally and one of the undead prodded his burden forward.

Victoria knew what was to happen, and braced herself. There was nothing she could do to save the victims . . . it was as if she were at the horrific Tutela meeting in Venice again, watching the starving, thirsty undead feast and ravage several young women. She gripped her stake . . . she could get one vampire, maybe two . . . but then what? There were five, including Lilith.

The smell of blood permeated the chamber, and Victoria felt her head began to swim as the heavy, iron essence filled her senses. As saliva pooled in her mouth, she swallowed, shook her head, felt her limbs growing loose and weighty.

The girl's screaming subsided into soft gurgles and gasps of breath, and Victoria found herself struggling to stay in her chair, to sit upright. Lilith lifted her head from the distended vein of her victim's neck, looking at Victoria. She ate daintily, and even when she smiled a knowing, horrible smile, her teeth gleamed pure white.

"You fight it even now," Lilith said to Victoria, then waved her hand in dismissal. Her vampire minion dragged away the unconscious girl, and the second one moved forward into her place. As before, the servant held his mistress's meal steady while she fed. This time, Victoria couldn't tear her eyes away from the long, slender teeth sliding into the whimpering girl's neck.

She hardly felt the stake in her hand any longer; all of her attention and focus were gathered up in a net of bloodscent and need. Blood racing, bounding through her . . . her vision blossoming red . . . her fingers trembling as she curled them around the edges of her chair. Only that death-tight grip kept her in her seat.

Lilith finished eating, and the unfortunate girls were taken away. Now the vampire queen looked at her remaining captive with relish. "Perhaps I should taste you again, my dear. I see that the bloodscent has set your own veins to singing . . . it could certainly help the process along. And I do like the taste of a Venator . . . even if it is swamped with Beauregard's blood."

Victoria tried to fight them off, even brandishing her stake. But it was knocked from her fingers, clattering hollowly to the floor and rolling quietly away as the two Guardians dragged her to stand once more in front of their mistress.

"Think about how much easier it will be when you

give in," Lilith sighed like a lover against Victoria's cheek.

She strained to break free, but her vision was still colored and the scent of blood and roses from the queen's mouth beckoned and teased.

"Think of how much easier when you have only to think of yourself. Only to do what is right for you."

This time, she bit into the top of Victoria's shoulder, at the juncture of neck and collarbone. It was painful, but pleasure seeped into her almost immediately. Liquid, hot, coursing pleasure . . . the delicate touch of lip to flesh . . . the brush of skeletal hands over her hair . . .

Victoria felt dizzy, the words of Lilith piling into her mind, crushing reality, destroying her conscience . . . she felt her body weakening, the bloodscent filling her awareness . . . and the release of pressure against her skin.

The last thing she knew was a pair of blood-soaked lips covering hers . . . and then she tipped into a hot, red oblivion.

When she awoke, Victoria found herself sprawled once again on the floor. She dragged herself up, her head light, but, blessedly, her vision had cleared of all but the faintest pink tinge.

Slowly, she climbed up onto her hands, then her knees, using the wall for support. As she became more upright, the room shimmered less, her head felt more stable, and her strength returned. The cloying smell of blood had faded to a bare essence, weak enough for her to ignore.

Turning slowly, she faced the chamber, expecting to see Lilith seated on her throne, watching with those laughing eyes.

But the throne was empty.

The room was empty but for a single Guardian vampire, who stood at the door. He looked at her, his eyes ruby pink, his fangs exposed in a lascivious smile.

Victoria scanned the chamber quickly, spotting her stake not far from the chair on which she'd been sitting. She pretended not to notice the vampire; her mind was working now, and she'd keep it straight and focused in order to make her escape.

Feigning a weakened state and staggering heavily, she made her way toward the forgotten stake, tumbling to the ground on top of it. The slender wood in her hand made her feel powerful again, and she waited, breathing long and deep like Kritanu had taught her . . . long and deep . . . long . . . deep.

She felt for the *vis bullae* that, so far, had brought her greater strength than anyone could expect. The cool silver, warmed on one side by her flesh, sent a wave of power radiating through her and Victoria knew she was ready. Keeping the stake hidden in the folds of her gown, she put her plan into action.

Pulling slowly to her feet again, as if in great pain, she staggered more, slowly, randomly, but deliberately toward the Guardian vampire. She saw through her lashes that he watched her, but with amusement rather than wariness.

All the more fool he.

When she drew near enough and nearly fell at his feet, sliding against the cold, rough wall next to him, he gave a short chuckle. He'd barely wheezed his breath back in when she surged to her feet, stake in hand.

He had enough time to raise his arm and open his mouth in surprise before the lethal weapon drove into his chest. The stake was a slender thing, but powerful enough to force through the heavy shirt he wore.

His ruby eyes froze wide before he shattered into ash and dust.

Victoria stealthily tried the door—who knew what or who was on the other side—but it didn't move. She dared not try to force it, for there could be too many to fight on the other side—Lilith included.

Besides, she had another plan.

She rushed toward the throne, moving quickly for fear that someone would return before she was able to hide away. Quickly, she unbolted it from the floor and moved it out of the way to reveal the hidden door behind it—a door that she was certain Lilith knew nothing about . . . for she would have retrieved her copper ring if she had.

Unsure what lay behind the door, Victoria hoped she could at least hide there, giving the impression of an escape . . . and, perhaps if she were lucky, there would be another way out.

As she worked, Lilith's taunts echoed in her mind . . . almost as if they were attempting to slow her movements and distract her mind.

You already feel the tug of consciencelessness. The seed of everything evil begins with self.

When one places oneself before every and all, evil spreads.

Already, you've done so, even when you knew it was wrong . . . have you not?

Involuntarily, as she climbed through the hidden door, Victoria thought of leaving Bemis Goodwin to the vampires —so that *she* could be free of the disruption he caused; of drugging Max—so that *she* didn't need to worry over him or protect him; of early on in her visit to London, speaking with Gwendolyn in her private parlor, and the fury that bubbled deep inside . . . and how *she* didn't care to listen or hear about her friend's plans.

But . . . those events didn't mean that she was turning evil. Did they?

Leaving Bemis Goodwin and his companion to die . . . perhaps. Incapacitating Max? Not evil, no . . . how could it be evil to protect someone else?

Even when she knew it would destroy him.

Because it would be easier for *her*.

Forcing those dark thoughts away, she huddled in the small space and looked out at the dislodged chair. She had to pull it back into place or her hideaway would be revealed immediately. Then her eyes fell on a metal rod near the door. It had a hook on the end, like a shepherd's crook. In the narrow slit of light from the room, she also saw a piece of marble; it looked just like the top of the ornate bolt that fastened the throne to the floor. Only, there was no bolt. It would easily sit atop the claw-foot of the chair so that once she pulled it back into position, it would look as though it were bolted down.

Apparently this door had been used as a hiding place more than once, and the tools were there to assist. The fake bolt in its spot, Victoria squeezed back into the small doorway and used the metal rod to tug the chair back into place. As it moved, the door was forced closed until only a narrow opening was left—just enough to draw the hook back into the room.

Satisfied that the room would appear untouched, she closed the door and turned to feel her way around the pitch-black area. Working her way along the wall, she was forced to duck to keep from banging her head—a tactic she discovered after having scraped against rough stone above. She quickly discovered that the chamber was not a chamber, but a passageway.

And one that, from the faint brush of cool air, she believed would lead to freedom.

Nineteen

Wherein the Marquess Receives a Visitor

The passage did indeed lead to freedom, and Victoria was able to find her way out of the sewers without confronting any other undead . . . but for one, whom she surprised when he (or she; she didn't even have the chance to see) came around a bend in the underground tunnel. She staked the vampire and continued on, realizing, to her consternation, that she was able to see better than she should be able to in the darkness.

A chill that had nothing to do with the portent of an undead crept over her shoulders and trailed down her spine. Vampires could see very well in the dark.

She slogged through the stream of waste as quickly and silently as possible, and soon found her way to the surface. The dawn was just breaking, which would explain why she'd met a vampire on his way back to the place they obviously gathered. It was a miracle she hadn't met any others.

Once out of the sewers, she hurried through the streets, looking for a familiar landmark. As she wandered, she realized that she had no idea how long she'd been gone. Was this the dawn that had come after the carriage ride in the park . . . or the next one? Or the next?

Victoria arrived at her town house when the bottom edge of the sun rested on the horizon. She raised her fist to knock on the door, but it was drawn wide before she had the chance.

"Kritanu," she said in relief. He was alive and well.

"Victoria!" He was as pleased to see her, if the wide spread of white teeth was any indication. But his delight faded almost immediately.

"Before I tell you my story," she said, moving into the house and closing the door behind her, "is Max well? Is he still . . . here? How long have I been gone? Did anyone—George and Sara—anyone try to attack?"

"This is the second morning after you left. There were no attacks here," Kritanu replied. His face had sobered when she mentioned Max, and she felt a thrill of apprehension. "Max is . . . the same."

"The same?" Victoria went cold. "He is unconscious? For two days?" She started to dash off, but the older man grabbed her arm.

"No, no, he is awake. Has been. I meant to say that he is where you left him." The accusation in his face was unmistakable. "As you ordered. Victoria," he said, his voice turning harder than she'd ever heard it, "you are *Illa* Gardella . . . but never ask me to do such a thing again."

"You didn't release him." She wasn't certain if she was relieved or terrified that Max was still safely where she'd put him.

"I was prepared to do so if you had not returned today." His eyes carried concern and admonishment. "You should never have done that."

"I'll release him now," she said, turning away. It had

been for the best. She didn't expect Kritanu to understand; he didn't carry the same burdens she did.

For all of her hurry to get to the sturdy wooden door surrounded by silver crosses and blessed with holy water, Victoria found herself frozen when it came time to lift the bar that had blocked Max in. What would he say? What would she say?

She took a deep breath. The heavy slab of wood had been wedged tightly in its brackets; a sign that someone had violently shoved at the door, and its moorings creaked as she forced it from its place. Automatically, she stepped back, half expecting Max to come blasting out.

Nothing happened, so with clammy hands she opened the door.

He was sitting on the bed, his long legs spread out in front of him.

"Max."

At the sound of her voice, he moved. With the grace of a jungle feline, he swung his feet onto the floor and stood, then strode toward her. Not particularly quickly, nor casually. But with general purpose.

Victoria braced herself for the onslaught—the railing, the anger, the accusation.

He walked past her and out into the hallway without a word, without an acknowledgment.

"Max," she said again, turning after him.

He didn't pause, but continued on his way down the hall.

She would have thought him deaf or blind if it had not been for the expression in his eyes: dark and angry.

The hackney lurched to a violent halt, and Victoria heard the clatter and subsequent roll of a wooden stake by her foot. She looked across the dark interior, catching Sebastian's eye. "Shall we?" she asked.

"Most definitely," he replied, bending to retrieve his weapon. There was relish in his voice and amusement in his eyes, and she knew that the carriage ride home would be far more interesting than the one they'd just completed. Perhaps, at least then, he would keep his stake well in hand.

The pair slipped silently from Barth's vehicle, well hidden by convenient shrubbery that lined the wall of St. Heath's Row most distant from the house. Shadows, in concert with the sliver of a waning moon and dark clothing, made them invisible.

Victoria led the way along the wall to a particularly dark corner. A robust oak spread its shadow over the area, and blocked any view from the rear of the house. Sebastian stood flush against the tall stone relief and she climbed up to stand on his shoulders; then, once atop the wall, she reached down to pull him up.

Once over the cross-studded wall, she led the way to the second servants' entrance, where she knew the door would be unlocked. Verbena had been playing matchmaker with the lower footman at Grantworth House and the belowstairs maid at St. Heath's Row, both of whom were taking a postmidnight stroll through the gardens at this very moment.

Verbena had assured her mistress that the footman and the maid would be much too busy examining the night-blooming pink primroses to notice any trespassers. She had also ascertained, when arranging the assignation, that the Marquess of Rockley was expected to dine at home that evening and intended to remain in residence that night.

He had, in fact, declined any invitations for dinner or

parties since the ill-fated carriage ride during which they'd gone to view the night sky.

When Victoria had returned from her brief captivity this morning and begun to attend to matters other than Max, it had been with great skepticism and suspicion in regards to James. Either he had been fully aware and involved in her kidnapping—which would make him a vampire or, at the least, a member of the Tutela—or he had been ignorant of it, as he claimed.

According to Kritanu, James had called on her home the morning after the nighttime carriage ride, explaining that there had been an accident, he'd been knocked unconscious, and when he came to, Victoria—Mrs. Rockley, as he'd called her—was missing. According to Kritanu, the marquess had appropriately wrung his hands and paced the parlor as he accepted the blame for whatever had happened to her, begging that word should be sent to him the moment there was any news.

Victoria listened to Kritanu's description of the man's agitation with a skeptical ear, and decided that, instead of returning his call or sending word of her return, she would find out the truth her own way tonight. Unlike Max, Sebastian had been delighted to see her, and more than delighted to join her in the excursion.

Max she had not seen since he stalked past her, and she had no need for his company anyway. She'd kept herself busy the rest of the day, and had sent an urgent message to Wayren by pigeon. She prayed that the wise woman would have some advice or information about Lilith's prediction.

The unobtrusive servant's door was well oiled in preparation for late-night assignations, and Victoria led Sebastian through the narrow hallway. She'd never had occasion to traverse the backstairs area of St. Heath's

Row, but she obviously knew the layout of the portions of the house common to the marquess and marchioness.

When they came to a hallway that gave an option for right or left navigation, Victoria started off to the right . . . but a firm hand on her arm drew her back. "This way," Sebastian whispered, close to her ear.

"How do you know?" she whispered back. "You haven't spent as much time here as I have." She pointed. "The stairs are to the right."

An amused smile tipped his lips and she thought he was going to kiss her right there, to which she would have put an immediate stop. But he resisted, simply responding, "You might recall that I visited your maid in the servants' quarters while you were still staying here. She did, in fact, sleep four floors directly above us here. To the right is the kitchen. To the left are the stairs."

Chagrined, and reminded that Max had also had to correct her navigation more than once—she always seemed to get turned around when inside a building—she followed Sebastian as he swiftly moved down the left passage. And soon they came upon a narrow, steep staircase. He glanced down at her, but she sailed past him, nose in the air. Even *Illa* Gardella wasn't perfect. Once they were on the third floor, Victoria knew her way around the bedchambers.

Somewhere in the house, a floorboard creaked. A clock hummed, gearing itself up to toll the hour, and moments later, as they reached the third floor, Victoria heard the rolling strokes of two o'clock.

And she realized that the back of her neck was cold. She smiled in the dark.

He was here. He wouldn't need to drink the elixir at night, unless he expected to be near her.

Which he obviously didn't.

Stake in hand, holding it close to the loose black trousers she wore when she moved about at night, Victoria continued on her way. A myriad of thoughts ran through her mind as she, with Sebastian close enough behind that she felt the brush of his coat, eased through the rear hallway.

Of course James could be lying in wait for her, expecting such a visit. Or the undead she sensed might not be the new marquess at all. But there were ways to find out, and tonight she would do so once and for all. She knew he was in the house; the only question was what condition she might find him in.

When she and Sebastian reached the door to the marquess's dressing room, she opened it and slipped in. Once inside the chamber filled with clothing and the smell of male grooming, Victoria turned to Sebastian and planted a hand against his chest in a clear message. She'd already told him that this was her task, and that he needed to be watching for any unforeseen problems. This was a reminder that she expected him to stay put.

In the darkness, he grasped her wrist and she thought for a moment that he was going to silently demand to go with her. Or to tell her to be careful, or to try to kiss his way into changing her mind. None of which would be effective. He drew a breath, his chest expanding under her hand, and squeezed his fingers around her skin in a quick little caress. Then he reluctantly released her.

Good. At least the man had learned something.

Victoria cracked the door from the dressing room to the bedchamber. The back of her neck was frigid, and unless James had company in his chamber, she knew she had found her daytime vampire.

Silent as a spirit, sticking to the shadows, she moved across the floor. The thin soles of her black slippers slid across polished wood, and then found the cushier texture of a fringed rug. When she stood at the side of James's bed and heard his even breathing, she had a moment of doubt.

What vampire would be sleeping soundly during the night?

She'd at least expected to find him awake, watching her with those red eyes.

But he was actually snoring.

Victoria looked down at him, adjusting the stake in her grip. She could shove it into his chest with a quick thrust, and it would be all over. If she wasn't mistaken.

But why should she be? The last time she'd tried to stake someone who wasn't a vampire—not counting the time Sebastian had inserted himself between her and Beauregard—had been more than two years ago, when she'd mistaken Max for an undead. It had been her first time, and she'd been misled by the stereotypical description of a vampire that came from Polidori's novel.

Victoria raised the stake.

Then she pulled it back. If she was wrong, the stab would kill a mortal James.

She sighed. There was no help for it. She'd have to awaken the man.

Fumbling in the deep pocket of the tunic she wore over her trousers, she pulled out a small vial of holy water. This was as good a way to awaken him as any.

The splash on his forehead sent up a soft sizzle and a curl of steam, and his eyes flew open—wide and red.

"Good evening, James," Victoria said calmly. She had placed her hand around the front of his throat, using her weight to hold him down. She held the stake fisted directly over his chest. "I do hope I didn't wake you."

"You." He growled in a voice that sounded deeper and

more guttural than the one she was accustomed to. His fangs shot out, pale in the darkness.

"Before I drill this into your heart and send you to your fate, I do hope you'll answer one question for me." He didn't respond, and she tightened her hand around his throat. He coughed, but an undead couldn't be strangled, so it was merely a discomfort, not a threat. "Are you really James Lacy, Kentuckian?"

He smiled and shifted suddenly. She allowed him to throw off her hold, to let him think he might have a chance to escape. He'd probably tell her more if he did. They eyed each other; he had risen onto his knees on the bed, and she'd stepped back as if cowed. "What do you think?" he replied.

"I think not. You were much too gullible." She glanced at his nightshirt and her lip curled. "I don't believe I've ever had the pleasure of meeting an undead dressed for bed."

His smile widened, and those fangs poked into his lower lip. "If I had known you were coming, I wouldn't have bothered. Perhaps you'd like to join me?"

He lunged, and yanked her onto the bed next to him. She sprawled for a moment, then rolled onto her back, keeping the stake behind her hip. "No thank you. What did you do to the real James Lacy?"

The undead reached for her tunic, grabbing a good handful of the material, and jerked her up as if she were a doll. Victoria sagged, yet she was ready beneath her feigned weakness. It was a game, now. How much information could she get before he became suspicious or bored?

"It was our plan from the beginning—caught him when he got off the ship from America. Insisted that he take a ride, and relieved him of his papers and clothing. Then we fed on him." He laughed. "In fact, I'm feeling a bit hungry at the moment, Victoria Gardella. Did you think you could sneak in here and get away without me knowing?"

She rolled her eyes. "You were snoring. I could have turned you to ash before you even awoke."

"Is that so?" His eyes burned bloodred, and his fangs gleamed sharply.

She pulled her arm from beneath and met him as he lunged, shoving the stake into the center of his chest. "Yes, indeed," she told him as he froze, and then poofed into dust.

There was movement behind her, and she whirled to find Sebastian standing there. His stake was at the ready.

Victoria frowned. "I told you to stay back."

"I did. Mostly." He smiled, and her anger could do nothing but sap away. This was Sebastian, and either he wasn't as confident in her abilities as Max was . . . or he cared more.

She thought she knew which one it was.

"Should we clean up the ash?" he asked. "It stinks."

Victoria nodded. "Let's. And then there will be another strange disappearance of the Marquess of Rockley."

They brushed the dust onto a pillowcase. Then he poured it into the cold fireplace.

Victoria was waiting when he finished. The back of her neck was normal; there were no other vampires in the vicinity. The daytime vampire—at least, one of them— was dead. And so was the real Marquess of Rockley.

The hackney was parked at the prearranged location, and they made their way back to the vehicle without incident. No sooner had Victoria clambered in and settled in her seat, the door closing firmly behind Sebastian, than Barth started them off with a great leap.

Whether it was by accident or design, she'd never

know, but the lurch sent Sebastian onto her side of the vehicle instead of the bench politely across from her. Once
gracefully settling into his seat, he turned to face her. His
knees bumped gently against her right leg and his arm sidled along the back of the cushion behind her. His gloveless fingers jutted into the long, simple braid she'd tucked
into the back of her tunic, his thumb smoothing over the
sensitive skin at the nape of her neck.

The carriage was very dark, and there was only the
ambiguous illumination from the lantern that swayed at
the front of the vehicle. She didn't have the chance to
speak, or even to think—for, all at once, Sebastian was
there, kissing her.

His kiss was hungry, one that surprised her with its in-
tensity. One moment they were climbing politely into the
carriage, and the next, it was a tangle of lips and tongue,
and hands that seemed to be everywhere.

Hot and sleek, his mouth covered hers as he held her
face steady so he could delve and taste. Warm fingers settled at the base of her jaw, and Victoria raised her chin to
gasp for a quick breath before slipping back into the kiss,
fighting to keep back the red-edged memories threatening
the corner of her mind . . . the lull of pleasure snapped by
the sharp thrust of fangs . . . the pull of her blood as it
coursed through her veins . . . the bizarre sensation of
cold and warm lips against her skin.

She moaned softly, half in horror at the remembering,
at the inability to stop it . . . half with melting pleasure,
for this man knew where to touch her.

Battling back the horrific images, she forced herself to
explore Sebastian, to remind herself that it was he, and
not Beauregard. . . . She wove her fingers desperately
through his thick curls, arching up against his hard belly
and insistent erection as he straddled her thigh, the edge

of the bench slicing into her skin from beneath. His weight pressed gently against her hips, and she moved her hands so they eased up over the smooth muscles of his chest to curl at the top of his shoulders. Wide, strong shoulders beneath the coat, and under the dark linen . . . smooth, golden skin. Sebastian.

A light brush of hair stroked her cheek when his lips lifted, then fell to trace the curve of her jaw, nibbling and licking. His breath puffed hot and hard against her neck, and Victoria was aware of her own breath rising to meet his as she focused on the moment . . . the man. The sensations. Not the memories.

Barely aware of the carriage wheels rumbling beneath them, at last she allowed herself to fall into a spiral of urgent, slick kisses and to feel the skim of fresh air over bare skin as her tunic was lifted . . . warm, sure, possessive hands smoothing on her flesh, exploring and coaxing as she closed her eyes. The sensations mixed and whirled, and the coach seemed small and intimate as he stripped off his coat. She pulled his shirt from the waist of his pantaloons, at last feeling the warmth of flesh and the pull of muscle beneath a light dusting of hair. Her fingers slipped around, rediscovering the unyielding silver of the *vis bulla* that dangled from the hollow of his navel.

Release, relief, pleasure slid through her, loosening her limbs, making her feel liquid and warm. His mouth settled over a breast, bared by the tunic piled over her collarbones. The way his lips closed over her tight nipple, sucking gently and drawing it deep into slick warmth sent her shuddering and shivering on the bench.

He pulled away, settling himself over her, his face close. His linen shirt brushed over the tips of her breasts and she could see, just so, the half smile on his face.

"And so," he murmured, his mouth close, "it is yet another carriage ride for us."

She smiled and then gave a little gasp as his hand moved down between them, sliding beneath the band of her trousers. He watched her, his face jolting and swaying with the motion of the hackney as his fingers, sure and firm, found the place they sought. Victoria's breath caught at the first touch, and then she felt herself gathering up, tight and ready, as he stroked and slipped and slid down in the heat.

"Now this," he said, his voice filled with amusement, "is the perfect way to end a night on the hunt."

She closed her eyes, fell into the pleasure that surged and opened inside her, pushed away the worries, the memories, the image of dark, angry eyes . . . She tensed, and reached between them to lift his hand away.

Then there was a sudden lurch and near tip as the carriage barreled around a corner and Sebastian, half on top of her, lost his footing and nearly sprawled on the floor. The unexpected motion brought her back to reality, and when he would have pressed back down against her, she placed her hands on his chest. His heart raced beneath her fingers; she felt it through the linen shirt.

"Sebastian," she said as he would have bent to her again. "I . . . it's . . . I can't."

He stilled against her, and she felt his chest rising and falling, as though he had to decipher her words. "What?" His voice was . . . wounded. He didn't sit back, but remained poised next to her, nearly on top of her. "What is it, Victoria? What's changed?" He gave a little laugh; it sounded forced, she thought. "You always made it a bit of a challenge, of course, and it was fun for both of us . . . but this is . . . different."

"I . . ." She didn't like that she sounded weak, but she

knew . . . she couldn't continue on the path they were going. She was confused, and frightened . . . and empty. She couldn't banish the image of those black, furious eyes.

Then, suddenly, before she could think of how to respond, Sebastian said something in French, so violent and sharp that she knew it was filthy. He grasped her shoulders now—not in a gentle, loverlike way, but with the need to know. "Beauregard. Was it Beauregard? Did he . . . touch you?"

Yes, yes, he had . . . but she remembered few details. She didn't want to remember them, didn't want to know enough to be able to answer his question. Victoria closed her eyes; what had happened with Beauregard had been ugly, horrific . . . but it wasn't the reason.

It wasn't because of Beauregard that she felt empty and lost.

"My God, you're shaking," he said softly. "Victoria, I'm sorry." He gathered her into his arms there on the bench, pressing her face to his chest, and wrapped her tightly. "I didn't know."

Suddenly, before she could stop it, her emotions burst forth and the tears came. The sobs of worry and angst, of fear and horror . . . what was happening to her . . . what had she done . . . loneliness . . . sorrow . . . confusion . . .

Sebastian held her, let her weep into his shirt until it was sopping. His face pressed into the top of her head, the warmth of his body comforting. The strength of his arms, and the feel of his hands, cupping the back of her head.

He murmured something into her hair, and pressed a soft kiss onto her scalp.

So unlike Sebastian . . . to be serious, to hold her without wanting more, to be silent.

"What did you say?" she said, pulling away and swiping angrily at her tears.

"I don't have a handkerchief, but I still have your glove," he said, giving her a rueful smile. "The one I tricked from you at the Silver Chalice."

She blinked, her eyelids swollen and her nose streaming unattractively. "My glove."

"I've kept it, and the other one I took later, too. Unfortunately," he said, his smile wavering in the uncertain light, "they aren't a matched set. I seem to have a penchant for baring your left hand. Among other places." He brushed the hair from her face. "I'm in love with you. I think I have been ever since you showed me your *vis bulla* in order to find out where the Book of Antwartha was."

"You tricked me into showing you," she said. Her mind spun.

"It wasn't a trick . . . I gave you what you wanted. Even though"—he chucked her lightly under the chin—"you still haven't given me what I want."

"What is that?"

"Don't you know?"

Her heart thumped madly, and she curled her fingers around his hands, nestled there in her lap. She nodded. "I think I do. But . . ." She drew in her breath. There were so many things. . . . "I don't know what's going to happen . . . to me." Her voice caught, but she forced herself on. "I may not be . . . myself . . . much longer." She couldn't put the thoughts into words.

God, please let me hear from Wayren soon!

"Lilith may be right," he said, "but she lies well. And either way, Victoria . . . it would not be the first time I have loved a vampire."

Twenty

Wherein Lady Melly's Machinations Meet an Unexpected End

Victoria woke late the next morning with swollen eyes and the remnants of dreams she didn't care to recall.

There was no word from Wayren, and Max had not made an appearance. Sebastian had reluctantly left her at the town house early that morning to return to wherever it was that he was staying.

Kritanu gave her the impression that he was aware of Max's whereabouts. But when Victoria broached the subject, she was met with a gentle shake of the head and closed lips.

Well, if Max wouldn't give her the chance to apologize, to explain why she'd been so certain—and that she'd been *right!*—that the evening had been a trap meant for her as well as him, so be it. He could sulk and brood and stay away.

Victoria had more important things to concern herself with. Besides, if Max were around, she'd be forced to confess the whole situation to him, including Lilith's frightening prediction. Which she felt no real need to do.

She hadn't forgotten the fact that he'd been holding a stake, ready to put it to use when she woke up back in the Consilium.

And that was what she kept telling herself, over and over. And over.

Max was out of her life. For good.

He doesn't want anybody.

Instead, she had to face the facts. Her night vision had become much clearer. If Lilith was right, and the vampire blood was taking over inside her . . . was it something she could fight? Something she could stop? Or was she destined to become undead?

The possibility was simply too horrific to consider. It just couldn't happen.

She wouldn't allow it.

The fact that Wayren hadn't responded to a message sent by pigeon caused Victoria even greater trepidation. Wayren's pigeons were trained to find her anywhere, and always seemed to do so, and to provide a response within twenty-four hours regardless of where she was. Thus Victoria began to fear that the wise woman had abandoned her as well.

Late that afternoon she sat grumpy and fidgeting in Lady Melly's parlor, listening to the three cronies discuss the details of George IV's coronation ceremony, which was to be held in a matter of days.

It was no surprise that the topic dominated their conversation, for the coronation of the man who'd been known as Prinny, nearly eighteen months after he'd ascended to the throne, was to be the greatest, most expensive and flamboyant crowning of an English king.

"What will you wear, Victoria?" asked Lady Nilly, leaning forward as if in anticipation of some great fashion secret.

"I don't believe I've been invited," she replied tartly, unconcerned with civility today. "And I do not plan to attend."

"But of course you have been invited! The only person of Quality in all of the land who is not to attend is the queen herself," Lady Melly chided her. "And if you stay away, you may be aligned with her in the eyes of the ton. That would not be fitting for the Marchioness of Rockley, Victoria, to take the side of Queen Caroline."

"It is *abominable* that the working and trades cheer that disgusting creature whenever she goes about the City, giving her false support," Lady Nilly said, her nose raised as if she smelled something objectionable. Perhaps it was the bouquet of daisies on the table near her tea. Victoria had always disliked the smell of the sunny flowers.

"It's only because they despise Prinny—er, His Majesty—that they love her. Or claim they do, which I freely doubt. If any of them got within a king's yard of that smelly sow, they should run the other direction and reexamine their thoughts," Lady Melly said primly.

"If the woman would wash or change her undergarments, or even comb her hair, perhaps His Majesty would allow her near him . . . but she does not." Duchess Winnie's multiple chins trembled, but she was not in danger of being accused of living in a glass house. "It's a simple matter of grooming," she said, smoothing her perfect skirts pointedly. The duchess, who was also a woman of large proportion, was always supremely clothed and coiffed before she stepped from her chamber. "I vow the queen's goats are better groomed than she."

The other ladies laughed, and even Victoria couldn't hold back a little smile. The gossip about the queen wasn't completely mean-spirited. The woman had made no friends from the moment she arrived from Germany to wed the man who at the time was the Prince Regent.

Victoria remembered the story of Caroline of
Brunswick's first meeting with Prinny, in which the
prince had come face to face with the sloppy, putrid
woman and said, quite loudly, to the Baron of Malmes-
bury, "Harris, I do not feel well. Pray get me a glass of
brandy." He'd not ceased drinking for the three days up to
and including the wedding. He'd passed out on his wedding night, and Caroline had left him on the floor.

It was no wonder there was enmity between the two.

A knock came at the parlor door, and Lady Melly
straightened expectantly. Victoria tightened her fingers
around an innocent teacup, knowing that her mother's anticipation could bode no good for her.

But then she recalled that it couldn't be James. He'd
been turned into a pile of dust and would no longer be at
the mercy of her mother's machinations.

Thus, Lady Melly was bound to be disappointed—in
more ways than one. The Grantworth House butler entered the room on command, carrying a silver tray, on
which rested a thick white paper, folded and sealed with
a blob of yellow wax and an unidentifiable crest. "This
missive for Lady Rockley," he intoned.

Victoria nearly knocked over a vase of sweet-smelling
lilies in her alacrity to seize the message. An excuse to
leave, she hoped, before the droves of afternoon callers
began their never-ending influx.

The message was simple, and in an elegant hand that
Victoria recognized with relief: *Your carriage awaits
without.*

"I must go," she said, without sitting back down.

"What is it?" asked Lady Nilly. But she was overrun
by Lady Melly.

"Surely not now!" exclaimed that genteel lady. "It is
too early."

Victoria fixed her gaze on her parent. "I'm sorry, Mother, but it is of an urgent nature."

"But you cannot," Lady Melly started, but this time Victoria was more firm.

"I must."

Her mother stood. "Surely it has nothing to do with that Monsieur Vioget you insist upon allowing to stay around," Melly said, her voice sharp. "He is no better than those clinging vines that we have to cut away from the chimney top."

Victoria blinked in astonishment that her mother was even aware of such a mundane occurrence.

"I must say, Victoria, that it is just too ridiculous that you encourage him! Why he has no title and isn't even British, and rather a bit slick in the tongue, if you ask me."

That was one way to describe it, Victoria thought as her lips threatened to twitch.

"His tailor is quite excellent," Lady Nilly offered. "And he does rather remind me of a kind gentleman who once saved me from a vampire . . . or at least, I dreamed he—"

"Do *hush*, Nilly."

"Mother, I suggest that you become used to seeing Sebastian about," Victoria said firmly. "For it is quite possible—*quite* possible—that he will someday become your son by law. And now," she continued rapidly, shocked that she'd actually said those words, let alone thought them through, "I really must leave. Don't try to stop me." Why had she said that?

"Victoria Anastasia!" Lady Melly shot to her feet. Teacups rattled and brown liquid slopped merrily. "How dare you take that tone—"

"Good-bye, Mother. I'll be in touch soon." And with that, Victoria whirled out of the parlor, fairly sprinting down the hall to the front door.

The sounds of screeching voices and gasping breaths faded as she darted out the front entrance in a most undignified manner. Her carriage was indeed waiting, its midnight blue paint sleek and shiny under the late-afternoon sun. Gold and silver trim gleamed when the coachman opened the door, and Victoria climbed in.

She didn't expect to actually find Wayren in the carriage, but there she was. The woman was of an indeterminate age—she appeared older than Victoria, but younger than Lady Melly. Yet she had been there when Aunt Eustacia had taken up the *vis bulla*. The satchel that always seemed to contain more books and manuscripts than appeared possible sat like a lumpy toad next to her.

A brittle brown-spotted scroll open on her lap, Wayren looked up from behind perfectly square glasses, squinted, and then removed them as Victoria settled in her seat. "Hello, Victoria. How are you?"

The words, so simple, and often spoken—and responded to—without regard to their real meaning, were said with such sincerity, and the expression in her gray-blue eyes was so kind, that Victoria felt the threat of tears sting, and the inside of her nostrils tingled with emotion. She blinked hard, and then answered with pure honesty. "I don't know. I don't think . . . perhaps not so well."

Wayren nodded. Gravity rendered her face smooth. "Aye, I can see that is so."

The carriage started with a gentle lunge, and Victoria looked at her companion. "You received my message. Can you tell me . . . is Lilith correct? Will I . . . am I . . . ?"

"The reason I did not arrive sooner—for I received your missive yesterday, of course—was that I spent some time with Ylito to see if he was aware of anything that might stop . . . or slow . . . the effect of the undead blood.

That would, you see, give us more time to determine a cure. If there is one."

"And?"

Wayren shook her head slowly. "There's nothing he can do. But Victoria," she said, and to her surprise, the older woman reached across the space and clasped her fingers around Victoria's wrist. Her hand was bare, and her grip closed over the skin above Victoria's gloves. The touch sent warmth and ease flowing through her; Victoria felt steadier than she had in some time. "You have already shown the strength to fight back the impulse of the immortal blood that threatened to take over. You are well armed, and you are strong. Though Ylito has nothing in his laboratory that might protect you, I believe that it is possible . . . more than possible . . . that you are strong enough to conquer this trial."

A deep wave of disappointment and fear washed over her, despite Wayren's comforting grip. There was nothing. Nature, in the form of tainted undead blood, would take its course. There was nothing that could be done.

Victoria drew back, and in spite of the warm summer afternoon, her flesh felt chilled when Wayren released her arm. Nausea churned in her belly. She'd expected, she'd believed, that Wayren would be the answer to her problem—that the mystical woman who seemed to know everything, or at least where to find out about it, would arrive with a potion or a serum that would wash away the vampire blood.

But of course. How could she be so foolish? If there were such an elixir, she could have ingested it after her experience with Beauregard.

She could have given it to Phillip.

Victoria blinked hard. So it would come full circle then. Her mistakes, her selfishness back to haunt her. Her fate would be the same as Phillip's, the innocent man. She just hoped someone staked her before she did something terrible.

The memory of Max, holding the stake when she'd awakened at the Consilium, refreshed in her mind. He would have done it without hesitation.

Wayren watched her with steady eyes, soft with worry. She didn't speak, as though knowing that Victoria had to assimilate it all on her own. She merely waited as the carriage rolled through the streets.

"Will I . . ." she began, then had to start again. It was better not to think of herself . . . but to keep the thoughts removed. "A vampire who drinks from a mortal is damned for eternity. Will you ensure that I . . ." Her voice clogged. All of a sudden, her future was becoming real to her. The possibility that she'd forced away, refused to consider, disbelieved . . . its reality was reflected in the expression of Wayren's eyes and in her thinned mouth.

"Victoria." The other woman's voice, stern and sharp, penetrated the fog of pink that threatened the edge of her vision. "You cannot let the power of evil slide into you. You cannot succumb."

"But vampirism isn't a choice; it's not something that can be fought off. I know that."

"No," Wayren said. "It isn't. Once the vampire blood is ingested, it overtakes the mortal blood in the human and . . . you know what happens. The person becomes undead. But that didn't happen with you, Victoria. Against every odd, and every expectation, it didn't happen." Her eyes were serious. "Why?"

"Because of the two *vis bullae*."

"That's what we suspect, yes," Wayren replied. "But we don't know for certain. Ylito and I have discussed your situation, and there is no real explanation for it, other than the two *vis bullae*, and the power and strength—both physical and mental—that goes along with them. That's the only thing it could be. But there's something else to consider, and this is why I think there could be more hope than you think."

Victoria was almost afraid to ask, so she remained silent.

"Normally when one is turned undead, when they awaken, as you did, the vampire blood has already taken over the entirety of the body and made the mortal immortal. But when you awoke, that wasn't the case. You were still mortal. You'd been spared. But now, that vampire blood is still within you, fighting to take over. That is what makes your situation different, Victoria. You're awake, and aware, and the battle for your soul is waging within you. The two strength amulets you wear have bought you the time . . . time for you to fight the urge to become immortal, and evil. Both physically and in your soul. Your mind."

Victoria shivered. "Is there a chance, then? With this evil growing inside me . . . is there a chance?"

Before Victoria knew it, Wayren was next to her on the seat. She grasped her shoulders with strong, slender fingers and looked deeply into her eyes. "Every mortal has the portent for evil deep inside them. Every man and woman makes choices for his or her self, for *self*, Victoria. It is only when those decisions outweigh all others; when they become the driving force, the normal state for that mortal, does evil win. *Self-service drives all malevolence*—but it will only succeed in winning if you allow it. *Do not allow it.*" She gave her a little shake, and the red mist faded. "I believe you can fight this away . . . physically. And spiritually. Do not allow it to take over, Victoria. I believe you can stop it."

* * *

Despite her nebulous information, Wayren showed no indication that she meant to leave London. In fact, she told Victoria that she'd sent for two of the other Venators, Brim and Michalas, to come immediately to London from Paris, where they'd been investigating some heightened demon activity. Victoria knew the two men well, and rather than being annoyed by the wise woman's presumption, she was relieved that she'd done so. They should arrive within a week, and would be able to provide extra support in light of Lilith's presence in London and whatever her plans were.

And although Wayren took her own quarters when she stayed in London, she remained with Victoria into the evening and they dined together with Kritanu. They had just finished dinner when Sebastian was announced, and, despite the fact that the Venators rarely paid attention to the rules of polite society, Victoria and Wayren met him in the parlor.

If Wayren was surprised at the way Sebastian greeted Victoria—with an embrace and a lengthy, well-placed kiss on the back of her hand—she gave no indication. Even when he took his place next to Victoria on the sofa, as if he were a love-struck swain—which was so far from Sebastian's persona that Victoria chuckled to herself at the thought—Wayren didn't appear to notice.

"I've just recalled something that I believe you will find very interesting," Sebastian told Victoria.

She sipped from the blush-tinged sherry she had poured, feeling the comfort of his warm thigh brushing next to hers. "What is it?" she asked, throwing aside the gloom that had threatened her since Wayren's arrival. "Have you found a new way to tie a neck cloth?"

"But of course not," he told her lightly . . . yet there was a bit of real affront in his voice. That surprised her, and she looked more closely into his tigerish eyes. A prickle began to worm its way down her spine. He'd been more . . . sensitive? serious? . . . as of late, and while Victoria had been deft at keeping their kisses to little more than kisses, and her corset fastened, she knew something was going to change. Soon.

She felt as if the decision had been made for her that afternoon, when she confirmed their engagement to her mother.

After all, he loved her. Or claimed he did . . . there was still a niggling suspicion about Sebastian; she'd refused to trust him for so long.

The only problem was the uncertainty of her future. Victoria felt a chill wash over her, and the unpleasant roiling return to her belly. She took a bigger gulp of the sherry than she'd intended, and realized that Sebastian had continued.

"When George Starcasset was in Italy this last year, not only did he make the acquaintance of Queen Caroline . . . but he became one of her favorites." He raised an eyebrow and gave Victoria a complacent smile. "It's more than a bit convenient that he and Sarafina Regalado have returned to England at the same time the queen has . . . after having been fairly banished for years."

Understanding burst over her, and she caught her breath. "And how telling that she should return from her self-exile in Italy just in time to see her husband crowned King of England." They looked at each other, and Victoria grasped his hand.

That was it. It had to be Lilith's plan: to invade the coronation of the king, where all of the most powerful men in England, the most powerful country in the world, would be gathered at one time.

But why?

Twenty-one

Wherein Our Heroine Takes a Swim

If Lady Melly found the evaporation of Victoria's reluctance to attend the coronation odd, she was too well-bred
to say anything in regards to the change of heart. Most
likely she assumed her sage motherly advice had
achieved the appropriate influence. Moreover, her attention was taken up by the equally sudden disappearance of
her favorite candidate for son by law.

Victoria, of course, remained mum on the topic of
James Lacy, except to promise her mother that if the man
attended the coronation, she would allow Lady Melly to
finagle a seat for her in the presence of the marquess. And
that she would be her most charming.

She felt that was a safe promise to make.

While Melly and her cronies dithered and dressed,
gossiped and coiffed, Victoria was making plans.

She'd seen no sign of Max this last week, and although
she almost missed his arrogant, all-knowing comments
related to her plans, she realized she didn't need him
there at all. Her feelings were bruised and raw, but there

was little she could do but focus on now, and then the future. She reminded herself that, although Max had walked away from her and the Venators in the past, he had done so only temporarily. He'd always returned.

But this time, she suspected he would not. He had no reason to; he was no longer a Venator. And he'd made it clear he wanted nothing to do with Victoria in any respect. And apparently, with Kritanu and Wayren's blessings—if their reticence in discussing the subject was any indication.

Wayren, Sebastian, and Kritanu had talked with Victoria about their suspicions and what the threat could be, and how it might be carried out. They'd all agreed it was likely not so much a plan to control members of the crème de la crème of England, as to kill some or all of them. Queen Caroline (who, Victoria suspected, based on her interaction with George, was either a member of the Tutela or a vampire herself) certainly hated her husband enough to do so. Perhaps the queen had offered Lilith protection. After all, that was the purpose of the Tutela, was it not? To protect, and serve, vampires.

But nothing was certain, so all they could do was be in attendance at the festivities, and be prepared for anything.

The day of the coronation was a hot, sticky one, as is common in July.

Victoria abhorred the fact that she was expected to dress as befit her station instead of in something more comfortable for fighting vampires or other threats. At least she wasn't counted among the king's closest advisers and compatriots, for they were required to follow his majesty's example and dress in the style of his predecessors, the Tudors. They would be wearing heavy brocaded and laced ensembles with sleeves slashed to show different fabric beneath, neck ruffs, and abominably wide and stiff farthingaled skirts. Not for the first time, Victoria wondered how her ancestor, Lady Catherine Gardella, could ever have been an effective Venator with such fussy and heavy gowns.

Yet Victoria's own dress had to be not only fitting to her wealth and title, but also serviceable in the event that she had to be more active. In this case, Verbena had come to her aid by supervising the creation of a frock that had a skirt split into wide trousers. The trouser legs were full enough to be mistaken for the bell of her skirt, and there were two flaps of fabric in the front and the back that fell like aprons over the split of the gown. They looked like embroidered decorations, they blended so cunningly with the rest of the dress. If necessary, Victoria could remove them to give her greater freedom.

"It's a shame that Brim and Michalas haven't yet arrived—Wayren expects them any day now—but I don't expect anything to happen at the coronation itself," Victoria said to Sebastian and Kritanu in the foyer of the town house. She pulled on her gloves and checked to make certain the several stakes were arranged on her person. Her *kadhara* knife she slipped into its sheath under her skirt. They were waiting for the carriage, which would take them to Westminster Abbey. "But it's best if we're prepared in any case." She glanced at the crossbow Kritanu carried, and counted more than a dozen wooden bolts in the quiver he would wear under a cloak.

"Of course not," said a peremptory voice. "The vampires won't be able to enter the holy space of the abbey."

Victoria's stomach flipped and she felt, to her great mortification, warmth flush over her cheeks. But one look at Max, who'd materialized from the back hallway near the servants' quarters, served to destroy her surprise and delight.

Although he was dressed appropriately for attending the coronation—in a splendid ruby-and-garnet brocade waist-coat, with a crisp white shirt and black neck cloth, and a coat that rivaled Sebastian's perfectly tailored attire—he didn't acknowledge her presence by even a supercilious glance down his long, straight nose. Instead, he directed his comment to Wayren, who, to Victoria's surprise, had appeared along with him.

"Normally, I would agree with you, Max," she said coolly, determined to force his attention to her. "But with the use of the special elixir, the vampires have been able to do many other things that they normally cannot. I prefer to make no assumptions in this case."

He looked down at her then, his expression carefully blank—even his eyes. They remained flat and dark, without even the hint of anger from before. His mouth was hard and thin. It felt odd—as though they were the only two in the space, as though some subtle struggle was happening . . . something that she couldn't quite identify.

"I hardly think that Lilith has allowed her entire army to partake of that dangerous serum," Max replied loftily. "It would rather be like cutting off one's nose to spite one's face. But, nevertheless, to the abbey we will go. And, after that, to Westminster Hall where the feast shall be held."

He turned as though by some magical means he'd sensed the arrival of the carriage. Or perhaps he simply faced the door, whose glass sidelights exposed the sight of the vehicle.

To Victoria's surprise, Wayren joined them in the carriage. "I am not able to fight," she told Victoria. "But I will ride there to learn the direction and survey the area, and then return to the house in the event that Brim and Michalas should arrive."

Not for the first time, Victoria wondered about the ageless woman, but now was not the time to allow her mind to be clogged by questions she'd never have answered. Instead, she and Wayren sat across from Sebastian and Max, while Kritanu insisted on riding on the exterior jump seat, serving as footman. Because of the potential threat, Barth had been asked to play coachman today, which was evidenced by the abrupt launch of the vehicle.

Sebastian had been uncharacteristically quiet, and Victoria felt his attention settle on her, lift, and then return. He looked magnificent, with his rich golden neck cloth tied in a ridiculously intricate knot and a bronze-and-copper waistcoat beneath a chocolate coat, and dark trousers. Rich leonine curls, tighter in the sticky heat, contrasted with the dark squabs of the interior of the coach, gleaming like honey on the window side, and lush brown on the other. He looked like a burnished topaz statue, but the mischievous smile that usually lit his eyes and tweaked his full lips was gone.

Victoria glanced at Max, who was glaring out the window. Taller in the seat than his companion—though just as broad of shoulder—he was a dark foil, with his sharper features, swarthy skin, and slash of dark brows. He'd pulled his hair back in that unfashionable club, rather than letting it fall in thick, unruly waves; perhaps it was too long for him to let it hang free. His jaw appeared hard and set as usual, but he'd relaxed his mouth since their exchange in the foyer. Victoria felt a little shiver run through her belly at the sudden, unexpected reminder of the one time he'd kissed her, against the cold, wet stone wall. He'd barely looked at her since, and certainly hadn't tried to repeat it.

Unlike Sebastian.

She looked between the two men without appearing to do so, a strange prickling rolling down her spine. Odd to see them, next to each other, facing her—as though to showcase their contrasting personalities, appearance, history. They were so different, and yet . . . much alike.

Her heart was beating harder and she didn't know why.

Or perhaps she did.

Her stomach filled with butterflies, and she looked away.

The speed of the coach had slowed because of the crush of spectators. They surged and waned like ocean waves, held back from the canopied walkway that had been erected for His Majesty. "Two million yards of Russian duck fabric to cover it!" she remembered hearing Lady Winnie screech, her small eyes round with disbelief.

As a peer, Victoria should have been part of the coronation procession, but of course it was more prudent for her to remain apart and prepared to engage. No doubt Lady Melly would have something to say about her absence, but that could be attended to later.

They arrived at Westminster Abbey more than an hour before the king was due to arrive. This gave them time to look around and observe the site. Wayren left with Barth shortly after, promising to send him back with the carriage as soon as she returned to the house.

Victoria and Sebastian happened to be near the main entrance to the abbey when a large, ornate coach arrived, thirty minutes before the king was due to make an appearance.

"Her Majesty, Queen Caroline!"

Exchanging looks, they hurried over and watched

the corpulent queen clamber heavily down from her conveyance.

"Good God, she looks ill," murmured someone next to Victoria.

She and Sebastian hurried closer, stakes at the ready.

As the queen approached the massive entrance to the abbey, the crowd falling back to allow her passage—or, perhaps, to move upwind—the doors slammed closed. Five burly men, dressed as pages, stood in front of them, barring her way.

"As Queen of England, I demand that you remove yourselves," proclaimed Caroline in her heavy German accent.

"By order of the sovereign king, we refuse to allow you entrance." The five men, much too large to be pages and who were later admitted to be prizefighters, stood nearly as wide as they were tall, effectively blocking her entrance.

Victoria and Sebastian moved closer, swiftly pushing through the crowd, heedless of civility. They were in time to see the queen beckon to her cortege, and six members of her party moved forward. "Remove them from my path," ordered the queen. "No one shall prevent me from attending *my husband's* coronation."

Her guards did as they were bid, and when Victoria saw the ease with which they shoved away and held back the five massive prizefighters, she looked at Sebastian. Clearly, they were undead, complete with superhuman strength and the benefits of the special elixir.

The queen had planned well.

Victoria needed only a moment to decide what to do. Taking advantage of the tumult caused by the queen's insistence, she darted off to the side. There was another door near the front of the abbey, and she was able to slip through quickly.

Smiling grimly, Sebastian was close behind her, and they made their way to the inside of the main entrance.

The doors were opening, and those inside the abbey didn't realize it was the queen attempting to gain entrance. Victoria and Sebastian hurried over to the door, pushing through throngs of people talking and choosing seats as they awaited the king and his procession.

When the doors at last surged open, Victoria stood on the side of the threshold. She was close enough to see the details of the queen's heavily beaded robe as she put one foot forward, onto the holy ground.

And then stopped, as though struck.

Shock and surprise flashed over her face, and she tried again . . . but the pain must have been too much, for she could move no further. Her face twisted in a horrible grimace, and her porcine eyes squinted in pain.

Max was right again. Of course.

Victoria eased forward, facing the queen, for everyone else had fallen away and was watching in horror and shock. Keeping her stake hidden in the folds of her skirt, Victoria said in a low voice, "You cannot enter here, Your Majesty." This was not the time or place to engage openly with an undead.

"Get out of my way."

Caroline looked at her, and Victoria knew at once what was happening. At this close proximity, she could see the way the queen's skin sagged, as if dripping from her skull. In fact, the entire massive person of the royal sagged, looking gray and quite unhealthy. She was dying, and Victoria knew it had to be because of the elixir. She'd probably been taking it for months while in Italy. It was just as Lilith predicted.

Would her other prediction come true?

Victoria pushed that unpleasant thought away, and remained facing the queen. As she looked at her more closely, she saw the flash of a shadow in her eyes. She'd seen a glimpse of something similar in James's irises on occasion, but had thought nothing of it until now, when the same look flickered in Caroline's. The sign of an undead, noticeable only at close proximity . . . there one moment, and gone the next. A look she thought she'd seen somewhere else as well. But where?

She could worry about that later; now Victoria moved slightly, showing her stake to the queen. "Step back, Your Majesty, or I will be forced to use this." Again, she kept her voice low, and only for the ears of the royal.

Assassinating the queen, vampire though she was, would be difficult to explain.

Caroline focused her eyes on her. They were burning red now, and the very tips of her fangs were revealed, poking into her lower lip. But there was nothing she could do.

"You cannot enter," Victoria said again, and moved closer. Glancing at the gathering crowd, she added, "The king has decreed it."

The queen had no choice. She stepped back, her face a mask of fury and pain. There was no grace in her movements as she turned and lurched heavily down the stairs to her waiting carriage. No one dared approach her, and as the crowds watched and whispered behind cupped hands, Victoria felt Sebastian's arm slip around her waist.

He urged her off quickly before anyone could ask why and how she had managed to keep the queen from entering Westminster Abbey when five prizefighters had not been able to.

And, as it turned out, the official report published in the papers and letters described the altercation as happening outside of the abbey, on the steps, with the five men holding off the queen's procession on their own. There was never any mention of a beautiful young woman with dark hair and a stick in her hand.

Shortly after the queen's disappearance came the news that the king was to be delayed due to a torn piece of clothing, and after that, the rest of the coronation ceremony—though horribly long and boring in Victoria's opinion—passed without incident.

Not until nearly three o'clock did the party move from the abbey to Westminster Hall, with the newly crowned king and his twenty-seven-foot train. The train was embroidered with gold thread, and the pages (real pages, not the prizefighters) who managed the long length of fabric kept it spread wide so that all of its glory could be admired.

The king tottered a bit when he at last left the abbey; sweat streamed down his face and he looked pallid and gray. However, Victoria knew that was not due to anything other than an excessive amount of fancy clothing— including unseasonable ermine fur—and an extremely long, hot day. The king of England was not a vampire.

Nor was he dead.

But Victoria was quite certain that he, and possibly others of his trusted advisors, were in great danger.

In the hall, three hundred people ate from long tables that traversed the length of the vast, high-ceilinged space. Victoria consumed little in her attempt to move about and keep her attention honed for any unusual happening. Still, it was daylight, and the more she thought about it, the more she realized that if anything else was planned, it would happen after the sun went down.

"When the sun goes down," said a deep voice in her ear, almost an echo of her thoughts. Victoria nearly jumped and turned to find Max behind her. He still wore that hooded expression, and refused to meet her eyes. He seemed, instead, to be fascinated by her earlobe . . . or, more likely, something beyond her shoulder.

"Of course," Victoria replied stiffly. "Lilith wasn't foolish enough to think that the queen could enter the abbey, even if Caroline herself thought she could. I don't believe for one minute that that was the extent of Lilith's plan."

"The king," Max continued as if she hadn't spoke, "should be leaving the hall shortly to return to Carleton House. The sun will just be setting. I suspect that will be the time we'll need to be our most vigilant."

"I've already come to that conclusion," Victoria snapped, then realized he'd gone, slinking away into the crowd before she could reply. "*We?*" she added in the direction to which he'd disappeared.

She turned away and found herself face-to-face with Lady Melly, who wore a forbidding expression. "Where have you been?" she asked with a smile on her face and a bite to her voice. In fact, the pleasant smile necessitated that her teeth remained ground together, and the words came out rather . . . clenched. "I've hardly seen you since we sat for dinner, and you certainly didn't attend us during the procession."

"I told you, Mother, my slipper became soiled and I had to return home just before the procession started in order to change it. You wouldn't have wanted me to attend the coronation with soiled slippers, would you?" Victoria lied blithely.

"Gwendolyn Starcasset has been looking all over for you," added Lady Melly in a slightly mollified voice. "Do come and make your greeting to her so that she will stop prattling to me about her wedding plans. I daresay," she continued over her shoulder as she started off, towing Victoria behind her, "it's as if no one has ever married an earl before. And Brodebaugh isn't all that is, but she certainly can say nothing but praise for him."

Victoria allowed her mother to drag her through the crowds to their places at the long table. To her surprise, she found Sebastian present, with Gwendolyn and Brodebaugh. He appeared to be fully enjoying his meal, and Victoria realized how hungry she was, despite the bit of food she'd already had. It had been a long day, and, if she and Max were correct, it would be even longer before the night was through.

Thus convinced to ease on her vigilance for a time, Victoria sat next to Gwen and proceeded to field questions about where she'd been and what she thought of the ceremony . . . and had she seen Rockley?

Victoria could only answer in the negative, and instead turned the conversation back to her friend's favorite topic: her nuptials, which were to take place in three days.

"I daresay, I've slept nary a wink, between plans for the coronation and my wedding," Gwen said, smiling. Victoria thought her expression still looked a bit weary, and she wondered if all was well with Brodebaugh.

Or George. He and Sara were conspicuously absent.

But before she had a chance to ask Gwendolyn about any of them, she caught sight of Kritanu. He was in a balcony overlooking the diners, and he tended to stand out due to his darkly complected appearance. He seemed to be gesturing to her.

"Excuse me, Mother," Victoria said, leaning toward Melly. "I thought I saw Rockley." The excuse was guaranteed to justify her exit, and when Lady Melly's face snapped toward the direction Victoria indicated, her daughter took the opportunity to escape.

Kritanu met Victoria and said, "The king is readying to leave." She glanced toward the table where George IV sat, and her companion continued, "I heard the order given moments ago. I've managed to obtain a position as footman to one of the coaches in the procession."

Victoria nodded. "Be safe," she told him. "Do you know where Max is?"

"He'll be there." Kritanu disappeared in the crowd of people, leaving Victoria to try to catch Sebastian's attention.

Outside of Westminster Hall, the sun had dipped to the edge of the horizon. As the king was climbing into his coach, the news came floating back to the bystanders: two overturned carriages had created a great accident, blocking the route by which the king usually drove to Carleton House.

He would have to take a different course, through the slums of Westminster.

Victoria caught Sebastian's eye and nodded. This had to be it.

With Barth's assistance, they obtained saddled horses and started off in the direction the king would be traveling, able to move faster and more easily than a coach and procession.

"We'll get there first and scout out the area," Victoria said to Kritanu as they rode past him and down a smaller side street so as to escape notice from the crowds. The sight of a lady riding astride—thanks to her split skirt— would cause just as much attention as the king's cortege; possibly more.

Victoria hadn't ridden astride in a saddle for years, and doing so immediately reminded her of Phillip. The sum-

mer she'd first met him, long before either were old
enough to be thinking of marriage or courting, he'd been
riding haphazardly through the meadows between their
families' adjoining estates. She'd met him when he fell
from the horse and he received a scolding from her . . .
and then, later, he promised to take her riding.

At any rate, Victoria was a confident enough horse-
woman to make her way through the streets, although Sebastian was far ahead of her. Since the attention of those
who were interested in such things was on the king's path,
the side streets were deserted of bystanders and the riders
were able to move swiftly and attract little attention.

But when they arrived in the dirtiest, most dangerous
part of Westminster, where the crowds had already
formed in anticipation of their sovereign's unprecedented
trip down their streets, Victoria felt nothing out of place.
No sign of undead, no prickling of the neck . . . nothing.

She and Sebastian traversed the streets, too high in
their saddles for pickpockets, and not nearly interesting
enough for other thieves in light of the coming procession. They heard shouts in the distance, behind them,
heralding the approach of the royal cortege.

Just then, the sound of pounding horse hooves drew
Victoria's attention. She turned, and around the corner
flew Max, barreling toward them on a large mount.

"The bridge!" he shouted, galloping past them.

Of course! The Thurgood Bridge, which spanned one
of the canals. Old and dangerous, and in a particularly
dark section at the edge of Westminster, the bridge stood
near the end of the king's route. It would be the perfect
place for a royal catastrophe.

Victoria slammed her heels into her mount and raced
off after Max, Sebastian thundering behind.

When they reached the bridge, the back of her neck

iced over almost immediately. Dark shapes filtered beneath the rickety structure, which wheezed and creaked even when no one crossed on it. Tiny red orbs glowed in the night, mostly beneath the edges of the bridge.

It was a narrow span, just wide enough for a single vehicle. Built over a canal barely two wagon lengths wide, it was made of wooden trestles that created a web of dark beams above and below the bridge. The underpinnings cleared the canal's flowing water by only a few feet. Brick buildings in various stages of disrepair staggered near the bridge and along the canal, looming like awkward shadows. They seemed to be converging on the narrow crossing, keeping it dark and close.

Max was already off his horse, and Victoria tore off the apronlike coverings to her skirt as Sebastian roared up and leaped off his own mount.

The vampires were taken by surprise by the sudden onslaught of stake-bearing Venators. Victoria clambered down the mucky slope at the side of the canal, feeling cold mud ooze into her slippers as she came face-to-face with an undead.

She kicked and caught the vampire in the chest, sending him falling back onto two others that had been climbing up the bank behind him. As they struggled to right themselves, she turned to another undead that had leaped down from the bridge. Her stake found its mark, and the female poofed into dust.

"Under the bridge," she heard Sebastian shout, and turned to see him and Max disappear into the darkness under the span.

In the melee that followed, Victoria was barely aware of the hordes of undead; she focused only on staking and stabbing as she worked her way along the mucky bank toward the inky shadows under the bridge. Once she found her way there, even in the dark she could see what was intended. The undead were clambering up and around the trestles under the bridge, ready to swarm the rickety structure when the carriage crossed over. The span's weakness would allow for the weight of only one vehicle at a time, leaving the king's coach to cross without its guards.

Victoria could only guess at the vampires' plan, but when she saw a low, flat shape in the shadows below, thanks to her improved night vision, she recognized it as a boat. Then it made sense: when the carriage was unprotected on the bridge, the undead would take that opportunity to seize the king and make off with him via the water below, taking him, no doubt, to Lilith, where he would be killed.

Hanging by one arm over a rough wooden beam, she kicked out at a vampire, propelling herself toward another in time to stake him. He exploded in a satisfying puff of ash, and Victoria was able to swing her feet and pull herself up onto one of the trestles.

She turned in time to see Max struggling with a vampire across the underside of the bridge. He was crouched on a beam, holding onto a rafter above him while battling a red-eyed undead with one free hand, and his powerful legs. As Victoria watched, a second vampire landed behind Max, effectively trapping him between the two undead.

She didn't hesitate, but swung herself toward the altercation just as Max knocked the first vampire off the trestle. The undead splashed into the canal below, and was carried away by the sluggish water.

Max turned in time to see Victoria slam her stake into the second vampire, leaving her panting on the shaft next to him. He whirled on her furiously, his dark face close to hers. "I don't need your bloody help." Then he leaped away to knock another undead from the bridge, putting distance between him and Victoria.

The sounds of the approaching procession reached Victoria's ears, which were ringing from battle and from Max's unpleasant words. She stared after him, fury pounding in her ears and her knees shaking—not with fear, but with pure anger.

Suddenly, something shoved her from behind, and she lost her grip on the wooden trestle. The next thing she knew, she was tumbling through the air, and landed with a splash in the water below.

Twenty-two

Wherein a Taut String Snaps at Last

When Victoria broke through the surface, she realized the gentle current had carried her away from the bridge. Her clothing was heavy and clinging, and though the water's temperature wasn't a shock, it was muddy and smelled unpleasant.

She wasn't a strong swimmer, but the summers she'd spent wading and splashing in the small lake at Prewitt Shore came back to her, and she was able to keep afloat and paddle awkwardly toward the edge.

She'd hardly gone far downstream, however, when her foot struck the mucky bottom of the canal near its bank. One of her slippers was gone, and the other one sank into the sludge. Her stake had disappeared when she fell, but she half swam, half slogged her way to the shore, knowing that she had others hidden. When she clambered to the top of the sloping bank, her split-skirted attire was plastered to her body, making movement awkward and slow.

By the time she got back on land, and rushed as

quickly as her sodden clothing and bare foot would allow, the king's cortege had reached the bridge. Crowds of people surged toward the carriage, and she could hear frantic shouts from the center of the procession.

"Keep close! Keep close, by God!"

She recognized the king's voice ordering his guards. He was known to be leery of large crowds, especially ones that verged on moblike behavior, for he didn't want a repeat of the kinds of horror toward royalty that occurred during the French Revolution. She couldn't blame him in this case, for the entire environment of close, looming buildings shadowing a narrow bridge, and the thronging crowds, would have made anyone nervous—especially someone like herself, who knew there were more than mortals to be leery of.

Victoria hurried toward the crowd, stones and sharp-edged bricks cutting into her foot. She saw that the king's carriage was broaching the bridge, ready to cross. The mob was pushed away and the coach started over the span. Even from her vantage point, Victoria could hear the creaks and groans of the wooden trestles as the royal vehicle rumbled across.

But she couldn't see any gleam of red eyes, either above or below the bridge. The back of her neck was no longer chilled, and despite the fact that she was soaking, nor was the rest of her body. It was a warm night, and the sludgy, rank mud had already begun to dry on her skin.

About the time the carriage reached the other side of the bridge, Victoria felt a presence behind her, and heard the long, deep breaths of someone who'd been working hard. She turned to see a dripping Max standing there, also watching the coach traverse the canal.

"Safe," he murmured.

"I can swim," she said tartly. "Even in a gown. I didn't need your help."

"I was speaking of the king, Victoria. He's safe. We can go home now."

Pressing her lips together in annoyance, she looked at the bridge. Now that the king had crossed, the crowd was beginning to disperse. The threat did appear to be over, for the remainder of the route to Carleton House was through safer, more well-lit areas. And it wasn't more than a short ride.

Then she recognized a familiar silhouette as he hurried toward her. He was not wet.

"All right, then, Victoria?" asked Sebastian as he approached. "They're gone. The ones we didn't get have run off." He looked at Max. "Get a bit wet, Pesaro?"

"Felt good," Max replied. Then, with a curt nod, he walked away.

Victoria turned to Sebastian, fully conscious of the smell emanating from her person and the press of stones against her bare foot. "I have to return the horse Barth borrowed for me."

He looked down at her. "Will you bite my head off if I suggest that you go home with Barth in the carriage so you can divest yourself of those wet clothes? The horses are Brodebaugh's; Kritanu and I will take them back. Much as I'd like to be there to assist you with your toilette . . ." His head tipped to the side, blocking out the moon behind him. It had waxed into a new quarter in the last week, and it shone bright and bold, casting a silver gilt over his curls. " . . . I think I shall pass on the opportunity this evening."

"I do smell rather rank," Victoria agreed. "I daresay the canal water isn't much cleaner than that of the sewers."

"I daresay you are right." They both chuckled, and

Sebastian moved toward her for a kiss. Then he thought better of it and straightened. A wry smile ticked at the corner of his mouth. "Good night, then, Victoria," he said, something like regret tingeing his voice.

She felt him watching her as she walked away.

The dried sludge from the canal made Victoria's skin itch, and had saturated her hair, which had fallen in smelly, dripping strands about her shoulders. The special frock with the split skirt would have to be burned, and her remaining slipper was so stained that it no longer showed a hint of pink.

By the time Verbena had finished bathing her mistress and washing the stench from her thick mass of hair, it was past midnight. She toweled the hip-length curls as dry as possible, then coiled them into a loose, sagging knot at the back of her neck so that it would be able to dry without tangling too much. Victoria dressed, not in a night rail, but in the loose trousers and tunic she wore when training, along with soft slipperlike shoes. She had a suspicion that Sebastian might come to the house with Kritanu after they brought the horses back, and she thought it might be best if she weren't in her bedchamber if and when they did.

After dismissing her yawning maid for the night, Victoria went down to return the *kadhara* knife to the cabinet in the *kalari* training room. She was surprised to find it lit by a lamp that cast a golden glow over the area, and thought she might find Wayren within. But it was Max.

He was standing at one of the cupboards, apparently also returning a weapon to its rightful place. At first he didn't hear her enter, and she noticed that he was garbed in clean clothes similar to her own—trousers and a tunic in undyed linen, bare of foot, his dark hair loose and making damp marks on the back of his shirt.

Victoria felt short of breath, and realized that her stomach was coiling and loosening with nauseating speed. She stepped into the room, letting the door close silently behind her.

Max turned. She saw his attention flicker past her. "Where is Vioget? And Wayren?"

"So you cannot deign to speak to me if no one else is present?" Victoria countered, stepping into the room. For some reason, she felt as though she was in control . . . despite the fact that his face still bore that flat, empty expression.

But the rest of him . . . Her mouth went dry and, suddenly, her heart was thumping so hard she was certain it was audible. The sleeves of his hip-length tunic were rolled halfway up his arms, showing an expanse of swarthy skin and muscle that would never be revealed in polite dress. And the loose neck of the shirt made a vee below the hollow of his throat, exposing the same dark hair that grew on his legs and scattered over the tops of his long, elegant feet. He was still wearing the leather thong and silver cross she'd noticed around his ankle before, but no other adornment. Except, perhaps, a *vis bulla*—her *vis bulla*—beneath the shirt. Her lungs tightened.

"I was just leaving." He started toward the door, and she remained in place. He'd have to brush past her to go.

"I want to talk to you."

"I have nothing to say to you." Anger darkened his eyes and for a moment she was almost afraid of his expression. It was so cold . . . she'd never seen such blatant loathing.

"That's fine, for you need say nothing. I want—"

He exploded then. "I don't give a bloody *damn* what you want, Victoria. I want nothing to do with you. Stay away from me until I leave. Which won't be soon enough." Max stalked toward the door, passing her in a swish that stirred the air like a miniature cyclone.

But Victoria was angry now as well. She lashed out and grabbed a muscled arm, yanking him back before he could touch the door handle.

He whipped from her grip, and now they were face-to-face. His eyes blazed and his mouth compressed with fury. "Leave it, Victoria. You've done enough."

She closed her fingers around his wrist. She was strong enough to hold him, and he knew it. "Max, let me explain—"

"There is no explanation for what you did." He was facing her now, and he grabbed her shoulders so hard she knew his fingertips would leave little black bruises above her collarbones. "You had no right to imprison me. *No bloody right.*" He was nearly shaking her, and she raised her arms between them to break his hold, shoving his hands away.

"I was afraid for you—" She grabbed at him once more as he turned, and this time when he whirled, she saw that he was no longer holding back. His face was black with fury, and his teeth were bared in a nasty smile.

"Afraid. For me." He slashed down and broke her hold on his wrist, sending a numbing shock along her arm. "Poor helpless Max. You had to lock me in a goddamn room while you and Vioget and Kritanu went out to fight vampires? Damn you, Victoria. I'll never forgive you for that."

She shoved at him, hard enough to send him stumbling backward. "Listen to me, you bloody lout."

He caught himself and lunged back up at her. "You want to fight, do you?"

"You know I can best you, Max. Then you'll have to listen to me, instead of running away from it—as you always do."

"Try it." His smile returned, hard and unfriendly. His eyes glinted with challenge.

She kicked out suddenly, and he blocked her thrust with an angle of his powerful thigh, then responded with a shove that knocked her back two steps. Furious that he'd taken her by surprise, she twisted around and grabbed his arm, slipping it over her as she neatly flipped him to the thick mat on the ground. He yanked her leg, pulling her off balance so that she was forced into a somersault that loosened her knot of hair.

Then he was up, breathing easily, as though he'd just stood from a chair, dark hair loose, brushing his shoulders and falling in his eyes. He crouched, ready for her, and she matched his stance as they circled in the room. It wouldn't be a battle of pure strength, but one of timing and the unexpected. In that, they were evenly matched.

"I didn't want anything to happen to you, you blasted fool," she said, lunging.

He sidestepped and kicked around from behind to trip her. She caught herself and staggered backward, pulling him with her. Max tumbled and rolled neatly to his feet, turning once again to face her. "You bloody castrated me, Victoria. You did me no favors."

"Lilith wants you."

"And she wants *you*, damn you. Even more than she wants me."

"No—"

"But I didn't drug you. And lock you up. For two

days." He blocked her blow with his arm, using the momentum to twist her around.

Victoria spun back to face him. "No, you simply paid Sebastian to kidnap me last fall."

The fact that Max had asked Sebastian to abduct Victoria to keep her from questioning his seeming loyalty to the Tutela, and thus ruining his plans to get close to Nedas and his demonic obelisk, had continued to be a bone of contention between them. That had also been the first time she and Sebastian became lovers, in a carriage, of course—a fact about which Max never hesitated to remind her.

She balled up her hands into fists that, small though they might appear, held inhuman strength. "To keep me safe," she said, punctuating her words with spars that slapped violently against his raised palms as he blocked her, "as you *claimed.*" She whirled around suddenly with a solid kick toward his abdomen, which connected with his side as he lunged out of the way. "How dare you claim injury when you did nothing less to me."

Max laughed coldly, ducking her blows and responding with one of his own that spun the air by her ear. "You talk as though it was some great tragedy," he said, backing up into a crouch again, "that you ended up in a carriage with him. The way I heard it," he said, taking a swipe at her, "it was no hardship for you after all."

She kicked out, clipping the edge of his jaw. She heard his teeth snap shut and she tossed him a tight grin. "At least I didn't act the coward and *pay* someone else to do my dirty work." She leaped at him; he blocked her lunge and caught her by the arm. Ducking under her, he flipped her over as she'd done to him moments before.

She flew through the air and landed on her back, the breath knocked out of her for the moment before she sprang to her feet, brushing a long strand of hair from her face. He was already halfway to the door.

"Where are you going?" she demanded, throwing herself toward him. Her leap knocked him to the floor, and they tumbled there in a tangle of limbs. She landed on top of him, but he gave a great twist and she flipped onto her back with a loud smack, pulling him with her. "Coward!"

"I'm getting the hell away from you," he said, rearing over her. His head blocked the lamp and left him half-shadowed. "Because if I don't, God help me, I'll be doing this." And his face swooped down toward her, fingers once again digging into the soft spots on her shoulders.

It was a furious, ferocious kiss; a desperate smashing and grinding of mouths pressing against teeth, a slip-sliding of lips, the deep, long swipe of tongue . . . and then more and more, so that she became completely breathless . . . but unwilling to stop to breathe. Victoria's fingers grasped the sides of his face as if to keep him there, even to pull him closer, feeling the throb of veins in his temples, and the slight dampness of his warm skin, the rough stubble under her palms.

His hair was as silky and heavy as it looked, and she curled her fingers up onto his skull, the tendrils wrapping around her hands as she arched beneath him, feeling the pull of her hair trapped beneath his hands, pressing her belly up into his, curling one of her ankles around his hips to pull him down closer. Their legs shifted and moved, trousers crumpled, rough hair scraped against warm flesh, toes and heels thumped against each other and the mat as they rolled and continued their battle in the most elemental way of man and woman.

Victoria tore at his tunic, pulling it up, slipping her hands under the linen to feel the slabs of muscle on his back. Warm, they shifted and rippled beneath her fingers as he lifted onto his elbows and dipped to move his face along her jaw and to the hot, sensitive part of her neck. She turned her face away, eyes closed, as he kissed, devouring her skin with his firm mouth, sending exploding sensations through her as she tried to keep from moaning like a cat in heat.

Then suddenly, he stilled, as if caught. Poised over her, his face against the side of her neck, buried in her curls, his breath moist on her skin. She felt the brush of his lashes, the sift of his hair over her cheek, the thump of his heart reverberating in his body, so close to hers . . . but his lips had lifted. His rough breathing mingled with hers in the silence.

She tightened her hands on his body beneath the linen shirt, folding her lips together, ready to speak his name.

"Don't," he said sharply, his mouth moving against her neck. "Don't . . . say . . . anything."

Tension radiated; she felt it trembling beneath her fingers on the smooth skin over his ribs, in the deep, long breath he took, expanding under her touch.

She felt it when he gathered up, ready to pull away, and she tightened her fingers on him.

And then, after another long moment, as though released, excused, sanctioned . . . something . . . he moved again with a little shudder, a release of stilled breath. He brushed her hair away, and kissed her neck, gently now, languidly, with the same skillful lips that had done so three months ago. The tension eased beneath her fingers and, when he moved again, it was to find her mouth once more with his.

Her lips were swollen and pounding from the previous onslaught, but he took his time here. It wasn't tender, the way he kissed her now, nor desperate and angry, as before, but . . . long and slow and thorough, slick and deep, drawing so much from her that she moaned quietly behind it all.

There was no mistaking his desire for her; as their bodies arched and moved, the loose fabric left little unsaid between them. She pulled at his shirt, and he lifted away long enough for her to yank it over his head. Bare skin, at last. As he bent back to kiss her again, she saw the expression in those dark, oft unreadable eyes: burning and intense.

There was no mistaking what shone in them now.

She felt warm and heady when he lifted again, and before she could protest, or worry that he meant to leave, he picked her up, settling her against his bare chest, and brought her to the pile of cushions in the corner. Her hands smoothed over the square of his shoulders, down over the dark hair and muscle, and to the silver cross that hung from one areola.

He stilled when she touched the *vis bulla*, almost as if he waited for her response. The last time she'd seen it, Nedas had ordered it to be torn from her skin. She could only imagine how Max had retrieved it from the vampire. When she brushed her fingers over the silver, her amulet . . . the one forged specially for her . . . she felt a leap of power sizzle through her. A clean, familiar rush.

She flattened her hand against him, the tiny, ornate cross pressing into her palm, and remembered doing the very same thing last autumn after having been disarmed. Max had forced her hand there, under his shirt, grasping her wrist with impossibly strong fingers, risking his life as he forced her to take power from his *vis bulla*.

It was either her, or you.

That was what he'd said when she'd demanded to know why he'd slain Aunt Eustacia. She'd been filled with hatred and the same loathing for him she'd seen in his eyes earlier tonight, directed at her. At that time, he hadn't told her the other reasons—that he'd been ordered to by Eustacia herself, that it was the only way to save them all from Nedas's power, that he'd had no choice— for if he didn't slay her, Eustacia would have died anyway. And Victoria too.

It was either her, or you.

How had it taken her so long to realize?

Unwilling to wait any longer, to give him any chance to walk away as he'd done after that kiss . . . that first kiss against the stone wall . . . she pulled away and stripped off her own tunic, and then the light chemise she wore beneath it, letting her damp hair fall over her shoulders and back. Max wasted no time; his dark hands were on her immediately, large and capable over her slender torso. They pressed her back into the mound of cushions, then smoothed down below her breasts over the gentle swell of her belly. To the two silver crosses there.

He fingered them gently above the waistband of her trousers, shifting the *vis bulla* that had been his against that of Aunt Eustacia, then releasing them back into the hollow of her navel. Still silent, but for the quiet rasp of breath, he spread his hands wide to cover her belly, curling long fingers around her hips and sliding them gently up her sensitive skin to cup one hand under each breast.

His touch raised little bumps on her flesh and sent tingles through her limbs, curling into the center of her belly. She arched up into his palms, her hands back on his shoulders, her hair tangling under and around them, as he bent down to her. Her breasts were tight, her nipples gathered into little round peaks, and when his mouth closed over one of them, she sighed. Closed her eyes.

Sharp pleasure-pain arched down from where he

sucked and teased, coiling in her belly, then shooting lower between her legs. Victoria felt the gentle burn, the gathering of desire there, and when one long-fingered hand moved down beneath the band of her trousers, she gave a soft sigh of pleasure. He found what he was looking for, and slipped in and around languidly until she had lost all shame and was moaning beneath him, pressing closer, demanding what they both wanted.

After that, there was no more waiting, no more teasing. Trousers were ripped away, and his long, strong body covered her equally bare, ready one. She wrapped her legs around him as he settled against her, and they both gasped when he moved that first time. The fullness, the long, deep stroke made her mouth dry again, her eyes flutter closed, her fingers close over his shoulders, nails digging deep.

He lifted away just as slowly, then back again, and again, and more quickly and desperately, over and over, long and filling and deep . . . and suddenly the build exploded, leaving her shuddering and gasping and arching up again in a wave of pleasure and sunlight and stars. He groaned deep in his chest, and she felt him tense and tremble against her with one last, sharp movement.

He sagged over her, his face down, eyes closed, dark lashes and brows only a breath away from hers. One hand rested on the cushion next to her shoulder, the other cupped into the curve of her neck and shoulder, fingers curled around her neck . . . as though he had to hold on to her.

Twenty-three

Wherein Our Friends Are Horrified by Multiple Locks of Hair

Christ Almighty, what a bloody weak fool, was Max's first thought. The second was, absurdly, *Where the hell is Vioget?*

Yet he had to touch her hair again. So dark and heavy, it was a wonder Victoria could hold her head up when it was piled on top. It spread over the pillows and coverlet of his bed, curling down over and between their bodies.

Good God . . . in his room?

But he couldn't pretend not to remember how they'd come to be here, how, in the back of his lust-fogged mind, he'd decided to carry her to the bed in the small chamber reserved for servants. Not to hers. Not to the one she'd shared with Vioget.

And the rest of the night . . . for once in his bloody life, he'd not listened to conscience. *In for a penny, in for a pound* had been one vague thought as he went to her again. And again.

Now, early morning sun filtered through the window, here in the servants' quarters on the upper floor where he'd cloistered himself for the last weeks. It brought reality, regret . . . uneasiness. And it cast enough light for him to see the curve of her ivory shoulder, the peek of a pink nipple, the rise and swell of her hip next to him. The glint of his *vis bulla* at her belly. Full red lips, swollen and crinkled in the aftermath of a passionate night.

Bloody hell.

Bloody damned *hell.*

He eased away from her, cold and furious.

She opened her eyes. Surprise, pleasure . . . and then her lashes swept down to hide the flush that colored her cheeks. Devil take it, had she seen the bald fear in his eyes?

"I trust you're still drinking the potion from Eustacia," he said calmly. His fingers didn't want to release the thick curl they rubbed between their pads.

"How did you know about that?" She sat up and he looked. Christ, how could he not? All that dark hair fell forward and around, obscuring the details . . . but he knew every rise and fall of them. "Oh, yes, I forgot. You know everything. Yes, I'm still drinking the potion to keep me from conceiving. But I had already decided to stop taking it."

"I think it a wise decision. You are *Illa* Gardella, the last of the direct line." He drew subtly away, released the lock of hair. "And I think it best if we keep this . . . to ourselves."

She blinked at him, her brown-green eyes all too shrewd. It was too blasted hard to hide anything from them. "What do you mean?"

"I mean there's no bloody need to tell Vioget. Or anyone."

"Max, you're being obtuse. You can't think I'd . . ." Her voice trailed off, understanding dawning. Thank God she was smart, and caught on quickly. It would be much easier if he didn't have to explain. "This is like the time you kissed me, isn't it? You're going to walk away and pretend nothing happened. Pretend I goaded you into it."

She was too bloody damned smart. Dammit. "Victoria, you—"

And forever after, he wasn't certain whether the knock on the door was a godsend or misfortune.

Regardless, the interruption catapulted their attention far from the matter at hand. A wiry orange puff of hair preceded the maid's eye peering around the corner. She didn't appear surprised to see Victoria there; in fact, Max was struck by the combination of satisfaction warring with trepidation on her face.

"Verbena? What is it?" Victoria must have sensed it too, for her voice was sharp. Or maybe the hardness was for him.

"I'm begging yer pard'n, my lady, but I foun' this on the front stoop. I don' know when it came, as there was no one to answer the door . . . Charley's day off, y'know . . . an' so I foun' it when I went out to see . . ." Her voice trailed off as she offered a small paper packet around the corner of the door.

"What about Kritanu?" Victoria mused, reaching for the envelope. Of course she wouldn't be uncomfortable being undressed in front of her maid . . . but here, in his bed? Perhaps this circumstance was more common than he thought. The maid seemed to have known where to find them.

"He's not 'ere." Verbena shrugged, spreading her hands. "Ol'ver said he didn't return last night." And Wayren was . . . well, Wayren. She was likely closed up wherever she chose to be, studying an old manuscript or scroll. She appeared when she needed to. Obviously, Brim and Michalas hadn't yet arrived.

Victoria snatched the packet from her maid. It was thick, tied with a red ribbon and sealed by a familiar wax blob. And . . . "Christ," he said at the same time as she drew in her breath.

"That's blood." Victoria tore off the ribbon and flipped the seal open. When she saw what was inside, she drew in her breath sharply.

Pressed into the folds of the stiff paper was a thick lock of shiny jet-black hair. And beneath it, a matching lock of tawny gold curl. Both were sticky with blood.

The folded piece of paper accompanying them was unmarked but for an ugly brownish streak. It was stamped with the seal of the Earl of Brodebaugh.

Twenty-four

The Stakes Are Raised

"I hope you don't plan to go haring off—" Max began in that tone of his.

"I'm not about to go haring off," Victoria replied sharply. All of the pleasure and contentment with which she'd awakened had evaporated. Now she was cold and angry . . . but most of all frightened.

She looked at Max, who'd moved away from her and was already dressing, building the wall back up, brick by solid brick. Pressing her lips together, she looked away from his tall, muscular body. Later. She'd deal with him, with this—whatever *this* was—later. But for now . . .

"I have no plans to go haring off, Max," she said in a calmer voice. "That's what they want me to do, and that's what put me in Beauregard's control three months ago. He offered an exchange as well."

"But his copper armband was the deciding factor in your downfall," he said in an ironic voice.

"He wouldn't have had the copper armband to weaken me if I hadn't brought it along. I left the Consilium without realizing, haring off as you would say . . . but," she said, frustration coloring her voice, and grief, for the reminder that Zavier's life had been the casualty that time—quite possibly along with her own soul. She shivered. "What are they doing to Kritanu and Sebastian?"

"I should think it's quite clear: holding them for ransom, so to speak. The only thing I'm not certain of is who it is they want to lure there. And," he added, picking up a shirt, "I use the term 'they' simply because I cannot believe Brodebaugh is acting alone. Or if he is even willingly involved."

"There we agree." Victoria stood from the bed, neglecting to cover herself, and couldn't help a bit of smugness when he had to tear his gaze away, his jaw clamping suddenly shut. He wasn't a bad sight himself, standing there in only untied trousers that settled at his hips. "It must be your scorned lover Sara behind all of this, and George too."

Max stopped suddenly and looked at her. "Victoria, Sara and I were never lovers . . . in the true sense of the word." He pitched the bundle of cloth at her. "You're cold. Put this on."

"I'm not cold. And in regards to Sara—you made a good case for the contrary," she retorted, catching the shirt. Did that mean he hadn't loved Sara, or that he'd never been intimate with her? "And it doesn't matter now."

"No, it doesn't. But I knew you wanted to know. And . . . you should." He pulled out another shirt and shook it out, preparing to put it on. Then he stopped. "Victoria."

She had started to pull on his shirt, ready now to return to her own room and dress, but his voice halted her. His hand was on the silver cross that pierced his skin. "This is yours."

Her fingers touched the one at her navel that had belonged to him; she was able to identify the difference between the two by feel. "And this is yours."

Without another word, he gave a little twist, then a pull, and slipped the dainty *vis bulla* from his skin. "Wear it now. It might help."

Her attention flashed to him. Had Wayren told him about the internal battle for her soul? Or was this merely a way to rid himself of any attachment to her and the Venators? "Only if you wear yours again." She looked up. "Lilith is aware of our . . . exchange. She was not pleased."

His mouth settled into a thin line again, drawing deep grooves. "Shall I help you?" he said when he saw that she fumbled with the little silver hoop. His fingers were quick and skillful, warm on her bare skin—but they were impersonal, and didn't linger—as he removed the simple cross. Then he pulled taut the little lip of skin at the top of her navel and slipped her own *vis bulla* into place.

It was an oddly intimate gesture—odd considering what had passed between them last night. Victoria felt a twinge of remembrance and her stomach did the silly little flip it tended to do when she was surprised . . . or discomfited. But then the feeling ebbed, and she realized that having her own *vis bulla* back in place was . . . cleaner. More pure and solid.

Max moved away, holding his *vis*, hesitant. Then, with ease she'd not shown, he replaced it in his areola and breathed deeply. Perhaps he wondered if his Venator powers would be restored once he wore his own amulet. He turned back to the neat table on which his personal items were gathered, and Victoria watched as he slipped the heavy silver ring onto the middle finger of his left hand. As if girding himself for battle.

"Tell me how the ring will protect you."

"I'm certain you've already figured it out, but . . . there is a catch which, when moved correctly, opens to reveal a sharp blade dripping with venom. A simple prick will do the trick."

"To you . . . or to Lilith?"

"To me. Now, why are you still here? Should we not be planning how to save your lover?"

She'd suspected it . . . but now she knew for certain. Max was withdrawing again. He meant to foist her upon Sebastian again so that he could walk away. And use that bloody silver ring whenever he chose.

What about me?

She bit her tongue, holding back the questions, the demands, the comparisons. After all, hadn't he despised Sebastian for turning his back on the Venators? There would be time for that later, time to force him into a conversation he wished to avoid. She wasn't about to let anything happen to Sebastian and Kritanu.

The rest of Max's comment brought to mind something he'd said earlier. "What do you mean, you aren't certain who they are trying to lure? It's you, of course. Lilith wants you back and Sara nearly delivered you to her. Two in exchange for one. Which is why there can be no 'we' about this."

Max raised a brow. "Indeed? I happen to disagree. I believe Lilith wants you more than she does me. After all, you're still a threat to her, unlike me—as you've made quite clear so recently. And you've escaped her for a second time, only days ago. I can only imagine how much ash exploded after that—and after last night, when we foiled her plans to kidnap the king. And if she believes you are some sort of rival for my . . . affections . . ." His expression and tone indicated how absurd that thought was.

"Don't be ridiculous. Is this some kind of twisted way for you to try and take control?" She realized she was still standing there with the shirt in front of her. She yanked it over her head. It smelled of him. Her knees weakened.

"No." He gestured to the packet, which lay on the mussed bed, open to show the glint of two shades of hair. "Apparently you didn't notice that the message was unaddressed. It's not clear for whom it was intended."

She opened her mouth to speak, then closed it. "It doesn't matter, Max. You're not as well equipped to face her as . . . as you used to be."

If she expected anger from him at her statement, she was disappointed. "There's one thing you're forgetting." His lips stretched in a humorless smile. "No one would ever think that I'd be moved to save Vioget's life. It's a game. And you're meant to be the prize."

Victoria would have laughed if the situation hadn't been so horrible. In fact, she did give a snort of disbelief. "That's just it, Max. You *would* be moved to save his life. The life of anyone, even someone you hate—"

"I don't hate him."

"Even someone for whom you have a great amount of antipathy. Because it's the noble thing to do," she added sharply, remembering her own poor choices. Leaving Bemis Goodwin and his companion to die. Drugging Max. Hating Gwen for her happiness. "Ever the hero, aren't you, Max? Always selfless. Do you never do anything just for you?"

She realized suddenly that the red haze was nudging the frame of her vision. Her heart was racing, and she felt a surge of ugly anger bubbling inside her. Automatically, she took a deep breath, touched her *vis bullae*, and shook her head as if to clear it. Yet that nobility, that steadiness, was what she loved most about Max. The strong, impassable line drawn between right and wrong, black and white.

Loved.

Her knees trembled anew.

It was the reason she'd been able to forgive him for Aunt Eustacia's death. The reason she'd never stopped trusting him. Had known he wouldn't forsake the Venators, even once stripped of his own abilities.

In her own mind, that stark black-and-white line had always leaked a bit into charcoal, or to fog . . . but that had recently begun to bloom into a wide stretch of gray. . . . Was that why he retreated from her? Because she wasn't as good?

By now the rosiness had faded, her pulse had slowed. The surge of malevolence had gone. Was it getting easier to fight it back? Or was it her imagination, wishing and hoping?

It also hadn't escaped her that last night, when she and Max were fighting . . . that vulgar evil hadn't attempted to take her over. That reddish haze and surge of wickedness hadn't teased and fought to control her. Why?

Was it because she hadn't been fighting for self-preservation, as she had other times? Her self hadn't been in jeopardy; she'd not been battling for her life? She'd not *needed* to be selfish to win.

The seed of everything evil begins with self.

When she felt steady, Victoria looked up and saw that Max was watching her. His attention scored her, as though trying to decipher what it was that had sent her off into the whirlwind of her mind.

Before he could speak, there was another knock at the door.

It was Verbena again, and she held a small white box.

A red ribbon tied it closed, and when Victoria accepted the container, an awful feeling of foreboding rushed through her. Max took one look at the brownish streaks on the outside and swore. It bore the same seal of Brodebaugh.

Victoria couldn't get it open fast enough, and when she did, she nearly dropped it. "My God."

Inside were two fingers, their bloody stumps sticky and oozing into the sides of the container. One had skin the color of coffee, and the other a few shades lighter. This second one bore a small golden ring that Victoria recognized. She didn't need to say anything; the look of revulsion on Max's face mirrored her own.

The message was perfectly clear. Time was running out.

Victoria arrived at the Brodebaugh residence as though making an early social call. The house wasn't as large as St. Heath's Row, but grander than Grantworth House. Situated near Hyde Park, the grounds of the home were walled but the rear was adjacent to a small finger of the park. Neighboring houses were far enough away to give privacy, due to the unusually wide side gardens.

The moment the door opened, she smelled blood.

"Victoria!" It was Gwendolyn, her eyes wild and her face tinged gray and streaked with tears. Her hair fell in ungainly clumps, and she was still dressed in the gown she'd worn to the coronation yesterday. "You've come! I was afraid . . . I'm so afraid!" She clutched desperately at her, pulling her into the house. "You have to help us!"

Victoria's heart was pounding. She'd suspected, but now she knew for certain.

As Gwendolyn closed the door, Victoria fought to ignore the heavy iron scent in the air, and to keep her mind steady. Instead, she focused on the comforting stake deep in her pocket, her own *vis bulla* beneath her clothing, and her surroundings. The foyer of Brodebaugh Hall was empty, fairly ringing with its silence. The whole building was silent.

"Where are they?" she asked, battling the smell of blood, the horror that now gripped her, the edge of pink at her vision.

"Did you . . . you came alone?" Gwendolyn sniffled, looking around wildly. "How could you . . . how . . ."

"I can handle it myself," Victoria told her firmly. "Where are the servants?"

"They're all gone," Gwendolyn said fearfully. "They—*she*—took them all away." She looked again, over Victoria's shoulder, out the door, as if expecting to see an army there. "There's no one but you? But, Victoria—"

She'd had enough with the hysterics. The stake was out of her pocket and Victoria had slammed Gwendolyn up against the wall before the girl took another breath. Or made another fake sob. Her hand closed in a tight vee under Gwen's throat, and she poised the stake against her chest. "Tell me where they are, or you're dust."

Gwen dropped all pretense. Her pretty face, which had turned gray and tired from the overuse of the elixir, curdled into a malignant expression. Her eyes bulged, and turned from blue to red in an instant. "How did you know?"

"I'd suspected for awhile," Victoria told her, realizing that the back of her neck had cooled. Gwen wasn't the only vampire in the house. "You were always there when a daytime attack occurred. I could see the elixir taking its toll on you, in your face, but I just thought it was exhaustion from your wedding plans." She tightened her fingers around Gwen's throat, causing the girl to cough and to scratch at her hand, trying to tear it away. "But when I saw the queen yesterday, I realized there's a certain shadow in the eyes of a daytime undead. They all had it: James, Caroline, her guards. And you."

"James." Gwen kicked out, but Victoria was ready. The little pointed foot, strong with undead power, merely grazed the side of her target's leg. "You killed him too! You killed my love."

"So that was it." Victoria knew she was taking up valuable time . . . but she had to know more. And why. "You helped set him in place as the new Rockley heir."

"I had no choice, since the first one was dead. I wanted to marry Phillip and you stole him from me. I'd seen him first, and then you made your debut, and immediately he was stumbling all over his feet for you. I didn't have a chance." Gwen's voice was rough from the hand at her throat, but her tone was petulant. "And now James. We were going to be so happy together. Eternal youth! And wealth."

Victoria looked at the girl who had been her friend and wondered how such a lovely young woman could have turned so evil.

Self. The seed of everything evil begins with self.

"You never intended to marry Brodebaugh?"

Gwen gave a squeaky laugh. "Oh, yes, we were to wed. And then he would die a sudden death, and I would find solace in the arms of the Marquess of Rockley. We've been planning this for months!" she ended on a shriek.

"How long have you been undead?"

"Only since George returned from Italy. He brought Malachai—you knew him as James. And when I met him, I knew the Tutela wasn't enough for me. I wanted immortality." Her laugh was grating and malicious. "I wanted revenge on you for years, Victoria Gardella . . . since you married the man I desired. I planned for you to die when you came to the house party last summer . . . when the vampires came for Polidori. But you fought them off. You and that blond Frenchman."

"You're dying from the elixir, Gwen. Did Lilith tell you that?"

Victoria felt, rather than heard, the front door open silently behind her. The gasp of fresh air was a relief.

"Ah. I see you've confirmed your suspicions," said Max. "There's no one about on the grounds; all the servants appear to be gone. And I wasn't seen, for the windows are shrouded."

"Good," said Victoria.

"You lied!" screeched Gwen. "You didn't come alone."

"So sorry." Victoria gave her a cold smile, and slammed the stake home. Dusting her hands off—gloveless, of course—she turned to Max. He'd pulled his hair back into a tight queue, and his countenance was tight with focus. "I probably could have gotten more information from her, but she was becoming tiresome. There are other undead here. Five or more."

He gave a sharp nod, and they started off down the main hallway, following the smell of blood.

Just as they reached the end of the corridor, facing two massive wooden doors, Max stopped. He took Victoria's arm and turned her to face him. Her heart started to pound. "I know you're in charge, and we have a plan," he said quietly, "but listen to me." His eyes burned with determination, and Victoria's mouth went dry. She knew what he was going to say.

"Max, no," she began, anger surging.

"Quiet," he said, his voice still soft, but with sharpness. His hand tightened on her arm. "You have to get yourself and Vioget out of here. You're Gardellas. That's the most important thing."

"We have a plan," she began, but her protest was cut off by a man's agonized cry. It came from beyond the doors. They both turned, and Max released her.

There was no more time for talk.

As before, Max remained out of sight, sticking for now to their plan. Victoria was the one who threw the doors open and stood boldly in the entrance.

The stench of blood hit her like a wall, filling her nostrils, slogging into her lungs.

"At last. Our guest has arrived. *Benvenuto*."

Sara, of course. She stood directly across the room from the doors. Her smile was beatific, her hair properly coiffed, her day dress a simple yet stylish pale green lawn. There was blood on it.

"*Cara mia*, Victoria," she said in a shocked voice, looking at her tunic and trousers. "Whatever are you wearing? It is *abominevole*!"

Victoria scanned the chamber quickly. What she saw made the red blossom over her vision, coloring her whole world for a frightening moment. She focused on the feel of the stake in her hand: its square edges, the smooth wood, the inlaid cross on the top. With her focus, the haze ebbed, leaving only the faintest tinge.

The room would have been used as a small ballroom, or for a musical performance. It was large, with little furniture, and a polished wooden floor. The windows were shrouded, blocking the sunlight. Several lamps burned, however, so the chamber was not the least bit dark, revealing every detail of the garish scene.

To the left were several creatures: Brodebaugh and

George Starcasset, along with four or five vampires with blazing red eyes—she didn't have time to count. George and the earl were sitting in facing armchairs. Brodebaugh's face was streaked with blood and his clothes were mussed. George, on the other hand, appeared patently uninterested in his surroundings, and had adopted a look of boredom on his boyish face. Two vampires stood near them. But that wasn't the image that would later give Victoria nightmares.

On the other side of the room, just out of sight until she stepped in, were Sebastian and Kritanu, also flanked by undead. The two men were seated in chairs at either end of a rectangular table. Their bodies faced the doorway, immobilized by a labyrinth of crisscrossing restraints. Kritanu slumped in his seat, sagging forward, held in place only by the straps around his torso. The vampire next to him held a heavy knife. Its blade was bloody.

Sebastian was looking at Victoria, fury in his face. There were fang marks, many of them, on his neck and the part of his arm bared by a rolled-up sleeve. He was pale. He, as well as Kritanu, had the hand closest to the table strapped onto it. Blood pooled on its surface, dripping from the edge to plop onto the rug below. Victoria tore her eyes away, but not before she saw the stump where Kritanu's hand had been. It was still bright with fresh blood.

"Get out of here, you damned fool," Sebastian shouted, veins bulging in his temples. Gone was the charm, the confidence, the irrepressible gleam in his eyes. He was bloody and dirty, his clothes were torn, his hair hung in his face but for the space where the lock had been snipped in the center of his forehead. The hand fixed to the table rested next to a dark stain.

"*Silenzio*," Sara said with a coy smile. "Be grateful that she arrived to keep you from the same fate as your *compagno eccellente.*" She glanced at Kritanu, who appeared to have fainted from pain or blood loss, moving her lips into a little moue and *tsk*ing. "He has been so quiet since the last stroke of the blade."

Victoria swallowed hard, choking on the bitter taste at the back of her mouth. *Calm. Breathe deeply. Fight the red. Remember the* vis. *Your* vis. "I'm here. What is it you want from me?"

"*Grazie*, for you to respond to my message," Sara replied ingenuously, her brown eyes wide. "Oh, and . . . *mi dispiace* . . . for the lack of servants. And there was no one to greet you at the door? They all have been dismissed. Permanently. Lilith wished to have them . . . for dinner." She giggled, but Victoria didn't see a hint of humor—or even madness—in her eyes. She was very lucid and very determined. Cold fear gripped her. "It has made the preparation of our meals rather *difficile*. For we who don't dine on blood, *naturalmente.*" Then Sara made a point of looking around as if in confusion. "But where is your dear friend?"

"Those are my friends," Victoria said. She looked at Sebastian and Kritanu. "And you'll pay for what you've done. Release them or you'll die."

"But what about your *amica* Gwendolyn? That silly chit was to greet you at the door. She could not have failed in her task. It was so simple."

"I regret to inform you that Gwen is a pile of ash."

"You killed my sister?" George cried. "How dare you!"

"*Silencio*," Sara ordered. "Have I not told you she slays at will? After what happened to *mi papa* . . ." Her eyes narrowed at Victoria. "*Davvero.* You are a smart one. It is no wonder he loves you."

"And so are you. Smart enough to know when you've overstepped. Release them now, and it will go easier for you."

"And so you've come charging to the rescue—*da solo.*" Sara chuckled as she walked over to the vampire near Kritanu. "How difficult it must be for *fusti* such as these to know that you—a mere woman—must save them. A shame, that. But you neglected to bring anything for barter. Now I shall be forced to continue with *mio divertimento.* And it may be quite an . . . *inconveniente* . . . for your friends." She took the large knife from the vampire and, smiling at Victoria, moved to stand next to Sebastian.

Her hand moved to touch the top of his head, as if she were caressing a pet . . . then slid down to his shoulder and along to grip the arm fixed to the table. She looked up at Victoria, her brown eyes gleaming with pleasure. "Have you ever heard him scream?"

"Stop. You needn't play the game any longer. I'm here. What is it you want?" Victoria's mouth was so dry she could hardly form the words. The stake hung uselessly in her pocket.

"You fool, Victoria!" Sebastian shouted suddenly, urgently. "You have to *go.*"

The blade flashed as Sara raised it. She was still watching Victoria. "What have you to offer me? *Pronto!* Before my patience is gone."

"One of the Rings of Jubai," said Victoria quickly. "Lilith will be delighted for you to return it to her. She will reward you greatly."

The blade wavered. A trickle of perspiration rolled down Sebastian's face, yet he glared at her. The room was silent. *Where was Max?* If he didn't make the disturbance soon . . .

"I know not what it is." But Sara was interested, and Victoria was glad to have her attention. *Just keep the blade up.*

"There are five of them, made of copper. The Venators are in possession of one of them, and I can retrieve it for you in exchange for Kritanu and Sebastian—unharmed any further."

"How do I know you do not lie to me?" The blade shivered and Victoria held her breath.

"Ask them." She gestured to the vampires clustered around Brodebaugh, who apparently was under their watch. After his outburst, George had remained silent. This was, clearly, wholly Sara's game.

One of the undead, a woman ironically, nodded when Sara looked at her. "Describe the ring," said the vampire.

Victoria did, quickly, her eyes on the blade the whole time.

"Where is this ring?" asked Sara.

"Sebastian retrieved it. He knows where it is." *What was the delay?*

Sara looked at her with distaste. "You expect that I shall release him to enable you to retrieve the ring?"

Just then—at last!—a sudden *boom* from the next room startled the occupants. The two windows near that wall shattered, sending glass shards scattering. Sunlight streamed in through the torn curtains, and chaos followed. A nearby vampire fell to the floor in agony, his skin peeling off in angry strips as he writhed in the sunbeam.

Chaos reigned—Sara was shouting, half in Italian and half in English, waving the knife, giving sharp orders. Two vampires launched themselves at Victoria as she started toward Sebastian, pulling the stake out of her pocket. She stabbed one, missing his heart but slowing him nevertheless, and vaulted over the table as the knife blade flashed.

As Victoria slammed Sara to the floor she felt the knife slice along her arm. Blood burst from her skin— *her* blood—filling her nose and turning her vision scarlet. The small woman beneath her had no chance to withstand Victoria's strength; it took only a single blow to the chest for her to release the blade and slump to the ground, unconscious.

Panting heavily, Victoria tore herself away from the woman she *hated*, blinking the red away, willing it away, as something heavy landed on her back. It smashed her to the floor, and it was alive.

Galvanized, Victoria rolled over, grabbing the vampire from behind and tearing at his grip even as he tore at her with claws and teeth. Her blood . . . Sebastian's . . . Kritanu's . . . filled her nose, her vision, sat on her tongue . . . It became a whirlwind, a maelstrom of kicking and fighting, of driving fury. She slammed and staked and scratched and elbowed until at last she was free. She grabbed the knife Sara had dropped, pulling to her feet.

Max was there at last, panting, his hair loose from its queue. He appeared to have done some damage if the streaks of blood on his face were the sign of a victorious warrior. As Victoria moved to free Sebastian, she saw Max lunge for the last remaining vampire and place a stake in the center of its chest. Even without the power of the *vis bulla* he was lethal.

As she sawed away at Sebastian's bonds, she heard a soft oath behind her. Her skin prickling, she turned to see Max, frozen, wearing a stricken expression. He was looking beyond her, and Victoria turned slowly.

Sara could barely stand, but the gun in her hand was steady. It was pressed into Kritanu's back, at precisely the location where neck met shoulder. "Now, we will negotiate." The fact that she spoke in Italian indicated the level of her distress. But, still, she held the gun, and Victoria was powerless unless she wanted Kritanu to die right then.

"The Ring of Jubai. You will bring it to me, if indeed it exists," Sara said, her voice warming. "Maximilian will accompany us. I'm certain Lilith will be delighted to see him. And will be appropriately appreciative to me. George." She looked over at her companion, who'd risen from his chair during the altercation, presumably in an effort to remain out of the way of violence, as he was more of a gentleman's Tutela than an adventuresome one. "You take him." She gestured to Max with a jerk of her head.

Now, Victoria noticed that Brodebaugh sat slumped in his chair, his head at an unnatural angle. He would be no help to anyone, ever again. George rose from his seat, moving toward Max with alacrity. "I'll tie his wrists."

"No," Sara said, her eyes crafty. "No, he will carry his friend. As added insurance." She smiled that cool smile. "He wouldn't risk harm coming to the old man, though he might not care what happens to himself."

For once Victoria was in agreement with Sara, disagreeable as it might be. For a man who was willing to take his own life rather than be subjected to Lilith's will again, it would be nothing for Max to risk trying an escape, even with a gun on him. But he would not endanger anyone else, especially Kritanu.

Victoria was ordered to give the knife to George, who then gave it to Max—presumably so that she and Max would have no chance for private communication—and it was he who cut Kritanu free. Under Sara's watchful eye and gun barrel, he hoisted the elderly man up over his shoulders as gently as possible. He, too, had vampire bite marks on his neck and on any exposed flesh. Blood still streamed from the stump of Kritanu's arm, and the man groaned quietly. He had lost a lot of blood . . . and he hadn't the Venator powers, although he wore a small amulet that gave him some protection from the undead.

"Now." Sara positioned herself with the gun next to the two men and faced Victoria. "You have two hours to bring the ring to Lilith, if indeed it does exist. I need not tell you to come alone, need I?"

"And if I bring the ring, then you will give me Max and Kritanu?" Victoria asked, knowing full well that Lilith would never willingly release Max.

"You need not be so greedy. You may choose *one* of them to free, in exchange for the ring. Although I cannot guarantee either of them will remain unscathed. Two hours is quite a long time." She smiled again and, as before, she seemed calm and lucid. Not a hint of madness. Just cold calculation. "And the old man is likely to attract quite a bit of attention upon arrival."

The message was clear, and Victoria's stomach contracted. The vampires would be on Kritanu the moment he arrived. She looked at Max and read the comprehension in his expression. He, on the other hand, would be relatively safe.

Until Lilith got her hands—and fangs—on him.

Victoria's mouth dried. The determination on his face told her he would use the silver ring at the first opportunity. Even before she had a chance to arrive with an item to barter. And even then . . . it was impossible to believe that Lilith would release all of them, even for the ring.

"Take me instead," Victoria said, suddenly calm. She was the one who wore two *vis bullae*; she was the one best equipped to hold off the vampire queen. She was the one fighting for her soul. And the one who knew of the secret passageway. "Take me to Lilith."

"No!" The single syllable exploded in tandem from Max and Sebastian.

But Victoria ignored them, even as Sebastian jolted the table and chair to which he was bound, trying to use brute force to pull free. She looked at Sara. "I am more valuable than he is," she said with a nod at Max. "He's useless and weak now. Lilith won't want him without his power. And I am *Illa* Gardella."

Sara was staring at her, consideration lighting her eyes. "An interesting idea."

"Victoria, no!" Sebastian jerked harder at the table. A pool of blood splattered to the floor. "Don't be a fool. *Victoria.*" His last word was an agonized command, and it rang there in the room, in the taut silence that had descended.

Then . . . "Damn you," Max said. Very quietly, as though he had no breath. His eyes were black pits, and she could see the renewed tension in his arms as he steadied Kritanu there. "You *cannot* . . . be so foolish."

"I cannot retrieve the ring without your assistance," Sebastian added suddenly. "You must come with me. I'm too weak to get to it."

Victoria could see the calculation in Sara's eyes, could fairly hear her mind whirring. Which would put her in the best favor with Lilith, which combination had the highest likelihood of obtaining the greatest leverage . . .

Refusing to look at either of her two comrades, Victoria waited.

"If you are so eager to be traded for them," said Sara at last, looking at her with a delighted gleam in her eyes, "then I am content that you will indeed come, bearing the ring. And at that time, I'm certain we can accommodate your wishes to be traded." Her dimple flashed. "You have two hours."

Victoria looked directly at Max, though her words were meant for Sara. "I will bring the ring. I'll be there."

After Sara and George left, with Max carrying his burden between them, Victoria returned to Sebastian's side to cut away his restraints. Long before he was loose, his unmaimed hand whipped out to grab her arm. "What in the bloody hell did you think you were doing?" he said, gripping hard, shaking her. "How could you do such a thing?"

"It didn't work, did it?" she replied sharply, still cutting ferociously.

My God, they had been taking no chances with him getting free. The bonds were so tight, she was surprised he could breathe. And all the blood, oozing from his skin. Her stomach twisted, remembering the look in Sara's eyes. She would have butchered each of them, piece by piece. She released Sebastian's left hand, bloody and missing half of the last finger. "I'm so sorry, Sebastian." She raised it to her face and his fingers closed around her hand.

"It's nothing," he said. "She didn't get the parts that matter." His smile was a bit lopsided, but genuine all the same. "Merely a badge of my long-questioned heroism." He looked up at her, his ravaged face already showing a mottle of bruising. "You don't really mean to bring the ring."

"Of course I do, Sebastian!" She was horrified that he would even suggest such a thing that she stepped away. "I should have gone in the first place."

"Are you addled? You're *Illa* Gardella!" He pulled to

his feet more smoothly than she'd expected, standing over her. His eyes burned golden as he took her shoulders. "What will happen to the Venators if you're killed, or captured? You can't." He wrapped her against him, smelling of blood and sweat and Sebastian. "You can't."

"And as such it is my duty to protect." They bumped the chair. A leather restraint fell to the floor with a soft whump as those words echoed in her mind.

Duty to protect.

Indeed . . . a duty to protect even when it wasn't easy. When the choice wasn't simple. In fact, when the choice was impossible. That was what mattered.

Could she do it? Could she be selfless in protecting the mortals she was charged to save? Even one for whom she might be bound by hatred and loathing?

It had been easy . . . so easy . . . to offer herself for Max and Kritanu. She'd seen the flash of expression on Max's face when Sara produced the gun: sick with fear. He'd known his fate then. Not fear that he would die, but knowledge that Lilith would have him once again. And this time, without the strength and power of his *vis bulla* to help him fight her thrall.

Victoria knew that Kritanu would not last. Lilith had no use for him, and the blood would be too much for the vampires to resist. When Kritanu was dead, would Max use the silver ring to join him? She had to get there before he did.

Sebastian seemed to read her thoughts. "Victoria, Kritanu is as good as dead. And so is Pesaro. He'll make certain of it himself."

"Where is the ring?"

He sighed, tightening his arms, and then released her. His damaged hand smoothed along her cheek as he tried to smile. But it faltered. His fingers trembled. "I knew better than to hope you'd listen to me. This is who you are. This is who you've become: changed from the selfish, superficial Society girl, poorly disguised in man's clothes and playing at a double life . . . to *this*. And . . . I love who you are, Victoria. I've never met a more fascinating, intelligent woman."

A wave of guilt and affection overwhelmed her, and at that moment she drew in her breath to speak. But he shook his head sharply, the same way Max would have. "Don't. Let's get the ring. And hope that Brim and Michalas arrive soon." He released her and stepped back, that charming smile unsteady on his lips. "But perhaps we should think of a plan first."

Relieved that she could concentrate on the rescue, Victoria returned his smile with a grim one. "I already have."

Twenty-five

The Vampire Queen Receives Her Guest

When Victoria and Sebastian left the Brodebaugh home, there was an additional surprise, and something that gave Victoria an even greater sense of urgency. They found Kritanu in a heap on the front stoop. He'd been left there for some reason—a happenstance that was both relieving and terrifying. She couldn't imagine why or how, and assumed that Max's cleverness had somehow achieved it.

Thus they would be able to save Kritanu's life; but that left Max on his own, with no one to protect. No one to stay alive to protect.

He knew she was coming. She'd told him. But, would he wait? Could he, in that hell?

Should she expect him to?

Do you never do anything for yourself?

This might be the one time he did.

She wouldn't be able to blame him.

During the retrieval of the copper ring from the rooms Sebastian had rented, and the trip back to Victoria's town house, Sebastian tried to argue with her. He wanted to approach Lilith in her stead, or at least, *with* her. But Victoria was adamant.

"You and Brim and Michalas—if they've arrived at last—will come in through the secret passageway, which, God willing, they've not yet discovered. If you have to fight your way in, at least they won't be expecting three Venators."

When they reached the town house, they were relieved to find Brim, the mountainous, coffee-colored man with barely a brush of wiry hair and a *vis bulla* in his eyebrow. Michalas, the lithe, whip-slender Venator with tight, burnished curls, had also arrived. They, in fact, had been making ready under Wayren's direction to travel to the Brodebaugh residence and provide their assistance.

Victoria couldn't have been happier to see them. Her confidence surged as she told them her plan.

"I need not tell you to take care," said Sebastian, a short while later, as the hackney left Victoria off near the entrance to the sewers. His face looked marginally better, for he'd washed away the blood and sweat, and had changed clothes. However, nothing could hide the mottling purple and red on his skin, and the strain in his eyes. The last knuckle of his maimed finger was bound and poulticed, thanks to Wayren. "And I need not tell you why it is important that you return."

Brim and Michalas nodded. But they said nothing.

Indeed, there was nothing left to be said.

Victoria slogged through the sludgy underground canal as she and Sebastian had done weeks earlier.

The back of her neck was cold. Red—and some pink— eyes burned, glowing in the darkness of the sewer tunnels, but none made a move toward her. They blinked, and there was impatient rustling in the shadows, but Victoria ignored it. Lilith was too smart—and complacent—to rush things.

When she came to the dead end of the sewer, where the rush of water fell down into darkness below, she easily found the narrow walkway that led up and along the side of the tunnel to the underground abbey. To her uneasy surprise, she realized she didn't need a light. Her eyesight in the darkness continued to improve: a morbid reminder of her tenuous hold on mortality.

Once at the top of the ramplike walkway, Victoria slipped through the narrow crevice. She slunk across the small space, then faced the first door, which led to the antechamber that had been empty during her first visit, and where she'd fought with the vampires while Sebastian hid the secret door. To her surprise, the door that had been bolted when she and Sebastian came was unlocked and easily swung open. But that made sense . . . for Lilith was expecting her.

This chamber was still empty but for a pile of rags in one corner and a broken wooden chair. The back of her neck was frigid and her heart slammed in her chest. She walked across the room and pushed open the heavy door to the throne room.

At first, it seemed as though her entrance had gone unnoticed. There were few occupants in the space—a small cluster of vampires sitting in chairs. Sara, standing nearby like a lady in waiting. Lilith, who sat in her large stone throne with her long, slender fingers curled over the arms, was talking to Sara.

And Max. Thank God, Max.

He sat next to the vampire queen on a low stone stool. His shirt was missing, his feet were bare, but he still wore the same trousers he'd donned this morning. Unbelievably, his skin was unmarked, though she saw a faint sheen of sweat on his forehead. The silver *vis bulla* glinted use-lessly in the midst of the dark hair on his muscled torso.

Victoria looked at him, willing him to notice her. To see that she'd come, and would get them out of there, or die in the process.

But then Lilith looked directly at her with red-blue eyes, and Victoria had to blink away in surprise before the thrall trapped her.

"Nearly two hours, Venator. We'd begun to think you weren't going to come." Lilith smiled and reached over with a slender white hand to touch Max. He didn't move. Languidly, she laced her fingers through the thick dark hair that fell in straggling waves around his face. He still hadn't looked at Victoria, and that made her uneasy. Very uneasy.

He didn't appear to be restrained; his capable hands rested on his knees. Her palms became sweaty.

"I've brought the Ring of Jubai for you. I want Max."

At that moment, he shifted, as if it were a casual move, as if he hardly noticed her presence. Or cared about it. He looked straight at her, and she was struck by the look in his eyes: fury, frustration. He was angry that she'd come.

She could almost guess his thoughts: *Bloody hell, Victoria. It would all be over by now if you weren't so damned bullheaded and let me die in peace.*

But he didn't understand. She would never leave him to this, or to die. She wouldn't let him go.

Lilith smiled, her fangs fully extended. "I thought that might be the case. I see that you've given him back his *vis bulla*. But," she added thoughtfully, "first we must see how *you* are faring, Victoria Gardella."

She had been prepared for it, had known it was in-evitable. But when Lilith grasped Max's head and tipped it to the side, bending to the tendon at the junction of shoulder and neck, Victoria felt the slam of her heart vibrating crazily through her, suddenly taking over. As though it struggled to be released, to control her.

This was the same scene she'd witnessed before, the same scene that still haunted her, which, she knew, was only the edge of what he'd suffered: brilliant coppery hair spilling over his bare torso, next to his dark head, the grimace of pain mingled with shameful pleasure that flushed his face, parted his lips in a silent groan.

And the sounds: the soft gulps, the faint whistle of suction. The palpable alertness of the other undead in the room.

Victoria had expected it, steeled herself for it . . . but the *blood*. The smell of it.

Max's blood.

Her vision went hazy and pink, and she swallowed back the saliva that surged in her mouth.

Lilith looked up at that moment, daintily wiping a drop of crimson from the corner of her mouth. "I see," she said. Laughter and delight tinged her voice. "You're further gone than I'd imagined."

Victoria couldn't look at Max; she could barely breathe. *Oh God, help me.* Her fingers trembled, the stake lay untouched in her pocket.

Lilith swiped a finger over the marks on Max's skin, bringing away a fingertip tipped with red. Victoria could see it glistening from where she stood, and swallowed again. "Come, taste," said the vampire queen.

Victoria's stomach rebelled, lurching sharply . . . yet she couldn't draw her eyes away from the crimson trickling from Max's shoulder. Her heart beat strong vibrations to her fingers.

And then Lilith's laugh, echoed by Sara, trilled over the back of her mind, and she used its horrible sound to pull out of the depths . . . of wherever she'd been. Her heart still pounded, her fingers trembled . . . but the tug had loosened enough for her to regain control. For the moment.

"I'm here to negotiate," she said, aware that her voice was perhaps not as strong as it could be. "Do you want the Ring of Jubai? Or shall I leave?" She swallowed, and the saliva did not return in the same salacious manner as before. The red in her vision eased to the edges, lingering, but no longer burning.

"Of course I want the ring . . . but I'll get it eventually. Soon, you won't be able to deny me anything. And this is so much more entertaining. Are you quite certain you don't wish to join me?" Lilith moved her hand possessively over the front of Max's chest, her long nails threading through hair and over the plane of muscles, carefully avoiding the *vis bulla* on one side . . . then back up into the thick strands that brushed his neck.

He remained unmoving, stoic, but unwilling to meet Victoria's eyes. Yet she saw the pulse in the veins of his throat, and the visible tension in his arms as they tightened, the press of his lips. She felt the revulsion and horror emanating from him, and yet he displayed no reaction.

She realized in that moment that whatever had happened with Beauregard three months ago, whatever he'd done to her—and she'd accepted—during his attempt to turn her, had been nothing compared to what Max experienced at the hands of the vampire queen. Her stomach pitched at the thought of such ugliness.

"I didn't think you were willing to share," Victoria replied, trying a different tack, concentrating on her breathing. Keeping it easy, slow, smooth. Trying to ignore the smell of blood.

"For a Venator turned undead, I may perhaps make an exception," Lilith admitted. "You are very close, Victoria Gardella. Can you not feel it burning inside you? The need? I see it in your eyes."

"You see nothing," Victoria told her, wondering how much time had elapsed. Sebastian and the others should have been able to find the entrance to the secret passage behind the throne by now . . . they could be nearby. She simply needed to kill more time. "You merely see what you want to see."

"Indeed." Lilith sat straight in her chair. "Let us find out about that." She stood abruptly. Her long emerald gown, which was more in the style of Wayren than her cohort Sara, cascaded to her feet.

The vampire queen gave a subtle jerk of her head, but Victoria was ready. She whirled as two undead swarmed behind her. Stake in her hand again, she knocked away the hands that grasped for her, grabbing one of the vampires and shoving the creature toward the other. Then, quickly, before they could regain their balance or react, she stabbed one. He poofed into ash, and the other stumbled backward. Victoria followed him with her own lunge, pushing him to the ground then following through with her stake.

Standing in the pile of ash, she faced Lilith. "Keep your goons away from me."

The tall vampiress looked at her with burning red eyes. The blue had narrowed to the thinnest circle. "That was incomparably rude, Victoria Gardella. But don't worry . . . I won't allow you another chance to misbehave. Come with me, or I shall take out my frustrations elsewhere."

Max stood as though pulled by a puppet string, and Victoria did not miss Lilith's implication. She watched him move, still smooth and graceful, yet reluctance belabored every step. The vampire queen was tall, nearly as tall as he, and she circled his wrist with her skeletal fingers.

Sara moved toward Victoria, and she saw that the blonde woman still carried the pistol that had stopped their escape earlier. Using its barrel, she pushed Victoria toward the door at the opposite side of the chamber.

Victoria hadn't been in this room before; in fact, she'd hardly noticed the entrance to it the two previous times she'd been in the throne room. The smell of blood was stronger here, and the space was lit, unlike the other, by two massive fireplaces—one at each end—and wall sconces. The flames danced black shadows on the stone walls so that they seemed to undulate in every direction. This chamber was much warmer than the other, nearly stifling with its heat.

Or perhaps it just felt that way because of the thick bloodscent, the leaping shadows, and the warm light.

The furnishings in this room included a long, low divan piled with cushions, tables and chairs, and, in the center, a dark shadow in the floor. On the other side of the shadow was another doorway.

A low growl caught Victoria's attention, and she turned to see three pairs of red eyes burning near the floor in front of one of the fireplaces. Six pointed ears cocked toward them, and then the three dogs rose, massive nostrils quivering.

The hair on the back of Victoria's arms lifted. They were huge wolflike canines with vampiric eyes and long fangs that curved outside their muzzles when closed. The head of the smallest one would be as high as her waist.

They streaked over to Lilith, who commanded them with a mere flick of her fingers. The dogs sat promptly, but their attention, Victoria now saw, was focused on

Max . . . on the fresh blood that oozed down his skin. One of them was furiously licking, half biting, at the finger Lilith had drawn through the blood moments before, but the other two sat at attention: eyes sharp, ears perked, mouths closed, fairly vibrating with bloodlust.

"Now," said Lilith almost kindly. "We shall see how strong you are, Victoria Gardella. And then it will be all over."

A cold web of fear covered her as she breathed hot, bloody, sluggish air and felt a drop of perspiration roll down her back.

Everything happened very quickly, but Victoria could have done nothing to prevent it. Sara's gun barrel poked her in the side, and the dogs sat sentry in front of her as three vampires moved forward at Lilith's command. They placed heavy, clinking manacles on Max's wrists, crossing them together at his lap. When they first approached, he stepped back, his teeth baring ferally . . . but when Sara prodded Victoria with the gun, he acquiesced.

"That's it, Maximilian. Don't put an end to the experiment before it begins," said Lilith. "And you need not worry, Victoria Gardella. I have no intent of harming your lover. This is merely a precaution so that he does nothing foolish."

Victoria looked at Max. His stony face gave no indication of what was in his mind. Even his eyes were flat and emotionless, and though he met her gaze, he gave her nothing else.

Nothing for her, but also nothing for Lilith.

The shadow in the middle of the floor turned out to be not a shadow at all, but a pit. As she realized this, Victoria turned cold again. She knew what awaited her.

Before she could think further, the three vampires who'd chained Max came toward her. She fought them with stake and foot and red-clouded desperation, but in the end she was subdued by two of them. She took little satisfaction in the pile of ash that the other had become. Red burned her vision and her body trembled. Her mouth salivated. It took them all of their might to hold her steady when Lilith approached.

Her fangs dipped into her thin lower lip. It was purplish in color and the incisors left little dark dents, revealed when she smiled. Victoria held her breath, expecting anything . . . but not the sudden swipe of nails over her cheek and neck.

She felt the three claws dig into her face, and the burst of blood that followed as though it had been simmering below the surface . . . waiting.

And then, before she knew what was happening, she was flying through the air, falling down, down, down . . . into the black pit.

Twenty-six

A View from the Stands

Max saw the scarlet weals of blood erupt on Victoria's skin. It would be over very soon. Whatever it would be.

Damn her. Why in God's name did she come here?

At the scent of such fresh blood, the dogs surged to their feet, heedless of their mistress's command. They snarled and drooled and tore after Victoria, leaping into the hole where she'd been flung.

"Open your eyes, my dear Maximilian," crooned Lilith near his ear. Her breath was hot over his flesh, almost liquid in its promise . . . and malignance. The scent of roses was nauseating. "You needn't worry that she'll die down there. I have the utmost confidence in her abilities. Now, come closer, so you can watch her at her best. She truly is magnificent."

She prodded him forward, and he obeyed. He understood what Lilith meant to do, and his palms grew damp as his insides churned. Hot tears burned his eyes. The silver ring was heavy on his finger, yet useless, dammit. Bloody useless.

If there'd been one chance to get close enough to Victoria, he'd have lashed out, sliced her with it, eradicating Lilith's opportunity for entertainment.

Damn you, Victoria. Why didn't you stay away? It could have been over by now.

He didn't want to look in the pit, yet he could not keep from doing so. *You'd be safe.* It was a mass of snarling teeth and writhing fur, slender white limbs, flashes of pale skin and fabric. Victoria had her stake; he saw it rise and plunge, awkward and desperate, even as the dogs snapped and bit and surged. He cringed at her gasps and cries, and hoped when there was a canine squeal or shriek. God, he hoped.

Rather than mauling her all at once, the mastiffs seemed to come in waves . . . one after the other, lunging, biting, snarling, scratching, then rolling or dodging away in the pit to let the next come. The attack was so fast and relentless that Max could make out no details . . . only that Victoria had not been able to rise from beneath them. And her stake had not yet been effective.

He didn't realize he was jumping forward, down, until a horrible jerk on his wrist manacles whipped him through the air, then slammed him back onto the ground, fairly yanking his arms from their sockets. Rough stone tore his skin raw as he skidded across the dirt and rock. Blood oozed from his wounds as he crawled rapidly back to the edge of the pit, feeling the strain of hard breathing coursing through him. If he could get down there, he needed only a moment, and the ring would do its job.

But another powerful drag pulled him back, sending him sprawling onto his spine, head whipping back hard onto the stones. He breathed heavily, looking up into the furious face of Lilith. "Do not try such a foolish thing again," she said. "Or I'll release them fully."

Max clambered to his feet, head pounding, fists clenched. He wanted to beg, his mouth formed the words, he drew in the breath to plead . . . but he knew it would do no good. Lilith would lap it up like her vampire dogs and stroke him like the pet he was . . . and she would do what she wanted anyway, reveling in his pain and using his weakness to control him, to destroy them both.

Christ Almighty, his weakness was two bloody women. The vampire and the Venator. The seductive evil incarnate and the feminine warrior.

There was a sudden sharp squeal and a soft explosion. Then quiet.

He surged to the edge again, looking back down into the blackness, hoping. . . . Her white fingers were there, bloody, digging into the small cuts on the side of the pit, pulling her battered body up . . . not so far from the edge, and Max plunged his chained wrists down to help drag her up, heedless of Lilith standing behind him, of her triumph in seeing his weakness. There were no dogs left . . . only the smell of vampire dust on the air.

Victoria collapsed onto the ground at their feet. Her clothing was bloody and torn, her eyes glazed, her loose hair in a long, witchy tangle about her, red-streaked fingers still clutching the stake. Yet she pulled raggedly to her feet and blinked hard; Max could see her struggling to maintain her composure, to clear her vision.

He saw it . . . he recognized the struggle going on beneath her skin, deep within. The need to go on, to destroy, to annihilate. His fists tightened. There was nothing anyone could do for her. She had to fight through herself. Wayren had told him all of the details that Victoria had not.

Holy God, let her be strong.

She drew a deep, shuddering breath and faced Lilith. Her eyes burned with anger, yet there was no red. Not yet.

Thank God, not yet.

Then, suddenly galvanized and hopeful, he fumbled with the ring, reaching toward her, ready to end it before she had to make the fatal choice . . . before she was battered any further, tortured, maimed, beaten . . . pushed over the edge.

But his chains were yanked again and he lost his fingering on the ring as he was forced out of reach of Victoria, tripping and stumbling into a heap. He closed the signet quickly before it cut his own flesh. There was only enough for one of them.

"Marvelous," said Lilith, speaking to Victoria. "Absolutely marvelous, but nothing less than I'd expected from you. And quite efficient as well. I rather thought you might take longer than you did. Although I shall grieve for the loss of my companions, the outcome will be so much more valuable. And besides," she said, her fangs pressing into her lip as her smile returned, "I have more to spare."

As if that were a signal, the door on the other side of the pit opened and in walked the man Max recognized as Bemis Goodwin. He was holding the leashes of four more slavering canines, their ears pricked forward, their eyes burning red as they scented the blood.

"And now we shall finish this," said Lilith.

Her eyes burned with excitement, and Max felt as though he were going to vomit. The room shifted and he tried one more time to lunge toward Victoria, releasing the tiny lethal blade of his ring . . . he needed only one small cut, just the barest nick. . . .

But something caught around his foot, pulling back, and he slammed into the ground.

And then a woman screamed.

Twenty-seven

The Choice

Victoria was barely aware of Max slamming to the ground at her feet. She felt the need, the anger pulsing through her . . . red burning her eyes, blazing through her.

Her heart still pounded, sweat poured down her back and underarms. Lilith's red eyes glowed at her knowingly. Reveling in the battle as it billowed and surged inside her. She drew in a deep breath, touched the amulets beneath her torn tunic, and gasped with the power: pure, clean power.

The red faded, the rampant violence eased, she felt as though control was in her grasp. Triumph blasted through her. Lilith had been wrong. She'd underestimated Victoria, and now she'd come through whatever this test was—

And then she saw the four dogs. And Bemis Goodwin, standing on the other side of the pit. The dark, deep, horrible space. Slicing teeth and deep claws, the smell of evil, wet dogs as they came at her again, and again. Not to kill . . . to maim, to torture, to tear into her, but not enough for relief. Not enough to kill. Victoria couldn't hold back a shudder. It rattled her, made her weak-kneed and dizzy and dry in the mouth as she remembered fighting them back, and back, and back. . . .

She felt the brush at her feet as Max tried to lunge back at her, and she focused on him, saw the blood and scrapes on his shoulder and chest, the torn flesh at his wrists. Yet her world was vague, and she moved as if in a dream . . . as though underwater, fighting through heavy waves, struggling to breathe . . . and then a sharp scream cut through the air.

Victoria whirled in time to see Sara shoved off the edge and tumbling into that horrible pit. The four dogs lunged after her, leaping down into the darkness. The scream filled her ears and Victoria raced to the edge of the pit. The dogs were on the woman, tearing into her as she tried to fight them off. The report of the pistol echoed in the small space, eerie and useless against vampiric canines.

Victoria inhaled bloodscent, felt the rush of fear, heard the screams, and fought it. She turned back to Lilith and found her watching with a slight smile on her face. A smug expression.

Screams, howls, barks . . . Victoria did not want to go back into that horrible place. Those sharp teeth, tearing and mauling . . . Sara begging and crying . . . the soft squeal of a dog hit by the butt of her pistol . . .

The red burned . . . images warred . . . Sara with the knife . . . sharp teeth . . . Sara standing over Sebastian, smiling . . . the blood . . . the smugness . . . cold calculation . . . the tearing of teeth into her flesh, she knew what it felt like . . . the pain, the release of blood. . . . She couldn't do it. She couldn't. . . . Kritanu's severed hand . . . the snarls filling her ears and face . . . pain . . . Victoria felt herself moving away from the pit. . . . She couldn't go back there . . . pain . . . but Sara . . . her screams . . . she couldn't bear it . . . she deserved it . . . she would have cut them all . . . teeth, scoring . . .

Victoria leaped, praying and sobbing, falling down, down . . . she fought the fear, battling the red that threatened to overtake her . . . she landed on a furry back and barely had the presence of mind to use her stake. She heard a shriek above her, the fury of Lilith . . . and somehow that penetrated and gave her strength. She'd won.

By God, she'd *won*.

As she battled those monsters, slashing and fighting, praying and slashing, the red eased . . . it released her from the tension. She felt purity blaze through her, white and clear, pushing away the drive to kill relentlessly . . . the pleasure in pain.

The dogs seemed to sense her renewed purpose, and they became more feral, no longer holding back. They no longer teased and tortured as they had done before, but lashed out, all at once, pulling at her, tearing into her flesh. Her stake tumbled from her hand, rolling to the ground and Victoria felt the soft paws pressing into her face as teeth and claws tore at her legs and arms, pulling at her hair. She rolled and kicked, thrusting at them, struggling to pull her other stake from beneath her trousers . . . and at last it was in her hand, heavy and solid, and she lashed out with it.

She was *Illa* Gardella.

Power blasted through her, and she kicked and fought, free now, free to be as savage as she could, for she no longer feared the evil. It had dropped its hold, broken by her sacrifice, bleeding from her wounds, pouring out of her with each strong exhalation . . . stronger and purer. . . .

At last . . . silence.

Silence but for gasping breaths, and Sara's soft sobs and keening cries.

Victoria staggered to her feet and looked up.

Max's handsome face, still dark and taut, scraped and bloody, stared down at her. She saw the expression in his eyes, read what was there, what he'd tried so hard to hide . . . and then he was gone.

Victoria wasted no time. She heaved Sara's mutilated body up and over the top of the pit, on the side away from Lilith, clambering quickly after her before the vampiress could act.

Sara groaned, and cried out in agony as she collapsed on the ground, a torn, mangled mess. Victoria pulled herself up over the edge. On the other side of the pit—nothing more than a long jump—she saw Lilith, fangs bared, teeth long and lethal.

"You were wrong," Victoria said, triumph in her voice as she leaped over the pit. She landed solidly on the other side, steady, her feet planted on the ground. Sure. For the first time certain of her power. Knowing she had won.

From nowhere, from some invisible signal, came a horde of vampires, streaming into the room, swarming toward her. Victoria readied her stake, and the last thing she saw before the red-eyed creatures attacked was Lilith bending to Max.

Her world became a melee of fangs and claws, of pain and thrusts and stakes. She caught glimpses of the room around her as she fought to keep them away, from tearing her . . . but she was no longer afraid of the red and the blood and of herself.

And Max had his ring. He would be safe.

They covered her, as the dogs had, but larger and heavier, though no less feral. She screamed once, when she collapsed on the ground beneath tearing fangs.

"The ring . . . Max!" she cried, shoving her stake up into the red eye of an undead.

She rolled over and glimpsed Lilith's green gown and white body against Max's dark one . . . and the impression of blood and lips and tongue, and then the burn of red-blue eyes as the vampire queen turned to look triumphantly at Victoria.

Then her view was cut off when a large undead closed his hands over her throat, squeezing, as another captured her legs, pinning them down as she writhed and fought for air, her stake flailing . . . and suddenly her legs were released and the smell of vampire ash poofed through the air.

A war cry filled the room and she was free. There stood Sebastian, his golden eyes furious and horrified, finding hers from behind the shoulder of an undead . . . the vampire vanished and there he was again, reaching to touch her—just once, a quick caress—and then turning away to fight the undead.

Brim let loose another battle cry, and now he lunged and leaped, throwing vampires out of the way with his massive arms. The silver *vis bulla* glinted in his dark eyebrow against his black skin, his muscles bulging as he took an undead by the legs and swung him around, knocking vampires to the ground. Michalas was there too, his stake slashing and moving. Victoria and Sebastian backed up to each other, battling the vampires, cutting them down into piles of ash.

At last . . . there was nothing but the smell of foul air and heavy breathing. Victoria looked over and saw that Max was gone . . . and so was Lilith. She cried out and started toward the door, the only way they could have gone, but Sebastian pulled her back. She stumbled against him, her hand flattening over his chest, and saw that he was pointing her toward the other side of the pit.

Max was there, freshly bloody, his hands still chained. He knelt next to Sara, bending close to her.

He turned away and looked at Victoria, then pulled to his feet. Her stomach rebelled for a moment, and then she saw what he'd done. The silver ring was gone from his hand. Sara, a mutilated, torn, agonized bundle, curled her fingers around it. She made a jerky move, one hand against the other.

And then she slumped, relaxed, her hands falling to the stones beneath her.

Max carried Sara's body over his shoulder, perhaps, Victoria thought, as a last tribute to a woman he'd cared for . . . at least to some extent.

"Lilith's gone," said Brim. "She slipped away."

"But she didn't get the ring," said Victoria. Nor did she get Max.

They left in silence, necks warm, filing out through the throne room where the chair was tipped over from the Venators' entrance . . . and out into the empty antechamber.

Victoria was last, and it happened when they were walking down the narrow ramp that led to the sewer canal. She noticed, to her great relief, that she could see nothing in the darkness without the torches Brim and Michalas carried. The rush of water echoed around them, and suddenly she felt something moving through the air, rushing down from above her.

It crashed onto her, something warm and human, and she lost her balance.

They fell, tumbling off the walkway, down . . . down to where the water splashed below.

Twenty-eight

A Battle Is Lost

Sebastian heard the noise behind him. He turned in time to see the dark figure land on Victoria, falling with her down into darkness.

"Victoria!" he cried, and jumped after them.

The fall wasn't as deep as he'd expected . . . yet far enough to be fatal if rocks were hidden there.

He heard the other splash moments before his own, heard a struggle in the water, gasps for air, but he couldn't see anything. She was already weak, dammit, and she'd been taken by surprise . . . if she'd hit her head on anything, or crashed onto the rocks that he kicked against . . .

He couldn't see, but heard . . . he could hear, and he fought his way through the rush of water to the sounds of struggle, unsure who or what he was swimming toward because it was so dark.

Where were the others? There'd been no other shouts, no other splashes. Did they even know he and Victoria had fallen? The others had been quite a bit ahead of them.

Groping in the water, at last he found hair, strands of

hair, and from the soft glow of light, saw Victoria's white face, eyes closed. She wasn't moving and he pulled at her. There was something dark on her face, dark and sticky. *Oh God.*

"Max!" he shouted, his voice echoing in the darkness. "Brim! Down here!"

Then he felt another body bump against him, but before he could say anything—was it Pesaro? Brim? There'd been no other splashes—strong hands pushed him underwater. Then he felt the slice of something sharp scoring his arm, then down his leg. His blood surged into the water.

Above he heard the faint echo of a responding shout, and managed to bellow out another call for help as he fought and struggled in the rank pool. He was weaponless against this mortal with the blade and feeling renewed pain from his missing finger. At last a new beam of light from above—finally!—illuminated the man's face. He recognized him.

Bemis Goodwin, damn him. Bemis Goodwin.

Rage sliced through him, rage and hatred for the man who would take her from him. He held onto Victoria while battling the man back, grappling in the water, protecting her from the knife that slashed into him. She slipped from his grip, from the slippery hold, and disappeared.

Sebastian cried another warning aloud, choking in a mouthful of water, just as he noticed a light moving near the edge of the pool. Pesaro, and Brim, at last.

He pushed Goodwin underwater, holding him there until the man stopped slicing and kicking. Sebastian released him then, splashing toward the faint white he saw in the distance. At last there was another splash behind him. He heard Michalas call out and could barely respond.

At last his hand touched something warm and human again . . . and then hair. He pulled, felt her come up against him. She wasn't moving, she wasn't breathing. He pulled, keeping her face from the water, dragging her to the side, onto the bank where Pesaro and Brim were clambering down the rocky edge.

Light danced behind him as he turned her onto her stomach, her face to the side. Blood everywhere, her face bruised and cut, her hair a mat of curls, her body cold and white. "No, Victoria, dammit," he breathed.

He felt the others come up behind him, down from the rocky wall, carrying torches. He kissed her cold face, brushed the hair from her eyes, willing himself not to think of Giulia . . . not to think of losing yet again.

Not to Bemis Goodwin. By *God*, not to the likes of Bemis Goodwin.

He struck her hard between the shoulder blades, and gave her a desperate shake.

Victoria coughed, and Sebastian rolled her to the side. Water spewed forth and she coughed more, her body wracked and shaking. Someone—Brim—handed down a dry coat and he wrapped it around her. The golden light encircled them, illuminating her face, the bruises, the three slices down her cheek, the myriad of other, smaller ones.

Her closed eyes were shadowed but at last fluttered, opening. Sebastian breathed easier. . . . She opened them, looked up at him. She looked at him, and he smiled, feeling the tug to one side of his mouth.

And then her gaze moved on, beyond, her eyes falling somewhere behind him. Her lips moved.

Sebastian recognized the look. Read the word, the

simple name on her lips. Saw the expression on her face. It was his hand she clutched, her cold fingers gripping tightly. But the look was not meant for him.

He'd suspected . . . for far too long. Perhaps he'd always known, and that was part of the reason for the animosity, the discord, the enmity. He'd hoped, simply hoped he was wrong.

Hope drained away, leaving him empty.

He'd lost.

Twenty-nine

An Au Revoir

Wayren embraced Victoria, sending the warmth of something like maternal comfort washing over her . . . then pulled away to look into her eyes. Searching. "Yes, indeed," she said, relief in her voice. "It's gone."

Victoria looked at her. "You could see it?"

The woman nodded. "A shadow . . . perhaps not so different than what you saw in the eyes of the daytime vampires. I admit, it's more obvious now that it's no longer there."

It was late that night after they returned from Victoria's near drowning in the sewers. Aunt Eustacia's parlor was crowded with an unusual bulk of Venators: Brim, who was by far the most massive, Michalas, Sebastian, Max . . . and also Kritanu, who, despite the loss of his hand and the number of vampire bites, still seemed almost more complete than the latter two. He sat in the chair that had been Eustacia's, near the piecrust table, silent and watchful.

Victoria looked at Michalas and Brim, then turned her

attention to Sebastian. He watched her steadily, as though gulping in the sight of her. She wanted to flush. "It took you long enough to arrive," she said, humor in her voice, trying to sound light . . . when inside she was a turmoil. She ached; her body ached and burned and still oozed blood. She'd easily be dead if she weren't a Venator. "I'd begun to wonder if something had happened."

"You knew we were coming," he replied. "It was your plan, and it worked flawlessly . . . except that that blasted carriage of Barth's broke a wheel and delayed us."

Brim laughed. "Sebastian was fit to kill the man, as if it was his fault that the wheel broke."

"The way he drives, it likely was," said Max from the corner. "It nearly cost us everything." His bitterness settled in the air.

There was a charged silence, and then Victoria spoke. "But it did not," she said smoothly. "Not only did we ruin Lilith's plan to assassinate the king, but I'm certain she's not foolish enough to stay here in London any longer. Nor did she get the Ring of Jubai, which, thanks to Sebastian, Wayren can now add to the collection at the Consilium."

The others nodded.

"And so the Queen of England is a daytime vampire," Brim said, disbelief in his voice. "How has no one realized this?"

"She's been taking the elixir since she turned, I venture to say, which can't have been very long ago. So she's dying," added Victoria simply. "I doubt she'll last another week or two." She shrugged. "We could find a way to help her along, I'm certain . . . but I see no point in doing so. Why should we take the chance of being involved?" She frowned grimly. "I had a bad enough experience with the Bow Street Runners and Newgate that I wish to remain anonymous for awhile."

"And Gwendolyn. How long had she been undead?" asked Michalas.

Victoria suddenly felt impatient with the questions. She wanted everyone to leave . . . she needed time alone. So much had happened, so much had changed. She could hardly keep from looking at Max, gauging every scratch and scar and bruise on his face. And the rough bites on his neck . . . the ones that wouldn't heal nearly as quickly as hers. But at least they were merely bites from Lilith, and nothing more.

And he, for his part, brooded in the corner, saying little. Sending her black looks that certainly did not bespeak affection. He was furious with her. Dark and angry . . . in a way he'd not been before.

It made her question what she'd seen in his eyes in Lilith's lair. Had she imagined it?

And Sebastian . . . Victoria felt her stomach squeeze. He'd become aloof. Still cocksure and engaging, but . . . aloof. Since he'd pulled her from the water and rescued her from Bemis Goodwin, something had changed.

Affection surged in her . . . and apprehension. She had to talk with him. Her eyes fell to her scarred hands and she let Sebastian answer Michalas's question with his own conjecture.

"It's not certain how long she'd been undead, but she couldn't have had the elixir for very long, of course. She must have begun taking it as soon as her brother returned from Italy—with the queen, and the serum."

He seemed to need to speak, whereas Max did nothing but glower from the corner. Victoria could feel his impatience, his need to get away.

"I have the suspicion," Sebastian continued, "and perhaps we'll never know for certain, that Gwendolyn was already part of the Tutela when Victoria and I were at her house party with John Polidori. She must have been planning something for a long time—and then she had to wait until we returned from Italy."

"But she sent her brother after you," said Max.

Michalas nodded, his eyes light with humor. "It was all the women, wasn't it? Lilith, Caroline, Sara, Gwen . . . all stymied by our Victoria."

"You're weary," Wayren said, standing suddenly. Perhaps she sensed the undercurrents, perhaps she merely understood that Victoria was, indeed, exhausted. Heartsick, worried, weary . . . yet hopeful. Ridiculously hopeful. "We can discuss this at another time."

No one argued with Wayren; Max was the first one out the door. He limped, moving a bit gingerly, but still graceful. And he was gone.

Sebastian stayed when Victoria closed her fingers around his wrist.

The door shut and they were alone.

He said nothing, just looked at her.

"I . . . Sebastian," she began, but he raised a four-fingered hand . . . whether he used that one purposely or not, she didn't know. It would be just like him to, as he put it, play up his heroism. She smiled. She did love him.

"No, don't. Please." He gave her a crooked smile, one that still had the power to send a tingle to her belly . . . just not the *right* tingle. "My pride cannot handle it."

"How . . . did you know?"

He settled his golden hands on her shoulders, one finger stretching up to caress the side of her neck. "It's been there for all to see . . . for whoever cared to look. I chose not to . . . and so has he. Victoria." His voice became urgent, his fingers tightened. "He's not worthy of you. He hasn't the ability to . . . feel. I don't want you to be hurt. And yet—no." He shook his head sharply. His sensual lips firmed so that a humorless dimple appeared. "I can't wish you well, or wish you to be with him. I simply cannot. He's made it clear to me that—" He stopped, squeezed her shoulders, bent to kiss her.

It was a farewell kiss—she read that much in it. Or, at least, an *au revoir* kiss . . . rather than an *adieu*. An "I'll wait for you" kiss, rather than a good-bye.

When she pulled away, he was breathing unsteadily, and so to be honest was she. Sebastian made her feel . . . yes, he did. He turned up the spark, he curled her insides, he made her soft and liquid . . . but it wasn't enough.

And as he looked down at her, she saw the understanding in his face. And she knew that in this, as always, he'd be the gentleman.

Victoria knew where to find Max.

She knocked, but didn't wait for his answer before she opened the door to the small bedchamber. The same room in which she'd awakened only this morning.

"What do you want?" His voice was sharp. Annoyed.

She'd surprised him. He was sitting in a chair, reading a book.

Reading a bloody book, the bastard.

The skin on his face and neck, and what little she could see under the loose shirt he wore, was scraped and raw. The bite marks from Lilith were no longer oozing, but the marks were there, angry purple-red ones, despite the salted holy water Wayren had poured on them. At least they would heal.

When he looked at her, his eyes were flat, devoid of emotion, even anger.

"Are you all right?"

That was the wrong thing to say; she realized it as soon

as the words came out. His eyes went darker and his face became even stonier.

"You shouldn't have gone there, Victoria. You should have bloody well stayed away and let things happen." He stood, anger rolling off him in waves. "You were nearly killed, you stupid, addled woman!"

She swallowed and her throat squeaked. "I told you I would come. I wasn't about to leave you with her."

"I would have taken care of myself," he thundered, slamming a hand down onto the table. A glass and carafe rattled against each other. "When will you learn to do what's right for everyone—not just what you want to do? Blasted stubborn, infantile woman. You take risks for no bloody reason."

"You should speak," she said, just as angry now. "You—"

"You're *Illa* Gardella," he shouted. "I'm no one!"

She'd never seen him angry like this . . . it was different from the cold, deep fury when she'd drugged him and locked him up. That was silent and deadly anger. This was . . . uncontrollable. Almost uncontrollable. And laced with desperation.

That was it . . . desperation. And . . . fear?

And that gave her the impetus to push further.

"Must you remind me constantly?" she said. "If you had it your way, I'd be locked up in some blasted tower while the rest of the Venators fight and risk their lives."

"I'm no longer a Venator, Victoria." Bitterness. Oh, such bitterness.

"You are in every way that matters," she said. If she thought that sentiment would ease him, she was deluded.

"I don't want your damned pity, Victoria. Just go away. Leave me be."

"I don't want to leave you alone, Max."

His eyes blazed. "I can't give you what you want. Vioget can. He can protect you, take care of you—"

"*Protect* me?" Now she was shrieking. She took a deep breath, pulled back on the anger. Calmed her voice. "I don't need anyone to protect me."

"Victoria," he said, moving toward her. He grabbed her, then shoved her away as if remembering what had happened the last time he'd gripped her in anger. His fingers closed into fists. "You nearly died . . . or worse. Didn't you see it? Didn't you see what she was doing to you?"

"Yes—"

"She was pushing you . . . she nearly pushed you the wrong way. And, Christ, look at you! And those bloody dogs, tearing you to pieces." His voice was rough, unsteady. "She'll do it again. She'll be after you—"

"Yes, and I had to watch her put her hands on you, drink from you, Max. I saw it, saw the look in your eyes."

"And she'll be after me again . . . and again. And she'll use you, Victoria. She'll use you to get to me."

"I don't care. Max, after what happened . . . what happened between us—"

He reared away from her at that, literally took two steps back. "Don't be a bloody fool. I told you we needn't mention it to anyone and we won't. Vioget need not know."

"He already does."

"Then I'm sorry for him, but it won't matter. The man is so damned infatuated with you, you could put him last in the line of your lovers and he'd not care."

"And you don't?"

"No."

She took a step toward him. "You're lying."

"Victoria, you'll do nothing but cause your own bloody embarrassment if you keep on this route."

"You were going to give me your ring, your only chance of escape from Lilith . . . so that I'd die before I turned. I saw you, Max."

He sneered. "I'd have done it for anyone."

"I saw the look in your eyes when I saved Sara. You can't deny it."

He hesitated, then shutters came over his face, cutting off all expression. He breathed deeply and there was a charged silence.

"Max—"

"What do you want from me, Victoria? A declaration of undying adoration?"

His face was suddenly close to hers, his eyes flashing with anger and frustration. His fingers dug into her shoulders, and then he shoved her away, turning his face for a moment. Then, hands on his hips, a great space between them, he looked at her.

"All right," he said, glaring. "I'll say it." His face grew even darker, burning with impatience. "I didn't want to love you, but I can't help it. I don't want to be without you, but I bloody well *will*. Victoria, I'll not go through this again. I'll not risk your damned neck again. It's the way it has to be."

Relief seeped through her, then was replaced by annoyance and raging frustration. "You're mad! What about Kritanu and Aunt Eustacia? Did he walk away? Did she?"

"I wish I could lock you up, and know you'd always be safe . . . and I know that can't bloody well happen. But I won't be part of it, I won't make it any worse than it has to be. *I can't do it.*" His voice was rough.

"I never took you for a coward, Max."

"Coward?" His laugh was sharp and humorless. And a little crazy. "When it comes to risking your life, yes, yes, dammit, yes, I am. I'm a bloody damned coward."

He spun away, slamming the door behind him. The glasses on the table rattled.

Victoria looked at the door and a slow smile pulled at her mouth. Now that she knew the truth, she was determined.

That would be the last damned time Max walked away from her.

Author's Note

One of the best things about writing historically set novels is the ability to play with actual events and to build a story around them.

But sometimes things don't fall into place exactly the way my plot demands, so, as an author, I take a little bit of liberty.

In *When Twilight Burns*, which is set during the summer of 1821, I center Lilith's plot around the coronation of George IV, which was, as described, a great and extremely expensive event. The details about his wife, Caroline, and her attempt to attend the coronation are true (with the exception of the fact that it was Victoria and her stake that kept the queen from entering Westminster Abbey), as is the fact that she died several weeks later.

However, one thing didn't fit into the timeline: the appearance of Comet Encke. In reality, the comet didn't appear until a year later, in 1822. Thus, for the purpose of the story, I tweaked a little and had it appear a bit early for Victoria and her companions so as to give them a legitimate excuse for a "moonlight drive."

The details about the toshers and the bone pickers beneath the City of London are true. The entire underground recycling industry of that time is fascinating. For anyone interested in finding out more about it, I recommend *The Ghost Map* by Stephen Johnson as a great starting place.

And by the way . . . there really is a Carmelite Abbey beneath the streets of London. Just in case you were wondering.

Colleen Gleason
March 2008

Read on for a sneak peek at the next volume of
the Gardella Vampire Chronicles

AS SHADOWS FADE

Available from Signet Eclipse in March 2009

She hadn't even pulled all her skirts up and into the carriage, saving the hem from being trod upon or caught in the door, when he pushed past and sprawled on the opposite seat, settling in the center of the bench in an arrangement that clearly indicated his desire for solitude there.

The footman closed the door, and Victoria heard it latch into place. Inside the interior felt dark, close. Her corset suddenly felt more restrictive.

"You're losing your touch, Max," she said, sinking into her own seat across from him. She took her time smoothing the skirt over her legs, perversely allowing it to whisk against his pantaloons, which, in the way of fashion, were held neat and straight by narrow straps beneath his feet. At least he'd dressed properly for the occasion.

He raised a brow in question, his face half-lit by the small lantern that hung in the corner above Victoria. Of course he'd choose the side that wasn't as well-illuminated.

She took the brow quirk as an invitation to explain. "That message," she said, gesturing at his long, sprawled body, "doesn't have your normal subtlety."

His lips moved in what looked like a suddenly checked smile.

"In fact," she continued, "it's a rather clumsy and obvious shield against something you wish to ignore." She drew off the single glove she still wore and looked expectantly at his stony expression. Her throat had dried and she swallowed gently, trying to ignore the sudden . . . awareness . . . between them.

"Are you going to tell me what you were doing with George Starcasset, or are you going to continue to look for meanings that aren't there?"

"Since you were the one who sought me out, on a matter of some urgency, I should think you'd be more eager to share your news. What on earth was so important that you braved a Society dance fraught with— What do you call it? Social frivolities?" One of her slippers was very close to his shoe. She edged her foot over slightly, just enough to touch him, and waited.

"Brim and Michalas have left," Max told her. The other two Venators had come to London to help Victoria, Max, and Sebastian foil Lilith's plot to kill the new King of England.

"For Rome?"

He shook his head, and moved his foot. Away from hers. "Back to Paris. We received word tonight that another demon was sighted. They went to conduct an investigation."

Victoria considered him for a moment. Wheels crunched and ground along the street below, and the floor beneath her feet rumbled. The lantern above her jolted, swinging its light gently from side to side, casting larger, then smaller, larger, then smaller shadows over his face. "And?" she asked when he said nothing further.

"And Kritanu thought that you should be advised immediately."

Victoria smothered a smile. And thus Max, who was so biddable and who adored social functions, leapt at the chance to join her at the duchess's party. Even for Kritanu, who was as close to him as an uncle?

Not, as he himself would say, bloody likely.

"So why was it necessary for me to leave the dance?" she countered. "If that was the extent of the news."

"Your hair is mussed, you're missing a glove, and there's a streak of blood on your neck," he replied. "You look as though you've just returned from some sort of assignation. A violent one."

"As it happens, I have." Of course her hair was askew. She'd not quite gotten the technique of pulling the small, hidden stake from her coiffure without messing it up.

"And along the way accosted a vampire? Or was that the purpose of the meeting?" He seemed to relax more, settling those wide, square shoulders against the velvet squab behind him. "You might wish me to believe that you had a téte-â-téte with George Starcasset, but the thought is utterly ridiculous."

"If I were to have an assignation in a carriage, it would most definitely not be with George Starcasset."

His elegant fingers, spread over the back of the seat, straightened. Then curled. "Viog—"

"Nor would it be with Sebastian," she continued coolly, refusing to drop his gaze.

"Victoria—" His voice was strained. Laced with

anger, real anger. He looked away, out of the window. His fingers relaxed again.

She wanted to reach across the gap between them and grab those shoulders and shake him until some sense filtered into that stone-filled, honor-bound, *cowardly* skull of his.

And she could do it, too. She was so much stronger than he.

But what good would it do?

Silence, full and heavy, sat in the carriage with them.

"This reminds me of the night we had to go to Bridge and Stokes," Victoria said after a moment. "Do you remember?"

"I remember," he snapped, still gazing out the window. "We had to save your husband from a vampire attack."

She took the opportunity to shift in her seat, arranging herself subtly, so that the small lantern light fell just so, cutting a swath of pale gold over the front of her gown. "I had to change in the carriage, remember? Into men's clothing, because it was a men's club, and of course I couldn't enter dressed as I was."

"My memory is perfectly clear; you needn't review the details."

"Then I'm certain you recall having to unlace my corset—"

"Victoria." Now he looked away from the window. "What are you about?"

She couldn't make out the expression in his eyes; they were muted by shadow. But by the set of his mouth, she knew he was angry. She knew how his eyes would glare, flat and black and cold.

"I've always wondered about something," she continued, as though he wasn't looking murderously at her.

"When I was undressing, and you were sitting shoved back in the corner, studiously looking out the window, or with your eyes closed as you claimed . . . did you peek?"

She heard what sounded like a stifled snort. Then . . . "Of course not."

At that moment, the carriage eased to a halt and Victoria realized in dismay that they'd arrived at Aunt Eustacia's townhouse already. Max fairly leapt to his feet, looming like a full-winged bat in the small enclosure.

But although he stood in such a way that did not permit her to rise as well, he didn't leave. Instead, he turned to face her, looking down from his half-stooped position. His hands moved to the wall above her head—a position of power that he must have felt he needed—and he looked down, his feet spread on either side of hers.

For the first time since they'd climbed into the vehicle, she could see his face clearly. Emotionless, sharp, closed. So empty it made her heart ache.

Her head tipped back, her neck cradled by the top of the cushion. Her fingers twisted in the shadows, burying in her thin, silky skirt, and her heart thumped audibly in her chest. At least, it was audible to her.

"Max," she said. Whispered. Begged.

"I can't, Victoria." His voice was just as unsteady, but deep.

"You *won't*."

"Don't be a fool." He'd regained control, and his words were clipped, cool. "You are obliged to do what's right for the Venators—just as I am. And what's right, Victoria, is for you to be with Vioget. A man who is your equal, who can stand at your side and doesn't have to hide from the bloody queen of the vampires."

"Max—" she began.

But he spoke over her. "Victoria, understand, you are the last of the Gardellas. You have to do what's right for them, for the world. It's your duty, your calling. You can't ignore that because we"—here his voice dipped even lower—"spent the night together. I told you then: It changes nothing."

"Coward!"

"Good night, Victoria."

He snapped open the door and was out before Victoria could respond.

She pulled herself to her feet, suddenly frustrated to exhaustion. How could a man who did what he'd done, faced what he'd faced . . . made the decisions he'd made . . . be such a bloody coward?

Then all other thoughts fled as Max's head came back around into the carriage. His eyes were fierce and dark as he reached forward to grab her by the arm. "Victoria, Wayren's gone missing."

COLLEEN GLEASON

RISES THE NIGHT

The Gardella Vampire Chronicles

In Italy, a powerful vampire is amassing the power to control the souls of the dead. Lady Victoria Gardella de Lacy—a vampire slayer for just over a year—races across Europe to stop what could be the most deadly army the Gardellas have ever faced. She is accompanied by Sebastian Vioget, a man as tempting as he is untrustworthy.

But when Victoria discovers that she has been betrayed by one of her most trusted allies, the truth will challenge all her powers as a Venator—and as a woman.

Available wherever books are sold or at
penguin.com

COLLEEN GLEASON

THE BLEEDING DUSK

To gain access to the secrets of a legendary
alchemist, Rome's vampires have allied
themselves with creatures as evil and
bloodthirsty as they are. The new leader of the
city's vampire hunters—Lady Victoria Gardella
Grantworth de Lacy—reluctantly turns to the
enigmatic Sebastian Vioget for help, just as
Maximilian Pesaro arrives to aid his fellow
slayers, no matter what the sacrifice. Desire
puts her at the mercy of Sebastian, while
loyalty binds her to Max, but she does not
know if she can trust either. Especially when a
seductive vampire begins luring her into
the shadows...

"A decidedly dark, decidedly unsentimental Regency
heroine who stakes the undead with the best
of them."
—*Detroit Free Press*

**Available wherever books are sold or at
penguin.com**

Penguin Group (USA) Online

What will you be reading tomorrow?

Tom Clancy, Patricia Cornwell, W.E.B. Griffin,
Nora Roberts, William Gibson, Robin Cook,
Brian Jacques, Catherine Coulter, Stephen King,
Dean Koontz, Ken Follett, Clive Cussler,
Eric Jerome Dickey, John Sandford,
Terry McMillan, Sue Monk Kidd, Amy Tan,
John Berendt...

You'll find them all at
penguin.com

*Read excerpts and newsletters,
find tour schedules and reading group guides,
and enter contests.*

Subscribe to Penguin Group (USA) newsletters
and get an exclusive inside look
at exciting new titles and the authors you love
long before everyone else does.

PENGUIN GROUP (USA)
us.penguingroup.com